The Seven Isles of Ameulas

Read *The Bot Story* by Casey Fahy
Also available from **Writers Club Press**

THE SEVEN ISLES OF AMEULAS

Casey Fahy

Writers Club Press
San Jose New York Lincoln Shanghai

The Seven Isles of Ameulas

All Rights Reserved © 2001 by Casey Fahy

Cover art by Kyushik Shin

No part of this book may be reproduced or transmitted in any form or by any means, graphic, electronic, or mechanical, including photocopying, recording, taping, or by any information storage retrieval system, without the permission in writing from the publisher.

Writers Club Press
an imprint of iUniverse.com, Inc.

For information address:
iUniverse.com, Inc.
5220 S 16th, Ste. 200
Lincoln, NE 68512
www.iuniverse.com

ISBN: 0-595-19161-4

Printed in the United States of America

"To judge a man most truly, imagine the world if he were king."
—Elwyn Gheldron

Contents

Part One

Chapter 1 Home Again	3
Chapter 2 Temptation	13
Chapter 3 The Old Philosopher	19
Chapter 4 Love	24
Chapter 5 A Party for Trinadol	34
Chapter 6 The Sea Monster	45
Chapter 7 The New King	52
Chapter 8 The New Queen	69
Chapter 9 The First Defense	81
Chapter 10 Wyndernia	98
Chapter 11 Strange Hope	110
Chapter 12 The Second Defense	120
Chapter 13 Ameulas	132

Part Two

Chapter 14 Here and There 155

Chapter 15 Pigg 169

Chapter 16 Checkmate 187

Chapter 17 A Message Heard 198

Chapter 18 The Council of Ameulas 214

Chapter 19 Revolution 241

Chapter 20 Under Way 264

Part Three

Chapter 21 The Fog Lifts 281

Chapter 22 The Race Is On! 307

Chapter 23 Caught 321

Chapter 24 Healing Wounds 332

Chapter 25 A Damsel in Distress 350

Chapter 26 Nightmares 364

Chapter 27 The Living Isle 374

Chapter 28 Drugor 405

Chapter 29 Reunion 417

Chapter 30 The Fate of the World 426

Part One

Chapter 1

▼

Home Again

As he sailed by the mouth of the Serrid Strait, Trinadol Gheldron heard a demon call his name.

He steered *Stargazer* between the narrow cliffs that rose a mile to a river of stars, and after sailing deep into that freezing chasm he saw a giant swell rolling toward him in the gloom.

He grabbed the mast as the dark wave lifted his boat halfway up the cliff to an icy ledge where the demon was waiting.

"Gheldron!" it screamed—a fossilized Winteg that broke out of the face of the cliff. The beast's bones crumbled as it lunged at him, and a diamond crown toppled from its thorny skull.

Trinadol almost caught the precious crown, but the angry wave carried *Stargazer* on its crest all the way out of the Serrid Strait and pushed her onto the open sea. Then a dark wind came out of the sky and caught *Stargazer*'s sail, driving her north three days and nights over mirror-like water.

On the third night, Trinadol rose and hauled the sheets in defiance, and the ocean boiled around him all the way to the horizons. He fought to bring *Stargazer* about and fixed her course on the red South Star, determined to claim the Winteg's crown, but *Stargazer* broke his grip and swung like a compass needle, knocking him onto his back.

The sea became smooth as glass again and reflected the stars as *Stargazer* sliced a straight line toward the blue North Star.

"Almighty Gairanor!" Trinadol beseeched his ancestors, whose eyes peered down from the heavens, and he howled a rage that finally fell sad and broke into sobs of bitter laughter. He fixed *Stargazer*'s lines and slumped beside her tiller. His long black hair twisted around his pale, chiseled face as he glared at the northern horizon. *Stargazer* was taking him home, to Ameulas.

The young Cirilen took an enryd out of his kit, cut a frown in the purple-skinned fruit and chewed the wedge of beefy flesh. His young eyes smoldered as he tasted home.

Ameulas had played a central role in his family's history. Long ago, the *Khalwairn* warrior, *Drugor*, who was the only one of his terrible kind to survive the first war between the *Khalwairn* and the Cirilen, had made his hateful return to the Hala World of mortals. He enchanted an army of Wintegs and sent them to slaughter the 48 Cirilen clans. Only the Gheldrons had escaped.

Trinadol's grandfather, Elwyn, led the Gheldron clan on a voyage halfway around the world in order to escape *Drugor*'s wrath. They settled upon the uncharted island of Trillan, which the Gheldrons made invisible to all but Cirilen eyes. Yet Elwyn knew that *Drugor* would not rest until he found him, so he journeyed north from Trillan all alone and came upon the kingdom of Ameulas.

The Ameulentians made him their king after he married the fair Apriscia, daughter of their elderly monarch who had eagerly relinquished his crown to the mighty Cirilen.

Drugor did find Elwyn, eventually, but Elwyn feared Ameulas could not survive their confrontation, and so he fled Ameulas, and met the fierce *Khalwairn* alone on the newly discovered continent of Ghenten, far to the northwest. There, the two mortal enemies perished in a white conflagration that laid waste to that virgin land.

Since then, Elwyn's son, Senadol, had ruled Ameulas, and Trinadol was Senadol's only child. Without admitting it to himself, Trinadol knew why

Stargazer was defying him now, for it was the only reason she ever would: his father was dying.

The 17-year-old Cirilen cut another wedge of enryd as he stared at the dark horizon. All his life, Ameulas had hung over his head like a crushing weight. He chewed the enryd's meat grimly as he tried to remember the place he had left eleven years ago.

He dipped his fingers in the cold, rushing sea and smiled at the first memory that came to his mind. It was a buttery enryd pudding with nutmeg, which he had eaten at a feast in a wicked mayor's lavish hall when he was three years old. He also remembered making the mayor close his bulging, bloodshot eyes just as he made for his mouth with a yellow hen's leg. The mayor had poked his fat jowls with the greasy drumstick and scowled at the giggling prince.

Trinadol discovered how to close people's eyes at a very young age. He found he could trap people with themselves by closing their eyes, a harsh sentence when they were being foolish, as they so often were in front of children—especially ones like him.

He remembered, most of all, how lonely he had been in Ameulas. He dreaded people who treated him like a superior, and that was how everyone had treated him there. He called the kingdom "the Boredom" and brooded miserably through six years of pageantry and ceremony until, at last, his father arranged passage for him to the island of Trillan, and rescued him from his misery.

The day he left Ameulas he was only sad to say goodbye to his father, who had stolen chances to fish with him on the sea and who taught him his first spells. For the world was all ahead of him, and the six-year-old Trinadol, with his already serious face, huge black eyes, and night-black hair, eagerly boarded a big ship that was loaded with 260 enryd tree saplings bound for his family's faraway isle. He remembered how his heart had raced as the vast sail filled and pulled the ship up giant blue dunes of windswept sea.

Courtiers had done their best to entertain him on that long voyage, but they were too doting. When Trinadol was a child, the *Wynderne World*, from which his kind's power came, burned through his skin and normal men saw him as through a bright mist. Yet the mariners were not afraid of Trinadol and they were eager to see what sort of things he could do. Midway through the voyage, he had decreed that no more members of the court should bother him so that he could play with the mariners, instead.

He remembered the magical morning when he had looked through the porthole of his cabin and saw Trillan for the first time, the island of steaming jungles and waterfalls, flowers the size of wagon wheels, and animals as smart as children. He chewed another wedge of the enryd, which had grown on one of the trees that accompanied him on that voyage long ago, and he could taste the perfume of Trillan's soil now as his thoughts drifted to that radiant place.

On Trillan, each day was a journey of discovery. Learning to obey nature so he could command it, Trinadol saw his studies and training crystallize into an overarching universe of knowledge and power. His kin had groomed him and adored him. And yet, after eleven devoted years, Trinadol decided he had had enough of theories and abstractions, and a towering boredom menaced his heart once again.

"The world is not made of parchment!" he cried to Dantair the Elder only six days ago. "I want to conquer evil, Dantair, not cringe and cower behind a book or on a throne, waiting for evil to come to me, like my grandfather!"

Dantair, the Patriarch of the House of Gheldron and Elwyn's brother, was astonished by his prize pupil's outburst.

"I have wasted precious years here!" Trinadol had charged. "My father grows weaker by the minute and yet my life has not yet begun! If the Crown of Arnarus is lost at Serrid, why couldn't one just find it? And if the diamond skull of King Peltor truly lies at the base of the falls of Esher, why couldn't one just detect it and hoist it from the sea? I can do these things, Dantair! I know just how! It's an evil waste of precious time to read forever of such stones languishing in the world! What great good could be done with these lenses, Dantair? The past and future hides in those jewels. Why have you trapped me here in this paper dungeon?"

Dantair had cautioned Trinadol not to act rashly, but Trinadol had left that night in the boat he had made with his own hands as part of his Cirilen training.

And now, after three days of freedom, *Stargazer* was taking him home.

He gazed over the gunwale and pulled his numb fingers from the water. Tiny blue, green, and yellow lights twinkled like millions of stars under the sleek boat. Trinadol realized he was passing over the reefs of southern Ameulas, and he threw the core of the enryd into the sea. He sat up to look over the prow.

An island rose under the North Star and he recognized it with a sense of dread: it was the Dimmrock.

His grandfather had moved the throne of Ameulas to this small island over four centuries ago. It had been called the "Dimmrock" for so long no one knew why. It was said to have been a prison in ancient times, Trinadol recalled now, ironically.

Two hundred miles south of the great southern gulf of Ameulas, the Dimmrock was ten miles long, rectangular, and had a square, choppy bay in its southwest shore. The glowing reefs made the island inaccessible to deep-drafting ships from the south. The Dimmrock's cliffs, dark slate slashed with green shale, rose 400 feet above the sea, crowned with luxuriant emerald fields that shone blue in the starlight.

On the southern cliff of the island, the Lightstone Tower shimmered, a 380-foot column made of a substance only Cirilen could conjure.

Some stones, like diamonds, Cirilen could not create. Yet there was one stone nature could not create, called *lightstone*, which Cirilen made from sand, roses, seawater and gold. Most Cirilen who worked their whole lives could never conjure the quantity of *lightstone* Elwyn had created for the Tower in a single afternoon four centuries ago.

When ordinary men beheld the Lightstone Tower, they saw a prism of all the colors surrounding it, for the surface of the Tower produced a mild optical illusion that could not be attributed to light or shade. Yet a Cirilen's eye could unscramble the puzzle of light and see right through the shimmering pinnacle.

On the ground floor of Elwyn's Tower sat his father's Throne.

His father had been a good king and was much loved by his people. Senadol's law was simple: he ruled that no man might be the ruler of another. He believed that no virtue could be unchosen, so he had left men free to choose. His kingdom prospered accordingly, leaping and bounding with energy, industry, imagination and generosity. Senadol preferred this—tyranny was dull.

The inspired works of free men, the colossal hilarity of their innocent blunders and the burden of their tragedies was enough to keep any ruler amazed, amused, and saddened, without much interference of his own. Moreover, Senadol knew that nations could only be temporarily wounded by tragedy, but were forever aged by law. So Ameulas, though ancient, still seemed young, and was kept so by an aging monarch who still loved youth.

Trinadol looked at the Tower that gleamed like a tusk on the Dimmrock's jaw as his musings and memories collided with the present. His shoulders were wedged against the taffrail as he lay with his umber robe open, revealing his leather tunic and tight trousers of purple eelskin that were tucked into his tall black boots. He smelled the incense of the forest and heard the breakers on the cliffs. He struggled to sit up on the aft thwart, sensing *Stargazer*'s urgency.

Stargazer was already entering the Dimmrock's bay, where he saw several ships anchored. Trinadol watched a heavy swell that rolled before his bow until it crashed in a long jumble of phosphorescence on the shore, receding before the gleaming figure of a knight.

Stargazer crested a wave and rode it in, and as the wave shrank and laid her high on the beach, the knight suddenly moved and lent a weak yet steady hand.

He wore silver armor open only at the wrists and neck. He looked at Trinadol after he pulled himself out of the wet sand, and Trinadol gasped to see the man's face—a livid skull sheathed in cracked and wizened skin. Yet the man's eyes were living and bright in his hideous face, and long hair of shining silver flowed around his head in the sea-wind. "My son," he hissed.

"Father?" Trinadol whispered, and he knelt in the sand before Senadol. His father had already died, and had remained inside his corpse for Trinadol's return.

"Late!" Senadol hissed, clenching bony fingers on Trinadol's arm. "Come."

Trinadol followed his father as his armor screeched with sand until the joints worked out the grains, and he saw the deep imprints in the sand where Senadol had stood for days and nights as the tides washed round his feet.

"Never mind," said Senadol, looking sidelong at Trinadol as his enchanted armor walked forward. "My flesh carried me. Now I carry it."

The First Moon lit a rocky ramp that led from the beach to the forest on the cliff. As Trinadol helped Senadol onto the path, he heard a sound like knives being sharpened and turned to see thousands of the silver crabs Senadol had created for the Dimmrock scrambling toward them over the beach.

"Go now, and remember me!" whispered Senadol from the path, and they scurried down the sand and leaped into the foaming waves.

Senadol paused and gathered his breath, and he pointed his withered hand at the trees above. "Elms twice my age live in that forest. Golden instruments were placed in their branches by your grandfather to make the wind sing."

"I remember, Father."

"Wait!" The old Cirilen's young eyes sparkled in his ruined face. He pointed his finger over the bay. A dark wind, like smoke, moved through the air. The wind crossed the path ahead of them and passed into the forest. The pipes lowed and the chimes shrilled in the woods above, and Trinadol even heard the iron bell toll in the heart of the forest.

Senadol grasped his arm. "Everything is so clear now, my son!" he said. "He came with you, like a wind in your poor boat's sail. He pretends to be a Winteg's ghost to trick the Gairanor."

"Who, Father?"

"Listen to the wind!"

Trinadol looked at the churning forest as the gale blasted the pipes and bashed the chimes.

"What does it sound like?"

Trinadol frowned. "It seems most vandalous."

"It is hatred driven mad by endless dreams of vengeance."

"Father! What is it?"

"It comes for you, my son."

"Why?"

"It wants to ruin you. It wants to be you."

Trinadol smelled the reek of his father's breath as he leaned close to hear him over the howling gusts.

"Old things crouching in the twilight love your youth and power even more than you do, Trinadol. You are evil's ending, or evil's beginning. Beware the crimson!" Senadol coughed black blood on his chin. "Beware the crimson…"

The wind shrieked.

"We must go." Senadol pulled his son forward as his armor marched up the path, and they entered the thrashing woods as the branches creaked and snapped around them.

The pipes, bells, and chimes in the forest shrieked, howled and rang in a ghoulish bedlam as Senadol moved forward like a machine.

"Father, let me dash this spirit away!" cried Trinadol.

"No, it is not so easy," wheezed Senadol, pausing and hanging on Trinadol, his frayed fingers snagging in his cape. "Even with the Scepter, I could not…"

"Rest, Father!" Trinadol flung a finger in the air. A cursed wind sent against a Cirilen? He met the wind with a white-hot pride: "Be gone!" was all he spoke.

The wind held its breath.

The branches were still.

They heard the waves sighing softly on the distant beach.

Senadol turned his head slowly and frowned, his sunken face livid in the moonlight. "Do not believe this flattery, Trinadol. This sugar it sprinkles upon you is not for your tongue!"

Trinadol shrugged and shook his head. "Father, it is gone. What haunts you so?"

A distant scream scratched the sky.

Senadol's eyes rolled heavenward.

The pipes squealed and a gust struck down through the forest and swallowed them both like a dark ghost, sucking them through the tunnel of trees.

Trinadol saw his father somersaulting beside him as a descending scale of panicking chimes screamed by them. On the great lawn at the forest's edge, the wind spilled Trinadol, and he rolled and climbed to his feet to see his father carried off into the sky by the seething shadow.

For a moment he wondered if it was taking Senadol to his bed in the Tower's pinnacle, but then it dissipated and let Senadol fall.

Bolting across the field and vaulting the stairs, Trinadol found his father's body crumpled on a terrace beneath the Tower.

He pressed his hand on Senadol's breastplate and the armor cracked and fell apart. He lifted his father into his arms and howled as he lunged over the last steps to the Tower.

He dashed through its arch, instinctively dodging to the right, and he shouldered through a door that led down a curving, torch-lit corridor.

He came to the landing of the stairs and scaled the Tower three steps at a time on its spiraling staircase.

When he staggered into the uppermost room, a chamber 30 feet wide, a solitary candle's flame pointed to Senadol's bed.

Trinadol laid his father down and waited with frozen tears.

"What a treachery…what a murder this is!" he cried, shaking his fist heavenward. "I will repay this hard violence one-hundred measures to one!"

His father's eyes opened, alive in the candlelight. "Trinadol," he sighed, and blood spattered his lips. "I've much to tell…and no time to retell it…"

"Speak, Father." Trinadol bowed his head between his arms, and his tears thawed and poured over his face as he clasped his father's brittle hands.

"Nothing," Senadol rasped, "gains easier passage to the heart…than that which is closest."

"How can anything be close to my heart now?" cried Trinadol.

"Trinadol! I am a Prophet Cirilen! The future I foresee nearly always comes true, and I have foreseen a terrible fate for you, my son. That which is closest to your heart will be your doom! The thing you love most will be your curse! But you will know the source of this treachery by a sign: crimson. Beware the crimson." The Cirilen stiffened.

"Yes, Father!"

"Beware the crimson…"

Senadol's head rolled on the pillow as his last breath extinguished the candle's flame.

Dawn glowed faintly in the *lightstone* walls as darkness fell on the new king of Ameulas.

*   *   *

Chapter 2

Temptation

The sun seeped through the walls, bathing Senadol in eternal amber.

Although Trinadol was horrified by the sight of his father's shattered corpse, he had been staring at it for hours.

He turned away and strode to the high-arched window.

He pulled open the shutters and the bracing wind swept back his black hair.

His face shone white, absorbing the sun into a hotter, inner energy. His proud nose was chiseled at an angle to his upper lip, his chin beardless, like all Cirilen. His dark eyes still burned in his haggard face.

He lifted his father, and descended the Tower, passing galleries, salons, libraries, apartments, and servants' quarters before coming to the mouth of the stairs.

The curving hall before him was lit by cool watercolors distilled through *lightstone*. The torches that were ablaze the night before had now been doused; servants must have tended them. There were many people on the Dimmrock, Trinadol knew, though it seemed completely deserted.

He passed now into the Throne Room, a wedge-shaped room 40 feet high that made the crystal thrones of King and Queen seem huge upon their dais.

Over the ornate, tall-backed thrones, banners woven in Demoldan gold and bright Ameulentian silk splayed over the wall. These ancient standards bore the devices of two kings: Gieron, Bondairtlen founder of Ameulas, and Elwyn Gheldron, first Cirilen-Lord of Ameulas. Thirty-three monarchs and a thousand years had passed between these two kings, and yet their staffs were crossed, symbolizing their royal union of their bloodlines.

Trinadol quickly left the Throne Room through its high arch whose ash-wood doors had never been closed and he took in the view that embraced him outside.

The curving verandah dropped 20 feet to two semi-circular terraces. Below these terraces, a round courtyard of swirled blue-and-cream alabaster encircled the Tower. Below this was a square courtyard of grass encompassed by stone walls. The stairs before Trinadol reached the north gate of this outer courtyard, beyond which a broad lawn stretched to the forest. Beyond the woods, Trinadol saw blue-green fields rolling to the island's edge. Ameulas could be seen from the top of the Tower, but here it was hidden by the sea's blue horizon.

Trinadol descended the marble staircase, crossed the greensward and entered the musical forest, which was bright and lovely and showed no sign of the night's chaos. The path, rimmed by boulders painted white, had been raked clean. When he came to a fork with one path leading west to the beach, Trinadol took the northern path through the woods.

Each part of the forest played only one note in every key on a variety of golden instruments. After exploring Cintairn Gheldron, as the forest was known, one learned which note came from each part. A shimmering tone from the southern edge would rise in a scale as the wind flowed north and shift chords as it crossed boundaries. Along the forest's edge Elwyn had hung the charms in harmonics of three notes, producing mellow chords that varied with the wind.

Golden bells, perched high in pinwheels, spun, flashed, and tinkled. Golden rattles shook in exotic rhythms, measuring the summer breezes. Rippling chimes serenaded lazy sunsets. And great pipes throbbed in hollow trunks, turning winter tempests into operas and, sometimes, even the iron bell that hung on the fig tree in the forest's heart tolled, when the weather was dangerous for men and mariners.

Today, the melody was meek and bright, with rhythms meandering in springy refrains. Pheasants watched them from branches as they passed and black squirrels and silver possums crept behind them down the path. Gray toads, fat and overeager, strained to keep up with Senadol's lonely procession, and a blue owl rolled its yellow eyes at them from the hollow of an elm.

Trinadol saw a crimson buck pause on the path ahead. Riding on the elk's back was an ugly monkey-like creature that looked sullenly at Trinadol before the buck lunged over a boulder and disappeared through the trees.

As he waded through the swirling fields of orange wildflowers beyond the wood, Trinadol floated somewhere between grief and dread, numb to his own weariness. When he reached the edge of the island he looked at the sea that beat the cliff in slow fury 400 feet below.

"A great and good man," he said to the sky, "is dead before his time! Who are you to dare this Cirilen, and me in the bargain, I wonder? Come forward, and without a lens of diamond I will chase every trace of you from Hala. Come! I've seen you before at the Serrid Strait and you were weak." Trinadol scoffed at the sky. "Mark this well, before the watching Gairanor this day: I will be your doom, if you would be mine!"

He leaped high then and cast Senadol over the edge.

Recalling the Spell of Passage, he cried, "Senadol awake, *too-oh-nair!*" before his feet had touched the ground.

His father's body hovered and his soiled robes caught fire, flaming into ashes.

With a thunderclap, an eagle's wings swept aside the white cinders. Its beak and talons were gold, its feathers like pearls, its eyes like burning moons. Seabirds dove around the eagle as it sang a cry of freedom and turned toward Ameulas, pumping against the wind as ashes streamed from its wings.

It wheeled suddenly and dropped three rings from one of its talons: the rings of King, Husband, and Father.

Trinadol caught them all in one hand as the eagle gazed at him one last time and then tucked its wings into a dive.

The wild bird swooped barely from the sea, dipping its beak in a cold crest and shivered droplets from its neck as it beat its wings. It climbed a spiral past Trinadol and high into the heavens, where even the gulls could not follow.

And Trinadol sat on the edge of the cliff and watched until the brilliant avatar melted in the dazzling blue.

*   *   *

When Trinadol left the cliff, the mid-morning sun was edging the leaves with gold and gilding the bumblebees. Lavender blossoms shaped like globes of tiny buttercups burned on the wind-churned grasses, flowers he recognized, now, like long-lost siblings. The orange corkscrew blooms pirouetting in the wind were called "Dimfires," he recalled.

He saw a flock of wild sheep in the distance, their heads high as they looked at him over the tall grass. There was a gusty warmth of summer in the air mixed with a chill of anxious fall.

Trinadol felt a great weight lifted as a new and ominous burden quickly replaced it. "That which is closest to your heart will be your doom," he murmured, remembering his father's words, bitterly.

He felt an arch and terrible confidence then. Surely, nothing was dear to him now. There was nothing to part with, nothing to lose—nothing he loved! And this could be the unexpected downfall of his assassin. I have the advantage of contempt, he thought, contempt for the crown that binds my freedom. I shall stand my ground and protect myself with scorn like a sword. If anything comes too close, I will simply smite it away for good sport. What a simple challenge is this prophecy, after all! Nothing shall ever be close to my heart, he decided.

With this earnest resolve, young Trinadol strode down the path in Cintairn Gheldron when he overheard the high, clear laugh of a girl through the trees.

He sensed rushing water nearby.

A few strides ahead, a path broke off to the right; he took it.

He came to a grove of trees with hand-like leaves and cobalt flowers that scented the air with vanilla perfume. The grove opened into a glade surrounded by trees in whose branches Elwyn had placed a full harmonic of reeds and bells. The ebbing breeze produced mellow, shifting chords around the clearing as Trinadol made for a grotto at the far end, where a waterfall cascaded into a swimming pond.

As he approached the pool he saw shelves carved in the rock for sunbathers on the far bank. One of these ledges appeared to be wet. Trinadol leaped over the jade pond to look.

On the smooth gray stone before his boots was the watermark of a maiden's bare body. So beautiful was every secret detail pressed on the rock before him that he was heartbroken as the image evaporated and disappeared in the sun.

He felt her eyes and looked up, and he knew it was she though he saw only her eyes and nothing more. Neither of them could endure the thrill of that stare and yet neither would surrender it. At last, he looked away and hung his head, organizing himself for their introduction.

"Sir, you startled me!" she sighed, looking eagerly upon him as she held a linen robe closed at her throat.

He looked at her raven-black hair, shell-white teeth and pomegranate lips, and got caught in her eyes that were blue riptides of beauty. "I am most sorry!" said Trinadol. He was dumbstruck. "What is your name, milady?"

"My name is Neuvia. And what is your name, good sir?"

He bowed. "Trinadol." He expected her to gasp. She did not. Indeed, it seemed it might have been any name to her.

"Then you are the Lord of the Tintilisair, now," she nodded. "I'm glad." She kneeled, bowing her head. "For the country," she smiled, rising.

He was thinking of a response when she began hunting her sandals. She found them and sat on a stone above the waterfall, lacing them to her ankles. When she finished, she stood and pulled her fingers through her wet hair. Her eyes were like shards of summer sky. "I must go, my lord. I'm a servant girl and will be missed in the kitchen." She paused. "Do you have a favorite dish? I'll make it for you."

"I remember scrambled eagle's egg and Dimmrock leeks..."

"You shall have them!" she smiled. "And black biscuits."

He stared as she walked off through the woods, using no path.

*   *   *

Chapter 3

▼

The Old Philosopher

The day of coronation drew near, and with each day's passing, ten ships bore more Ameulentians from the mainland.

The Lightstone Tower flew the long green buntings of Ameulas. The yellow banners of the Demoldans, spun of gold, were hung beneath them, for in Elwyn's time the gold-rich island of Demold, along with Ameulas and Ghenten, formed the united kingdom known as the Tintilisair. Now, only Ameulas and its neighboring isles remained of the Tintilisair, yet the gold banners were brought over a thousand miles as a gesture of lasting good will by ambassadors of Demold which lay between Ameulas and the lost continent of Ghenten.

Ladies and lords celebrated, danced, supped, and drank wine on the sunlit terraces and lawns beneath the Lightstone Tower. Fruits indigenous to all regions of Ameulas adorned the tables, and wines made from succulent berries and grapes were kept chilled in great blue jugs encased in glacier ice from the larders in the Tower's cellar.

Sweetmeats, sour breads, and rich, complex cognacs were abundant, but none of these could induce Trinadol to mingle with his future subjects, who craved no greater indulgence than his presence.

He looked down from the window of his father's room, cataloging and scrutinizing all the things he wanted to do. He spied a group of mariners swinging mugs of cold beer in rowdy, guarded clusters, sea captains boasting and horseplaying like overgrown boys. He loved those mariners once.

Now he flinched at each gesture they made as his father's words chided his heart.

He decided to call for the mysterious beauty as soon as affairs were more settled. He knew she posed a threat to him, that she might approach his heart and possibly seize it in her beautiful hand. But he had not been able to put her out of his mind. He must study her, he thought. He must study all things that threatened to come close to him.

If Neuvia was the agent of some enemy, it was all the more important for him to watch her. He would parry her charms with suspicions and use her very loveliness as evidence against her. As soon as he detected the first stirrings of desire he would freeze the heat inside his chest and remain invulnerably cool. And yet, he wondered, how could beauty so fair and spirit so pure conceal death and doom?

The bell rang. "Yes, enter!"

The heavy trapdoor rose and an attendant poked his grizzled head into the room. "Your lordship, a man is here to see you regarding your Coronation. His name is Artimeer."

"Who?" He had seen seven obsequious oldsters already today and had been excessively drilled on the elaborate proceedings of his coronation. He had been measured, choreographed, versed and blessed, and could not imagine what else they could do to him besides stuff an apple in his mouth and cook him.

"It is Senadol's court philosopher, Artimeer."

Artimeer, thought Trinadol. Artimeer was one of the very few he could remember from his father's court. Artimeer had never treated him like a superior, and even seemed sympathetic to his peevish sense of humor. Ah, Trinadol sighed, how nice to discover a friend here! Then dread filled him with suspicion. "Let him enter," he said.

Artimeer climbed the ladder and slammed the trapdoor behind him with a casual flourish.

The old philosopher appeared much the same though time had sculpted him leaner, like the face of a mountain. He smiled uncertainly to see Trinadol, who was now a young man he did not know. Fidgeting with the green cape he had been persuaded by court-minded fools to wear, Artimeer straightened up and studied the Heir Apparent. He seemed to read the weird intensity in Trinadol's face and trace the stressings. Concerned, he looked away. "My lord, welcome home," he said.

"I have no home," said Trinadol.

"It must be difficult."

"Yes. It is difficult."

"My lord, and Senadol is free?"

"You are that familiar with the practices of the Cirilen, Philosopher?"

"Yes, my lord, having learned of them from Senadol."

Trinadol nodded, respectfully.

"And then there is the question of milord's numen, which shall be revealed at Coronation," said the sage.

"What concerns you, Artimeer? Why should you worry over what colors my heart?"

"My lord, I beg pardon." Artimeer marked the quickness of Trinadol's defense. "But it is a subject of popular conjecture. The numen of your grandfather was bright gold, and his ruling age was golden. Your father's numen was pure white, like silver, and his ruling age was silvern. When the Scepter, with the Cronus Star clear and dormant, is passed to you, the people will await the numen of the new lord to manifest itself in the scepterhead and presage your reign."

"This is impudent! To imagine the color of my soul, and conjecture its value as one might judge the fairness of the weather or the ripeness of a fruit is deeply offensive to me, Artimeer." Trinadol stood tall before the old philosopher with his hands at his hips.

"Milord, you do not know the color of your numen?"

Trinadol folded his arms, looking through the *lightstone* wall. "I do not wish to know it." He looked harshly at Artimeer. "My wise teachers have never let me touch a stone of power. But it does not matter now. My heart cannot be any hue, for love is a curse to me, Philosopher. My heart must always remain empty."

"My lord, is that possible? Even when we choose nothing, still, we are choosing," said Artimeer.

"Do not riddle me with philosophy! Speak plainly."

"Hatred and love are edges of the same blade which cuts both ways, lord. If a man values his garden, he hates the snail; if he loves life, he hates the killer. If a man hates everything, including himself, he must love something that he believes cannot exist. And if a man loves everything, both good and evil, then he must hate the good, since evil is that which harms the good."

"So even a killer is a lover?" Trinadol mused.

"All killers are lovers, lord," shrugged Artimeer rhetorically. "But are they lovers of death, or of life? That is the question."

"Life! It must be life she loves, and goodness, Artimeer…" Trinadol waved his hand as if to erase his confession. "How does an assassin look? Surely, the mark of death must be inscribed in his very frame, in his contemptuous posture, in the miserable wrinkling of his features…"

Artimeer turned toward the window, unable to see through the wall as Trinadol did, but able to see through Trinadol well enough. "My lord, there are two kinds of killers. There is the kind who kills in the name of life, and he may look radiant, and the bitterness in his eyes may glitter bright as hope. And there is another type of killer who is far more common. He kills in the name of death, and he will everywhere disrespect man and woman and seem foul. However, a man may appear sickly, though his heart shines with goodness, and a man may look wholesome, though his deeds are full of malice. The evil man cannot affect the aspect of a good man, however, in actions, words and appearance without becoming a good man himself."

"Your law seems simple, yet rich with implication," said Trinadol. "I must ponder it." He nodded at Artimeer.

The old philosopher smiled. "My Liege, I believe your numen will be blue and pure. That you would ponder good and evil bodes well for Ameulas."

He bowed and left Trinadol to his thoughts.

*   *   *

Chapter 4

▼

Love

The reason one hates is that one loves, yet my father has foreseen that love will destroy me. Does this mean I must hate love? This kingdom is both my prison and my poison and my reign a life and death sentence. Bitterness, it seems, is my only armor.

Trinadol put his pheasant quill in the inkwell on his desk and blew on the page of his journal. He glanced down through the window at the mid-morning festivities from the room atop the Tower and he decided at last to descend among his people and refrain from choosing his poison, indefinitely.

*   *   *

Avoiding the Throne Room, Trinadol passed the kitchen and noticed a white-haired woman in the hall ahead of him. She wore a green uniform and rubbed her hands on a blue apron. As he approached her, Trinadol recognized Ardolia, his personal cook when he was a child. Time had only added flourishes to her indomitable face.

She sighed and rushed toward him.

He was cold to her kiss.

"Lord, forgive me, but I can't help but remember the little lad who loved my black biscuits and yellow gravy! How you've grown! Such a handsome young King there never was!"

Fond memories of Ardolia and the wonderful food she had cooked for him filled his heart, and he reminded himself not to lower his guard. "Indeed, I did love the foods you made for me, Ardolia."

She smiled, melting in maternal joy. "But you look tired and travel-worn. Let me cook breakfast for you again!"

"I think not. There is a girl in your kitchen. Her name is Neuvia. Let her cook my breakfast and bring it to me on the verandah. I choose to dine with her this morning." I don't love you, he told himself as he turned away and left Ardolia trembling with heartache as he strode down the corridor like a stranger.

He brooded on a stone chair by a stone table, looking from the verandah at the dark, white-capped sea. He had enlisted a few surprised men-at-arms and sent them around the bends to block this part of the Tower's curving verandah from visitors.

Preceded by the sumptuous aroma of Ameulentian herbs, Neuvia emerged from the Tower.

She was dressed in her green cotton kitchen dress. Her face was a radiant shade of white, her eyebrows dark over her sky-blue eyes. The wind stroked her black hair, threaded with crimson strands. There was a little sweat beaded on her upper lip. "I thought you would call," she said.

Trinadol was speechless at the vision of her.

She set a platter on the table with a great golden dish of fried sparrows' eggs, Dimmrock leeks, thick bacon, and enryd cut into little circles and fried in red butter. On a side dish, his favorite black biscuits with yellow gravy steamed invitingly.

Trinadol sighed to see the familiar food, hypnotized by the lovely memories its spices revived. He checked his heart as a cruel thought chilled his mind: poison! He looked into her eyes. "I asked for an eagle's egg," he said.

Neuvia curtsied. "I thought you might prefer fried sparrows' eggs, my lord. They are fresh and especially delicious. The marmosets bring them to me." She smiled, revealing her exquisite teeth.

"How did you guess I preferred fried sparrows' eggs to scrambled eagles' eggs?" he frowned.

"A cook's intuition," she pouted. "Nothing more…or less, my lord?"

"And you brought none for yourself?"

"I have eaten breakfast, my lord. But if it is poison you fear, I will taste each course from your own plate!" She laughed brightly and sat in the chair nearest to him. "There is not a soul on this island who would not taste your food, for not a soul would poison you! Be sure of that, at least…my lord?"

"Yes, of course. What…where did you come from, Neuvia?" he asked, looking down at his stiff hands.

She took the spoon from the platter and tasted the eggs. She offered him half a spoonful. "I am Ameulentian. I was born on Ameulas, of humble farmer stock. My mother is a cook here and I have lived here since I was seven. You may taste the eggs, now, if you like, lord."

He sampled the spoon of eggs and was reminded of his hunger. "Delicious!" he grunted.

"Thank you, my lord." She smiled and took a bite of bacon, offering it to him.

He pointed at the other end.

Surprised, she turned over the strip and gently bit off the other end, licking her red lips.

Trinadol swallowed as he took the piece of bacon from her and bit the same end, chewing the savory meat as he looked at her fair skin. He looked down at his plate. "How old are you?"

She tasted one of the black biscuits dipped in gravy. "You may eat these now, my lord. Seventeen. How old are you, if I may ask?"

"The same." He ate a whole black biscuit sopped in gravy and more eggs and bit into a strip of bacon soaked in yolk.

She sipped his black coffee and mint-leaf apple juice. "You may drink these now, my lord," she smiled, raising an eyebrow wryly.

He sipped the coffee and wiped his lips on the soiled sleeve of his tunic, clearing his throat. "Has anyone ever spoken to you about me, Neuvia?"

"Yes! Of course. But why do you ask, my lord?"

"You are not part of any plot?" He watched her closely, his eyes narrowing. "A plot to slay me?"

She looked at him as though he were crazy. "No!"

Trinadol glanced at the Tower, seeing through it, and he sighed in pain.

"How could you think such a thing?" she asked.

He looked into her eyes her fiercely. "Why then, sweetest maiden, if you know nothing of me or my heart, did you lie in wait for me in the forest?" he demanded. "What kind of trap did you have in mind?"

Neuvia cried out, wanting to strike him, but of course she could not. She smiled wickedly, instead, and rose. "I have duties in the kitchen," she said. "I will be missed!"

"You have none." Trinadol gently caught her hand as she turned away. "Sit down, milady."

She did, confused, and wiped a hot tear from her proud cheek.

They stared then into each other's eyes, like killers.

"Do not torment me so..." he whispered, closing his eyes and holding her hand gently.

"I do not wish to," she whispered back as new tears ebbed in her eyes. Her lips trembled, but she steeled them in defiance. She left her hand in his and shook her head slowly, hating him, and yet pitying him, unexpectedly.

"Who told you to wear the things you are wearing?" he said.

"The cooks!"

He opened his eyes. "Who showed you how to put your hair?"

"My mother!"

He squeezed her hand sharply. "Who taught you how to hold my hand?"

"I—" She took her hand away, bewildered.

"Who made your eyes like my dreams, your lips like fairies dancing in my mind? Who carved your nose so fine and fierce, and shaped your body so fair and unforgettable that it plagues my sleep and invades my dreams? Eh? Who taught you how to turn your face from me now with such splendid pride!" He touched her jaw reverently as though he were admiring the genius of an assassin.

"I do not know!"

"Who taught you how to weep? How to weep without surrendering?" He touched one of her fierce tears in awe.

"No one!" she shouted, and she rose in rage.

"And how to be in every way so lovely to me!" he denounced her, rising and seizing her shoulders. "Who taught you? No, milady, you are too perfect for me to be innocent!"

She clawed his ribs through his tunic. "I have dreamed of you coming home to the Dimmrock since I was a little girl! You are a Cirilen with strange powers, and it is I who should fear you! And yet I do not. But you fear me? I am in the dark!"

"This must be some magical crime," he cried, laughing in anguish. "How could nature create a creature so perfect for me to love and bring her to me now, when love is the thing I am forbidden?" He stroked a strand of crimson in her hair.

She recoiled from him in contempt. "Yesterday I thanked the Gairanor for sending my dream to Hala. Now I wonder why they sent my nightmare!"

He softened his grip on her arm and looked into her eyes that filled his heart with adoration. He closed his eyes and smelled her lovely scent, smiling bitterly. "Who told you to wear that perfume?" he asked.

"I do not wear perfume," she whispered.

He shook his head, and opened his eyes.

Tears of hope blinded them from all doubts as their smiles met in a kiss that seemed like the first true thing they had ever known.

* * *

They ran down the main path of Elwyn's forest and the world smoldered with beauty around them. At last, their bursting hearts spent, Trinadol took her hand and they walked down the dappled path, catching their breath.

"You see these elms?" He gestured at the giant grove of jade-leafed trees around them. "They are twice the age of my father. I climbed each kind of tree in this forest when I was a child. Elms, eucalyptus, oaks, jacaranda. I built a tree house in a perfect enryd tree when I was four."

"Your tree house is by the brook?" she asked.

"How did you know?"

"I played in your tree house, Trinadol, when I was a little girl. I know more about you than you think. I explored every room so I could find out everything I could about you."

He grinned and pulled her close.

"What are you thinking of?" she asked, boxing him in the side.

"Fate and foresight."

She frowned. "I wish you wouldn't puzzle me with riddles."

He laughed and nodded. "I dislike riddles, too. When I was a boy, I placed a charm on my tree house—a charm that rendered it invisible except to the girl who would be my Queen."

"I placed a charm on your tree house, too!" she said proudly. "A love charm over Trinadol, the handsome heir to the throne who left across the sea when I was seven. So who's to say which one of our spells truly worked?"

"Yours, I fear," he growled playfully.

"I burned a flower for my spell," she bragged.

"I burned a lizard!"

She wrinkled her nose.

"It was already dead." He shrugged. "Boys have different spells than girls."

The forest bloomed around them as the chimes and pipes played a winsome melody. "Is all the world competing for my heart today?" Trinadol laughed, softly. "Kiss me, Neuvia. I want you to win my soul!"

"Yes, milord." She curtsied like a proper servant girl and kissed him.

Then she led him through the trees to the grotto where they first met.

Vanilla wind stirred the trees around the glade. Neuvia kneaded his stiff shoulders before the rippling pool. "Do not think doubtful things, Trinadol," she said.

He turned to her.

She kissed his smooth chin, unclasping the cape at his throat. She took off his cape and laid it on the grass.

He smiled.

She took off his dagger and unbuttoned his vest, then unhooked his tunic, soaked it in the water, and laid it out in the sun. She began unlacing his trousers.

"Hold!" laughed Trinadol. "My viper!"

"I shall, soon," she winked. She frowned. "Well, you can't go swimming in these clothes, and my lord must take a bath! You haven't washed for weeks!"

Trinadol laughed, blushing.

"Goodness, Trinadol! I cared for seven boys, and each I bathed from infants. It isn't my doing if you didn't bring a swimming cloth with you."

He sighed as she rolled down his eelskin trouser legs. "Would evil not choose a subtler path?" he grinned with a heavenward glance.

They capered on the edge of the pond, sloughing off their clothes, and inevitably they lost their balance and fell into the water, with Neuvia's stockings still on her legs and Trinadol's left boot and pants hanging off one foot.

They tossed these, sopping, beside the pool, and sipped cool water from each other's lips as they bathed each other, tenderly.

Trinadol charmed some of the tiny tinfoil minnows to jump through a hoop he made with his thumbs and index fingers. Trinadol and Neuvia laughed at the innocent fish and praised them as they leaped so well.

They crawled onto a smooth stone shelf to dry in the sun, caressing each other in dizzy joy as the still-mesmerized fish leaped from the water beside them until Trinadol noticed them and rescinded his spell, remembering they were simple creatures best left to their own devices.

The afternoon was at that perfect stage of light and shade, heat and breeze.

Neuvia thought about the spell Trinadol had cast on his tree house. She tugged his ear. "If I am to be your Queen…"

"Yes?" He sat up and crossed his legs. "Could it be so?"

She did the same. "Which I am quite sure should be so," she said, "then I must get out all the demons of a boy's loneliness, all the desires grown wild in a young man's lusty heart, for I have been taught that boys must do this before true love can be between men and women." She said this honestly and plainly, looking straight into his eyes.

"Hmmm." He rose and pulled her up and took her naked into his arms beside the pool. "I am young," he said. "My demons are few and I wish to share them with you for the rest of our lives rather than be cured of them today. I doubt you could exorcise those demons, anyway, sweet maiden, nay, set them free, instead, and multiply them in pandemonium, eternally," he grinned.

"We should begin, then!" she whispered in his ear, and kissed it.

*   *   *

Aglow in the aftermath of their first passion, they noticed the shadows leaning long over the glade like disapproving old prudes.

"I am at odds, Neuvia," Trinadol said. "My father warned me to distrust that which I love most, yet I am filled with love! If I love that crimson sparrow sunning on a rock, will it stab my eye with its beak? If I love this pond red-spotted with moss, will it drown me? I guess we all must choose our poison, Neuvia. So I choose the whole world. I will love that which is good, as all men must, and stand against evil, as all men must, for it is as Artimeer said: we can know good from evil! I do not know how or why I love you, Neuvia, but it is as though I have always known you. I cannot imagine loving anything more than I love you as long as I shall live, for I shall keep loving you more, and nothing will ever be able to catch up. If you would be my doom, so be it. I would not choose another fate!"

"My lord, I will fight beside you against your foes, for yours is my fight now, and always will be! I will not be your doom, nor will I allow fate to make me so."

Trinadol knelt and took her hand. "Marry me, Neuvia," he said, touching her fingers to his hot brow.

"Marry me, Trinadol," she smiled, and a tear spilled down her cheek.

And they kissed, and their kiss had a tiny lifetime of its own, dying young and furious.

"Come then, Wife!" he laughed, and he tugged her hand. "Tonight and a million after we shall have for our secret feasts. Why don't we mingle with the good people of Ameulas? Dare I say it: with *my* people, Neuvia? I shall confuse this foe of mine by embracing all." He smiled and stroked her ear.

"Splendid!" she smiled, hiding her sadness at Senadol's dark prophesy and concealing her own determination that it would never come to pass. "First," she said, "I shall get your clothes and dress you." She placed the point of her finger on his lips. "They should all be dry by now, and a little fresher, no doubt, my sweet lord."

He watched her as she got his clothes, enslaved with joy to see the glow on her ravishing face and the wild, lustrous way her hair dried in the warm wind.

*　　　　　*　　　　　*

As they were walking back through Elwyn's forest, they spied a child zigzagging through the trees and kicking a blue ball.

"Ho, Trinadol!" shouted the boy as he kicked the ball in their direction and scrunched his apple face, buckling down and pumping his legs. He reached them and skidded to a stop as he caught the rolling ball under his scuffed boot. Then he dropped to his knees and panted, holding his stomach.

"You've run too hard, little one," said Trinadol, fanning the dust. "What's the emergency?"

Neuvia pulled the boy to his feet and dusted him off.

"Lord Trinadol!" he huffed. "Won't you come and join the par-tee?" The pug-nosed brat grinned through chubby, freckled cheeks.

"Well, of course!" said Trinadol. "And tell them there that I bring the new Lady of Ameulas—her name, a surprise for all!"

The redheaded rascal gasped and his blue eyes bugged at Neuvia. "A Queen, too? I'll tell them, your Majesty!" he cried. He turned, booted the ball, and bolted toward the Lightstone Tower shimmering in the distance through the treetops.

*   *   *

Chapter 5

▼

A Party for Trinadol

When they reached the greensward, the ladies and gentlemen of Ameulas flocked to greet, congratulate, and bless Trinadol and his betrothed.

Surely, it was a wondrous sign that Trinadol had chosen an Ameulentian girl for his bride, and a fair bride she was, though dressed in plain servant's clothes. Their fair Neuvia of the raven hair to wed Trinadol, the keen-eyed young lord—a great beginning!

"Good lords and ladies of Ameulas," said Trinadol when he and Neuvia had ascended the musicians' dais before the outer courtyard wall. "My father passed splendidly away—his shape a strong eagle of pearl and gold. The beauty of land and sea went with him to the Gairanor."

A cheer of awe swept the crowd, for some had seen the bird shining high up in the sky.

"Now I ask you to welcome me to this mighty kingdom," said Trinadol. "For I will rule with a light hand and a heavy fist, as did my father. Together we will live to improve our land and make our strong people as free on earth as in their dreams. This I promise, as did my father and my grandfather, as long as I am King."

"A toast to Trinadol!" cried one impassioned mariner, with a blue-black beard, who stood tall in an aquamarine cape. "Long live the King!"

The women and men of the Tintilisair raised their flagons and toasted deep.

"I wish to make an announcement," said Trinadol, grinning at Neuvia and stroking her index finger. "The radiant Neuvia is to be my queen. On the morning of my coronation, we shall be wed!"

Nothing could whip up the crowd like his own announcement of the rumored engagement.

Gifts were spontaneously conjured for the young queen: gold silks from Demoldan emissaries, perfumes from Ameulentian traders and whalers, and fabulous jewelry from the necks and waists and wrists and fingers of wealthy dowagers who lovingly surrendered their treasures to her.

Neuvia giggled as her fellow servants became her servants, suddenly attending to her every need, and they seemed to take it all very seriously, to her surprise.

Court officials, who congratulated him and spoke warmly of the coronation and wedding, swarmed Trinadol, and they invited him to visit their provinces on Ameulas.

The contingent of mariners, meanwhile, Trinadol noticed, kept a respectful distance.

Trinadol listened good-humoredly to the courtiers, but there was a hint of the courtly hobnobbing he abhorred as a boy, so he presently held up a hand to one Ameulentian who was describing the hunting in his forest and said, "Dear sir, I should simply visit your good province, and let my arrows sing there, rather than tease my ear too much with sweet promises. You make me wish I were there and I do wish to be here! Come, let me speak with those who represent the mariners of Ameulas for whom I admit I have a special favor."

"And we've a special favor for you, my lord!" said Karlock, a seasoned mariner with a short gray beard like cropped silver wires framing his keen, bronzed face. The captain advanced now, sporting a silver fox cape, green tunic, gray pants, and long black boots. He planted a spiraling cane of narwhal tusk with a handle of crimson wood. "I'm Karlock Isopika, Captain of the *White Shark*, the finest vessel afloat if I do say it my very self." He glanced at the other captains. "And I do!"

Arrghs and groans rose from his colleagues at this.

Karlock crumpled his feathered hat in his leathery hands with sudden discomfort. "Lord, we've been meaning to ask you a question for the last few days. You were indisposed, and such, but it's been gnawing on us. You see, ever since one of our vessels bore you to Trillan, and you favored the mariners to your own courtiers and listened to our tales and learned our skills like the best of our sons on that long voyage, we've held you to be like a foundling son to us, and…well…maybe we remember some of the things you did for us?"

Trinadol cocked his head. "Eh?"

Karlock swallowed. "We have many tales, lord. Perhaps too tall!"

"Here, you will tell me, won't you?" said Trinadol, pointing to the younger fellow beside the captain.

"I am Nil Ramesis, lord, second mate of the *White Shark*," said the tall man whose hair was very black, almost blue. His thick beard was cut short on his strong jaw, framing the proud, defiant frown of his mouth. "We have many tales of your Majesty saving ships and rescuing men in the storm, sending dolphins and seals for drowning sea dogs like Lince, perhaps." Nil winked at the bald first mate, who looked glumly at Trinadol. "And, your lordship, some say you lit landmarks with lightning in the fog and blew sails to save a reefing, or cleared—"

"Indeed?" Trinadol raised his hand and shrugged at Neuvia who was looking at him, intrigued. "I used to have dreams about mariners when I was a child…" he said. "But I…"

"We believe you did these things, lord, when you were a boy!" said Lince. "A statue of you as a lad is mounted over the crow's nest of every ship in Ameulas—it's a lucky token to us mariners."

Trinadol was taken aback. "I'm most honored," he said, unable to understand how the mariners could come to believe this about him. "Of all the citizens of Ameulas, however, I will favor the mariners with my influence, and bend it over the watery world where nowhere is home for men. I will represent the mariners as though they are my own constituency. Please, tell me about the trade winds, the hazards, and the bounties of the sea that are most important to you. And I shall listen well and do all that I can to assist you."

A faction of mariners departed to a private clearing in the forest to speak with Trinadol.

Neuvia, meanwhile, mingled with the people of Ameulas and the emissaries of Demold, and she was not overwhelmed, but instead her composure was regal and soothing, as she had always been, even as a cook's apprentice.

*   *   *

The mariners of Ameulas stood around Trinadol in a hidden clearing of the forest. "Are the reefs dangerous?" Trinadol asked Captain Karlock.

"Yes and no, lord. There are places where the reefs are too shallow—places where ships pile up on the bottom and make the reefs grow higher. However, the reefs are also where the red minnows school. And they are home to green abalone and striped shark, and oysters, squid, red tuna and black mackerel. The reefs are more our friend than our foe!"

"I believe I can lower the dangerous parts of the reefs," said Trinadol. "Are charts available that show the locations of the dangerous reefs?" asked Trinadol.

"Nilly, here, is the best chartmaker in Ameulas!" said Lince.

"The best *cartographer*," corrected Nil with knitted brows.

"But cartography isn't Nil's real ambition," ribbed Karlock.

"Eh? What is?" smiled Trinadol.

"He wants to wright a ship that can't be sunk. Don't ya, Nilly?" grinned Lince.

Nil blushed.

"A great dream," said Trinadol.

"'Tis what you said to me long ago," said Nil, a look of surprise on his face.

There was something familiar about Nil Ramesis, but Trinadol could not place it.

Nil nodded modestly, for he was proud. "I can draft a chart of the southern reefs for you, lord."

"Good, please do, as accurately as possible! The Crown shall pay you a thousand Gierons of gold. Then maybe you'll have enough gold to build that ship."

"He'll draft the smartest chart you've ever seen, lord!" said Lince, the tattooed eye on his bald head peering at Trinadol as he grinned a scimitar of pearly teeth at the Cirilen.

"I've no doubt!" Trinadol laughed.

"Lord," said Nil.

"Yes, Nil Ramesis?"

"Do you remember?" asked Nil.

"Remember?"

"The tales," urged Lince.

Trinadol shrugged. "Things have probably been exaggerated…" Oddly, he was starting to see some of the unlikely events these mariners described in his memories, though they could not have really happened. Then it came to him!

He remembered a dream he had told his father about when he was a boy. In the dream, Trinadol had seen a sailor with a blue eye on his head blown from a ship in a typhoon. The sailor was tangled in lines and barely kept himself above water with his great arms. Trinadol remembered the chill of pity the big blue eye on the sailor's head had stirred in him and he remembered taking hold of the lines and pulling the man over the swells. He had set him on a wave that carried him over the welldeck, where his friends grabbed onto him. His father exalted at his little son's great dream, impressed with the character in Trinadol's hidden heart. "I remember!" said Trinadol, and he gripped Lince's hand, amazed.

Lince smiled from ear to ear, blushing and shaking Trinadol's hand. "Thank you, lord," he muttered, stepping back and nodding at Nil.

Trinadol did not understand how his boyhood dreams could have had such effect, or what effect they had had. "Please, Captain Karlock, take me sailing tomorrow. Perhaps I can charm your vessel," he said, wanting to spend more time with the mariners.

Karlock's eyes widened. "To do what?"

"Well, I could make my statue over your crow's nest glow whenever there is danger…?"

Lince laughed, slapping the tall and gangly Nil on the back. Nil smiled in awe.

"That would be fine, lord," Karlock nodded.

Trinadol rose. "Tomorrow, then, bright and early, we shall go sailing. I would like Neuvia to accompany me. Perhaps we can fish for something? Something big, eh?" Trinadol winked. "If the *White Shark*'s up to it!"

Lince's brows peaked.

Karlock grinned. "Tomorrow at dawn then, lord!"

*   *   *

When Trinadol and the mariners returned to the lawn, the sun was setting in an orange sky.

Trinadol summoned his numerous attendants. "Have torches lit around this lawn, and have the tables brought out. We must tend to the feast and have the roasting pits kindled. And bring Neuvia to me—oh, and one more thing," considered Trinadol. "Could someone find me a very cold mug of Ameulentian beer?"

The attendants dashed off in various directions.

Neuvia was led to him through the gathering gentry. She kissed him openly, and it brought a sudden applause and gossip of approval from the court. They shrugged warily at each other and turned toward the musicians' dais, which had been raised against the outer wall of the courtyard.

They climbed the stairs, clasping hands, and from the dais Trinadol addressed the people. "It's such a welcoming night—such a clear night, I thought we should feast outdoors on this lawn below my grandfather's tower. If you are worried about insect aggressions—" Trinadol waved a hand over the field and gasped, closing his eyes. He opened them. "There shall be none," he smiled, waving a hand.

The crowds purled with pleasure, for this was the familiar blessing Senadol had bestowed on fairs and festivals.

"Here's your flagon of beer, lord! Poldur Herrig, the best draft in Ameulas!"

"Many thanks!" Trinadol toasted the crowd. "Let us dance and dine under the stars, my people, but pay close attention, for mysterious entertainment might dance in the sky tonight!" he bowed with a mischievous flourish, and the Ameulentians clapped their hands and rang handbells.

Trinadol's table was set on the musician's dais, and the musicians moved in front of the dais, which would cause complications, but such is life, thought Trinadol. And lo, they move! Trinadol thought as the musicians were ordered to move and just as Trinadol wondered who might be responsible, Artimeer, in his black-and-white robe, came walking through their midst waving his arms.

Artimeer climbed the stairs to the dais and took his seat to the right of Trinadol, though all others waited for Trinadol's approval.

"Thank you for joining me, Artimeer, my friend. I trust you," said Trinadol.

"I am very pleased," Artimeer nodded, smiling against the grain of his cautious face.

Trinadol's attendants asked him to choose the guests of honor for his table. Trinadol invited Neuvia's mother first, to sit on Neuvia's left. She had been offered courtly gowns but the old cook would have none of it. She proudly wore the green dress of the maidservants of the Lightstone Tower, like her daughter. Such servants were chosen from the very best Ameulas had to offer and were paid in gold for their talents, so the green dress was a prouder thing than any fancy frock to Nardleen Fenstridol.

Neuvia's father had died in a freak accident in a feud with a Great River beaver. The beaver's dam had bordered her family's farm for close to 30 years when Drok, the young buck of the beaver family, killed the friendly patriarch. Drok, with his huge head and close-set eyes, took over the dam and let it deteriorate. He liked to spy on Neuvia, for he had become enchanted by her. Drok had tried to catch the five-year-old Neuvia one day while she filled a white basket with blueberries, but she smelled Drok's bloody scent from behind a tree trunk and screamed. She pulled out the small hunting knife her father always put in her basket. Drok jumped out in front of her and clapped his flat tail against the tree. Neuvia's father heard her scream and came running. When Drok had reached for Neuvia, she stabbed his paw clean through. He yelped and pulled back, the knife still stuck in his paw, and he ran snarling through the trees as her father, armed with a pitchfork, chased him all the way to the beaver dam. Drok gnawed through the dam's central beam and the old dam broke, flooding the farm and killing Drok and her father.

That was why Nardleen and her daughter Neuvia had journeyed south to work as house cooks in the bustling city of Gwylor, where they had no problem finding employment in the most fashionable houses of Ameulas. Nardleen was a cook of extraordinary diversity and taste, having been trained in the superior northern disciplines, which, due to the hardships faced by its practitioners, made the most of many ingredients. And Little Neuvia delighted the old gentry with her sparkle and depth, a black diamond. So, after Senadol sampled a feast they had catered, he inquired boisterously for the cook, and the hosts winced as Senadol stole Nardleen and her charming daughter away from them with a royal offer.

In addition to Nardleen's exquisite cooking, however, Senadol had also been thinking about his son, and how it would be a good thing to have such a beautiful and deep-spirited young woman as Neuvia on the Dimmrock when Trinadol returned from Trillan.

Trinadol then asked the counselors of twelve provinces of Ameulas to dine with him, and lastly he asked Nil Ramesis, Karlock Isopika, and the bald mariner, Lince Neery-Atton, to complete his table.

Neuvia and Trinadol stood on the dais and raised their hands to the revelers. A dull thud of thunder rippled the starlit sky. "Ameulentians, behold!" cried Trinadol. All at once, the heavens were cut loose from the horizon, and they spun dreamily overhead.

There were yells, whoops and a general fright. Many lost their balance and grabbed onto each other as they looked at the sky.

Trinadol laughed and put his arm around Neuvia, holding out a calming hand. "My people, it is only an illusion! Not even I can move the stars; only we on the Dimmrock may see a sky such as this tonight. But watch closely."

With a far off crackling, four glowing forms appeared like firebrands on the sky: a blue ship, a white horse, a red bird and a yellow lion on a ring above the horizon.

"Five times tonight the horse will be due north, the ship due south, the bird due west, and the lion due east, and the stars will be right over Hala. Every time this occurs, all must say 'cheers!' or drink twice the amount in their cups!"

Trinadol pointed and the ship began tossing, the horse galloping, the bird winging, and the lion pouncing at different speeds in different directions around the horizon.

There was a hubbub as the people plunged into a controversy of wagers and disclaimers, and the musicians played a mystical melody to suit the stargazing contest. They had witnessed festive illusions in the sky conjured by Senadol, but never anything so fantastic!

"There, you missed it!" cried Trinadol. "Everyone must drink!"

The smell of roasts braised with honey wafted over the lawn. Two great lobsters as big as men and tender veal were served at Trinadol's table, with black breads, white-nut gravy, green spear vegetables, and the onions and butter all so distinctive of Ameulentian fare. Lince proposed one boisterous toast after another, as he was a salty dog with a chest like a keg of beer.

Trinadol clanked his own mug against his every time, matching him as the night progressed.

At one point, Neuvia kissed her lover's ear and whispered, "My lord, if you drink anymore tonight we won't be able to make love!"

This helped Trinadol get a hold on himself, and onto a fork so that he could eat some vegetables.

But Lince managed to hammer him with one more: "To Trinadol and Neuvia and all the sea and everyone in the whole willy-wolly-wonderful *wooooooorld!*" toasted the mariner with a broad swoop of his pewter mug, which Trinadol met with a foamy *thunk!*

"I think that's the toast to end all toasts, Mariner," said Artimeer, bending an eyebrow like a crossbow and zinging a sharp glance at the sailor. Artimeer gripped the table's edge with both hands as the slowly spinning sky made the world too like the deck of a wheeling ship for Artimeer's taste.

Lince blushed. "Say no more, sir!" he muttered. "The joy's overflowing, that's all! I understand the royal lad has more than grog to attend to what with a fine young molly like Neuvia waiting on him!"

"That will do, Mariner!" said Artimeer.

Neuvia laughed. "Oh, he's blushing, Artimeer!" she laid her hand on Lince's big tough hand that seemed like a crab's claw. "Thank you, dear sir!" she said.

Lince grinned at Artimeer.

"Neuvia, would you be so good, however, my dear?" Artimeer gestured toward Trinadol.

"A walk will do you good, milord!" she whispered in Trinadol's ear.

The cheers of the celebrants rose at the fifth and final alignment of the wheeling heavens, and, with a peal of far thunder, the magical sky winked and the true sky appeared once again, to everyone's relief. And the Second Moon smiled over the well-wined and dined delegates, guiding them to their welcome beds.

*   *   *

Trinadol observed the effects of the alcohol, which he had never experienced before, and rewove his mind to compensate for the imbalance. By the time he and Neuvia returned from their walk he was clear-headed and he looked at her as desire began pumping icy fire in his chest. It was, after all, his duty to honor the pre-nuptial tradition and make love to his betrothed.

They climbed the steps of the Tower together, buoyant and rosy from the flowering day and enamored with the rapture they had in store. They passed the servants' floors, and an old matron spied them crossing a doorway. "Lord Trinadol! Wait, me lord!" Benelvia came to her door by the stairs.

Trinadol waited impatiently with Neuvia on his arm.

Benelvia's face was as craggy as an arid mud-flat, with a nose like a cactus. "Will me lord be spending the night with me Lady?" she asked.

Trinadol sighed. "Since I'm sure it's very much your business, mother, yes, we will be spending the night together!" he bowed.

"Well, me lord, it is very much my business! I put a new bed in your father's room, a little perfume on the linens, and a new candle, which I lit as he told me to." She winked as though she understood all about it and smiled the sweetest mother's smile Trinadol thought he'd ever seen.

Trinadol kissed her on the forehead, much to her astonishment. "Good night, fair mother!" he said with a teary eye.

Neuvia reached out and took Benelvia's knobby hand. "We will remember this night, and you, so fondly. Thank you." Neuvia kissed her hand.

They ran up the stairs under the soft regard of the royal matron, and soon they lay in each other's arms, no crowd, person, robe or jewelry between them, but only the jewels of their eyes, the pearls of their teeth, the sable of their hair and the silk of their skin as they treasured each other that night. Together they came to the threshold of joy's house, and they flew as one into its light, and Neuvia sighed as her sight pierced the *lightstone*; for it seemed she floated with Trinadol among the stars.

*   *   *

Chapter 6

The Sea Monster

The *White Shark* smashed the back of a rolling swell and slid into the next, cleaving it like an ax spraying sawdust. The frowning shark figurehead under her bowsprit foamed at the mouth as it cut into the crest. A single white sail rippled over her decks.

Neuvia wore black woolen tights on her long legs and a black leather waistcoat adorned with yellow feathers. High boots of deep green chameleon covered her legs, and a gray fur cape of an ancient forest bear was clasped with an emerald at her neck. She stood with Trinadol by the starboard rail of the welldeck, conversing with the officers and crew.

Lince, the first mate, champed at the bit.

Nil Ramesis looked at the sea with a nervous grin.

Karlock seemed willfully subdued. "The seas are a bit rough today, lord. Bear it in mind," he said. "What kind of fish are we looking for, might I ask?"

Trinadol's eyes glittered like obsidian in the sun as the ship bashed into the slathered shoulders of royal blue. "Is there a beast of infamous history in your waters, Captain?" he asked. "Is there a terror, in legend no matter how obscure, who has earned the wrath of men, going on to yet more crimes against mariners without justice? Come, say frankly that monster's name, for that's the fish I wish to catch today."

The men *harrumphed* and grumbled.

"There's Knot!" offered Lince.

Others groaned at Lince's suggestion, for most did not believe the sea monster Knot had ever existed.

Nil frowned. "Knot's been dead for centuries, Lince. If she ever existed at all!"

"Tell that to Bon Tonnel-Burr, who died in Knot's jaws not five years ago off Logger's Port!" growled Lince. "Nay, Nilly, it's easy for young saplings like you to doubt your elders' wrinkles are etched by experience."

"Oh, Lince," sighed Karlock, Lince's elder, shaking his silver head. "Knot's a myth and nothing more."

The crew laughed.

"Knot lives, Captain!" insisted Lince. "Ancient and slow, sure, but cleverer and sneakier, too! She steals sailors in the night when the waves are rollin' like her own black coils. Milord, Knot is the very same serpent that stole Gieron from his people a thousand years ago! Aye, 'swallowed his skiff whole, aye, and took him down like a trophy for her mountain of pretty skulls, in her sea-crag, down away!"

"'Tis a popular myth, lord," said Artimeer, who stood stalwart but sallow with seasickness.

Lince gaffed a look at the old philosopher.

Artimeer looked wearily at the sky. "I think I'll go below for the day's activities, my lord." Artimeer bowed and crossed the heaving deck straight as a stayline to the aftercastle.

Trinadol produced a pink stone from his trouser pocket and held it for a moment, closing his eyes. Then he threw it far out onto the sea.

As the pebble skittered into the deep, the mariners wondered what strange message it might be delivering.

"What did you tell the stone, lord?" Karlock asked.

"I told it to challenge the mightiest beast with the greatest hatred of Man lurking in the depths and inlets and deep sea grottoes of southern Ameulas to fight a duel with the *White Shark*."

"Knot," Lince grunted.

There was argument and agreement.

"The great Knot monster, killer that she is, aye!" Lince growled, striking fear into the fresh converts.

"Was I too bold, Captain?" asked Trinadol.

"Perhaps, lord!" nodded Karlock, who put no limits on the sea.

"I suggest we ready what gear we have, then, to greet whatever meets my summons."

"Avast! Man the harpoon and ready the longboats! Haul out the net and run it out starboard, mates! Haul in the starboard sheets and cut a circle nor'ward, helm!" Lince's voice was like a hull grinding on coral. He sprang into action himself, with his great crab's arms seizing the starboard line at the head of the starboard crew.

"Ho, Captain!" cried Garello from the crow's nest. "Whitecaps to the north, making hot for us!"

"Double-check it, lad, with these seas!" yelled Karlock.

Trinadol aimed his father's gold spyglass north and glimpsed a row of fins arching like the oars of a galley through the side of a swell.

The longboats shoved off, drawing the weighted nets on their blue-glass floats in a northward embrace as they rowed over the sea's shrugging shoulders. The harpooners grasped long spears with iron pikes, gaffs and blades, looking nervously at the horizon from atop each wave.

A faint gray thing, a thing older than color, twisted into daylight and plunged back into the sea.

"What sort of beast was that, Captain?" Trinadol asked.

Karlock looked down at the deck. "It's Knot."

"Aye," Nil sighed.

Lince shrugged, nodding.

The creature snaked under the waves into the center of the trawl that had been dropped into the sea.

Serpent-like, her serrated spine sliced curving, creamy scars in the water as she recoiled before the net. She lifted her steaming head from the sea like a great old shark with a pointed nose and a frowning gash of teeth. Her two octopus arms coiled in avid symmetries around her head. Her eyes were brown, maybe, and they pulled like riptides. Unmoved by the waves, she gazed at Trinadol.

Lince wondered if he had overestimated the young Cirilen.

"Man the harpoon, Nilly!" Karlock cried. "Keep her eye fixed!"

Nil cranked the aiming mechanism, fixing the serpent's eye.

The grimy seabirds that made their living following the ancient sea worm croaked as they landed on the rigging of the *White Shark*.

"Should you call her away, lord?" asked Karlock. "This beast is very old and wise in her dark ways!"

"Not yet," Trinadol said, trying to draw Knot's drowning gaze away from Nil's. Trinadol thought he had seen a crimson sparkle inside her greedy eyes, but she was staring at Nil now as her jaws undulated and drool foamed around her gray teeth. Her arms gestured mischievously and she slipped under the sea.

Passing beneath the net, she dove under the ship.

Everyone ran to look over the port side, but the sea was dark. Nil swiveled the harpoon and pointed it down. The dirty birds perched on the rigging suddenly flew away.

A flashing streak appeared in the water and Knot shattered the surface, arching like a twisting, glistening pillar over the ship. Her muscular arms streamed behind her, grasping at the mast and yardarm.

Trinadol was surprised by the sudden attack, but with a hot pride he twisted his right hand and spoke: "*Kair Talo Ga!*"

A thunderclap smote the air and the serpent was pushed higher, her arms just missing the mast. She snapped her jaws at Garello in the crow's nest as she fell on her back through the air and came down to meet the sea off the starboard rail.

Waves washed over the longboats as she landed, and her arms groped wildly out of the frothing water. She lifted her tail, swathed in the black net, and beat the sea with it.

"Close the net!" commanded Trinadol. "The beast is stunned. Now is the time! When she lifts her head, fire the harpoon, Nil!"

But Nil was lost in Knot's gaze, for she had already raised her head and had ensnared the mariner's eye.

"Stay here, no fear," Trinadol whispered to Neuvia, and he sprang across the deck to the harpoon.

"Let me man it, Nil! She's charmed you!" Nil staggered aside as Trinadol sat in the wooden seat to fire the crossbow.

It was aimed crudely by eye and could be swiveled and tilted by the harpooner. Trinadol spoke to the harpoon as he turned it, winding it down and finding the beast's eye in the site. "Always right, the aim of this bow!" he whispered, and he felt the timbers creak and tighten.

A bloody light sparkled in Knot's lidless eyes. Her head was covered in net, intentionally, Trinadol suddenly realized. She was winding herself in the net for another leap, and this time she would pull the net and the boats around her like a shawl. "Gheldron!" she hissed; and the crimson light clearly burned in her eyes.

The harpoon sailed straight, and the mariners watched it cross the sea as if time had slowed down.

The next instant, the thick shaft had gored her left eye, piercing her crouching brain.

A convulsion jerked a great loop of Knot's back out of the water, rippling down her length, and her neck and arms fell forward, sending a wave over one of the nearby boats and capsizing it.

The men quickly righted the boat and climbed in, securing the net and bailing furiously.

Knot's head rose again from the sea beside the boat, and she snapped her jaws wildly, chipping her filthy teeth. A gush of blood as black as her myriad murders poured from the spar sizzling in her skull and one arm coiled around the shaft, pulling wildly. Blood rasped from her throat as she exhaled a reeking breath over the men. Her other arm blindly seized the chest of a red-haired sailor and lifted him out of the longboat.

The sailor screamed as Knot brought him before her jaws.

She lunged at him even as her arm slackened, and he slipped from her grip into the sea as she sunk her teeth into her own coiled arm.

Her head plunged into the sea.

Then her body stretched out, long and straight, ripping the net and freezing rigid. Her muscles winched tight beneath her gray skin until some central mooring finally sundered and she rolled loose on the sea, turning over on her back.

The red-haired sailor emerged from the water, to a hail of cheers, and he climbed onto her orange throat, straddling it as it gulped over the swells. He plugged his nose and raised his fist as the men cheered.

Neuvia ran to Trinadol and kissed him on the forehead as he sat at the harpoon. "What a wonder, my love!"

Artimeer emerged from below and set agog eyes on the sea beast heaving limp upon the waves.

The dark gulls that followed Knot to share in her killings turned with the wind now and tore off bits of her meat, a treacherous feast of poisonous flesh that would soon dispatch them with their deadly mistress.

The mariners led a cheer for Trinadol, and some began composing songs on various instruments to remember the undoing of Knot.

* * *

The *White Shark* hauled the sea monster to the bay of the Dimmrock and longboats dragged her past the breakers. Then the waves rolled her out of the sea onto the shore. She stretched 100 yards on the sand.

Court engravers and painters gathered to capture the scene for posterity, racing Senadol's silver crabs, which quickly closed in to strip her ancient bones and tidy their beach.

As Trinadol and Neuvia climbed the rocky ramp to the forest, Trinadol turned and looked at the villainous creature smoking on the sand below, remembering its crimson eyes. "She may have swallowed stones, that old one. They say Gieron carried a scepter!"

"One legend per day, my love," winked Neuvia. "If there are prizes in Knot's gizzards, they will wait for your discovery. But there is more in life than stones of sorcery!"

Trinadol turned. "Would you rein me in, like a gelding, Neuvia?" He thought he had heard Dantair's censure in Neuvia's words and was reminded of how, for all his life, he was kept from reaching his limits, or from touching a stone of power. "Is there something wrong with my power, Neuvia?"

Neuvia was surprised and paused on the path. "No, indeed, my love! I am sorry that anyone has given you that cruel doubt—please be rid of it, my lord! I glory in your power! I only meant to say that each part of life informs all others." She kissed him to prove her point.

He sighed. "Of course." He touched her mouth. "You are right. What a splendid guardian for my heart." He looked into her deep blue eyes, admiring her exquisite beauty that simply stole his soul away.

*   *   *

Chapter 7

▼

The New King

Throughout the forest, Senadol had placed plants from all over the world, which he hoped to cultivate on Ameulas. He had made some sections of the forest ever-moistened by steaming pools and fountains spraying high to suit exotic specimens from tropical climes, and he had made other sections open to the sun and filled them with sand and planted slow-growing cacti of dream-like shapes. Trinadol even noticed plants native to Trillan twining amidst the forest's greenery.

Marmosets lived on the island, existing elsewhere only on Demold thousands of miles away. The little monkeys had wandered into the island's young forest long ago and factioned into a dozen groups which could be known by the colors of their splendid headdresses and by the kind of trees in which they lived.

During one of their days in the forest of unfolding surprises, three days before their wedding, Trinadol and Neuvia came across a bronze statue of Queen Conilair, Trinadol's mother.

Trinadol knelt and bowed his head. "I never knew her," he said. "She died giving birth to me. I used to sit here and ask her questions, but she never answered me. She never forgave me."

Neuvia looked at Conilair's bronze face, which was stern and gentle. Conilair's hair was short under a small, high-fanged crown. She wore tights and a jerkin. An ivory snake with amethyst eyes was braided like a necklace around her throat. "She does not appear to be a woman who would blame another for her choices," said Neuvia. "I think she was as proud of you as she was proud of herself."

"Perhaps your words are true." Trinadol lifted his head, and a shifting ray dispelled the grief that shaded his face. "And yet," he paused, looking down again. "That which stalked and killed my father was really here for me."

"What is this, Trinadol?"

"Neuvia—speak of it to no one. I trust only you. Something has stalked me since my birth. Those around me have suffered. My mother. My father. I am afraid for the things I love: for you, Neuvia."

Neuvia looked up at the stately Conilair. She took his hand. "My promise is complete, my lord. I will brave death for love, as we all must. It is the way of the world." She smiled. "But you will be King and I Queen of a kingdom of loving subjects. We will have great power and you will have your father's scepter to defend us."

"My father's scepter. Yes! Neuvia, I had not thought of it. When the Scepter is mine, my power will be magnified ten thousand-fold. Neuvia, no evil will ever be able to harm us…"

Neuvia squeezed his hand. "Then we do not need to live in fear?"

"No!" He laughed, touching his fingertip to her chin. "Then we can live for love, no matter what fate my father has foreseen."

* * *

As the sun set on the day before their wedding and Coronation, Trinadol and Neuvia wrote their marriage vows at different desks in Trinadol's room in the pinnacle of the Lightstone Tower.

As was tradition, each told the other a line, and the other finished it with a rhyme secretly, then wrote another line, and so on.

"'And if you wander from the road…'" Neuvia said.

Trinadol wrote down a rhyme, hiding it. He gave her his, "'And if the burden bend you low…'"

She laughed and wrote down her vow, hiding it from Trinadol. "Stop sneaking a peek!" she cried. "'And if a star shines bright at night—', Go on, that's it!"

Trinadol grinned, stroking his long hair back from his brow. "That's a challenge." He wrote, hiding his parchment. "All right!" he said at length. "Here's yours: 'For you are polestar in my sky.'" He looked seriously at her.

Neuvia's eyes welled brightly. "All right." She wrote her rhyme. "'I'll trim the wing, you point the prow,'" she whispered, thickly.

Trinadol stared solemnly at the page for a while as he pondered her vow. "'For having you just doubles me,'" he finally said.

He smiled and she laughed.

He took her hand and he felt her heart beating in her hot palm.

They were hardly breathing when Nil Ramesis was suddenly announced below.

Trinadol called him up and the mariner pushed open the trap door and climbed humbly into their company, a few wooden tubes under his arm. There was something familiar about Nil Ramesis, Trinadol decided, though he could not identify what it was.

Nil cleared his throat and presented the polished tubes. "Charts of the southern reefs, my lord. The most accurate in existence." He grinned starwhite teeth in his midnight beard.

"Ah," Trinadol reached his hand out. "Thank you ever, Nil Ramesis." He spread one of the charts on his great curving desk. "'Tis beautiful work, indeed!"

"Thank you, my lord. May you find good use for them!"

Trinadol rolled the chart and replaced it in its tube. "I shall. I will see you after coronation tomorrow afternoon. Here!"

Nil accepted a heavy bag of gold and grinned. "Till the morrow then, milord! The mariners send all blessings for the slaying of Knot. She rots on the sand like a graveyard filled with ten thousand sailors, but a glorious wreak it is to us humble servants of the sea whom she so sorely used! Good even, lord! And sweet dreams, milady!"

Nil bowed and descended the stairs, closing the trapdoor behind him.

*   *   *

The old white cock, with his drooping yellow crest, stretched like an aging acrobat on the wall of the courtyard and heralded the day of the Royal Wedding and Coronation.

Trinadol woke. She was gone.

The ceremony, he remembered, rubbing his eyes.

The trapdoor rose, and Benelvia and Artimeer entered the room with food for flesh and food for thought.

Benelvia set a tray of breakfast on the low table beside his bed and took a hot wet towel from the tray, pulling his hair back and swaddling his entire head. "Wake up, me lord, we'll have to look lively today!" she crooned, unwrapping his head and swabbing his face while combing out Trinadol's tangled hair with the other hand.

"How many hands do you have, woman!" Trinadol grunted, too groggy to resist.

"Drink the black coffee, Liege," said Artimeer. "It's most invigorating."

Trinadol sipped the tiny cup of coffee and felt his chest fill with morning fire. "Indeed," he grunted, smiling at Artimeer as Benelvia tugged his hair back. He poked a cube of fruit with a silver spike.

"A fine day for a wedding, lord!" Artimeer said, nodding.

"A splendid one, me lord!" said Benelvia, her round face blushing.

"Such harmony of ceremony, a wedding and coronation! They are so familiar they might always be together, and the better!" mused Artimeer, clapping his hands nervously.

"You seem less logical than usual, Artimeer," said Trinadol, flinching at Benelvia's comb.

"I am, lord! But you have chosen love! That is certain. That's the basis of your destiny, which I, with my romantic's logic, believe to be a fair one for Ameulas. I am happy for my friend, your father, and for you, a clearly more ambitious and yet virtuous king who shall lead an able people on a bold and noble journey. I see great good, if I see all!"

"Great to hear such good words, Artimeer," smiled Trinadol, wincing.

"The balance of the ceremonies strikes me as right," enthused the sage. "The perfect union of symbolism brings a smile and a tear to a long and cold face. Do you have any last questions about life, son? Any at all?"

"Any and all." Trinadol rose. "I am ready."

"Your clothes are laid out for you to choose in the room below, me lord," said Benelvia. "I'll leave you to it, then. Come along." Benelvia winked at him around her big nose as she climbed down the stairs.

"If I were a prophet like your father, I would see a brilliant future, I think," Artimeer smiled. Then he pulled down the round door behind him.

After Trinadol chose his clothes and dressed in the finest raiment, a shirt of gold-embroidered silk, a leather vest worked with sculpted trees and an eagle with lapis lazuli eyes, blue cape, black leather trousers with a stripe of gold on each side, and tall black boots. Benelvia rattled the bell below and Trinadol descended the stairs to the third room down where she was waiting. "Your broach is upside-down, Trinadol!" she groused. "I'll get it." She fussed under his chin. "There it is. The sign of Elwyn Gheldron. With the diamond and all. Better right-side-upways, if you pardon, me lord." She winked.

"Is Neuvia ready?" He marked how foolish he sounded.

"Nervous as you, me lord—not quite—steady now—happiness and more—such a big day ahead!" She slipped each comment between straightenings of this and buttonings of that.

"Thank you, Benelvia!"

"Down you go," she said. "Halfway down, at the baths, the girls are waiting. They'll bathe, oil, and dress you up again. Soothe you nicely. Artimeer will be waiting at the bottom of the stairs, so be along now. It's a tight schedule!" She sent him down the curving stairs. "Long may you live, lord!" she called after him, melting in motherly joy as he disappeared around the bend.

*   *   *

At noon, Trinadol, in scented robes and rosy-skinned, his tresses curled and starred with lines of tiny white wildflowers, emerged from the arch of the Throne Room onto the verandah.

From the top of the stairs, Trinadol saw two rows of people decked in clothes of brightest dyes and embroidered patterns lining the stairway. At the end of these two lines, alone before the woods, stood Neuvia.

Even at that great distance, he felt her eyes, and held them as he descended the stairs.

She stood perfectly still, watching as he passed the throngs on the lawn.

He saw what she was wearing as he drew nearer. Her dress was made of white silk and purple velvet, and over her breasts stretched a gossamer fabric starred with gold embroideries, revealing the nourishment and maternity of the Crown. A silver circlet, fashioned like a delicate snake with amethyst eyes, clutched its tail at her throat. Her midnight hair was brushed back with diamond pins in its deep currents. Her face was radiant as morning snow.

Trinadol took her hands. "You are the name and shape of my own heart," he whispered in her ear.

"And you are mine," she whispered, a private wedding.

They strode back down the long aisle hand-in-hand as minstrels strummed guitars, drowned out quickly by the hurly-burly of the guests.

Children ran behind the lines to climb through legs and sneak another peek at the King and Queen as they passed, and old women who prided themselves on matchmaking fainted as they glimpsed the royal wedding party, and they had to be hoisted up by old men and boys as little girls fanned them with pigeon feather fans. Dogs bayed, pet Browner Pigs chortled, and parrots screeched, adding to the choir as the forest piped a winsome march in the lively breeze.

The Royal Wedding Party climbed the stairs to the verandah beneath the arched door of the Lightstone Tower, where Artimeer stood waiting.

Artimeer handed Trinadol the ring of wife, an amethyst set in glinting gold. Then he gave Neuvia the Ring of Husband, a thin band of cool platinum. They both stepped away and faced each other.

Trinadol began: "Upon this day I wake to see…"

And she responded: "Your eyes looking back at me. And what I see, I'll seek to make…"

"Fairer 'fore the new day's break. And when I see your every pain…"

"I'll seek to make it well again. And if you wander from the road…"

"I'll look for you down paths unstrode. And if the burden bends you low…"

"I'll carry the yoke and eat the crow." She winked at him and they laughed, and the crowds gently chorused their nervous mirth. "And if a star shines bright at night…" she continued.

"A sister to your eyes, I write. For you are polestar in my sky…"

"So far to fly for you and I. I'll trim the sail, you point the prow…"

"I'll lift us high, you'll show me how. For having you just doubles me…"

"Twice the world and twice as free. What today we make as one…"

"No Hala god…"

"Shall make undone…"

"And Death could not…"

"Tear us apart…"

"For I am half…"

"Of my own heart."

The people wept like a tossing sea around them.

Trinadol embraced her, laughing next to her ear, and when they kissed, the heralds blew their horns in spontaneous fanfare and silver confetti spilled from the high windows of the Lightstone Tower.

Artimeer winked as Trinadol gasped for air, and the old philosopher chuckled as the crowds reveled on the lower terraces. He said nothing to take away from their moment, tending instead to the servants who were readying the Throne Room.

Trinadol held Neuvia close as the cheers of the Ameulentians rose like starlings in the sky.

*   *   *

The Throne Room bulged with all the honorable guests who could be squeezed in as Trinadol and Artimeer waited outside. Neuvia went in to stand by the Queen's Throne, which had been empty since the birth of Trinadol.

The Lightstone Tower was radiant and let a phalanx of buttery sunbeams shine over the long aisle to the dais. An apple-scented incense perfumed the air. The two curvaceous, crystalline Thrones of King and Queen gleamed smiles of light on the regal banners of Gieron and Elwyn.

Outside, Trinadol stood with Artimeer, who held the Scepter of the King of Ameulas concealed in an onyx case. The wind was crisp from the sea.

Trinadol looked at Artimeer. "We shall see the color of my heart now, my friend," he said.

"The music of your vows will be the harmony of your reign." Artimeer smiled and bowed solemnly.

"Thank you, Artimeer. You go first, I believe."

"Yes, my Liege."

Artimeer wore no jewel or plume or ornament. His black-and-white robes and green cape flowed as he strode before Trinadol down the aisle, carrying the heavy case of the Scepter.

Artimeer ascended the dais and stood to the left of Neuvia between the royal Thrones.

Trinadol stopped on the step below the dais.

"Trinadol Gheldron, Third King of the House of Gheldron, born in the Tintilisair and wed to her Daughter this very day of splendid days, you are destined, promised, desired, and rightful heir to the Crown of the Tintilisair." A Bearer offered Artimeer the golden, emerald-tipped Crown on a blue silk pillow, and Artimeer set it upon Trinadol's head as muffled praise swept the royal audience.

Neuvia found Trinadol's ring in a pouch at her hip, pinned there by the boys who had bathed and dressed her. She gave it to Artimeer.

"The Ring of King, of amber nostalgic, tempers his mighty hand," recited Artimeer. He put it on Trinadol's right index finger. In the amber jewel was a narrow scarab of silvery purple, which had not lived for countless ages.

"And Neuvia Gheldron, Third Queen of the House of Gheldron, born in the Tintilisair and wed to her Son this very day of splendid days, you are destined, blessed, and rightful heir to the Crown of the Tintilisair." Artimeer took the high-fanged Crown of Queen, wrought of platinum over nine centuries ago and worked with pearls, diamonds and amethysts, and he lovingly laid it upon her head.

Trinadol found her ring in a doeskin pouch pinned at his hip and gave it to Artimeer.

"The Ring of Queen completes her offices with leverage all her own." These words not even Artimeer completely understood. He slid the ring down Neuvia's right index finger above the Ring of Wife.

"Now," said Artimeer, opening the onyx case. "Let the ancient Cronus Star on the Royal Scepter of the Tintilisair reveal the numen of your mighty reign." Artimeer held the Scepter high before the people.

The Scepter's stone and metal were icy silver though the handle was wrought of all precious metals mingled in a swirling alloy. The handle's shape was strong yet an intricate design spiraled around the shaft to the scepterhead. The metal sometimes shone like pearl, other times dappled silver and blue, still others like an iron thing, and sometimes like blue-veined copper. Only in Elwyn's hand was the metal all gold.

Eight platinum thorns held the Scepter's diamond. The Cronus Star was oval and its surface was cut into long, narrow facets. Seven inches tall and five inches wide, the diamond weighed three pounds.

Artimeer waited for his response, but Trinadol's eyes were set on the jewel. "Clear as water and cold as ice," said Artimeer for Trinadol. "You shall take it…"

"Take it in my hand," Trinadol nodded, remembering his line. "To show my soul to all…"

Trinadol took the Scepter in his hand; everyone watched the stone.

The Lightstone Tower grew dark as clouds passed over the sun.

A prismatic luster rolled deep inside the gem, faster, brighter, and shone facets of light over the people's rapt faces as they watched.

Artimeer nodded, and Neuvia smiled in awe beside him.

A speck of color bubbled, catching and spreading from the center.

At first, the people did not acknowledge the color, though they saw it with their own eyes. Their confused minds judged it to be blue, purple, or even gold. Yet when the hue blushed so deep and bold a match for blood, staining all who stood before it, they looked at each other and cried out, wondering how the joy of centuries so surely promised could be traded for a bitter age, so neatly, and without some violent infamy. They looked on the King in pity and shook their fists at the impossible, sneering light inside the Cronus Star. Then, as their eyes beheld him, they became bewildered with fear.

Artimeer studied Trinadol without expression.

Neuvia shook her head, staring incredulously at the stone.

Trinadol's heart plummeted as he looked into the gem, his face reddened in sick shame and futile rage. The evil his father warned him of was himself! His teachers had been right to keep him from such stones. They knew but did not tell him…!

Everyone seemed to shrink away from him now, and many rushed through the *lightstone* arch, weeping in horror. "Be gone then!" he yelled after them.

"My lord, no!" implored Artimeer, seeing the strange light in the young King's eyes.

"You, too, Philosopher!" Trinadol pointed his finger, ringed with the rings of King and Husband. "I mean you no harm. Leave my side! Leave this room! Leave this island, never to return! Be gone from me, with all your mortal's logic. On Hell's path am I, alas! Right is wrong for me, Philosopher, and love is hate. All I touch is doomed. Leave me and die in peace, as you deserve!"

Artimeer found his mouth would not open. He looked grimly and dearly at Trinadol. Then he turned away in anger, for he saw no place for reason here.

The philosopher, who had been such a loyal steward of the Gheldrons, sadly followed his fellow Ameulentians, who hurried to their lodgings within the Tower to gather their belongings and sail home to the mainland, with their grief and fears in tow.

*   *   *

The Throne Room was cleared before Trinadol noticed Neuvia beside him.

She sat coolly in the Throne of the Queen of the Tintilisair, which gleamed lavender underneath her.

He wavered over whether to send her away.

He sighed and stroked the diamond as though it were his wounded heart, staining all, including Neuvia, whose wedding gown seemed drenched in gore in its bloody eminence.

She rose, looking at the infected stone, and she thought she saw a jealous demon glaring back at her through its narrow facets.

She reached for the shaft of the Scepter, meaning to smash its head on the *lightstone* steps.

He heard her thought and seized her wrist. His eyes burned slitted fire. "Gone from me!" He flung her away.

"The jewel lies!" she said.

"It cannot lie!"

"There is evil in this stone, but it is not yours, my husband! I know your heart and I see none of it in that stone!"

"How could you know?" He fell to his knees before his own throne.

"I need no magic! Don't believe what you see! Believe what you know!"

He looked sadly into the diamond, wishing she could be right, but how could so plain a truth be denied? Here was his father's prophecy come true! His own power was evil, his very soul was cursed.

And yet, the power of this stone was all Trinadol had left to defy his doom. "You would shatter this stone, Neuvia?" he asked her. "A stone like the Cronus Star can battle destiny itself! My birth killed my mother, and brought evil upon my father. My red soul stains the scepter now, imperiling all I love. Yet with this stone I can turn my own power against itself. I can build a bastion before fate, and prevent doom's blow from ever falling! You, Neuvia, more than any, must leave me now, and forever! To cause you harm would destroy me more utterly than death." Trinadol shut his eyes and closed Neuvia's lips.

"I will never leave you with that wicked stone!" she said, her lips immune to his Cirilen will.

Then she strode across the red hall to the corridor that led to the Tower's stairs.

Her footsteps faded as Trinadol sat heavily on his throne in the vermilion shame of the Scepter.

Warily, he peered into the jewel, looking for telltales of deceit and illusion, for stones like this were full of memories and distortions he must learn to interpret so he could channel a momentum of forces inside its secret reservoirs.

He spied faded images in its depths from Ages past, when his earliest ancestors founded the Sarkish Empire, reigning and waging war, and he wondered to see pale glimpses of those lost times like reflections trapped inside a hall of mirrors. The Second Age ended as the Sarkish Empire fell, decimated by plague, but Trinadol's ancestors isolated themselves inside a snowy mountain in which they carved a vast city, using the Cronus Star to move the rock. For 200 years they lived there, expanding their subterranean sanctuary while the plague ravaged all of Sarkland. The animals and birds they knew perished, and they dared not venture down to where the grass grew for two centuries. The Cronus Star nourished them, providing their food and lighting their dark crops. Not until Bochael took the Cronus Star in his hand did they leave their shadowy halls to find the land deserted and overgrown by strange animals and flowers. Heartbroken, some went back to their mountain sanctuary never to be heard from again and some left across the sea, not heeding Bochael Ghealidrun's urgings to stay and help rebuild the land. Abandoned by his kin, Bochael set out alone with the Cronus Star to cross the sea, and through the dark age that followed the diamond passed from his hand on a line that led straight to Trinadol.

Trinadol's eyes searched the gem Elwyn used to woo the Winteg and raise the Lightstone Tower and the Jetty at Gwylor. In those days, the Scepter was called the Golden Hammer. In Senadol's reign it was called the Silver Moon. Through the diamond, his father had seen the world's tomorrows and persuaded the squirrels and birds of Ameulas to scatter the nuts, pits, and seeds of a hundred fruiting trees across the wild hills of Ameulas. And in his hands, what? The Bloody Scythe? And yet this august stone offered Trinadol alternatives fate could not imagine.

Looking into the sharded carnage of yesterday, the fevered memories of the jewel, Trinadol lost all sense of time and sank deep in red fathoms. For three days no one dared approach him, for the crimson in the Scepter burned through the *lightstone* walls of the Tower, menacing the hearts of all who saw it.

*   *   *

On the second day of the King's isolation, the sea captains convened aboard the *White Shark*.

Karlock Isopika called them to order.

"A grim day," he said.

All groaned agreement.

"Yet, my fellows, there lies within Trinadol a child most courageous and true of heart," said the Captain. "If he hadn't done so much good for us mariners when he was but a child I would myself wonder on my allegiance today. I say whatever burns the Scepter is no Trinadol! We saw that, helpless as we were to do a thing against this dark magic. He was himself ruined by the false light, proof it was a lie! But bide us well our time until the day we can rescue the King from the jealous god that's tricked him!" Karlock shook a stony fist. "Now, Nilly will have a word."

Nil cleared his throat. "I believe the King to have been tricked, as the captain says. Lince and myself have confirmed his best deeds. The killing of Knot was for all the mariners to see, as she lies melting on the silver sands alee. Whatever it was that stole the King's Scepter threatens Ameulas as well. Did he ask us to stay, so he could torment us? Nay! Not a one does he demand for his pleasure, not even the fair Queen Neuvia whom he loves like his breath, for no pleasure in this is his! Now he sends us away, fearing for us, even as he banishes himself to a life of loneliness and terrors everywhere. But things will be different, as they say—*someday*, mariners."

"Nil's said the truth for every mariner to hear it!" said Lince. "Tell it round and make it fast!"

The captains shouted their approval, for once in accord, and went to their vessels to sail for ports scattered across the coast of Ameulas.

*   *   *

Neuvia went to Trinadol's room to wait for him, and as she waited, and hours passed into days, she began to look through Senadol's books for some note that might free her husband's mired soul.

She found a page marked by a tiny white feather in a book entitled *General Observations*. Written in the old King's shaky hand was a curious passage:

> *A NOTE ON THE WIVES OF CIRILEN*—When a Cirilen marries a Bondairtlen, and if their love is true, the first time they make love and reach the peak of their passion together, a transfer of some power takes place.
>
> The Bondairtlen woman is then endowed with intuitions, even influences (depending on the individual) and, of course, she inherits the life span of a Cirilen at that moment. Though they are limited, with training, some of the faint powers acquired can be focused and amplified, especially with a stone.
>
> The fruit of such love-driven union between Bondairtlen and Cirilen is potent indeed. Alas, the birth of Trinadol was a cataclysm, and one my wife did not survive. After 186 years of marriage, there was no other woman for my heart of hearts.
>
> Wait for children, I say. Life is long for Cirilen, and it is best to allot ripe youth for those things that will enrich the reflective heart of old age. Yet I wonder if Trinadol's birth alone could have killed his mother, or if grief alone is aging me so fast.
>
> —*The Fifth of Foxtail, 1061*

Neuvia decided to take this book.

She also took a small red book with "My First Book of Magic by Trinadol Gheldron" written on it in his child's hand.

One leather-bound journal was entitled *After My Death*. She opened it and leafed through the pages. They were blank, but at certain angles her eyes caught writing. She saw the word "prophecies" on the first page before it faded away. As she flipped the pages she saw the words "take—this—book" on different leaves one after the other. She took this book, as well.

Thus armed, she descended the Tower to the deserted kitchen.

By now, even the servants had abandoned the Lightstone Tower. She took a few pots, some tins of food, a large amount of smoked meat, a sack of yellow rice, knives, rope, flint, a box of thick blue candles, soap, towels, three kidskin flasks of berry brandy and three of red wine, needles and thread, an extra uniform, and one for a man with pants, sheets and pillows, and every tool or item she could think of, throwing them all into two great empty carrot sacks. She lashed them together with rope and then dragged them down the marble hall outside toward the Throne Room.

A carmine eminence splashed the polished floor of the corridor through the open door. She stepped lightly on her bare toes into the room and saw him on the crystal throne, behind which spread curving bars of crimson light over the banners of Gieron and Elwyn.

Trinadol stared like a fool into the diamond, his mouth open and drool spindling red from his lips.

She pulled a pear from a sack she dragged and hurled it across the room. She slipped out the *lightstone* arch onto the verandah.

The pear sailed high and came down on his face, splattering and bruising his nose and knocking the Crown from his head. His chest filled with fury as he looked at the empty doorway. With a gruesome grunt, he pointed and the ash-wood doors that had stood open past any man's memory slammed closed. And the bronze bolt fell, tolling the Tower like a deep-toned bell.

Neuvia dragged the two bursting sacks over wet marble on her bare feet, her torn wedding gown fluttering as she looked over the confettied marble and lawns below. The tents and tables had been abandoned and their bright canopies were caught like sails, ripped and rippling.

She climbed down the stairs on her bare feet and shivered in the fresh rain, looking out over the forest at the ships departing on the sea. Gray scud sent lancing showers over the Dimmrock.

Using no path, she went into the dark, musty woods.

     *   *   *

At dusk, Neuvia watched a bloodstain spiraling up the Lightstone Tower as Trinadol climbed the stairs to his room.

She watched him with his own spyglass, which she had taken, as she lay on the bed in his own tree house in the room on its highest branch.

Trinadol opened the shutters of the north window and looked over the bay. "Take my voice and fling it far, carbuncle," he whispered, and a light beamed from his eyes as he looked into the gem and the Cronus Star burned like the South Star as he raised it over his head.

Storm clouds darkened the sky. All who were still on the Dimmrock saw the tip of the Tower burning red and heard a terrible voice made of rumbling sky:

"Leave this island and never return! Ameulas and Trinadol must never meet! Leave this island and never return or you will know wrath most merciless and complete!"

The blazing eminence of the gem seemed to feed his shame with defiance and encourage stronger words upon his tongue than he had wished to say.

He closed the shutters of the window and sat on the edge of his bed as he dove again into the churning eternity of the stone.

Day gave way to night; the weather worsened. Violent gusts shrieked, vandalizing the woods, and rain came down like gravel.

The tree house rode the storm like a taut boat as its seven boughs rolled and pitched, and yet Neuvia only woke when the storm bell started tolling. She found a silver squirrel sleeping beside her cheek and stroked it before returning to battle her nightmares.

     *   *   *

Chapter 8

▼

The New Queen

Trinadol's tree house was quite exceptional for one he designed, with help from two elderly court architects, when he was only four years old. Neuvia Gheldron knew it well, the secret castle of young Trinadol that no one else could find. No one believed her, either, and some thought she was make-believing that she had found Trinadol's tree house, though Senadol knew she was telling the truth and patted her head protectively at banquets whenever she precociously described visiting the Prince's "sylvan stronghold."

Trinadol's tree house was built in the sturdiest and most flexible variety of tree in the forest, a white star enryd, with seven main branches emerging from the trunk in a spiral. A rope ladder hung to the ground from the highest room 50 feet up, and when a person stood on the ladder's bottom rung, it unlatched a counterweight that gently drew the ladder up.

Neuvia had woken early to a dreary day and set to work making her new home habitable. She had just added a few more river stones to the leather sack of the counterweight after smearing all the leather parts of the ladder with lard to rejuvenate them. She stepped onto the ladder and it rose gently, and she caught the ceiling of the first floor with a light hand.

The first floor of Trinadol's tree house was low and wide, curving around the ivory trunk into which Trinadol had carved war mottoes like "Never Yield!" or "Heroes Live Longer Than Cowards!" Tarnished miniature swords, pikes, and a mace hung on racks on the walls. In this room, both Trinadol and Neuvia had defended the arboreal keep from imaginary sieges.

Neuvia deposited the last carrot sack of supplies here in this lowest room and unhooked one sack of stones from the line of the counterweight. Then she pushed down from the ceiling and rode the ladder up to the second story.

Wooden stairs corkscrewing around the trunk passed seven inner rooms, each built over one main branch. Outside these inner rooms, steps were carved on their mighty boughs, which split into five strong "fingers" that held outer rooms as though in muscular white hands. These fingers interwove above each of these outer rooms in thick green thatches starred with white flowers. Festoons of purple orchids and island mistletoe curtained the windows of these outer rooms.

Neuvia climbed the spiral stairs through the seven "stories" of Trinadol's tree house. Two rooms were game rooms, or one a war room and one a game room, and in inside them Neuvia found some of Trinadol's toys half-made and games half-played, sculptures of big monsters in clay, half-painted.

One room was apparently a magic room with simple charts and phosphorescent stars painted on the ceiling and childish fetishes like a goat's horn and a row of dried, red lizard tails looped over hooks on the wall. She found a collection of pretty rocks in a wooden box on the apprentice's dusty workbench and she remembered thinking they were magical stones when she was a little girl looking through Trinadol's things, and maybe some of them were.

A bathing room was plumbed with water from a cistern above and a lookout room was in the hand at the end of the branch. On the next branch up was a kitchen of sorts furnished with a seemingly make-believe stove—an iron grill over cobblestones. The outer room on the branch was a miniature dining hall with table and benches and miniature gables carved with scenes of hunters and animals.

The outermost room of the seventh branch was Trinadol's bedroom. This room had a small bed of goose down, like his father's. The room was round, like a crow's nest—or like his father's room atop the Lightstone Tower. The room's four windows were likewise aligned to the compass points.

Neuvia changed from her wedding gown into more practical clothes. She pulled on thigh-high socks of Dimmrock wool, gray and smooth as polished slate, and a billowing shirt of black silk with small stone buttons, and she silently thanked her fellow Ameulentians for the fine sundries they had so generously given her.

She looked through Trinadol's golden spyglass and saw the last three ships tilting for the mainland just before they disappeared in the murk.

She lit two candles and opened her books, and read them for the rest of the day, switching from one book to another.

In Senadol's *General Observations* she spotted a curious passage:

> *Today, my Queen successfully reversed a love charm against me. It fills me with quaint delight, for I incanted that my lips should taste like her favorite flavor, and suddenly, a few days later, I find her lips now taste like orange—my favorite flavor! And she said she did it by uttering the Sarkish phrase 'too-oh-nair' after reversing the words of my own charm. 'Too-oh-nair' means 'justice,' roughly, in Ancient Sarkish. It appears that magic may be generated by love!*
>
> —*The Twenty-Third of Wheat, 913*

Neuvia thought of Trinadol's charm that hid the tree house from all eyes but hers. She opened the small red book entitled *My First Book of Magic by Trinadol Gheldron*. She saw Trinadol's spell for closing eyelids. "Think 'look' to inword eye and close the lid while wundering why," said one note next to a simple diagram of the eye muscles, and she laughed.

There was a charm for making a flower bloom, but Trinadol noted that the charm only worked with Morning Glories. There was a lizard charm that would summon garden lizards. "Another cheap party trick," Trinadol noted parenthetically. There was a simple motion charm, the words of which a Cirilen could utter to move a plate or a book aside. "I think this spell is for old men," Trinadol noted, but he added "Good potenshul." In fact, this was the very spell he had used to repel Knot.

There was also a monster spell:

> *All Monsters remember me*
> *It took me, now three, to finish thee!*
> *When all is done, mark my words*
> *I'll feed your brains to the birds!*

Evidently, Trinadol had written the spell himself and tried to translate it unsuccessfully into Old Sarkish, but the work, thankfully, was unfinished.

Neuvia came across a love charm in the book. Trinadol had drawn red hearts on the vellum of the page in profuse geometries spilling from both sides at the top. Under this fountain of childish passion, he wrote:

> *This tree house never seen*
> *Lest by my future Queen!*

And he noted that one dead lizard had been burned for his charm.

Neuvia pondered the poignant spell as she looked out the window at the Tower.

*   *   *

Trinadol woke from a drugged slumber and rose from his bed. His white candle sought to fill the cloud-darkened room with clean light, but the Scepter blazed red and quickly stained its radiance. Trinadol fought back at the red glamour, deciphering its tint for a moment before the code of light shifted and reddened his sight again.

He thought of Neuvia and despaired. "You said you would not leave me with this stone…"

He held the red diamond to his heart. "Neuvia! Perhaps you are my doom's unwitting accomplice? Do you keep your promise and do you watch me even now? I feel sure that you do!" Trinadol turned to gaze through the Lightstone Tower, in duty mixed, his eyes searching deeper than mortal eyes could see. If she was on the Dimmrock now, he would surely find her.

*   *   *

As dusk fell, Neuvia saw a fresh stain of blood in the gauze cloud that swathed the tip of the Tower.

She flipped through Senadol's book of prophecies and saw words on a page long enough to read them: "She must do promptly what she can, or all is lost…"

Neuvia looked at the Tower and spoke an improvised incantation:

> *"While Cronus Star is blinding*
> *This place unseen by King!"*

And she added *"too-oh-nair!"* as Conilair had done to return Senadol's spell.

She looked at the Tower. The red seemed gray for a moment. She shrugged, thinking she caught a strange gleam in the stone of her wedding ring. She imagined proudly that her charm had worked as she settled in to spend the night perusing her library of amazing books.

*   *   *

Even with his vision focused through the Cronus Star, Trinadol failed to see her anywhere on the island, and he plunged into a daze of grief. She had forsaken him, he thought, and rightly so.

The Scepter stood ironic guard over his condemned soul as he plunged into the soothing amnesia of the jewel's omnipotence.

*　　　*　　　*

> *A NOTE ON WIZARD'S SHOES—The sleek craft a young Gheldron must build to complete his education, which is sometimes called a "Wizard's Shoe," is a curious creature, indeed.*
>
> *My own such craft, most sadly, was destroyed as my power waned and could no longer protect her. Sharpeye was not even at sea when her timbers were sundered. She was being transported over land to a tranquil lake, there to live out her days, when a crimson moon startled the horses and tipped the wagon. Yet, in our long voyage together I discovered many marvelous aspects of her nature.*
>
> *Such supple sailing craft not only follow stars but also act to protect their makers even if it means disobeying them. Many times, Sharpeye saved my unwary neck, even as I scolded her for her recalcitrance.*
>
> *—Senadol, The Fifteenth of Apple, 1051*

Neuvia finished the passage and flipped through the pages of Senadol's *Prophecies*. She had learned to do this. Even though the pages might be blank a moment before, she found that after reading something in one of the other books, a fragment of the *Prophecies* might become visible. She saw one now: "…she might help…" was all it said before fading on the page.

Trinadol had introduced her to his "Wizard's Shoe," the small sailing vessel he had built on the Island of Trillan. The proud craft had shifted her yard in a distinctly rude way, she remembered. Neuvia decided that she would pay her a visit in the morning.

She read some entries made in Queen Conilair's firm yet lovely hand, and she even found a poem Conilair had written about her pet snake, Toy, who had reposed around her neck like jewelry for 187 years, never growing, aging, or eating:

MY TOY

Caught in Elwyn's courageous hand
In Ghenten's green-leafed wold
Already eons old
With scales white as snow and
Eyes like purple amethyst
Sighing softly now he hissed
His wish and his demand
Though his venom could swift kill
O'er even Elwyn's will
He coiled coy 'round his hand
And crouching lithe and curvilinear
Begged to be his Queen's familiar
And shifting what he planned
Elwyn brought him to his Queen
And with gemstone eyes and scaly sheen
He slipped around her neck, and
Coiled like a chain bejeweled
For all the centuries that she ruled
More jealous than a wedding band
And when the Queen died one day
He left her neck, and slipped away

> *Returning from the Dimmrock's stand*
> *To guard my throat in my long reign*
> *Regaining regal place again*
> *'Till new Queen does command.*
> —*Conilair Gheldron, The Seventeenth of Whale, 1033*

"Toy," Neuvia Gheldron mused, imagining the deadly little serpent that was such a loyal servant to the Throne. Probably, the ancient snake had died. Even ancient things grew old, she surmised wryly.

After midnight she heard scrabbling in the leaves below. Looking down around the white branches, she saw a large beaver sniffing the trunk of the tree. She flung one of her throwing rocks at it, and it squawked and *tcched*, shambling off and plopping into the stream.

When she turned from the window, her heart pounding, the book of prophecies fell open, though the candle's flame was unstirred by wind. She read, "She should trust animals who offer friendship," on the opened page before the words faded away and the pages flipped, as though in a wind that seemed not to be there.

Neuvia sighed, unlatching the small windmill.

She had cut away the growth that prevented it from turning. Six large pails hung evenly spaced on a thick loop of rope that circled as the windmill turned. A pulley that was moored to a stone in the brook passed the buckets into the water and then up to Neuvia. She lifted the buckets off their hooks and into the room as each returned from the brook and she poured them into the sealskin cistern under the floor. In the morning she would open the valve and the fresh water would cleanse the wooden gutters and reveal where they needed repair.

As she worked that night to fill the cistern, squirrels and marmosets appeared, throwing bunches of berries and nuts on the floor beside her like emissaries offering tribute. She pulled back her sweaty hair and laughed whenever one appeared with whatever it had managed to hold onto during the treacherous climb up the smooth tree. "Thank you!" she said to each, in turn.

By three that morning, the cistern was half-full, which she thought was full enough.

She sat on Trinadol's bed and ate berries, nuts, and a small raw egg, which a bird had laid on the windowsill for her. She would make curtains later, test the plumbing, think about what to do about cooking and generally clean away a decade of dirt and dust.

But for now she would get a few hours of sleep before she set out for the beach to see *Stargazer*.

*   *   *

She was awakened by grapes, nuts, and apples rolling off the windowsill and bouncing on the floor. She looked out the window and saw it was very early in the morning, as she had hoped.

On the windowsill, she saw the culprit who had made the disturbance.

Wriggling with alarming speed through a bunch of black grapes was the rarest of all snakes, its proud face smiling and its eyes sparkling like sapphires: a Pearl Snake, like Queen Conilair's!

At first, Neuvia was frightened as the serpent slipped across the floor and reached her foot. But she did not flinch, as the snake's dark green tongue seemed to taste her naked toe. The long and slender serpent climbed her leg, spiraling around her thigh, and slid up under her shirt.

Smooth and cold, the sleek snake slid up between her breasts to her neck, and coiled around it, braiding its length fully three times. It grasped its hooked tail in its jaws, and promptly went to sleep.

"Toy," she smiled, and she felt the snake's feathery tongue on her throat as if it were tasting her voice. As light as a string he seemed, and smooth as ivory. "Thank you for waking me in time," she said.

She threw her bearskin cape around her shoulders in the chill morning.

Fog hovered in the treetops outside the window. She pulled on her boots that were lined by silken Dimmrock wool and she descended the rope ladder to the ground.

She laughed to see the bounty the animals had brought to her. As well as food, there were bundles of string and pieces of metal and glass brought by amorous magpies left in the nooks of the tree roots. A great horned owl had laid a rabbit before the tree for her, and no ant had touched its flesh. Indeed, ants had left black piles for her, which Neuvia found to be pepper kernels!

Near the rabbit was a neat stack of wooden beams of varying lengths, stripped of bark, with every bump and branch gnawed off smooth. Neuvia recognized the work of beavers and it frightened her, reminding her of the crazed beaver she had known as a child who had left her weird gifts.

She sat down in the pungent leaves with a sharp carving knife to see how soft the beams of wood were and if she could easily carve them into gutters to replace the rotted portions in the tree house. After she grooved an inch of one of the thick beams, she frowned. Replacing the gutters would be a long job, she regretted. She left that job for later, and set out for the beach.

*   *   *

Neuvia walked down the path on the rocky rampart to the beach, noting the gray ribs of Knot rising out of the sand like the peaked beams of a burned-out hall. The monster's huge skull was missing, probably taken by the mariners.

The wind was chill off the choppy bay.

Pulled high on the beach sat *Stargazer*, and Neuvia approached the proud vessel Trinadol had built, and *Stargazer*'s trident sail dropped and rippled.

Neuvia heard a whisper in her ear and realized Toy was speaking to her, feathering her tongue with its tongue. "She will help you!"

"Ah," said Neuvia. "Thank you, Toy!" Neuvia bowed before *Stargazer*, touching her knee to the sand.

Stargazer's sail snapped in the wind. "Why not look in Knot's bones?" whispered the air that slipped over her canvas.

"Yes, Mother!" Neuvia said before she realized where her own words had come from. What strange respect the people in her husband's magical world commanded, she thought. She rose and walked down the beach to the remains of the great sea beast.

Stargazer reflected a beam of sunlight among Knot's bones from a brass fitting at the top of her mast. The ray danced among the arching ribs and Neuvia was attracted to a glint of gold in the sand. She moved the sand aside with the point of her boot, and there, half-buried, was a jewel.

Digging out a golden handle, she lifted a precious scepter out of the sand, and turned it to see its square diamond. She brushed off the jewel, which was even larger than the Cronus Star. The diamond Gieron had set in this ancient scepter was cut into simpler facets, flawless and unusually pure.

The myth of Gieron's death, swallowed by the sea monster while sailing to the Dimmrock so long ago, indeed was true. And the scepter Gieron had possessed must have given the mortal king some of the certainty of his reign, Bondairtlen though he was. Certainly, it had extended his life, as it had extended Knot's life for so many centuries.

Gieron's scepter had withstood a thousand years in Knot's poisonous acids, and yet it shone like new in Neuvia's hands.

She heard the sail of *Stargazer* whipping and she hastened out of the ruins of Knot to her side.

"Cover the stone!" the wind whispered over *Stargazer*'s canvas.

"Take it to the tree house," Toy hissed, tickling her ear.

And so, guided by her strange allies, Neuvia covered the scepter and took it back up the path to the forest as the sun spilled through the clouds above.

*   *   *

Trinadol woke from an evil dream. A ship bearing soldiers had defied his edict and a party came ashore to confront him. They met him halfway up the steps to the Tower, where Trinadol had come to warn them away, but with the heat of a furnace his power poured forth from the Scepter and the men burst into flames and tumbled down the stairs, crumbling into embers. He cried out, and the great Tower shattered behind him in the sky and came down upon him in a grinding rubble.

Trinadol sat on his bed looking out the window of the Lightstone Tower at the sails that dotted the northern horizon. As each appeared, grew closer, and receded, his heart pounded a rhythm of dread.

*   *   *

Chapter 9

▼

The First Defense

When Neuvia returned to the tree house she found Senadol's *Prophecies* open on the floor of her room. Her eyes barely read, "It will be hidden in fresh water..." before the pages fluttered.

So, with a silver cord of braided spider-web, one of her wedding presents, Neuvia lowered the Scepter of Gieron into the vat of clear water under the top room of the tree house.

She then took a biscuit from a shy rat that must have stolen it from the Lightstone Tower, and she patted its head. She sat on the bed and nibbled the untouched white corn biscuit, looking through the white leather-bound book Senadol had entitled *General Observations*.

She heard three ravens calling around the tree house.

Sparrows with emerald and blue feathers lighted on the sills of all four windows.

Rusty gray squirrels sprang under them into the room, burrowing their heads under Neuvia's legs on the bed and switching their tails.

She heard the stout, unmistakable claps of the beaver's tail against a distant tree trunk and the great horned owl landed on a branch outside the window overlooking the brook, its feathers raised and ruffled in the daylight as it hooted low and one of its amber eyes glanced gravely at her as the other glanced out through the forest.

"The King," hissed Toy in her ear.

Neuvia focused her spyglass on the tip of the Tower.

The stone was pale; Trinadol had left!

*   *   *

Like a blooded bull, he charged down the main path of the forest. The coppery Scepter seethed in the tree-leaf dapples as bug and bird and beast alike scurried away before him.

Under his left arm, Trinadol held the *Cirilinicon* of Elwyn Gheldron, one of the most precious books in the world.

He had found the book after looking down through Elwyn's Tower for seven hours, searching every crevice of every floor. At last Trinadol had stretched back on his bed, and looking up he saw the Cirilinicon hidden inside the ceiling above him. After removing a series of nearly seamless puzzle pieces of *lightstone*, he had pulled down the ponderous volume, which was bound in the black hide of Sar, the furious cave devil his grandfather had slain in his youth.

In the thick volume Trinadol had found techniques he could use to build defenses around his lonely throne and make it impossible for anyone, no matter how well-meaning, to ever reach him and allow his curse to come true.

He imagined that meeting occurring, under numerous conditions, but always leading to the doom his father promised. If he never touched the world with his poisonous soul, he reasoned, he could not harm the world. If he let nothing come close to his heart, his fate would be postponed, indefinitely. Perhaps then he could live, at least, without cursing what was dear to him. Neuvia, after the brief lifetime of their passion, had wisely abandoned him, he was grimly certain now.

The sun burned off the mist as he reached the sandy beach. He passed the ruins of Knot, searching among them with piercing eyes. But he found nothing there.

At the end of the beach, the cliff curved toward the sea and from its base a broad vein of pink granite emerged, standing out from the dark rock as it met the sea. On the back of this promenade of pink rock was carved a round tidal pool.

The pool was called the Eye of Simairon, *simairon* meaning "sea" in Ardeyon, the language of Sentad, which had been the language of Ameulas since Elwyn was King. Shelves were carved into the rock around this pool facing the sea so visitors could gaze into the window at low tide.

The pool resembled an eye with a deep black pupil from which a trickle of hot water sprang. This warm ribbon of fresh water kept the pool from becoming too briny on summer days and too cold on winter nights. Three tides spilled over the granite bar each day, refreshing the pool and changing its cast of characters.

Though the rock was pink, the "eye" appeared blue-green, for the bottom was spread with anemones reaching turgid crowns into the undulating water. Bursts of violet coral followed white veins of quartz to the eye's pupil. Between the anemones and coral, in a thousand crags and arches and holes, were the armies of crabs and the tiny blue-and-yellow brittlestars, and the purple-and-pea-green sea cucumbers with their yellow-and-vermilion bouquets filtering the water for sea crumbs. And there were snails like painted porcelain baubles, ancient mail-plated chitons, keyhole limpets tipping their bright hats, green abalone, orange eels, tiny pink octopi, and the friendly red-and-white barber shrimp that groomed all creatures—except for the gold urchins which ate the fearless barber shrimp. The shrimp were protected, however, by the roaming squads of silver crabs, which Senadol had created to keep the beach clean, the kelp trimmed, and the voracious urchins at bay.

Each time a visitor looked into the Eye of Simairon, there were new marvels to see. Trinadol walked over the granite outcropping, eager to look into it and was startled to see the whole pool shining crimson before him in the bolting sun.

Then, as though it had been a cruel illusion, the pool seemed to blink and reveal its rainbow splendor.

When he got to the edge of the pool he noticed red fanworms rooted across the bottom—sea flowers that pulled in their red feathers at the slightest provocation. These flowers were spread further apart than they had first appeared, and they shied back into their wormholes at his every movement.

Trinadol sat on a bench carved into the rock overlooking the pool and set the Scepter on top of the *Cirilinicon*. He folded his legs, threw back his robe, and let the sun bathe his naked body.

*   *   *

"Spy!" Toy whispered.

"That's what I'm doing," Neuvia whispered back as she parted the ferns on the cliff overlooking the Eye of Simairon.

Looking into the tide pool, sitting naked in the sun with his hair flung back by the sea-wind, was Trinadol.

The great horned owl sat in the tree above her, fearless in the bright sun. A brown sea eagle sat on the tree's highest branch over the cliff, watching. The owl hooted. The eagle cried and leaped into the sky, its wings flashing.

She let the ferns close and lay flat.

Trinadol sensed something on the cliff behind him and pointed his silver spyglass. He saw an eagle flashing in the sun and followed the bird as it flew north along the cliff.

Neuvia extended her spyglass and slid it through the lacy leaves, resting it on a rusty fork and twisting the focus. Trinadol was reading a large book whose pages were bound in shiny black leather. He closed the book and seemed struck by something he saw in the pool. He rose and put his hands over his eyes as he gazed down. She steadied her hold on the spyglass, and then saw something in the pool.

A rare black nautilus swam in broad, fast curves, its creased shell like the hull of a ship cutting the water as jets propelled it above the surface.

The nautilus had been trapped in the pool by the tide and was searching for a way out.

Neuvia saw an orange hand floating on the green water near the nautilus. It was a starfish, one she had heard of but never seen. It was called a *rollock,* which meant "monster" in old Ameulentian. It could float and swim like a man with its fifth arm like a head that pointed forward tipped by a cluster of purple eyes. Neuvia remembered these starfish hunted the black nautilus. This one may have waited for weeks in the pool, like a spider in its web, until a nautilus fell into its trap.

The rollock stroked a few strokes and hung still. When the nautilus eventually curved over it, its orange fingers closed and cracked its shell. The rollock sunk with its quarry.

Trinadol waded out into the pool and reached into the water, lifting the nautilus and the starfish. He stood still as he looked at the grimly wedded creatures.

"Why can't I call him?" Neuvia asked in exasperation.

"Not yet," Toy's tongue feathered her ear.

"What is he doing?" she asked.

"I do not know!"

*   *   *

Nothing. Neuvia found nothing in the book of prophecies when she returned to the tree house.

She craved meat. The owl seemed to try something different each day to find out what she wanted, and the sea eagle brought her a fish at dusk every day. Generous birds even brought her three eggs each morning.

Would Trinadol see the smoke if she cooked? She took her books and climbed down the stairs carved on the ivory branch outside to the dressing room. She turned and walked down the spiral stairs around the trunk to the low-ceilinged kitchen.

She looked at the queer stove there—an iron grill with river cobbles piled under it. She had brought some pots from the Lightstone Tower with her. She looked through cupboards under the counter around the stove. There were corroded copper pots and cobwebbed, rusty utensils. Then she found a mildewed book with a yellow ear of fungus growing on its spine. She remembered the book from when she was a child and knew everything about the tree house, but now it was but a dim memory. She scraped the growth from the binding and separated the leaves of vellum to let them dry. *My Cookbook*, it said on the first page in Trinadol's childish hand. On the next page was this entry:

> *MY STOVE—Father helped me make the most wizard stove of all! I say "You Better Get Hot!" to the river stones. Then I throw one of them back in the Chuckling Wee. The rest get hot, with jealousy, Father says.*

She read the imaginative and imaginary recipes for Trinadol's favorite meals. He tried to cook fried sparrow's eggs with spices and butter gravy and even black biscuits, using unspeakably silly ingredients, and poor little Trinadol noted "less pepper maybe" or "no snail juice" or "doesn't work" under his failed recipes. He also tried frying the colorful tree snails that inhabited some of the forest's trees and, after proudly explaining his herb, meal, and grease formula as "delicious and fit for the very Gairanor!" he added, apparently the next day: *"Bleeecch!"*

As she leafed through Trinadol's delightfully twisted tome, she was warmed by the optimism in the child Trinadol, and she held the clever book to her bosom.

"The stove!" whispered Toy.

"Yes, Toy!" Neuvia smiled, stroking his ivory braid. Toy rode so sensitively on her skin that she forgot he was there sometimes.

She selected a smooth pebble from under the iron grill and went to the window. A branch had grown between the kitchen and the stream. So she pulled open the door on the outer wall and climbed the stairs carved on the white branch to the outer dining room, the miniature hall with a table and two benches.

Neuvia knelt at the window facing the stream and saw she had a slim shot. If she missed she would get more stones to throw. "You better get hot!" she said. She eyed the shard of water between the branches and flicked the stone. With a winking splash, it struck the water. "Ha!" she declared, and ran nimbly down the stairs.

She crouched as she entered the kitchen door, peering in.

The stones were as rosy as a fresh litter of puppies. She approached and tested the air over the iron grate and found it hot, yet the heat soon dissipated as she raised her hand. She decided that if she boiled things in water, she could cook without smoke! Looking up, she noticed a screened chimney built into the ceiling.

That night, Neuvia ate boiled rabbit with onions and potatoes and steamed flat bread. She was a master cook and even this improvised meal was better than the fare of most country hamlets. She sat in the dining room on the end of the branch, looking through the forest boughs chiming and fluting in the sky as she drank a hot cup of herb tea.

Across the Chuckling Wee, her eyes focused on a startling figure, a man-like animal covered with orange hair.

He hung in the trees and stared at her with piercing blue eyes. His legs were like great arms spread in different directions gripping the branches in hand-like feet.

She was soothed more than frightened as she looked into the powerful beast's eyes, and she remembered the "Orange Man" from tales, a very old creature who had dwelt in the woods since Elwyn's time even though he was rarely ever seen.

After staring for several minutes at Neuvia, the creature yawned and moved off through the trees as night fell and stars pierced the sky.

Neuvia smiled, glad to know he would be somewhere in the forest with her.

She lit a yellow candle and scanned the pages of Senadol's white book of general observations, and she came across a curious entry:

> *A NOTE ON THE WYNDERNAL REALM*—*Never have I visited the Wyndernal World. As far as I know, my father was the last Cirilen whose link to that magical world was substantial enough to open the eyes of his second life in that glorious realm. None of my living kin on Trillan have been there, except for Dantair, who only went once. My father Elwyn described the Wynderne World as the world of the possible, and "what this world might be."*
>
> *It is the fabled source of the Cirilen's power, this realm. By discovering how its possible forms may project through a gateway such as the Cronus Star, the Cirilen may bring forth into this realm the miracles of Wynderne. If a Cirilen succeeds in letting enough Wyndernal property into this world, his "second eyes" will open when his first eyes close, as the gateway weakens.*
>
> *The Wyndernial Realm is dangerous as well as beautiful, by all accounts, however, and it is not a place for the faint of heart.*
>
> —Senadol Gheldron, *The Second of Wheat, 894*

Neuvia looked through the dusky forest. Another world, she thought. If only there was one.

* * *

Trinadol's quill paused over a fresh page.

In a jar of seawater before him, the rollock was devouring a fish. Trinadol had begun the first shorthand subject descriptions of the starfish in Trillanic Runes, each rune specifying a certain category of color, shape, movement, senses, habits, and strength, using the Scepter to measure each of these properties. He would have to calculate their reconvergence in appropriate proportion and harness the levers in the sky needed to affect the incantation he was composing.

On Neuvia's desk he had spread the charts Nil Ramesis had drawn, which showed the most treacherous reefs between the Dimmrock and the port of Gwylor 200 miles north.

It would take three months to find the exact formula, the place, the moment, the words, and the position of stars and moons necessary to create the first of his defenses.

* * *

Eighty-seven days passed, with Trinadol leaving the Tower only three times to return to the tide pool with the rollock, taking measurements of some sort with the Cronus Star as he peered through its facets.

Twice a day, he hurled a jar out the window of the Tower, and it would return to the window ten minutes later full of fresh seawater, which he poured into the rollock's jar.

Neuvia watched him descend the Tower only four times, returning to the pinnacle with sacks of food that followed him up the stairs from the larder below.

He worked deep into the night, always outlasting her as she fell asleep fearing for his troubled soul.

She had, in the last months, developed a comfortable routine with the helpful denizens of the forest. She learned that she could summon things in a subtle way from the animals who lived there.

After showering in the bathroom of the tree house one day, she put her last bar of soap on the windowsill; the next day another appeared beside it.

So she now she set out a sample of what she needed on windowsills, and no matter what the item, it would arrive within a week after various teams of animals managed to locate the item and deliver it to her.

A golden necklace of summer days strung pretty links across the season, but one day had been particularly dark for her.

This was the day Neuvia came across the beaver, who often left her pieces of wood chiseled into the shape of rotted moldings, gutters, and beams she had thrown out of the tree house.

It reminded her of Drok, the crazy beaver who attacked her when she was a little girl and killed her father, though she did use each piece of wood the beaver milled for her to replace the ones she had discarded. Yet she had nightmares of the beaver gnawing away the trunk of the tree house while she slept.

She was bathing in the brook one day when the beaver appeared, tall as a man on the pink-clovered bank, sniffling as he looked at her, and it terrified her. She dove down and snatched a stone from the streambed. She flung it at the beaver and swam to the other bank, running naked to the tree house and riding the rope ladder all the way to the top. She shivered, crying on her bed for a time that she did not measure before she rose and pored over Senadol's book of prophecies. But its pages were blank.

In these months, Neuvia learned a good deal more in her books. She read about the halcyon days of the greatest island in the world, Sentad, mighty kingdom of antiquity that lay on the far side of Hala, and she learned how the fierce *Khalwairn* had conquered majestic Sentad, and how the Cirilen united in the great *Wynderne War* to destroy them. Centuries later, *Drugor,* the last *Khalwairn,* had returned with his hibernal servants, the Wintegs, and slaughtered 47 of the 48 Cirilen Houses. Only the Gheldrons, of whom she was now one, had escaped.

The Gheldrons journeyed west to found the enchanted island of Trillan. Elwyn Gheldron, who was their patriarch, journeyed north from Trillan in 669 to become the first Cirilen-Lord of Ameulas. He married the Ameulentian princess Apriscia, the daughter of King Gustomeer, and she had borne him one son, Senadol. In 839, *Drugor* came to exact vengeance on Elwyn. To spare Ameulas, Elwyn had fled to Ghenten, the virgin land to the northwest, and there Elwyn engaged *Drugor* in a final battle that laid that fair land to waste before it could flourish under the Tintilisair's flag.

The last incantation of Elwyn Gheldron banished *Drugor* from the Hala and *Wynderne* worlds with a curse that drew its power from the invincible Gairanor beyond both worlds, and it was this curse that ancient *Drugor* had not the strength nor guile to escape, tied as it was to the bloodline of his nemesis.

Elwyn had died in 840 with *Drugor* after delivering his invocation on a rocky gorge in southern Ghenten. Senadol traveled to Ghenten alone to find his bones, and he released his father's spirit to join the Gairanor as a white bull with golden horns that charged across the sea until it crossed the horizon into the sky. And so, Senadol retrieved the Scepter and bore it home to Ameulas. He was crowned King at the age of 140, ruling from 840 to 1064. He was 365 years old when he died. Now, at seventeen, Trinadol was King.

Neuvia also found that it was by delving into the high arts that the Cirilen and *Khalwairn* had opened the door to the *Wyndernal World*. What was natural in that weird world could then escape into this one, where it might be monstrous and evil, or miraculous and good. So, after *Drugor* was banished, the remaining Cirilen of the House of Gheldron assumed guardianship over the known magical stones that could open that gateway. As the keeper of the Cronus Star, Trinadol bore a grave responsibility over the stewardship of Hala.

Neuvia made special note of the privileged powers that she, as the wife of a Cirilen, might command. They were greatly limited compared to the powers of a true Cirilen, though with grace and wit they could be employed to clever and potent effect.

She learned that if she ever tried to use Gieron's scepter, Trinadol would surely detect it. A Cirilen could easily discover the existence of the jewel itself, even if it was not used. Neuvia had to keep the scepter in water, inside the tree house, which she had charmed so that Trinadol could not see it.

She could use the scepter once, however, in order to protect something she loved. Senadol had taught his wife Conilair how to cast the Spell of Protection over the world, cautioning her that she should save her option for a time of crisis. Conilair had not the opportunity to use the Cronus Star, for she was too weak to use it at her death. Neuvia memorized the spell Senadol had written down in his book of general observations, and she kept Gieron's scepter in the cistern under the floor in case she might ever need to use it.

*   *   *

On the 88th day of his seclusion, Trinadol emerged from the Tower.

Neuvia followed him through the forest despite the warnings of the eagle and the owl, which scouted for her above.

She reached the northern edge of the forest and crouched in the tall rush, focusing her spyglass across the field.

Trinadol walked in his red robe, his back to her.

She crouched down and started following him through the trail of bent grass his long strides had made.

"Don't let him see you!" said Toy. "Take off your cape. Your dress is green!"

Neuvia cast her cloak far to the right of the trail on the wind and crawled as fast as she could behind Trinadol.

After she followed him for an hour he finally reached the edge of the cliff and faced the sea.

She rubbed her battered knees. The sun was tilting just past noon. The wind was strong, whipping back his crimson robe and jett-black hair as he stood against the wind, his body thrusting toward Ameulas.

Trinadol raised the Cronus Star as he watched the sky, as though he were waiting for some imperceptible thing.

At last he turned and paced blindly toward her.

He stopped a few feet from her.

He looked in her direction as his eyes flashed crimson.

"He's blind!" Toy whispered in her ear.

Neuvia nodded.

Trinadol turned back toward the sea.

He looked at the sky again and whispered a few words. A high wail emitted from the gemstone as though in pain or demented pleasure.

A single red spark shot out of the diamond into the sky.

Black wisps of cloud materialized above, swirling together between Trinadol and the sun.

A chill of shadow gathered over him on the field.

He spoke something softly, his eyes closed, his head bowed, the stone crystal-clear in the Scepter.

The chimes of the forest jangled like an army riding in the distance.

The Cronus Star sent sparks in all directions which did not burn out but flew straight as arrows as far as the eye could see, changing color through the spectrum as they spread through the sky.

The ground lurched, and Neuvia dropped the spyglass.

"The animals were right," Toy hissed in her ear. "He'll doom the island!"

Neuvia held onto fistfuls of grass as the ground banged and rumbled under her knees. "What can I do?" she asked.

"I do not know!" Toy sighed.

Slivers of rock fell from the palisades all around the Dimmrock, slicing into the waves.

Loose stones fell from the courtyard wall and the great bell clanged in the forest as the birds circled over the trees.

A crack opened in the wall surrounding the square courtyard and a piece slid off into the gateway, smashing over the marble steps.

The statue of Trinadol's mother toppled from its base.

Neuvia rose on the field, trying to stay on her feet. "Trinadol!" she cried, but he did not hear her.

He shouted strange words and pointed the Scepter at the cloud above, which parted and let a ray strike the red diamond.

Neuvia took a step toward Trinadol but the ground split and a wall of steam shot up before her. She fell back, hiding her face from the scalding shower.

As the steam subsided she saw that the cliff on which he stood was thrusting away from the Dimmrock. A span three feet wide gaped between them, and the fault was 400 feet deep, reaching down to the sea. As if unlocked from jaws sealed since the beginning of time, the voice of creation roared from that grinning crack.

Trinadol convulsed in ecstasy, laughing in the dripping glow of the Cronus Star as the ledge moved away from the Dimmrock. A wall of steam blasted up again, and when it fell she saw he had collapsed. She remembered from her studies that the Scepter could not act when its master was asleep, except to defend itself. Neuvia leaped across the crack as it laughed wider.

She grasped the grass on the other side and pulled herself onto the ledge. Then she lifted Trinadol to his feet and pushed him over the chasm, shouting *"Kair Talo Ga!"*—the spell of force she had heard Trinadol use against Knot.

Trinadol seemed to be propelled forward slightly, to her grateful awe, and she leaped behind him onto the Dimmrock, catching his arms as the soft ground crumbled under his chest. She dragged him over the edge and even Toy pulled on his red robe with his tiny jaws.

Safe on the cliff, she sat with him, panting as she looked at the great piece of the Dimmrock sliding into the sea.

The ocean was boiling around the Dimmrock, though the island no longer trembled. The new island continued to move away, sinking as the field on top caught fire in orange sheets that sent brown smoke over the sea.

Neuvia thought it best to drag Trinadol further away from the edge of the cliff. The flowers shivered around them as he lay in a cold sleep with his head on her lap. His knuckles were white around the tarnished Scepter whose gem was now pale.

She touched the Scepter's handle and its stone flashed, singeing her finger with alarming pain. She cursed it and looked back at the island moving over the sea.

The new island left a wide wake over the heaving swells as it plowed north. She sat stroking Trinadol's brow on her leg as the cliffs of the new island glowed like coals. The waves hissed against its walls and waves of steam rolled away from its crimson shores. The cliffs melted and foaming banks of glowing mud emerged as the island's deep roots rose molten out of the sea.

As the island grew it stretched into a long, glowing finger of land, its points curving back toward the Dimmrock like a horseshoe in a forge as it moved north over the sea. She watched it until it finally cooled, fading in the dusk and distance.

A balmy wind gusted and fat, warm raindrops raised the spicy scents in the field around her.

"Leave before he wakes!" whispered Toy.

"Yes!" She kissed Trinadol, and his lips were ice-cold. "Will he be all right?" she asked.

"Yes," said Toy. "Elwyn did this, too. He will wake suddenly! The Queen must leave."

She kissed him once more and smoothed back his hair. She picked a wildflower and slid it into the hair above his ear. She left him lying on the grass in the warm rain.

*   *   *

When Trinadol woke, he rose on one elbow and looked from the moonlit cliff. As he suspected, a small portion of the field, when chiseled straight down into the island's roots, was a giant mass of land to work with. He could see the new island glowing on the horizon under the golden moon, just where he wanted it, fused to the treacherous reef on Nil Ramesis's chart.

The sky was clear, yet it must have rained while Trinadol was asleep. He passed his hand through his hair and found the flower Neuvia had placed there. He twisted its stem, smelling its perfume and thinking of her. Dread pressed his heart.

He rose to his feet and the Scepter pulsed weakly in his hand. He found the rollock's jar and brought it to the edge of the new cliff.

Then he pulled the starfish out of the water and held it in his left hand, the Scepter in his right. "Now, Rollock! Be my guardian!" he cried, and he gathered the Second Moon's light into the diamond over his head, turning the gem with a precision that gnawed ever so slowly toward each focal point in the sky. Employing the muscular coordination he learned on Trillan from his kin and letting the equation he must perform utterly possess his nerves and muscles, Trinadol aligned a star on each facet of the jewel and gathered the distant rays and gravities like ropes and pulleys from the heavens. Shifting his muscles, like the turning of the earth, he raised the rollock.

Trinadol looked into the Cronus Star and hurled the starfish like a discus over the cliff and a cat's cradle of twisting red beams followed it from five stars in the sky as it fell into the gloom.

A gush of greenish light leaped from the Cronus Star into the spinning starfish, which seemed to hang, spinning in the air without falling.

Then the sea sprayed around the starfish unexpectedly, revealing that it had grown giant as it fell and was now the size of five whales fused together.

The great rollock started to swim like a man, arm over arm and kicking, as one arm looked forward toward the northern horizon. It rotated a different arm to the head position every mile or so as it swam toward its new home.

Trinadol fell to his knee, and touched the Scepter to his forehead as he staggered away from the cliff as the Cronus Star pulsed weakly, like his heart, barely illuminating the path before him.

He passed through the forest and over the rubble of the wall that had collapsed over the stairs. Then he scaled the Tower, and finally fell upon his bed.

Lying on his back, he looked at the flower that he had found in his hair. It was blue and sweet, and he thought of her.

Never again, he thought, the caress of her presence? Never again, his young wife by his side? There was a monster, now, between them.

With the Scepter on his chest, he fell into an abyss of bitter sleep.

*   *   *

Chapter 10

▼

Wyndernia

Trinadol *woke on the Throne.*

The **Scepter** *was not in his hand, and he did not feel the urge to find it.*

He marveled, instead, at his surroundings.

The Throne Room was dappled by an undersea radiance of blue-green lapping over the lightstone around him, and the scent of limes lingered in the cool air. Trinadol's skin felt like it was wet under a hot sun. If this was a dream, it was as tangible as truth, he thought.

Soft pipes lowed and stirring chimes shimmered. He noticed the silhouette of a woman kneeling before him.

"May I approach, lord?" she said with a voice like smoke and perfume.

"Come," he said, breathing in her fragrance.

The woman came out from under the turquoise shadows so Trinadol *could see her. Her hair was gold as wheat and shining like pearls, and her skin was tawny as copper. She wore nothing but a palla of gossamer and* Trinadol *admired her slender body through the sheer cloth and looked into the green pools of her eyes. She smiled. "My lord, do you like what you see?" she asked.*

"How could I not like what I see? Yet I know it cannot be real. This is some strange dream, I am guessing..."

"Lord, tonight you are initiated into a higher order, an inner circle. In ancient days, many Cirilen won passage here through their mighty deeds. Not every Cirilen was able, but those few who were are heroes, every one. Your grandfather, Elwyn, was the last Cirilen to walk in Wynder. And now his grandson, so young, has crossed into greatness with the splendid feat you performed on Hala this day."

"What do you speak of? I have heard only myths of this world. Why would my teachers hide it from me?"

"My lord," she bowed again. "Your teachers were afraid the greatness of Elwyn had passed to you. And they were right, if only by half! This is not a dream. I am real. You are real. This world is real. This is your second life, Trinadol, and now you finally see with your second eyes. All great Cirilen have two lives, and one is their dream life, which for them is twice as real as the waking world. You will want for nothing that this world and I cannot give you. If it is love or lust you require, I will give you enough to satisfy your wildest fancy the instant it fires your imagination. Nothing shall be denied you, for here you are absolute master. This is the reward of greatness, lord! Indeed, my splendid Cirilen, you are the greatest living sorcerer in all of Hala, the most potent mage since Arnarus! You shine, my most wonderful lord!"

"Who are you, then?" asked Trinadol.

"I am the gift of the Gairanor, the most high council of your ancestors who convene in the nethers of heaven. I am justice, lord. They have given me to you, and they have unlocked the door of paradise for you. I am to assure you that this second life *of challenges and pleasures will be as real as the magic you allowed into the* Hala World *of mortal men today."*

"I wish to speak to the Gairanor!" said Trinadol, thrilling as he gripped the crystal arms of his Throne.

"I cannot summon them for you. Nothing can do that!"

"Come closer to me. What is your name?"

"My name is Zexethia, my most spectacular lord." She climbed the stairs and stood before him.

He stared at her body that trembled beneath lucid fabric. It was real! She was certainly real! And yet her eyes and face shone with a luster that mixed art into truth, her lips brush strokes of pleasure and passion. He touched her hand and squeezed it.

"Yes, lord. Flesh. Sweat!"

He smelled her hand. She smelled of green apples and cinnamon.

"Perfume," she smiled slyly, her indigo eyes slitted. "Now you see you never really needed her." She knelt and kissed his hand.

He swooned at the touch of those lips that were a confection of femininity on his hand as though his palm were a tongue and her lips were honey.

"Neuvia *could never understand your power or magnificence,"* purred Zexethia. "Or the extraordinary appetites of greatness and the solemn importance of providing you with even your lightest whim. She had no concept of your superiority or of her duty, as a mortal, to kneel down before it and to serve it completely, as I will, my lord on High and Master Most Supreme." She closed her eyes and lay upon the stone at his feet.

"Neuvia," he sighed softly, remembering her scent, which was not perfume...

Zexethia leapt to her feet. "Behold your Queen, lord!" *she presented Neuvia, who had been sitting silently on her Throne.*

He recoiled. She seemed craven and small. Her face was pale, her eyes dull and mean, her beauty blunted before the spectacle of Zexethia. There was a wicked gleam in Neuvia's eye!

"Stand up, Bondairtlen *woman!" Zexethia shouted, shining like gold before Neuvia, who rose at her command, and she was not as tall as* Trinadol *expected. Zexethia pushed Neuvia to her knees and slapped her cheek, turning to him.* "Nay, lord, she wishes only to pull your greatness down to wed with mediocrity! She wishes not to see you soar, but to see you bound to the muddy earth by her side." *Zexethia slapped Neuvia again.* "She clings to you like guilt, weakening your resolve!" *Zexethia struck her again and Neuvia wept weakly on her knees as she accepted each of Zexethia's blows, her cheek smudged by a bruise, a droplet of blood sparkling on her lip.* "She tries to draw you away from your power, my master, weakening you and preparing you for doom!" *The shining Zexethia slapped Neuvia again and her hair fell over her face.*

He looked at Neuvia, horrified to see her weak and groveling, as though guilty of all Zexethia charged.

"Look on her!" *cried Zexethia.* "There is nothing she can do that I will not do a thousand times better, rewarding in kind the magnificent deeds of your days with nocturnal splendors of equal magnificence. Neuvia is as worthless to you now as I am worthy. You ascend, and she holds your ankle like a weight." *Zexethia slapped Neuvia viciously once more, but Neuvia only bowed her head as though in shame before Zexethia.* "I will cut your bonds to that other world, lord, and set your wild spirit free in both worlds!" *Zexethia produced a glass dagger from her red boot, and in a flash, she pulled Neuvia's face back by her hair and slipped the crystal point to the hilt in Neuvia's throat. Neuvia's eyes glazed over as* **Trinadol** *gasped. Part of him was stricken, too, and seemed to die. Zexethia withdrew the dagger before his dumbfounded eyes and a broach of blood gleamed on the gorge of Neuvia's neck, splattering as she fell to the stone. Zexethia pushed her from the dais, and she slid limply down the stairs, rolling into the aisle.*

Zexethia turned to him, the dagger dripping in her hand. "Long live the Queen, my lord." She tossed the knife away and knelt before Trinadol, kissing the palm of his hand. He gasped as his hand filled with venomous pleasure and he heard her whisper as though his hand were his ear: "Long live the King!"

* * *

Neuvia was chewing a bite of pear and reading a passage by Queen Conilair about Cirilen husbands, a passage that was addressed to the future Queen of the Tintilisair and so commanded her attention, when Toy whispered, "Sleep!" in her ear. "The King is in danger!"

"Sleep?" Neuvia frowned.

"The Crimson has left the Scepter. Nothing guards the gate of the King's dreams. He is in the *Wynder World*, and the Crimson is there with him! The King is in danger! I can speak to the diamond! I can get you in to see the King."

Neuvia shook her head. "I can't just go to sleep! I am wide-awake now, Toy! What danger is the King in?"

"The Crimson Ghost has followed the king through the Cronus Star and will try to seduce him. You must sleep! I will worm a way for you to follow."

"But how?"

"Lie down!"

"I can't just go to sleep as though going into battle!"

"Yes you can…" Toy sighed.

She lay down on the bed and Toy began coiling, interweaving his braid around her throat. "Close your eyes!" he hissed.

His lengths loosened and tightened, sliding silken around her neck and squeezing and releasing the veins gently, an intricate caress of his complicated knot that made Neuvia drift deeper and deeper away from wakefulness. With a sigh she fell out of this world and into a dream…

She was in a dark room that seemed to have no walls, or whose walls were transparent and thick as infinity. There was a wooden chair in the room. That was all. She passed to the other side of the vast room and saw the ash-wood doors of the Lightstone Tower through a gloom of distance. They seemed real hanging in the nothingness. She ran and felt her body, her heart, and her lungs. She felt her feet on a floor of stone. She smelled an ancient breath of unstirred air. This was more than a dream, she knew.

Neuvia felt energy charging her body, as though her every urge was poised on the verge of reality. This was more than wakefulness, she wondered.

She pressed her hands to the ancient wooden doors and pushed.

*   *   *

Zexethia smiled at Trinadol *as she rubbed oil onto his feet. "So young and yet—so great," she said. "What greater things will you do? I wonder! Will you shine like* Arnarus? *Will you blaze like* Elwyn? *Can your star be as bright as theirs? I should perish, immolated by joy, if your triumphs were half as bold!"*

Trinadol *gripped the Throne, staring at the golden lioness of a woman who soothed, emboldened and burnished his brash manhood to vindication, by turns lavishing his every ambition, leveling the scales of his conscience and encouraging him to even greater boldness.*

The bronze bolt of the ash-wood doors burst in burning splinters as sun and blue sky flooded into the Throne Room.

Zexethia turned on her knees and scowled at the one who stood in the lightstone arch.

Only then did Trinadol *feel that a separate purpose had arrived, as though only his will had been influencing everything here, including the beauty of Zexethia, if not her very existence. Now, another will that was not his own influenced this strange world, coloring its substance with a different spectrum, and for a moment he dreaded it until he knew who it must be. For the body bleeding on the floor was smaller than* Neuvia, *who stood haloed in rainbow circlets and shafted sunbeams under the shining arch of the Tower.*

"Now is the test. Send her away!" said Zexethia, clutching his arm.

Neuvia *walked down the aisle in her green dress, black tights and leather sandals, her black hair rippling from her brow, loose and long. Her visage was splendid, blazoned by an angry muse and crowned by righteous rays. She stepped over the body that was supposed to be hers, and it turned to pearly mist as she climbed the stairs to the dais.*

"You are Neuvia*!" whispered* Trinadol. *He hung his head, bewildered. "I know not what to believe here!"*

"Then let me show you, my love." Neuvia *pulled Zexethia to her feet by her flaxen hair, and indeed* Neuvia *was taller and on fire*

with colors and motion, making Zexethisa look ghostly before her.

Toy, who appeared iridescent blue with a white belly and violet eyes in this world, unraveled from Neuvia's throat and coiled down her white arm, slipping his head over her finger.

Neuvia *pointed to the breast of Zexethia, and Toy bit her nipple through the gossamer, injecting her with his cold poison.*

Zexethia jumped back, clutching her breast. Her white teeth turned crimson in her mouth as she screamed a dark curdle of pain that broke like a wave of black glass against the walls. All at once the life left her and she fell like a doll on the stone with a wooden crack. Her flesh desiccated, falling in shreds from her bones and blowing away like ashes. Neuvia kicked her brittle bones from the dais and turned to Trinadol. *"She was a lie, my love. But I am real, even if this place is not!"*

"Neuvia, come let me touch you before you slip from sight!"

She ran to him and let him crush her in his arms. She combed her fingers through his hair as he kissed her eyes and felt the warmth of her ears and smelled her hair. "Are we all that is real here? Where is here? How did you come to me, Neuvia?"

"I am the Queen of a Cirilen, lord, and there are powers that come with my office."

Trinadol *laughed in amazed gratitude and held her by her shoulders at arm's length.* "Let me look at you! I thought I lost you—yet you find your way to my heart against all odds or means. Alas! The Scepter *could not guard my heart from you!"*

"The Scepter *could not, my lord. But something has taken the* Scepter *and does guard your heart from me and from all the waking world."*

"What do you mean? Tell me, Neuvia. I trust you completely!"

She sighed in joyous relief. "During your wakeful hours the Cronus Star compels you, my love. It uses your power more and more against you even as your power grows. I am your Queen. Trinadol, I never wish you harm. Nor do I believe you, my husband, could wish mine. You doubt yourself! You paint your ambition crimson too readily! I will flatter you with a warning. I have read Senadol's writings. You are more important than you know. You are the last of the great Cirilen, the last of the super guardians of Hala. If you do not guard the entrance to Hala from this wild world where we are now, wicked nightmares will invade the waking world. You have enemies older than you by thousands of years, hatching plots not in Ameulas but here where they hide from the Gairanor and seek ways into the waking world. They long for that world where they can demand worship and servitude from mortals. Here in this dreamscape, the Scepter, which is of the Hala World, cannot sway you. Here, you cannot reach for the Scepter and it cannot help you. And here, I tell you, you are most safe, because you are with me!"

"The other world is a nightmare," he said, closing his eyes, losing himself in her midnight hair.

"Yes, Trinadol." She bit back her tears.

"Let's spend this day together," he said. "I think I was here when I was a boy, when I dreamed. We can go anywhere. Anywhere on the Dimmrock, or anywhere in the world. Let today be our honeymoon! Let's ride horses across the sea and soar over mountains, and when we go tonight together into the Lightstone Tower, we will kiss each other long for courage before we sleep to wake in the other world. For it will only be a short time before we meet here again, in this paradise, I promise you.

How can the nightmare be too high a price for the next dream we have together?"

Neuvia *frowned. "Our day is night, our night is day."*

"Our sweetest dreams are real. Our bitter fate is but a dream. Come, my sweet wife. Let us be eagles!"

Trinadol *took her hand and they were eagles with feathers painted white and royal blue.*

They soared together from the dais of the Throne over the aisle and through the splintered doors, rising on the wind over the forest.

The flowers in the trees pulsed colors as if a heart of rainbows pumped inside the world. The birds were brighter, wilder, and wiser. The sea was a vast vat of colors intermingling around the Dimmrock. The salt in the air was citrusy and crisp, the sun gold and hot, and the wind was braided warm and chill.

Trinadol *and* Neuvia *flew over the Dimmrock for hours before he pointed at the sea and they plummeted over the beach, hooking over the Eye of Simairon, where* Trinadol *changed into an orange eel and slipped into the water.*

Neuvia *followed him and they danced, streaming like ribbons around each other in the briny grotto.*

That night, after they had made love as eels in the sea and hummingbirds in the forest and horses on the beach and tigers in the grass, they went to sleep in fresh linens, wrapped in each other's arms, and made love as man and woman, their long hair entangled on smooth pillows of Wynderniol silk.

*   *   *

She heard the faint crowing of the old white cock, and woke up.

"You're awake!" said Toy.

"Yes, Toy." As soothing as his whisper was, it still startled her sometimes. "Is this real now?"

"Yes."

"Very well." Sunlight confettied the forest outside. She rose and stretched her other body—for that's what it seemed like now after feeling her magical body in the dream world.

She remembered everything she had done there in that world of pure will, where all was sympathetic to and intuitive of any idea or desire; and now this world seemed pale, remote. But she recalled the limits of gravity and the stricter rules of Hala as she washed and went down to the kitchen to fix some tea. Before long, she could hardly remember the sensation of the *Wynderne World* at all.

"Thank you, Toy," she said as she sat in the outer dining room.

"The Crimson is ancient and very strong," said Toy. "But even he did not know about Toy! He killed my sisters."

"He?"

"Yes!" hissed Toy.

"Then the woman?"

"A shape he took!"

"Then you did not kill the Crimson?"

"No! I killed the shape he took. If he stayed in *Wynder* he would have died inside that shape. But now he will not let us pass. He dwells in the Cronus Star, not here and not there. He waits for a way to come out. Not into that world. I think the Gairanor hunt him there. He wants to find a way into the Hala World. He is almost as old as I am. He is too much for Toy. Only the King can destroy him, if he can be destroyed."

"Only the King?" she breathed.

"The King is young. The Queen must be with Trinadol in the *Wynder World*. She must bend his ear. She must sweeten his heart!"

"How?"

"She must council him in that careless world to have care in this one. We may pass through Gieron's Scepter."

"Good." Neuvia stroked Toy's smooth curves. "I love him enough for two lives, Toy," she said. "Or two deaths."

*   *   *

Chapter 11

▼

Strange Hope

Trinadol woke feeling a strange and welcome peace. The sun was hot in the *lightstone*. He half-expected to feel Neuvia beside him, but she was not.

He threw the blankets off him and breathed heavily as he looked through the ceiling at the sky. He felt a cleansed, innocent bliss in his veins. He had the strongest feeling that he'd had a dream, though he could not remember it. As he tried, the Cronus Star blushed, and the shock of its evil gore drove the notion away.

He felt the weight of truth crash down and he lay flattened, his conscience dripping red from the walls and ceiling. "Neuvia, Neuvia!" he groaned, pulling his hair as he sat up. "Why couldn't this be a nightmare so I may wake by your side each bright morning with myself innocent and the world fair! But this is the true world and dreams of you only add doubt that could mean my undoing. Forever missed and missing from my life, Neuvia, you will surely drive me mad!"

Trinadol rose from the bed. Enough of this, he thought. Dreams are for the night. He looked out the northern window at the island he had created, which lay near the horizon from the high vantage of his window. He used the silver spyglass he had rummaged from one of the rooms below; he seemed to have lost his golden one. He focused the inferior instrument and, finally, after his Cirilen eyes deciphered the lens and corrected the image, he saw the foamy ribbon that girded the new island's sooty slopes. In the island's lagoon there now resided a gigantic starfish.

Occasionally, he knew, it would swim out onto the high seas to hunt the black nautilus. Yet it would find the black nautilus much too small. So it would feed on whales and other sea beasts it could corner in its lagoon. Or, if the Ameulentians did not heed his command and sent a ship to the Dimmrock, the Rollock would intercept them, and consign them to the fate he had warned them of.

Trinadol remembered part of his dream, suddenly. He remembered that someone had told him there was another world, a windy world, or…a *winding* world? Someone had said that Elwyn had been there. Trinadol turned to the thick *Cirilinicon* of Elwyn Gheldron on his desk and opened the book, searching for any reference to such a realm, wondering why his teachers would have kept such a thing from him. After many hours of searching, he finally found something:

> *The Wynder World should not be discussed overmuch in the Hala World. Suffice that it must remain where it is, as must my life there. And they must never mingle. The laws of that world would demolish this tender world. Perhaps my last purpose is to protect this soft and yet infinitely more courageous world from that omnipotent and easy world, lovely though it is, yet filled with callow and arrogant souls who do not know the cost of whim and destruction in the Hala World. The Khalwairn came from Wynder, though most Wyndernes are not as full of avarice as they. The Wynderne World is infinitely reformable and life there is indestructible. Conduct which is noble there is ignoble, therefore, here in Hala.*
>
> *I confirm what the ancients have handed down. The Wynder World is the source of Cirilen power and our power lies only in discovering ways to release properties of Wynder into Hala. Thus, this general caution to all Cirilen I propose: The incantation should be regarded as*

a set of rules within which the Wyndernal forces unleashed in Hala may operate. The more successfully a Cirilen brings Wynder to Hala, the more Hala he allows into the Wyndernal Realm; and Wyndernes worship the Hala World. Therefore, the more magic a Cirilen conjures in Hala, the greater access he is given to Wynder.

This is an unholy market whose trade has driven many a Cirilen to madness and death. In order to buy greater time and powers in the Wynder World, some Cirilen have been driven to careless, wicked exercises of their power on Hala. Even good Cirilen who are stewards of men have faltered and taken any cause as their excuse to throw their brutal bolts, so keen were they on Wynderne glory. Without care, however, rogue spirits from Wynder can inhabit their creations on Hala, releasing great evil there.

Furthermore, while a Cirilen is in Wynder, he is exposed to treachery and harm in Hala, for he cannot protect his sleeping body while journeying there. This is why I moved the Throne of Ameulas to the Dimmrock. It is also why Arnarus's twin sister Cyrene built Solitaria, her great tower of marble and lightstone that staggers the eye of the beholder with its mountainous size. Before it cracked it held 500,000 rooms. She made the tower impregnable from the sea and let some ten thousand demonic guardians loose to wander its maze of rooms where pits and falling blades and catapults lay hidden in the dark. The tower spiraled into the heavens of Tropical Echargaia, and Cyrene was ever building it higher. She named her colossal citadel Solitaria, and surrounded herself with ferocious eagles that made lookout from the lofty parapets, swooping down on all invaders. Cats of great size and exotic colorings prowled the walls. All this so Cyrene would be safe while she ranged in Wyndernia, sleeping inside her welkin keep.

She tried to build two identical towers, one in Wynderne and one in Hala, and yet she could never match the height of the Wyndernia tower here on Hala. One day, when Cyrene tried to raise the Hala tower higher, hoping to bridge the gap between her two bastions and thus join the two worlds with an intermediary bridge, the Hala tower reached one brick too high, and a single crack bolted like dark lightning across the white lace of its arching windows.

One side of the tower slid into the sea, sending a tidal wave across the world and burying Cyrene under an island of rubble that, to this day, rises around the ruined pinnacle of Solitaria.

A Cirilen should not seek to impose everything that is possible in the Wynder World upon Hala, where the short and precious lives of mortals suffer an irreparable chain of consequences, and where time, wealth, wellbeing, and matter are finite and cannot be restored once their limits have been violated. Prudence is the way of this fragile world, each step testing the ground rather than stomping it in defiance, as some of my predecessors have regretfully done.

Beware giving this world up for the ecstasy of that one, for death here is death there, as well!

Only the Gairanor can restore life after death, though it is restored to a strange world beyond both of these worlds, which we surely know not.

—Elwyn Gheldron, *The Fifth of Oak, 835 After Sentad*

He regretted that his father had told him so little about Elwyn.

What reason am I to make of all this, Artimeer, he wondered. There is another world, that is sure, he thought, and I was there last night. But why is it only a pale dream? Does something block my memory?

Trinadol stared into the gory diamond. Perhaps this *Wynder World* his grandfather spoke of was the world where he belonged. Right was wrong for him and wrong was right. Perhaps this other world could abide his dangerous spirit and his passions would be innocent there, endangering nothing, and free of this world's twin curse of conscience and consequence.

He saw the withered blue wildflower on the rug beside his bed. He picked it up and it seemed heavy in his hand. "And Neuvia, this flower makes me think of you," he whispered. The sweet thought of her unmanned his purpose and he sat confounded in pain and doubt. "Alas!" he hissed, squeezing the Scepter's handle as grief of her dazzled him. "Are you somewhere near me, hiding out of sight? You threaten my sanity, my dearest love!"

The Scepter bled with sudden violence and the shaft burned copperine in his hand.

"Ah, Star: Perhaps you know what to do? Do it, then! If Neuvia is here on the island, find her! If this is not just a sick heart but something more, if Neuvia might somehow be concealed on the Dimmrock, even now, she might appear at a crucial moment and break my will, and bring fate's blow crashing down on both our heads. I command you, Cronus Star: Find eyes to see with in the forest and turn every leaf. Find Neuvia, and prevent her from crossing my path!"

The diamond flushed black and pink, and then went pale. He felt as though his blood were being drained as the stone flushed crimson, and he was reassured by its fire to have such a powerful ally in this lonely war.

He admired the Cronus Star as it shone rich red. Perhaps through this stone he could find another world where he could be free, even as he built his prison.

*   *   *

Pigg woke up.

He blinked as he looked around the forest with fully aware eyes.

He was an ancient creature for which there was no mate. He had no sex, yet he is called "he" so as not to offend the feminine, which Pigg surely had very little of in his nature.

Pigg was bred long ago, a failed cross between the enemies, an experiment by his father that went awry to his paternal horror, despair, and revulsion. He was sent here like a rat on a barrel by his father, pulled by a current in the sea, and dumped on the shore of the Dimmrock, unbeknownst to Elwyn Gheldron, who was then king.

He lived alone through these last centuries, put into the slow half-sleep of a sloth, riding his lineage of elks through the underbrush. He seemed to be a cross between a monkey, a boor, and a sloth, with less hair. Very skinny and scrawny, he was no more than four feet tall. His head was too small even for his narrow shoulders and it was covered with a wispy fuzz of black and brown hair.

The islanders named him "Pigg," after Slow Tim Pigg, the legendary codger who moved so slowly that he lived 150 years. But Pigg had lived longer than this celebrity had; he was 646 years old.

Pigg had ridden his latest mount for ten years, and his long curved claws had punctured permanent holes in the elk's neck and flanks so he could pierce the pain points of his bedraggled beast of burden. He did so now, and the elk sprang through the underbrush.

A girl, he understood Father to say. A Bondairtlen girl. A little cannibalism, eh, wondered Pigg, his jaw lolling open. His mother was Bondairtlen...

What a choice morsel his father had served this time! He licked his black, seemingly singed snout as he urged the red elk forward. Pigg was wide-awake now; Pigg could eat meat.

Every half century or so, Father let him eat meat. Strangely enough, only twelve years had passed since the last time, but Pigg didn't wonder at his good fortune.

The last time, Pigg remembered, he got to cook and eat a baby, the King's bastard son by the Gardener's daughter, who had seduced the widowed Senadol with the ponds and pools she sculpted in the forest. She had borne Senadol a son, half-brother of Trinadol, and left him by the Chuckling Wee one day in a canvas stroller whose wheels were locked by a lever. Pigg unlatched the lever and scurried away as the pram rolled down the grassy bank and tipped into the river.

The babe's head was dashed on a stone, and he floated downstream through the trees. At the edge of the western cliff Pigg was waiting to snatch the little body from a bloody swirl before it was hurled over the falls. And Pigg had danced a mountain jig he learned in Sentad when he was a piglet kept with his father's mountain raiders.

Pigg was omnivorous. He ate soap and wax sometimes, when he found them. Nothing was better than a two-week-old carcass writhing in a high maggot sauce, however. If there was anything Pigg loved, it was his food, and he loved it dearly.

Flies swarmed around his stinking head, and Pigg sucked them through his snout and swallowed them.

The old elk stumbled through the dense undergrowth. Pigg always traveled through the thickest parts of the forest, rarely crossing a path. He caught a scent of Neuvia in the tapestry of aromas and followed the silver thread as it unwound through the trees.

Pigg came to a bend in the Chuckling Wee and looked across to see the tree house. The Queen was inside, and she was not a girl but a woman in full bloom...

"*Hmmm,*" he wondered. A fabulous feast Father gives me today! A couple of days to ripen and then—a very tasty treat! He shuddered in ecstasy. "Oh yes," he sighed, rubbing his belly. "*Mmm,* goody, goody!"

Then Pigg smelled Toy and his blood went cold.

It was a tricky thing to mix with Toy. Pigg alone among beasts on Hala could stand a strike from Toy—but maybe not two. Pigg ate snakes when he found them, and their venom was like a marinade on his palate, tangy and spicy but rarely strong enough to give him worse than gas, which Pigg didn't mind—in fact he thought it was fun to have gas. But Toy? No, and thank you much indeed. He did not care for that sauce!

As Pigg wormed his lips, which he always did when he was thinking, the great horned owl swooped silently behind him. The owl hooted, and when Pigg turned his horrible face toward the sound, two talons grabbed his snout, pulling him off the elk and dropping him on his scrawny back.

Pigg's nostrils were cut and bleeding. His eyes glazed at the smell of blood and he snorted it in, sucking down every last droplet and swallowing it thirstily, whetting his appetite.

He went to the brook to splash his face off. His nose would probably get infected, but he would live. Plus, there would be more flies, he thought, and even some maggots, maybe.

He pulled his elk along the river where he could mount it and jump over the brook under a low branch where the owl could not get at him. But when Pigg tried to climb on his elk, a host of marmosets descended from the branch and hammered him like hailstones, scratching, biting, and striking him.

Pigg jumped into the river and they flew off him into the trees. Then three marmosets jumped onto his elk and commandeered it, riding it off through the woods.

Pigg coughed and spat. All this water would clean the stench right off him, and there would be no more flies for a good long while. He climbed the bank on the other side of the stream, but even as he sat in a muddy puddle, a silver squirrel threw a rock at his lacerated nose, stinging it like a bee.

He growled, blinking. The Queen has many friends, he thought. Well. Piggy-wiggy won't stoppity-stippity-stop till he eats her uppity-wippity-wup!

He drooled from his frowning lower lip under his snout as his beady black eyes twinkled.

The Queen was in her room high above, hanging clothes to dry over the windowsill.

Pigg saw her smooth white skin, like linen soaked in cream, and the red raspberry nibble-wibbles like his mommy-wom's. His little brain buzzed with grisly dreams.

He decided to try again, this time crawling on his belly through the leaves to the trunk of the enryd tree.

        *   *   *

Neuvia hung out a shirt and some stockings to dry on the bathroom windowsill of the tree house when Toy whispered in her ear.

"The Enemy!"

She stood back from the window. "Where? Who?"

Toy turned cold and shivered around her throat.

There was a ghastly howl of pleasure or pain, Neuvia could not tell which, below the tree house. She heard chattering and snarls of beasts in combat. A sharp crack struck the tree trunk. Then silence.

Neuvia chose one of her throwing stones and went to the window.

There, below, was the beaver, his fur raised as the paddle of his tail cracked the trunk of the Enryd Tree. Neuvia cast the stone down, and hit its back. It looked up at her and then shambled across the grass and plopped into the river, paddling upstream.

Neuvia stroked Toy, but he was ice-cold and seemed to be sleeping. She went to her room and opened the book of prophecy on her bed, but found nothing.

Her heart was not eased when she saw the red glow in pinnacle of the Tower as it moved down the spiral stairs.

        *   *   *

Once again, Trinadol marched through the forest, and Neuvia followed him with her eagle and owl as lookouts.

She spied on him from the northern cliff as he descended the path to the beach to gaze into the Eye of Simairon.

Neuvia peered through Trinadol's gold spyglass as he pondered an anglerfish he had caught in a jar. There was no sign that he remembered their time together in *Wyndernia*. She wondered, now, if it had really happened.

Trinadol took his specimen back to the Lightstone Tower and secluded himself, once again.

As dusk fell, she prepared herself for sleep, anticipating her time with him, but Toy, who had not spoken since the beaver prowled below the tree house, whispered, "The King may not pass into *Wynder* tonight!"

"Why not?"

"He must earn more time."

"How must he earn it?" She frowned, feeling her cause becoming impossible. "I must see him! Toy, you said I must protect him and counsel him there. How must he earn more time?"

"Magic."

"Oh no," she hung her head, sadly.

"When he brings more magic into this world, that world will let him return. Then you will see him. After a time, after much more magic, he will go there every night. But the King is very young."

Neuvia sighed, sitting on her bed. "Does he remember?"

"The King does not."

She felt her spirit crack like spring ice and she bit her lip. "Why? How could he not?"

"The Enemy. The Enemy is in his stone. The Enemy did not let his memory pass from there to here. After a while, even the Enemy will not be able to hide his time there anymore. Patience. The Queen is brave. The Queen has time. The Enemy is great."

*   *   *

Chapter 12

▼

The Second Defense

Trinadol studied the brown anglerfish he had taken from the sea, setting down its physical dimensions and determining the proportions of his incantation, according to principles he learned from Elwyn's writings.
After 67 days, he finally completed his last calculation.
He looked into the jar at the anglerfish.
Its yellow eye with leafy brown lashes stared back at him.
With the Scepter and the jar in his hands, he descended the Tower.

*   *   *

He stood on the sharp, raw edge of the Northern Cliff as another towering piece of the island slid away from the Dimmrock into the sea.
"Be still," whispered Toy. Neuvia held her breath as the island groaned like a wounded beast beneath her in the aftermath of Trinadol's assault.
Trinadol raised the spiny angler in his left hand as blood spiraled down his arm. After aligning the facets of the Cronus Star to the moons and first stars, he threw the angler over the cliff, and a laughing, mad soul passed through the Cronus Star into the fish, which seemed to hover in the air as it thrashed and wheeled. Then sea-foam blasted underneath the angler, which had grown into a leviathan as it fell.
The monster churned the water as it wagged from side to side, shooting across the sea toward Ameulas with shocking speed.

And as it swam, it seemed to change, and in the far distance Neuvia could see it had sprouted arms that were swimming like a man's.

Trinadol turned away and wandered blindly past her, the Scepter's light guttering bloody light as he made his way across the field.

She followed, and saw flocks of Dimmrock sheep, their unshorn wool matted and ragged, running in frantic circles in the distance.

The earth staggered, and then caught itself.

A long groan vibrated in the Dimmrock as a wave curled away from its rocky shores.

Neuvia trailed behind Trinadol as he staggered down the path in the forest toward the Lightstone Tower. She paused, heartbroken, looking after him. Then she turned into the woods, heading back to the tree house.

*   *   *

After 67 days, Pigg had finally devised a plan that enabled him to get to the trunk of the tree house, with no animal of the forest interfering.

He had covered a blanket he found with thorny vines, and, so far, it had fooled all the Queen's friends. Pigg snuffled as he swallowed a fat yellow slug that he had sucked from the root of the enryd tree.

He smacked his cinder-black lips and sighed. Not the candy the Queen's flesh would be, but a tasty snack to bide him over. His eyes glazed, half-lidded and blood-shot with pleasure. His curled tusks gleamed yellow to either side of his snout.

His nostrils caught her scent. His gnarled pink ear caught her step drawing near.

He jumped from under the blanket like a popcorn kernel off a pan onto the back of his unfortunate new elk and hunched down on its back as it sprang away from the tree house.

Pigg paused under some tall ferns by the Chuckling Wee and peered back at the tree house. He smelled her like a swirl of honey stirred in the tea of forest scents.

She stepped onto the rope ladder and rose like an angel, soft as a whisper.

Pigg's mind spun with humility and reverence. What a sloppity-slop-slop she will be for my belly, he thought. He decided to wait until she fell asleep, and try again.

*   *   *

Neuvia climbed from the ladder into her room and began packing her clothes into one of her sacks. She packed the spyglass and scooped the apples and nuts off the windowsill into the sack.

"What are you doing?" asked Toy.

"Be still," she said, wiping a tear away. "Do not speak another word to the Queen tonight!"

Toy bit his green tongue, vexed by the command. He watched in silence as she rolled blankets and put them in the bag. She raised a plank of the floor and reached into the water tank. She untied the spider rope from the golden handle of Gieron's scepter, wet a towel, and drew the scepter out of the water, wrapping it quickly in the towel. She put it in the bag, inside one of her tall boots. Then she pulled her bearskin cloak around her shoulders and fastened the emerald clasp at her throat, over Toy.

Toy said nothing and slipped his sleek head over her furry collar, sighing with a flutter of his tongue.

Neuvia tied the sack to the rope ladder and let it descend. Then she climbed down the ladder. She untied the sack from the ladder and hoisted it over her shoulder. The owl hooted a low, quizzical "Who?" She blew it a kiss as it tilted its head.

She went straight through the woods to the moonlit ramp that led down to the beach. When she set foot on the beach, she heard *Stargazer*'s sail flapping before she made her out on the beach.

Kneeling before the vessel, Neuvia felt tears come to her eyes, as though she were before her mother.

"Milady," she said. "Take me away from this island. I cannot help Trinadol. He does things which can only bring ruin, to himself and to Ameulas!"

As though the wind itself was using her canvas for lips, *Stargazer* answered, "Come then, child!"

Neuvia dried her eyes and jumped into the sleek craft, whose sail filled as she slid down the beach and met the welcoming waves.

Neuvia laid her bag of provisions against the after thwart and pulled out one of her blankets. She lied down against the sack and covered herself in the woolen blanket, peering over the gunwales at the sea parting around *Stargazer*'s sharp knife.

When she passed the northern point of the bay, with its grottos sucking and gasping, Neuvia heard words rippling over *Stargazer*'s sail: "You will live to be a thousand years old, if no harm befalls you!"

Neuvia's eyes widened.

"Who shall be your mate in life?" hissed the wind on the canvas.

Neuvia did not know what to say, looking up at the trident sail rippling above her.

"If you leave Trinadol, you will see 20 lovers go from blossom to dust!" said the wind.

A tear rolled down her cheek like quicksilver in the starlight.

"Trinadol is yours for a thousand years. Only you can save him."

Neuvia laid her head on her sack of provisions, looking at the stars that hung like jewels above. "Toy," she whispered. "You may talk now."

"The King is going to *Wynder* right now! If you hold Gieron's stone I can take you to him."

Neuvia reached inside the boot and unwrapped the scepter. Feeling its handle, she lay back on her improvised pillow and closed her eyes.

The huge square diamond gleamed on her chest.

"As Queen of the Tintilisair, Toy, I command you to put me to sleep this instant."

Toy coiled around her throat, finding the pulse points and restricting them as he lowered her as gently as possible into the *Wynder World.*

*   *   *

He came to her. They embraced on the verandah of the Lightstone Tower. Trumpets sounded from the terraces and green banners streamed like spring leaves from the Tower's pinnacle. The people around them were dressed in courtly clothes of festive hues that changed even as the wind shifted, and they applauded Neuvia *and* Trinadol *who were also dressed in sparkling raiment. They were truly King and Queen, and their kingdom shone in the benevolent sphere of their influence, making any other world seem like a crude fiction.*

Looking into each other's eyes, Neuvia *and* Trinadol *greeted each other and turned hand in hand to greet their subjects. The people were real, though not like any people who lived on* Hala. *They were* Ameulentians, *though they were* Wyndernalia Ameulentians, *like possible spirits and half-formed characters with different faces and names. They were childlike, though many of these beings were ancient. They crowded around and praised their new King and Queen and asked optimistic questions about the King's plans for Wynder Ameulas, and, of course,* Hala Ameulas, *in which they were all surprisingly quite interested.*

"How will you lead us, lord?" asked one Wynderne.

Neuvia *responded, "We shall reign without fear of our subject's freedom and we will ask only their loyalty in return."*

Trinadol *turned to her. "My Queen is the rose in the garden of my mind! So do her words unfold and blossom with perfect beauty. We shall trust the good in our people, for the sake of the good. Nothing shall pervert this law, as simple as it is true!"*

"Teach us the ways of right and wrong, lord!" said Theosophiclar, the Court Engineer who had helped Elwyn, Senadol and Trinadol marshal the resources for their Hala exploits and whose three blue eyes were bright under his waving brows. "For here in Wynderne there is no death for us and no damage that cannot be undone. What is good, lord? What is evil? Teach us!"

"We shall teach you," said Neuvia, "so that when the King lets some of your brave spirits free in Hala you shall love its laws and know their wisdom and serve his other kingdom well."

"My Queen has had another splendid thought! What an inspiration she is to us all! Even my illustrious grandfather did not think to prepare his Wynderne subjects with ethical instruction, for he preferred to trust his own strictures instead. I shall seek to win your trust and loyalty, therefore, so I may summon you in friendship instead of fear to my Hala service."

The people cheered, and trumpets sounded as Trinadol begged a moment alone with his Queen in the Throne Room.

He held her close. "Let me see you."

"And I, you," she said.

They embraced, out of time for a moment, before they ran to meet the miraculous day.

*   *   *

Wyndernia is a place of spiritual hedonism, where the will may express itself in infinite form as readily as it might be changed inside one's heart. The limitations of this place, therefore, are not of the material, but of the spirit that would shape it, and it is important not to exceed the limitations of one's spirit when visiting here. For the material limitations of Hala are the stuff our minds are made of. Our knowledge and our virtues are meaningless outside the finite world where life and its necessities are particular and destructible. When our earthly spirits are streaming through the Wynderne range, transmogrifying, we must fix in contrast in our minds the original world from which we came, like a lodestar, or there is the danger of going mad and forgetting the need to return to Hala, which is our mother and our body.

—Elwyn Gheldron, summer of 577, After Sentad

So wrote Trinadol's *grandfather in a book* Trinadol *found in the Wyndernalia Lightstone Tower. The book was made of* Hala *material, which* Elwyn *had allowed into Wynder through his acts of magic.*

Trinadol *discussed these topics at his table in Wyndor as he and* Neuvia *spent weeks there with their magical subjects learning from them the Wynder ways.*

They heard stories of Elwyn *and of* Trinadol's *more distant ancestors, some of whom had gone mad in Wyndor and were called out by the Gairanor. And they heard songs sung of* Trinadol's *achievements on* Hala, *songs honoring the slaying of* Knot, *the raising of the* Rollock *and the* Angha. *Strangely,* Trinadol *brought little memory of these last two deeds to Wynder.*

One day he and Neuvia *were in Wynder, the sky-borne navy of a Wynderne king, whom* Trinadol's *advisors told him was named* Blox, *attacked the Dimmrock.*

From the Lightstone Tower, Trinadol *spotted* Blox's *flying ships approaching the island, flying the flag of the forgotten land of* Ghenten.

Blox's aerial formations began swooping down from the clouds over the Dimmrock as Trinadol *watched.*

Trinadol *did not call his people to form an army, but instead he flew over the sea himself and found the flagship of his attacker: a great ten-masted sailing ship in the midst of the cloud-borne armada.*

He knocked on the captain's cabin door and entered, finding the surprised king dressed in shimmering armor. Yet Blox had the pallor and demeanor of misshapen clay with red stubble on his unshapely head. Trinadol *was scornful, for this was how the Wynderne had perversely chosen to appear, since he could choose any form.* Trinadol *strode across the cabin and seized the Wynderne in his hands and lifted him over his head.*

"Freedom is not enough for you, eh, Wynderne?" he asked the surprised upside-down face of his would-be conqueror. "You must have power over others, too, is that it? Then I shall send you down to Hala *where you will learn freedom's value! There you will have no special powers and you shall not rule others, but likely be ruled, instead, in humble, mortal's form! Then maybe you will learn how hard freedom is to come by, and how vile it is to covet the freedom of others, thou wicked king!"*

And Trinadol *cast Blox out in righteous wrath from the Wynderne World in which he had been born into the* Hala World *to learn the lessons of that harsh mistress.*

Having conquered Blox's navy in a single stroke, Trinadol *won a victory he had not anticipated: for Ghenten was then joyously reunited with Ameulas, if only in the Wynderne World, and his subjects rejoiced.*

For this and other deeds, Trinadol *was celebrated as a wondrous monarch, and even the Wyndernolian Ghenten folk dedicated themselves to their new lord and praised the reunion of the Tintilisair, though few Wynders remembered much of Ghenten or the Tintilisair with their hazy history and short memories. Trinadol's courageous deed was strange and marvelous to them, however, and they decided the* Hala World *was a place peopled with romantic souls who were ablaze with the valor, virtue, and love inspired by the scarcities and sacrifices of* Hala. *It was soon the wish of many of* Trinadol *and* Neuvia's *subjects to go to* Hala, *and serve them there, and it was the wish of all to have more of* Hala *in Wynderne.*

For weeks after the victory over the invading king, the first momentous event in ages beyond memory, the Wyndernolian Tintilisairians engaged in every kind of festivity and adventure, contest, and celebration.

Neuvia *was taken under the wing of courtly matrons and three Ladies-in-Waiting became her fast friends as they shared wild adventures; Kateri with red hair and yellow eyes, Tinefri with black hair and black skin, and silly Wethia, who had but a rope of brown hair sprouting from the top of her otherwise shaved head.* Neuvia *and these magical sisters jumped off cliffs and changed into birds, and ran as wolves, and swam as killer whales together. Wethia comically went as a narwhal when they toured the shores of the Dimmrock, exploring the island's briny coves.*

One night, they whispered crazy things to each other as they lay in the grass while **Trinadol** *conjured spectacles in the midnight sky beneath the scintillating Wyndor Tower. That was the same night* Trinadol *had picked a red rose, and the petals turned blue. When* Neuvia *related this poetic moment to the people on the gaming grounds around the Tower, they cheered and rose into the air, trumpeters, cats, and all.*

"Good people! Let us play a game I have thought of," cried Neuvia *to them, taking* **Trinadol**'s *elbow.*

"Let us entertain the Queen," nodded Trinadol, *and they all laughed in appreciation of her, arrayed in the air around them.*

"Let the ladies change into cherubs and all the gentlemen change into cupids, each cherub and cupid armed with golden bows and silver arrows. And let each arrow of pleasure earn a kiss!"

The Wyndernalians were ecstatic to hear Neuvia's *earthly inspiration, and felt the magic of the* Hala World *in her indulgence. At once, the entire populace of the court shape-changed into armies of cobalt blue cupids and lavender cherubs with gold-feathered wings, all laughing in chorus as some blew horns for the hunt. Their golden quivers were full and their bows were soon bent as all, including King and Queen, dove into the woods to dodge and stalk each other among the treetops whose chimes and reeds played a dancing suite under the breeze's brisk baton. And* Trinadol *and* Neuvia *gave many a kiss away to the eager Wyndernes, who sought them out with such sweet desire.*

*   *   *

For 27 nights in all, they slept and woke together in their second kingdom. Yet one night, Trinadol *dreamed as he slept in the Wynder World.*

He fell from a storming sky toward an obsidian sea until he found his buoyancy and stopped his fall. Below him, Trinadol could see a ship foundering on the waves.

Trinadol flew closer and saw the crew as they hauled the lines of the rolling caravel. Before the prow, blue in the night as though covered with frost, the great arm of the Rollock rose out of the sea.

The men pointed and shouted as though they recognized it.

Trinadol's heart turned icy cold.

He saw a man with a blue eye tattooed on his head fling a harpoon high over the prow. The harpoon barely missed the arm, which seemed to see it coming as it leaned to one side.

Trinadol remembered this man! It was as though he had seen him in this very place long ago. It was Lince Neery-Atton, the sailor with the blue eye tattooed on his head.

Trinadol flew down and confronted the arm, on the tip of which sprouted a cluster of eyes waving on stocks. "You shall not attack men who fish upon the sea!" he cried. "Attack only those who come searching for me!"

The greedy eyes curled away from him and the Rollock's arm disappeared beneath a wave. Trinadol heard a cheer on the deck, but he flew away, upward through the cloud to escape their sight.

He woke, then, his cheek on Neuvia's hair, and wondered drowsily for a while about his desperate dream. When he dreamed in Wynder, he realized, his spirit must somehow be able to go back to **Hala***. This must have been how his dreams had come true when he was a boy! Somehow his dreaming spirit had pierced through Wynder back into* **Hala** *where he had actually done the things he dreamed!* Trinadol *smiled in wonder as he laid his head on the pillow and smelled* Neuvia's *hair. He decided to sleep a little longer before he breakfasted on another day of bliss with his bride.*

When he woke, with the scent of Neuvia's hair still in his nostrils, his sheets were damp.

A storming night swirled around the Tower.

He saw the Scepter on the pillow where Neuvia's head had been, and the Cronus Star caught fire, staining the dark room crimson.

*   *   *

"Wake, my mistress," hissed Toy. "I wish it wasn't me to say it—wake now!"

Neuvia opened her Hala eyes, and the very weight of her body told her that she was back.

The ceiling glowed turquoise and she saw *Stargazer* had clewed her sail and stepped her mast so she could pass through the low arch of a grotto of glowing blue rock. She wondered how long she had been *there*, and how long she had been here.

"Cover the stone. She's taking us out!" Toy feathered her ear.

She wrapped the scepter of Gieron in a wet cloth, placed it in her boot, and stuffed it into the sack. Her muscles were weak and she felt very hungry.

Stargazer sliced under the arching entrance in a valley between the swells, and she ruddered herself out onto the open sea.

Her mast rose as though the wind lifted it, and her lines coiled tight as her trident sail dropped, and snapped full.

Noisy seabirds thronged the cliff side. The waxing Silver Coin was sinking behind the southeastern horizon in the misty morning sky.

"To Ameulas?" the wind whispered on *Stargazer*'s sail.

Neuvia smiled wryly. "No. Take the Queen home, milady," she said.

Stargazer came about. "The Queen is brave," she whispered as she conveyed Neuvia back to the Dimmrock's bay.

* * *

Chapter 13

▼

Ameulas

For six years Neuvia and Trinadol traded their loneliness in the Hala World for their brief reunions in *Wynderne*.

Seldom did they think of their forsaken kingdom in this time, and the Ameulentians, for their part, mostly left them to their solitude. Yet one day, while Trinadol was sleeping and dreaming in *Wyndernia*, his spirit emerged into the Hala World in a cloudy sky over the Gulf of Gwylor. His flesh was no more than a chalky blue light in the air, faint and far away from his first self, two worlds ago.

To the south, he saw the island he had just created—the fifth—its heart still smoldering on the gray sea.

On the mighty cliffs of Ameulas to his west Trinadol saw a cunning dark castle carved in the living granite. He remembered it from his youth.

Rain fell as he flew out of the sky toward the castle's turrets, which rose like crowned heads out of the cliff.

Trinadol alighted inside the window of the tallest tower, which was carved out of a vast vein of jade that streaked through the walls of the castle.

Trinadol found a long spyglass on a tripod in the top room of the green tower, and, peering through the eyehole, he saw that the lens was focused on the still-glowing island he had just raised.

He glided down the stairs of the tower like a ghost, wishing to spy on the castle's residents and see how Ameulas was faring.

He did remember this place, he realized. There were deep swimming pools in one of the castle's courtyards into which Trinadol had watched the royal divers perform amazing dives when he was a child. This was Castle Martharr, where his father had let him spend the day with the Martharr children, Teldon, Lelinair, and Nil. That's why Nil Ramesis was so familiar to him! But why was his last name not Martharr?

Nil had shown Trinadol a model ship that he had made and rigged to a pulley so it glided in the air on a string across his bedchamber. Trinadol had made the tiny ship's sails billow as it soared through the air on Nil's strings. He had liked Nil. He had been three years old at the time, but the memory was vivid. Nil had told him that he wanted to build a ship that could not sink.

Trinadol heard voices when he got to the bottom of the stairs and he looked through the crack in the door at a spacious hall that faced the Bay of Gwylor.

Amid the gathering of people, Trinadol recognized Poladoris Martharr, who was Mayor of Gwylor when Trinadol was a child. His older face was grim now, and those around him seemed filled with grief.

Trinadol saw Poladoris's late father, Lord Tormerick Martharr, in the giant portrait hanging over the tall fireplace of Castle Martharr's great sitting room.

Senjessi Tillow, who was present, had painted Tormerick astride a black stallion in dark oils that were still uncracked after half a century.

Trinadol remembered that Tormerick had designed Castle Martharr as well as the masterpiece of aqueducts, sewers, and canals that made the city of Gwylor one of the most hospitable cities in the world.

To those who saw his portrait, Tormerick's face seemed elated sometimes, and sometimes pensive, but now he looked angry as he looked at the grim day pictured in his window. The election for Mayor had been tallied last night and, after 20 years, Tormerick's son Poladoris had been voted down as Mayor of Gwylor.

Trinadol noticed Artimeer standing by the Lady Martharr, and he wanted to call out the old philosopher, but first he wanted to find out why this august gallery of Ameulentians seemed so grim and heartbroken. Even the family's hounds, Tecwyn and Acceber, seemed to sigh in grief, crossing their paws under long faces before the dying fire.

Trinadol looked at the beautiful Lelinair Martharr, who was a little girl the last time he saw her. She was tapping her restless fingers on the wooden bear-claw arm of her chair. Her sad eyes matched the mahogany. She wore jodhpurs of soft kidskin and a white shirt, her short boots laced up the side. No jewelry adorned her except for a masculine gold ring on her right index finger. It was set with a milky white stone streaked purple. Trinadol saw the same ring on her grandfather's little finger in the painting over the fireplace.

Their mother, Sendinia, whom Trinadol remembered from his childhood, was not present, for she had died three years ago, and yet their father, Poladoris, did not look his age and looked the same to Trinadol. His sharp-nosed face was kissed by the sun and clean-shaven, and his long black hair was threaded silver, swept back from his forehead and clasped in a brass ring. There was the suggestion of passion and happiness in the wrinkles around his eyes—the permanent happiness that imbues the creator of any beautiful thing. Poladoris's sculptures of great beasts, heroes, heroines, thinkers, artists, and villains in Ameulentian history and mythology were placed throughout the rooms and gardens of his father's castle in niches designed for them, as well as throughout Ameulas and other parts of the world where his work was prized. Poladoris had sculpted Trinadol's mother and father, including the bronze of Conilair on the Dimmrock, Trinadol remembered now.

Poladoris's ancient hand was too unsteady to guide a chisel now, however, and yesterday his fellow citizens decided that it was too unsteady to guide Gwylor, as well; Mayor Blox had been sworn into office that morning.

The mariners, Karlock Isopika and Lince Neery-Atton, looked crowded on a fancy couch that was made more for two young girls than two bow-legged sailors. Both held new caps in their hands and rubbed them raw, wondering who was going to talk first.

The Queen Mother sat near Lelinair. Nardleen Fenstridol's consternation seemed tempered by trust in her daughter Neuvia's good sense. The pressures of worry and faith had stalemated her lips in a straight line that never wavered.

Bulgar Bedrosium, the wealthy merchant and trader Trinadol remembered meeting before his coronation, sat on a couch with his wife Ninny, who looked as frightened and silly as her name. Bulgar's large nose curved down over a regal mustache of charcoal black. The circlet of hair around his head was tarnished silver, like a crown. He was short and broad as a barrel and wore a stud in his ear with a honey-hued gem as big as a bumblebee. He opened his mouth to speak—but then closed it, again, sadly.

Trinadol noticed Nil Ramesis, then, as he kneeled on one knee before Poladoris and kissed his hand, and then stood behind Poladoris's chair, then, gripping its carved back in strong hands.

Nil's real father and mother had died at sea when Nil was a child; Trinadol remembered Nil telling him this as the present unearthed the past. But what Trinadol did not know was that Nil had survived a shipwreck that had killed his parents and was discovered on the beach below Castle Martharr by Lelinair's mother. The Martharrs had raised Nil as though he were their own.

And yet, Lelinair and Teldon were twins, and Nil had always felt the third wheel, treated separately. And he kept, for his own reasons, the last name of his true father, Ramesis. He had insisted on using his birth name even when he was nine years old. His adoptive father attributed his stubbornness to an undying love of his parents. Poladoris never noticed Nil's ardent love for Lelinair, which Nil had felt like a fever, as long as he could remember.

By the age of 16, Nil Ramesis had already become a respected cartographer, having learned the craft from Poladoris, who was a master, having been instructed by Tormerick Martharr. Nil went on a few expeditions that were arranged by his proud adoptive father so he could "earn some money of his own." In the last few years, however, Teldon had excelled Nil at the business of cartography, having inherited a more artistic hand from his father, and he had set up his own chart-making business on the castle's premises.

By the age of 18, however, Nil had already announced his intention to become a naval engineer, still dreaming of his unsinkable ship. Poladoris arranged for him to be tutored by the best naval engineers of Ameulas, but Nil found them too insulated from experience to justify their calcified codes of building.

So Nil hired on to a fishing boat, at the lowest rank, to the vexation of Teldon and Lelinair, who thought it beneath their brother's rightful station, and Poladoris sighed, pursing his lips and raising his eyebrows in acquiescence.

Nil worked his way through the ranks of mariners from the bottom rung, and never betrayed the great house from which he came, using only his given name, which earned him no favor. Lord Martharr was perplexed and yet submitted to Nil's strange insistence on this point and never interfered on his behalf.

Nil came to know many sea craft during his rustic adventures, observing their weaknesses in storms or over reefs or pulling nets. During this self-prescribed apprenticeship, he had kept extensive notes. So, when Trinadol gave him a thousand Gierons of gold for drafting maps of the Southern Reefs, Nil bought his own shipyard and started building safer boats with ideas he had been working out all his life.

As Trinadol stood in the jade arch of the castle's tower, he perceived the tortured love between Nil and Lelinair, for Nil looked often at Lelinair and Lelinair never looked at Nil.

Senjessi Tillow cleared his throat, finally breaking the silence. An old, brown, bald man in his seventh decade, the painter sat with his wife, Merania, a vivacious girl of 18 whose hair was jet-black and skin snow-white, like winter at midnight. She had hounded Senjessi as though he were a hibernating bear until he submitted to his third and, Senjessi swore, final marriage. Merania was the old artist's fierce defender and the fountain of his youth.

"Blox is a pox on all our houses!" Senjessi cried, ripping open the pall of grief that hung over them all. "Who in Hala is this 'messiah' he's always yammering about then?"

"Oh, Senji!" sighed Merania.

"I think Blox is not even from Hala!" he charged forward. "He's some *Wundry* thing, and that's what I think!" Senjessi folded his arms and shook his head sarcastically, glancing at Artimeer. "But I'm no philosopher!"

Blox? Trinadol wondered as he heard the name.

Artimeer raised a hand. "Really, Senjessi! Blox, who is so gray and sorry of shape? I can't imagine a *Wundyrne* thing being like Blox!" Artimeer laughed softly.

"He's not at home in the Hala world, Artimeer, and that's the reason he cut off his right hand and shaves his ugly red hair from his lumpy gray head. *Guh!* He looks like clay before it is sculpted and yet he thinks himself divine! He cut off his own hand and calls this crime against nature art! And he calls my art obscene? He is from some other world, where things don't matter, Artimeer! I've heard there's a world like that." Senjessi shook his fist as though he were squeezing an orange.

"Calm down, Senji, please!" said Merania, pulling down his arm and dusting it off to distract him.

"What about what Senji says, Artimeer?" asked Lelinair. "Today, Blox promised us his Messiah-King, Nekkros, whom he has made famous with all of his handbills posted in the city. Blox promises us that Nekkros will be more powerful than a Cirilen-Lord. He says that his Messiah-King will look like Trinadol, but far from neglecting Ameulas, he will rule it in every way, bringing what Blox called 'total justice' to our realm. Does it not seem that Blox, depraved and ugly as he might be, though many think him fair, is the agent of magic things, if not himself a thing from *Wundery* places?"

Artimeer pursed his lips. He took his arm from over Lelinair's chair and sat in a scallop-shaped chair central to the gathering. He wore a white robe without adornment and thick leather sandals on his strong old feet. He folded his leg over one knee and rubbed his shin. "Your question reveals my own suspicions, as usual, Lelinair. Blox is the lackey of some nether evil, I suspect. Despite the seeming piety of his philosophy, I knew his purpose was evil the first time I noticed him laugh."

Some in the room chuckled at the image.

"Yet don't be too amused," Artimeer nodded. "Much can be told by a simple thing. Blox cut off his right hand and he shows his stump to the people—yet with his invisible hand he picks their pockets, covers their mouths, and snuffs out dissent! 'Live for something higher!' Blox cries, while reaching for something lower. It is all said by the laugh he shares with powerful men: he laughs at the powerless."

"Artimeer, the wise," grunted Karlock, glancing at Lince, who nodded.

"It is true," nodded Senjessi.

"Maybe not!" said Bulgar. "Perhaps Trinadol is wicked just as Blox says. I was at the King's Coronation, and Trinadol seemed little kind or good when he got his hand on the Scepter," said the businessman.

"I agree; how can we trust him?" wondered Ninny, her eyes wide and desperate. "Three expeditions perished trying to reach Trinadol!"

At this, Lince Neery-Atton, who was aboard one of those "expeditions," rose and untied his awkward tongue. "Trinadol is a good king, and I, fine ladies and lordies—er—know it's true!" He cleared his throat, his bald head blushing. "We was founderin' in a gale six years ago on the *Green Ghost* out of West Falls, and the Rollock, lords and ladies, eh, had been giving us chase for three days. We fought it off, with nets and luck, aye, even through the storm! We were all but finished and almost said the high goodbye when the Rollock reached up before our bows yet again. I flung our last harpoon, but missed her starboard by a hair, and I thought that was the last I'd see of this dear life.

"Then out of the sky came Trinadol himself, aye, like a blue ghost! He floated over the Rollock, darkling like, pointing his finger disapproving. And she backed off, she did, and let us be! We'd wagered we could get through in a storm, ya see, and wangle a quick audience with the King. But we turned back after that, and no fishing ship has been attacked for no cause by the grim guardians that wrecked those two s'peditions since then. Fer two it was, not three, since ours 'twasn't a s'pedition, nor was it lost!" Lince slapped his thigh with a thick hand. "I know brave sailors who've gone on their way through the Wizard's Isles, wishing no truck with Trinadol. Sailors have seen things, aye, and some have gone mad by things they've seen, 'tis true. A few captains have gone for glory and a piece of the Rollock, as well, and the Rollock won't abide offenses, no indeed, nor will the other strange things about. But seamanly respect has been rewarded with safe passage. That I'll say for the King. He saved my life twice, once when he was but a boy. 'Tis worth my allegiance!" Lince growled.

Trinadol was gladdened to hear Lince's words. But as he listened intently in the shadow of the door, he felt himself awaking, and despite his interest he was pulled away, back to *Wynder*, just as Bulgar began to speak.

"Nevertheless, the trade routes are crippled by the Wizard's Archipelago," said Bulgar. "Insurers are making a fortune. Ships run too close to reef and shore in order to avoid the menace of those isles. Fishing waters have been cut in half. The markets are slow, the prices high. People aren't eating fish as much as they used to! The ports of Tunce and Elbon have replaced our port as trade centers. The city of Gwylor looks the worse for it. And we have, with Blox's policies, attracted a host of bums, charlatans, and thugs who claim allegiance to Blox, swelling his vote and unseating our good Mayor!"

"Blox blamed all these problems on our Mayor during his campaign," said Artimeer. "Now he neatly shifts the blame to Trinadol. Certainly one cannot, in reason, condone whatever part the young King plays in this show of force against us—unless he means to avoid a more grievous clash he believes would result if he allowed our union. No, friends, I believe the King wishes no harm, as the mariners' stories prove. Indeed he secludes himself and warns all away so he cannot harm our land or people as the unwilling agent of some terrible evil. I think the King believes he is protecting his Kingdom."

"Indeed, I believe it—he's right!" said Senjessi.

"Aye," said Karlock and Lince.

"I think you're right, too, Artimeer," said Bulgar, nodding at Ninny reassuringly. Reason could always overturn Bulgar's opposition, which he merely offered to test notions, and Ninny's perpetual state of panic was the prod that made Bulgar test every idea—the secret of their success. "However, in Trinadol's absence, evil grows like weeds in a garden untended," Bulgar frowned.

"What will it mean?" asked Poladoris, sitting in his great chair before the window. He had not said a word before this. A cloud lingered over him since the news of his democratic defeat. "What will this mean for Ameulas, Artimeer?"

"Good Mayor, we know from Blox too much for his own good. He claimed today in his scurrilous speech in Bartering Square that his messiah would seek vengeance on unbelievers and bestow glory on the faithful. How does he describe his messiah to us? He will look like Trinadol, he claims. Odd! He will look like Trinadol. Yet his stone will be multi-colored, not crimson. O, friends! Many things are betrayed by his words, about his master's plans and assumptions, all aired too freely on an underling's tongue."

"What things, Artimeer?" asked Teldon.

Artimeer rubbed his knee. "Blox's god can't come *now*. But when he does come, he will look like Trinadol. Why?" Artimeer spread his hands as though clearing the air. "The King and Queen were very young when much was set upon them. Senadol told me a great weight was falling too soon. I am convinced, though they are young and too hard put upon, the

King and Queen are good at heart. This weird master whom Blox adores from afar may be preying on our King, even now, from some nether place. He lays traps around the Dimmrock to keep us from intervening while he weaves thicker his evil web."

"Pray tell, philosopher. You really should charge by the word," said Bulgar.

"The fact that Blox describes his messiah as carrying a scepter with a 'multi-colored stone' is a cheap ploy and yet—a costly revelation! If a stone can be colored many colors to please a superstitious eye, as a foreigner might judge Ameulentians, can it not just as easily be colored blood-red to frighten Ameulentians at a coronation? But, this last must have been plain to everyone."

"Always good to have you here to point out what is plain," Teldon smiled.

There was a murmur of admiration for Artimeer's mind and alarm at its conclusions.

Senjessi blurted, "What are we going to do? *Do!* That's all that counts!"

"Senji, we all want to do something. But none of us have had the chance," said Merania.

"We need to reach the King!" growled Bulgar.

"No ship can pass the Terrors," said Poladoris. "The two expeditions I sent had the best ships in Ameulas, and none returned."

Nil looked at Lelinair.

She did not look at Nil. Instead, she opened her hand and looked at her half of the *lightstone* pebble that she and Nil had broken ten years ago.

It was said that after lovers broke such a pebble, the halves of stone would grow in different ways each moment they were apart. Lelinair could not believe her piece would ever fit Nil's, after so many years.

A decade ago, she had told Nil he could never be worthy of her, plucked from the sea and owing all to her father, until he made his own name and house. It was a mighty challenge to an orphan, a challenge from which Nil had not shrunk.

Nil looked at the crate he had brought with him when this council was called. He glanced at Karlock and the bald-headed Lince.

"Go on," Karlock grumbled.

"Now or never, son," nodded Lince.

Nil swallowed and cleared his throat. "I'd like to show you all something. It could be what we need."

Nil lifted the crate and set it on the carpet at the feet of Artimeer and his father. He pried open one side with a chisel and lifted out a model ship, which he set on top of the crate before the gathering.

Nil had made the model himself, carving the planks, threading each miniature deadeye and pounding each tiny nail as though he were wrighting the real ship he had envisioned. Made of soft Demoldan mahogany polished with beeswax, brass fittings, and linen sails, the model shone, impressive in itself.

From the height of the deck rail, it was clearly a ship larger than any built in Ameulas before. It had two masts, very rare on Ameulentian ships, and a lateen sail that was unknown. Between the square mainsail and the bowsprit were two flying jibs for extra speed.

The lines of the ship were fast, yet her keel was lined with long spikes. Two catapults, of Nil's design, faced port and starboard, and there were four spring-loaded harpoons, two on the fo'c's'le and two aft, on bases that swiveled. Six great millstones were secured behind the mainmast. Fishing nets were strung, ready to be let out port and starboard.

One side of the model's hull broke away, as Nil demonstrated now, to reveal the officers' quarters in the fo'c's'le and the galley and mess in the aftercastle. The decks slid out for inspection. The long "Green Deck" was filled with hammocks for the crew, three longboats and storage for the ship's supplies. The hold was dry and held ballast and provisions, an unprecedented cargo space for a sea journey, arranged with ladderways fore and aft and two central shafts to the main deck. The hull was ribbed with black braces apparently made of cast iron like the hoops of a barrel, except that they were on the inside instead of outside.

"This is the ship that can reach the King," said Nil.

* * *

"What sort of sail is that? I've never seen that sail!" pointed Senjessi.

"And what are the millstones for? Sinking the ship?" lamented Artimeer.

"The spikes on her keel will slow her down and make her heavy!" said Lord Martharr, hiding his fatherly pride.

"It's too big!" cried Ninny.

"It would be very expensive," nodded Bulgar, his mind working like an abacus.

"It's beautiful!" Merania whispered in Senjessi's ear. She smiled at Nil, who blushed, unaccustomed to open praise from a beautiful woman.

Nil looked at Lelinair, but she was looking at the model with frozen, inscrutable eyes.

"It's a bit risky, Nil," said Artimeer.

"Why it's the craziest ship I've ever seen!" said the Queen Mother, Nardleen Fenstridol. She had lived under the ward of Castle Martharr since the self-exile of the King and Queen. Though her cooking was bold and inventive, Nardleen tended to be traditional toward other things in life. Yet hope was kindled in her eyes by the sight of Nil's wild ship.

"Something to behold, eh, milady?" Lince grinned like a wolf, showing his swag of pearly teeth at Nardleen, who laughed heartily. "I'd be a carpenter the rest of my days to feel her on the sea for an hour, I would!" Lince said. "I'm with you, Nilly! Hundred-and-sixty feet, right? Well, indeedy-do, that's a piece of vessel, my Royal lady!"

Questions and remarks sprayed up together and Nil held up his hands. Lelinair looked intently at the model.

"I shall explain her with more detail," Nil said, "if everyone pulls up a chair and gathers round. Stoke the fire, for the room is chilled by the hunting night. Don't you agree, lord?"

"Stoke the fire!" cried Lord Martharr. "The hunting night approaches!" And it seemed his foundling son had stoked the tired embers in his eyes and lifted the shroud of defeat from his shoulders.

Two servants threw logs of ash into the fire.

All listened as Nil described the *Sea Mare*, for that was her name.

"Two masts," he nodded.

"I've heard that an aftward mast would turn a ship in circles," said Senjessi.

Ninny whispered in Bulgar's ear.

"Or push it backwards!" said Bulgar.

"Not if the sail is of this design. It can be pulled completely around on a joint so it billows forward no matter which tack is taken. And the flying jib at the bow more than balances the aft sail. A second flying jib can be added as well, with the unusually tall bowsprit."

"How do you know?" asked Artimeer.

"From testing models on ponds on windy days."

"Models?" asked Lelinair, still staring at the ship. "On ponds?"

Nil nodded. "On windy days. I've had no opportunity to build a full-sized ship of this design, Lady Martharr, but I am certain the principles are the same," said Nil.

Lelinair looked straight into his eyes.

Nil almost looked away in surprise at the first gaze to pass between them in so long. "Have I finally gotten your attention, then, milady?"

"It's a gamble, all around," said Bulgar, shrugging.

"What are those anchor stones for, behind the mainmast?" asked Senjessi.

Nil did not break Lelinair's gaze. "Fishing nets may be used to entangle the guardians of the Dimmrock," he said. He pointed. "The anchor stones may be attached to the nets and released, dragging whatever is caught in them down into the depths."

"And why the spikes?" asked Bulgar.

"The Rollock will not be able to get a hold on the hull if it finds it too thorny."

"Perhaps," said Poladoris, rubbing his chin as fear competed with pride in his father's heart. "Perhaps not, also." He looked hard at Nil with his purple eyes. His bushy eyebrows and beaky nose gave Poladoris the appearance of an owl.

"I tested it, lord," said Nil. "Again with models and with a real rollock. You see the spiny nautilus was my clue. The spines on its shell either stop it from being devoured by rollocks or slow the rollocks down."

"And how will you stop it after slowing it down?" asked Lelinair.

"Nets, weights, harpoons, catapults, and fire. Hand-to-hand combat. The crew shall be armed, of course."

"And who is to captain this ship that sails into the maw of death?" she threatened even as she asked him.

"I shall be the captain of the *Sea Mare*, milady," said Nil. "I shall lead the expedition myself, when the ship is completed." He looked into her eyes, and smiled in surprise. "Do I finally have your interest, then?"

"Fleeting, Lord Ramesis," she replied, but she saw that he was splendid, chiseled like a god and swarthy as a warrior, dauntless before death and omnipotent because of it.

"Well, it's ambitious, very ambitious," said Bulgar.

"It's just too big!" said Ninny. "The boat's too big!"

"I'm with you, Nilly!" Lince winked.

"I cannot pay for the whole project. It's too risky," said Bulgar, pursing his lips and counting his fingers. "But I can give you supplies from time to time. It's nothing." Bulgar shrugged. "Really, nothing."

Nil shook his hand. "Thank you, sir! It shall be your best investment."

"I doubt that very much. But you are of this noble house, though not born of it, Nil Ramesis. I have learned to expect great things from this house, and now from you. To see little Nilly who chased Lelinair across the fields when you were tiddlywinks, now destined to be a sea warrior pitting his life against terrors bigger than this world—it's not a thing I readily pay to see. With luck, it will take too long to build your ship for you to captain her through the King's isles."

"Time will tell," said Nil.

"A little gold. You may need a little gold," muttered Senjessi. This model had moved his artist's soul—but he was uncertain about its soundness. He had always mingled what was and what might be on his artist's palette. At last, it struck him as something that might be, but he was not sure what persuaded him, his reason or his imagination. "The *Sea Mare*," he smiled, raising his brows and spreading his hands as if he could see her setting sail. "Yes, gold will help! I'll donate a little trust to your cause, Master Ramesis!" he winked at Merania, who kissed him on his spiky cheek.

"Of course, though my heart is mixed, I will contribute some money, as well," said Poladoris. "But I will not give you so much that you may complete this vessel too quickly. Time may counsel, as well as tell, my son."

Nil clasped his hand and knelt before him.

"It's a bold plan," said Teldon. "I'll give you the best charts of the area. Very little is known, but you shall have the finest charts possible before trying that cloudy course, Brother! In every way, I'm at your disposal."

"Thanks, Telly!" Nil clasped Teldon's hand, preassured of his loyalty, for there had never been any rivalry between them, and never had Teldon found it necessary to lord his bloodline over Nil. They were brothers in every respect, Nil the older and more adventurous, Teldon the younger, more cautious and artistic.

Lelinair rose, still staring at Nil. Her face was pale and her eyes were cold. She squeezed her hands into stony fists. Her eyes stabbed him deep before she turned and strode out of the room through the northern arch.

Nil rose.

Poladoris shrugged. "It's very natural. She fears to see her brother setting such a hellbound sail, Nil, as do I."

"Yet she is not truly my sister, lord," said Nil, staring after her. "I must know her heart." He bowed, kissed his hand, and strode from the room as the gathering discussed the daring voyage.

He pursued her up the same winding stair of the Even Tower that they climbed in their childhood so many times when everyone was asleep. The last time, Nil had been seventeen and Lelinair, sixteen. They had kissed long beneath a crescent moon for the first and last time. After they kissed, they cracked the *lightstone* pebble they had found on the beach that morning. Then Lelinair set a challenge for Nil, and he remembered those words as though they were carved in his heart: "Everything you are, Nil Ramesis, you owe to my father! I cannot think of you as other than a brother, and never as a man, until you make a name for your own house and into it ask my hand for marriage!"

Ten long years had passed, and neither had yet married.

Nil climbed the last few steps and took a breath, closing his eyes. When he opened them, there she stood atop the jade tower, wrapped in a cape under the pale gloom of the sky, glaring at him.

The wind blew strong and a colorless sun was setting in charcoal clouds. He went to her and kissed her. After a moment, after a decade, she yielded to his lips. After another, her lips turned cold.

She looked over the bay. "Captain!" she cursed. "How much must you prove? How wrong must I be? I waited, Nil Ramesis! Was that not enough for you? And now you would throw yourself away?" The fragment of *lightstone* in her hand cut her palm as she clenched her fist and struck the jade wall.

Nil grabbed her wrist and gently squeezed her shoulder. "The *Sea Mare* may be our only hope, Lelinair! And only I can captain that ship. But it will take two years to build her, and I don't intend to die." Nil knelt on one knee. "Lelinair! You are everything to me!" he confessed, in reverence now as he held her hands, bowing his head between his arms. "At sea, I saw you everywhere, your eyes in the night, your smile in the waves, your laugh in the surf. When I saw death shaking his fist at me, I thought of you and fought it back! You kept me right through these hard years, and made each obstacle surmountable, my love, no matter how steep!"

"So when did you think you would have time for me, Nil Ramesis? Now that you have plans for a name in history?"

"Now! I ask you now! Marry me, Lelinair! Be my wife, and fight with me for Ameulas!"

She looked at him, and saw his splendor. But as he kneeled prostrate before her, she held herself in disdain, seeing only the worst fate. She said to him: "Marry you? So I can be a widow in two years? I will never marry you or support any part of your plans, Nil Ramesis! You have tortured me by proving too much to a young girl's vanity, by never forgiving or forgetting a cut made hastily and not meant to stab a decade deep! I am mortal, sir, and you have spent my youth unwisely, needing to prove all in advance! Yes, you have faced the hard world every day, but did you not ever think of taking your reward? What of me? So devoted to proving yourself a master were you that you did not reach for the reason you were doing it—the reason I was waiting for you! So now, an enemy as great as love you have inherited for all your struggles, Captain Ramesis! Irony on top of irony!" Lelinair laughed, and it was like a knife attack to him. She opened her bleeding hand and Nil saw her piece of *lightstone.*

Nil opened his hand and showed her his half of the shining pebble. "Let us see if they still join, Lelinair. Our pride will make an irony of everything if we let it!" He reached for the stone on her palm.

She pulled her hand away. "I do not wish to know the answer now that you are planning this voyage into death!"

"It could be our only hope!"

"It's absurd! Ridiculous!"

Nil had never seen her cry, but now Lelinair's face seemed gashed by a ruinous blow. She wept though she was still proud and looked at him in anger.

"I demand we test the stone!" he charged, holding his other hand out for Lelinair's half of the *lightstone* pebble. "Show me our love is not whole!"

"No!"

Nil seized her wrist and she took the stone from her hand with her other hand and threw it from the tower.

The gleaming stone sank between the courtyard walls and Nil wept bitterly on her bloody palm.

Lelinair turned away from him. "When I look at the sea, I will remember you," she said. "For you are the tragedy of my life, as unforgiving as the sea that brought you to me and took you away."

Nil left her, his head bowed in grief.

She looked below the tower and noticed a dull glint on the grass in the courtyard below. With a crack of lightning's whip, a cloudburst showered the castle, and masked her tears as she closed her eyes.

* * *

Blox nestled in the high-backed chair of the Mayor of Gwylor, alone in the dark Council Hall, and he drummed his fingers on the point of the great wedge of mahogany that was the council table.

The door at the end of the hall opened with a squeak and his administrator, Rishen, slipped through, and strutted past the empty chairs that lined the triangular table. He approached Blox, seated at the point. "May I sit with you, Lord Mayor, for a moment?" Rishen smiled, triumphantly.

"No, stand instead," said Blox, whimsically.

Rishen frowned and stood, obediently.

Blox rubbed the gray bump of his nose, scratching it pleasurably with the nail of his left index finger. "New laws shall be manifest," he said, and he glanced haughtily out the Long Window, blurring his eyes to the stifling monotony of the Hala World.

Irritated, Blox glanced at all the aging things preserved and hung on all the walls of the hall. "The people of Ameulas are too attached to the Hala World, Rishen," he frowned. "Therefore, their property shall be subject to seizure and passed around." He raised his stump, gesturing. "Also, I don't like the fact that women of Ameulas are so...*earthly*. Beautiful and smart ones seem to think themselves better, and desire men of...*means*. They must be taught a lesson, I think. The smart ones and the pretty ones, and especially the smart *and* pretty ones, should be forced to marry humble men of no success or distinction. The ugly and dull ones should then be matched with those men who are exceptional in this Hala World and who fancy themselves wise in its ways and deserving of its desserts. What a perverse notion!" Blox laughed excitedly. "How it would delight Him! Alas, it's too far a goal to achieve, I fear, before His Coming." Blox tilted his head sadly at Rishen. "For the moment, however, there are necessities to attend to." He groaned, smacking his lips in disgust. "We need food, medicine and gold, again, for our hungry, sick, and poor followers. Therefore, enslave some of the fishers, farmers, doctors, and wealthy rich of Gwylor." Blox struck a wise pose before Rishen.

"Why not just take food, medicine, and gold, my Mayor?"

"You still do not understand, Rishen! Reason rules nature in this Hala world, instead of simple will. But those who rule men have power over this world. Men decipher Hala's stubborn substance to bring forth its tiny measure of reward, but for those who rule men, the harvest is rich! So, Rishen, my loyal right hand, men are the key to power, Gwylor is the key to Ameulas, and Ameulas is the key to Hala. One! Two! Three! Gwylor shall be made an example for the realm, preparing the way for Nekkros. We have done well. Go and tell the Disciples to post my decrees. By the time the Council of Ameulas convenes next year, we shall outnumber our surviving opponents as poor Ameulentians from the countryside flock to Gwylor and swell our votes."

Rishen bowed in reverence before the Mayor and left him in the dark hall.

Blox leaned back in his chair and curled his thick, clay-colored lips in a sneer. "Be damned, you Ameulas!" he whispered. "Soon everything your proud king was so afraid to touch will be shredded into ribbons of ash and sorrow!" He squeezed his *Wynderl* fist on the stump of his right wrist as he watched the rain splatter the long window, blurring and smudging the lights of the city below.

*   *   *

Part Two

Chapter 14

▼

Here and There

Seven years had passed since Trinadol was crowned King.

In that time, Neuvia and Trinadol had reunited in *Windryne* six times, one for each incantation he had cast.

Their time increased with each visit, but only two or three days passed on Hala for three or six months they spent in *Wyndor*.

Neuvia went to sea with *Stargazer* after Trinadol cast his violent spells so she could sleep peacefully in the Grotto of Blue Candles with Toy as her guardian.

Neuvia kept a journal of her experiences in the *Wynder World*. As soon as she woke from *Wyndornia,* she wrote down all she could remember on the pages at the end of Senadol's *General Observations*. Writing this journal occupied much of her time pleasantly in Hala. Sometimes she read the things she had written in awe, finding it difficult to remember or believe the events and adventures when looking at them later. Yet these memoirs were her one solace when the days in Hala grew most lonely. And just when she could bear the loneliness no longer, Trinadol always charged out of the Tower to fling another bastion around their strange sanctuary and win their way to *Wynder*, once again.

In *Wynderne,* Trinadol had read a history of *Wyndernia* written by his grandfather on a paper woven with Hala material. Trinadol and Neuvia read it aloud to each other in installments each time they went *Windering*. Throughout the book, Elwyn mentioned events in the kingdoms of

Wyndyrnes, who, though they lived forever, were prone to forget their own history, with nothing permanent to record it on. Elwyn also wrote about the Cirilen, who held great sway in *Wyndor* once, as had the *Khalwairn,* in antiquity.

At the end of the history of *Wyndernolia Tintilisair,* with all of its bright happenings leading up to the construction of the Lightstone Jetty at Gwylor and the Lightstone Tower, Elwyn wrote an overall synopsis of the history of the two worlds.

Here they learned that before the dawn of man and his cousin, the Cirilen, there existed only one race of Hala creature capable of journeying to the *Wynder World.* These were the Wintegs, smarter than animals and yet slower-witted than men:

> *Giant, shambling creatures with a simple society, Wintegs wandered the northern ice floes hunting the northern polar bears. The Wintegs were like white werewolves with dragon's jaws and gold eyes, but on Hala there are only skeletons trapped in stone or bodies in frozen glaciers that remain to tell us of these ancient creatures. Somehow they found a way to Wynderne and got lost there, their Hala bodies perishing as they did so. They were wild in the Wynder World and wreaked havoc there. They raped the Wyndernes and their terrible offspring were called the Khalwairn.*
>
> *The Wintegs went mad from the loss of the Hala World and were filled with sleepless hunger for it. At last, Ala, the only great leader in the history of the Wynderne peoples and the only one acknowledged by all, for a brief time, to be their king, gathered the Pearl Snakes, of which there were thousands, to hunt down the Wintegs.*
>
> *The Wintegs were assassinated by the Pearl Snakes or murdered by their own children, the Khalwairn—all*

except for two, who found a way through a vein of diamonds at the southern pole of Hala and possessed the eggs of an arctic bear pregnant with twins. The Winteg pups tore their way out of the bear's womb and devoured their surrogate mother. Thenceforth, Hala Wintegs descended from these two different and less intelligent beings that were even more ferocious than their distant ancestors.

The Wintegs' Wyndyrne offspring, the Khalwairn, were monstrous and beautiful, sweet-seeming and vicious, and able to negotiate the trade between Wyndernal and Hala substances. They learned the high arts for low purposes, plotting in Wynder to raid the Hala World, for which they had inherited a thirst from their Winteg sires.

Ala sent the Pearl Snakes after the Khalwairn, as well, eventually, but when they were discovered the Khalwairn slew all but three of the magical serpents. These found passage through magical diamonds that had formed in Hala rock in the northern waste. In Hala these three snakes continued to hunt Wintegs relentlessly across the snowy expanse, until centuries later, in the second war of Sentad, Drugor killed two of the snakes and won the Halarian Wintegs' servitude. The last Pearl Snake found its way to Ghenten and crossed my path in a forest there. Thereupon, I presented the last Pearl Snake to my Queen.

In the mists of history, Gaernathon settled the great continent of Sentad while the Cirilen still led the lives of nomads scattered across the world. The Khalwairn ruled the Windyrne World at that time, having changed King Ala into a monster and flung him into the Hala sea. Each Cirilen who parted the veil between the worlds found lethal opposition from the Khalwairn and their unwitting armies of Wyndernes. It was first through here that the two enemies came to know each other.

The Cirilen, more earthly in origin and thus more passionate than the quixotic Khalwairn, battled their jaded foe with righteous valor, and this fascinated and won over the Wyndernes who had never imagined such proud purpose before.

The Khalwairn conferred in Wynder and plotted to storm Hala and conquer their new rivals there. They invaded Wyndernolia Sentad and secretly populated Halarian Sentad, shrouding themselves from Hala men until they were ready. When they organized their forces, they attacked Gaernathon's great kingdom in the north of that vast continent, fielding armies of Wintegs and enslaving all they slew as soldiers in their growing legions. They killed great Gaernathon, Sentad's wise and good king, and they made him their General, and tragically he marched against his own people as a gruesome mummy.

The Cirilen knew the Khalwairn and knew good Gaernathon, and loved his that was the greatest of all Hala Kingdoms, and they knew they must come to the aid of his fallen nation in its hour of need. All 48 houses of Cirilen that then existed combined forces in the war against the Khalwairn. The Cirilen relied on the loyalty of men instead of their thralldom. This not only helped turn the battle's tide in Hala to their favor, but gained them favor in Wynder, as well. For, ironically, Wyndernes sought more eagerly to help the Cirilen win their honest struggle than to assist in the cruel whim of the Khalwairn, who fought in shallow lust. Wyndernes came to see the Cirilen as champions who were liberating

> them from the Khalwairn, who had conscripted them into their perpetually gory fantasies. For, however harmless the Khalwairn's atrocities may have been in Wyndor, the Wyndernes were grateful to be free of them.
> To most Wyndernes, the Hala world is a sacred place. Indeed, it is the Wyndernes' only compass point in an endlessly shifting world. They peer down through still pools and look in awe at its forms and noble souls always fighting back the chaos, and they see the hard seed from which their own world blooms. For Hala is the solid ground from which their fanciful flight doth spring, its particulars the stuff of all dreams. For this reason, I believe, the Wyndernians gave more generously to the Cirilen than to the Khalwairn in the Great War, and this sabotage cost many Wynderne lives, cast down into Hala mortality by Khalwairn inquisitors. Ironically, these fallen Wyndernes promptly became our allies in Hala and helped us win the first war of Sentad for the Cirilen.

Miraculously, Neuvia was able to recall these fragments of Elwyn's history from memory after returning to Hala, and she painstakingly recorded them on the blank leaves at the end of Senadol's book of general observations.

She even recorded Elwyn's last entry:

> Today in Hala, I died. Having sheltered myself in a vast cave in a wall of the Crimson Canyon on Ghenten, I reversed His charm on the Winteg that He possessed and sent to stalk me. When He came, I was waiting in the cave with my last incantation written with my blood on vellum scrolls and the Cronus Star smoldering eager in my hand. The Winteg seemed friendly to Drugor. Yet when He walked to the mouth of the cave, the Winteg

seized Him in its dragon jaws. I pronounced my last incantation and it did succeed, I see, in opening the two veils. From the Gairanor there did come an ultimatum of lightning and thunder that made law my enunciation: that He should never return to Wynder or Hala as long as my bloodline persists. For this, I paid with my life. I see that Wyndernes have come to prepare me for my journey past the Wynderne heaven and into the Gairanor's far circle.

Alas, I hope I gave as much as given by these two worlds to me.

Trinadol and Neuvia learned from Elwyn's writings that, ultimately, each night they went to sleep in Hala they would awaken to a new day in *Wynderne*, resting only when they slept in that world, provided they did not dream there and enter Hala as ghosts. In this dream state, they could see things transpiring on Ameulas with eyes more awake than they were in either world.

Together, they traveled throughout their *Wynder* kingdom, and Trinadol worked on *Wynderne* monuments, drawing on the elements of the Hala World he had brought forth with his incantations. These elements were as memories in the mind of *Wyndernia* and with them he could construct permanent things there, to which the *Wyndernes* were beholden and upon which their spirits seemed to feed. Apparently, they worshipped the Lightstone Tower, for it had properties only they completely understood, and which they seemed reluctant to describe.

Neuvia inspired Trinadol to prepare a loyal base of *Wynderl* spirits ready to call to his Hala realm, willing to respect Hala's fragility and the rules he set down when they came. For it was these spirits, his *Wynderli* subjects, that a Cirilen enlisted when he cast his spells into Hala. Evil spirits would take evil form. By preparing his subjects with moral, Halarian instruction, and winning their loyalty, they came to serve his Hala bidding with proud discipline. This pleased Trinadol greatly, for he was haunted in *Wynder* by his wish to protect Hala, on which he unleashed such terrible forces.

Surprisingly, even in *Wyndornia* there was evil, though property and material were practically inviolable. For there was a finite property there, after all, as unlimited as matter and mind might be. Each *Wynderne* had but one soul, one will, and that will could be taken away. In this place so free of limits there was the lust for power, the will to cage free wills and add them to one's own will, and make all the infinitely multifarious world match one idea, one theme, of one author's making. There were ravenous spirits unsatisfied with their own dreams or too satisfied with them, jealous of all love that was not directed to them or all activity that did not originate from them. These were the tyrants of *Wyndornia*.

So in *Wynder* there were rumors of war, and even battles with neighboring kingdoms that were ruled by *Wyndorls* who sat in thrones left empty by the *Khalwairn* and Cirilen. Such tyrants grew eccentric, and found great frustration in *Wynder*. Their mightiest battles amounted to symbolic squabbles, forgotten by the very participants a week later. No command could make any real or permanent effect upon anything in *Wynderne*, and so their power had no consequence, beyond delaying their subjects from eternity. These *Wynderne* kings contemplated victims where life could be threatened, property was precious, and time was finite. Scarcities would give their edicts an edge and their cruelty might find a meaningful home, some surmised, in the Hala World. For they had caught the fever of the *Khalwairn*. Blox, the king Trinadol had cast down into Hala, was such a *Wynderne*.

When Trinadol dreamed in *Wyndernia,* he walked the starlit streets of Hala Ameulas, wrapped in whatever rags he could find to hide his cobalt radiance. He walked down country roads in wild places, past coasts and wharfs, hamlets and hidden glades, smelling the heath and the grass and the wood smoke. He found his forsaken kingdom to be prosperous during the first years of his isolation. But then, in his vagrant's disguise, Trinadol spied decline, and with it ill deeds committed by roving rogues with shaven heads who called themselves the disciples of Blox. Yet he did not recognize this name as the name of the *Wynderne* king he had cast from *Wynder*.

One night while dreaming in *Wynder* and soaring over Ameulas, Trinadol discovered a garrulous gathering of Blox's disciples around a bonfire on a meadow near the Forest of Lind. He flew down and touched earth behind the crowd, his beggar's clothes cloaking his *Wyndery* luminescence.

Wailing people were being bound to pine logs as the mob of disciples, dressed in rough burlap, prepared to cast them onto the roaring pyre.

Trinadol moved among the raucous crowd and whispered in one woman's wide ear: "Why, Granny, do they punish this boy and girl?"

"They bear the mark of evil," snarled the woman, paying no attention to the stranger who asked. She jeered with all the others, and Trinadol's heart was sad.

"What is the mark of evil, old woman?" he asked.

At this, she turned. "Beauty!" she hissed. "People point to them as proof that Blox's word is wrong and that the Hala World is lovely!" The woman froze as she looked into Trinadol's eyes, suspicious. "Who might you be, stranger! Your eyes pierce me like icicles!"

Trinadol let his robe fall and shone before her. "Well they should!"

The others on the field turned and shrank away as Trinadol rose in the air.

"Let you know that this you do is wrought of evil counsel, not higher than this world, but jealous of it!" he cried, and with the motion of one arm he extinguished the flaming pyre. "These children shall be free and if you cannot take them into your hearts then take your hearts away from this world that you shun! Madness is not holy, nor is the treasure of this world evil! If you've no love of this world, leave it, instead of scarring it with your wicked wrath! Or if you still have love, repent this blasphemy, for you foul your own nest with it, most wrongly of all."

And the gathering of people, as superstitious as they were, scattered on the moonlit fields, renouncing their burlap robes and flinging them off. Trinadol freed the fair youths Blox's thugs had kidnapped, and he soared into the sky before any could approach him with thanks or ask him his name.

When Trinadol woke in *Wynderne* he had told Neuvia what had transpired in Hala and she had consoled him, though she, too, worried what might be happening in their neglected realm.

In Hala, the years had not weighed as heavily on Neuvia and Trinadol as on Bondairtlen men. They still seemed the same age as when they were wed, yet they appeared more timeless than youthful, faint and ghostly like shades under the sun, though it seemed that sorrow and fate, more than magic, faded them there.

Neuvia had watched Trinadol four times from the cliff as he chose specimens from the sea. He had taken a starfish, an anglerfish, a strand of seaweed, and a jar of clear water with nothing in it that she could see.

Around the horizon to the north, west, and east were spread the gnarled islands Trinadol had carved out of the Dimmrock. South and east spread the coral reefs that glowed and twinkled like fields of flowers in spring and summer. Due west, there was nothing but an open roadstead, for a wily gambler, straight into the Dimmrock's bay. Three ships had made for him down that avenue nearly four years ago, but two of his guardians, the Microsia and the Rollock, had dispatched them without mercy. Two years ago another of his snares trapped a second expedition, of five ships. The ghosts of those men, who had defied his decree, deepened the red miasma around his soul. No flotillas appeared on his horizon in any direction since those doomed missions.

Neuvia had watched four years ago through her spyglass as the Rollock, its limbs milling and kicking across the sea, caught the last of three ships from the first expedition that tried to reach the Dimmrock. The Rollock dragged the ship under, long before it reached the island. Attacking one of the other ships was a beast made of crystal knives and scissors. Its legs rippled and a long glass tail whipped over its back as ten claws on ten crystal arms snipped the ship's rigging.

Separate, always separate in their Hala selves, Neuvia and Trinadol never met each other there. Trinadol was blinded by the Scepter's glare, and Neuvia was always forewarned of Trinadol's presence by her menagerie of guardians. Senadol's book of prophecies had given her no guidance for years now, and Toy interpreted this as a cue to continue on the path she had taken, though she wondered if Senadol's vision had simply reached no further. Toy advised her not to make contact with Trinadol while he was under the Scepter's sway, but instead to be on hand when the moment came to act. When would that day come, she asked and asked, for surely Trinadol was in graver danger, with less chance of help, with each passing year.

One day, Trinadol had wandered to the brook within plain sight of the tree house, but he did not notice the tree house or her. He sat on the pink clover and bathed his feet in the stream, his stoic face pensive. He did not see the panicking animals that always surrounded him, calling out warnings. The Scepter cast his tired face in red tints as it filled his heart with fears and furies that took all his soul to master.

Neuvia watched him from her room atop the white tree. She could not bear to watch him suffer so, but Toy slid down her shirt and coiled around her breast, feathering her nipple, quelling the words that were forming on her tongue, and she was knocked off her purpose by his chilling compulsion. She watched Trinadol walk off through the forest, followed by 14 sealskins of water floating in the air behind him. She sighed as Toy went back up her chest to wrap around her neck, weaving his fine braid methodically.

*   *   *

On a blustery summer day in 1073, seven years almost to the day after they were wed, Neuvia woke to find the owl's head on the bank of the brook, its long-lashed eyelids drooping over lifeless yellow eyes.

She wondered who could have been so wicked in her forest as to kill this loyal friend and she felt a fierce, maternal rage.

She suddenly remembered the weird gifts the mad beaver left for her when she was a child, and it chilled her heart. She and the island's beaver had never been friends…

She buried the owl's remains and put a smooth turquoise pebble in the soil over his grave. Then she climbed the ladder to her room.

Toy whispered in her ear the news that Trinadol had taken *Stargazer* onto the open sea.

A storm was coming, though it was a brilliant summer day. She went downstairs to make herself some tea. She took a pot up to her room, closing the shutters of three windows, and sat in a chair by the window overlooking the stream. She lit a fat candle and pulled off her long boots, setting them under the sill, and then she curled up under a blanket on her bed. She read some of her books and waited, as Toy listened to far away things, parsing what Trinadol was doing in her ear.

At orange dusk, Toy announced that Trinadol had cast a great incantation north of the island. After a while, Toy reluctantly reported that the King had fallen asleep in *Stargazer* and was now in *Wundyrne*. She demanded to meet him, over Toy's protest.

Toy had no choice but to obey.

*   *   *

They were together again, after only a few months, and they lay on the air over the Wundyrnal Dimmrock watching a weightless ballet of mythical creatures wheeling over the greensward: a griffon, a hummingbird, a goldfish, a winged elephant and a dripping Blue Whale, each form taken by one of the Wondyrne Ameulentian players who had visited the Dimmrock to perform for the King and Queen.

"These Wondeyrl artists really know the Hala *detail, don't you agree, Love?"*

"Yes, even more so! They catch sparkles in sparkles and shadows in shadows and colors in colors! The goldfish wiggles, and sends sunlit droplets from its fins and fabulous tail...Behold the mighty whale, Trinadol! *When he tilts, the world tilts instead!"*

They laughed, indulgent, as though against the other world.

Trinadol and Neuvia *had grown so close in carefree Wynderne that smiling was as intimate as kissing, and their time apart kept their love always new. They gloried in their reunions, and regardless of* Trinadol's *deeds in the other world,* Neuvia *was thankful that they won them passage back to this place of redemption where she could have his ear and heart. But it troubled her that this world's pleasure was masking that world's pain.*

Now, Neuvia *frowned and took* Trinadol's *hand. "I've not inquired, but I must know, at last,* Trinadol. *What is the evil you fear in* Hala*? Is it truly yourself that you fear, because of your father's prophecy? Because the stone of the* Scepter *burns red?"*

"I do not wish to think of it."

"No, my love, you must! Tell me what Senadol *said to you."*

He looked inward, reluctantly. "He said to beware that which is closest to me. For that would be my doom. He said I would know it by its mark—crimson. He could not have known that would be myself."

"Or something else? The Scepter *is the symbol of your power."*

"My power that curses all."

"No, no, my love. Perhaps what preys on you has stained your power, since that is what it fears!"

"Who told you that?" asked Trinadol.

"My girlfriends, silly though they all may be. They see things more clearly than we, sometimes, I think. This crimson preys on you, and seeks you through your power, painting it evil so you would use it against yourself. You must not believe your desires

and ambitions wicked, my husband! Such doubts surely twist the flower of your mind into fierce and angry shapes, and prove your mean sentence after it was falsely passed. You are good, my love! How can you not know it? Let us live, curse or no!"

"You are wise," said Trinadol, touching his brow to her lips.

She stroked his ebony hair, shimmering many colors in her fingers. "Let us make from this hallowed world a passage to Hala daylight, and make that world ours again, as well. We have to leave this fair dream, and make Hala like here, only more so. I do beg you, my lord." She knelt before him and he stroked her iridescent hair.

"You believe it is possible for me to be in that fragile world? That I should call off my guard, breach my wall, and enter Hala unafraid and unashamed even though my ambitions may wreak havoc?"

"Trinadol, you must! I live on the Dimmrock with you. I have been there all along…" She felt a jolt of burning pain as though a rope tied around her heart had suddenly tightened. Her sight went black and her eyes flashed violet in agony before she ceased to be in the Wynder World.

Trinadol wheeled in rage, piercing his eyes through the distance in every direction.

She was gone!

*   *   *

She woke and found her wrists and ankles bound to the bedposts with rough rope.

A snarling creature with bubbling nostrils bared its tusks over her with a ravenous sneer. Its yellow eyes did not look into hers, but moved up and down Neuvia's flesh, drooling hot on her scepter's diamond.

How many hurts? Pigg reminisced as he looked at the patch of white skin on her hip. Lots of hurts, he remembered now!

His many foiled attempts to get the queen had garnered him countless bumps, breaks, bruises, and baths. But in these last seven years Pigg had eaten all of the silver-and-red squirrels that liked to help her. He had eaten some sparrows, hummingbirds and magpies, but that just made the birds swarm thicker whenever they saw him.

So, for the last few years Pigg had not touched the birds and they had kept a more respectful distance. But he managed to catch the mink, which had been slipping her things from the King's Tower.

Pigg kept the mink's fur with pride, shriveled on a stick in his deep burrow not far across the Chuckling Wee from the tree house.

He had also been able to dig up the burrow of badgers and he ate the whole family, after tossing the old patriarch into the river. Pigg snorted and giggled as he watched him dashed on the rocks below the cliff.

He had also rooted up the raccoon family. Only a few weaklings of their kind still existed on the Dimmrock.

The beaver was too tough for Pigg, but after seven years of bad luck he had finally caught the owl that liked to gouge his face.

He was very clever. Pigg found a piece of fishnet on the beach during one of his midnight forays, and later he pretended to spy on the Queen, standing out in the open with the fishnet bunched in his hands. When the owl swooped, he waited till the last moment, ducked and threw the net. The owl fell full into it, and Pigg twisted the net, breaking the bird's wings. Then he wrung its neck, and he left its head as a gift for the Queen this morning.

Now-nee-now-now-now, Pigg thought. I got the Queeny-weeny-ween!

* * *

Chapter 15

Pigg

Trinadol *reached for the* Scepter *before remembering he was Wyndering and did not have it. His eyes slashed the world like swords and when he was satisfied that nothing in his Wyndernalia Kingdom caused this, he tore himself inward through the hidden diamond of his* Hala *power.*

As he passed through the diamond's dusky chamber, with its empty chair, he looked around and saw no demon hiding there, as Neuvia had suggested—only the chair, in which he had never sat.

He emerged into his Hala flesh lying in *Stargazer*, scalded by Hala sensation as though plunged in boiling water. As the pain subsided, Trinadol stared at the ceiling of the blue grotto, having forgotten how to look through Hala eyes. Coated in icy sweat, he tried to think where he might be. He looked at the Scepter lying on his chest but did not touch it. Neuvia's words echoed fresh in his mind. Yet as he thought of the empty chair inside the Cronus Star he feared she had been wrong. If there was some evil lingering in the diamond plotting Trinadol's downfall, it must be his own. He clasped the handle of the Scepter and then he realized his mistake: he could not reach her in Hala! Why had he come back? Somewhere on the mainland she lay imperiled, even as great buttresses of magic surrounded him.

He must get back to *Wynder* and induce a dream into Hala so he could soar far and wide looking for her in every hill and glen of Ameulas, wherever she lay endangered. And then he could take her in his ghostly arms and fly back to the Dimmrock where they could live out their days, curse or no curse, surrounded by his walls of magic, so only she might be his killer, if that was fate's obsession.

He had no time to craft a subtle incantation; there was one he could use that was the basis for all the others, and could be left unfinished, in perpetual motion.

He sat up and ordered *Stargazer* forward, and the little boat knifed through a brief window in the grotto's arch and raised her mast as her three-pointed sail dropped, and she climbed a warm green swell.

He needed no scroll or stellar alignment for what he had in mind. After six islands he knew how to do this simple step without such precision. The Seventh Isle of Ameulas would not have many limits. So be it, Trinadol thought. May the most unruly of my *Wynderne* subjects come forth with this conjuring and inhabit my creation, he decided, for he had not care about a world that would threaten Neuvia's life.

Stargazer could not dissuade or resist his rage. The Scepter never burned so bright as Trinadol moved like a grievous wound over the sea. He beached his craft and ran up the rocky rampart to the forest.

*   *   *

Pigg had not spoken to anyone for hundreds of years. He tried to moisten his gray tongue and smack his lips over Neuvia so he might address her in a way he imagined befitted a Queen. "Lady, you see me, right?" he grinned.

She beheld him unmoving and, in fact, without the slightest struggle against the bonds Pigg had wound around her wrists and ankles. At first, she thought it was the beaver hulking over her, then a nightmare, then the awful smell of Pigg convinced her it was something she had never come across before in the forest. So she looked at the creature over her without expression, trying to imagine what it might be.

She is a Queen, Pigg thought. She was cool, composed and in control, even though he had her completely at his mercy. All he had done was creep up her tree and nothing bothered him. He had climbed on the ladder and it sprang upward 50 feet and slammed him into the ceiling of the Queen's bedchamber. She did not wake up, and Pigg, rubbing his head, climbed into the room and gawked at her.

Toy had been asleep and did not see him. Pigg spun his grimy cords around her hands and feet like a dirty spider. He dared not touch her scepter but, instead, reached down and pulled Toy by the head off her neck and gulped him down, head first, his entire length. And he felt him slither into his iron stomach as its terrible acids churned.

Pigg opened the shutters of all four windows and let a fresh ray of summer light the room. He climbed on top of her and gnawed her white cotton slip at the belly, ripped it open and pulled it out from under her. She was naked before him, except for the ropes, and Pigg drooled on top of her.

Toy woke inside him, and bit him. The pain dizzied Pigg's brain with strange pleasure; he knew the poison would be dissolved inside his impervious gut. But Toy's was not only a Hala poison, but a *Wynder* poison, too. Pigg wondered if he might be in danger if Toy struck too many times, even inside his iron belly. Cold sweat ran over his face, twigged with coarse hairs like a fly. "My Queen, your toy inside me stings me, so I must dine on Queen meat so sweet—pure like river water—so to wash out the poison, your Lady-wady-wade," Pigg stammered. "Oh, my Queen!" He scrabbled her porcelain belly through the ropes. "So pure and fresh of flesh, of fleshy-flesh so fresh and white! Now you are Tim Pigg's candy cream and saucy-sauce!"

Neuvia looked at the floor beside her bed where she had dropped the book of Senadol's prophecies. The pages were fluttering. Her eyes barely read a sentence: "Her wisdom might prevail..." Then she saw one word as the flipping pages paused: "Wait."

"She looks at blank pages!" said Pigg, nervously. "It's time to eat my Queen now. And you, so sweet and fresh will clean the Pigg from end to end. The poison is hot and sour! I need your candy in me quick! Thank you, Queen, sweet pastry for my tummy-tum-tum, and to your grace and glory may it be, I hope, and do pardon me, too, if you should please!"

The Scepter of Gieron was on her chest, touching her flesh, and she believed that she could use it. Yet she could not use it without alerting Trinadol that she was here on the Dimmrock. If Trinadol remembered all she had told him in *Wynder*, he would remember where to look for her. If not, he would not come, and for the best. But if he saw the scepter he would find her, anyway.

She could only utter the Spell of Protection once in her life and must measure that need against the course of centuries, as Toy had reminded her many times.

"Well, Master," she said to Pigg. "Where is your charcoal drawing stick?"

"What?" Pigg said, blinking in the glare of her gaze.

"What is your name?"

"Er…Tim Pigg, they call me."

"Why don't you draw the marks on my flesh, Master Pigg?" she inquired with sweet concern. "You can plan the cuts that way; the flank, for instance, the marrow of the shins and, of course, the delicate hands, which," she flourished her fingers, "if roasted in peanut oil and onion flowers should melt the tongue of Gieron. As a master cook myself, I thought you, such a prince among eaters, Master Pigg, would appreciate such things a little more! No matter, I can guide you. I'll show you how to use the nicest cuts for the most delicious meals and purifying remedies, which you seem so much in need of, after your many toils. But you must be quick! No more shilly-shallying! No more dilly-dallying! Where is your charcoal, Master Pigg?"

"Charcoal?"

"All butchers have it, those with the smallest pride, at least!" Neuvia looked out the window as though suddenly bored.

"They do?"

"Of course!"
"No!"
"Yes."
"Really?"
Neuvia sighed. "You mean you don't know it?"

Pigg's mind was dizzy as a pinwheel as he heard her savory voice. Did he have charcoal? No! And blast it, too! He looked from side to side. A piece of charcoal to draw on the Queen…He saw a stick from the Enryd tree on the floor and hopped down. Breaking off side branches, he lit it over the flame of her candle.

Neuvia looked at Senadol's open book of prophecies on the floor, but its pages were still and blank.

Pigg danced a strange jig as he watched the flame rise on the end of the stick. He let it burn as soot collected on its tip. Then he screwed his lips into an 'O' and blew out the flame.

He grinned as it smoked and looked down at her body. "Now, Queen, tell me how to draw the lines for the butchering part which I must do. Your little toy's having some fun in me gutsy-wuts. Show me how to make the cutsy-wuts, and sweetly serve your honey meat that I need to eat as I promised you I do, without a lie today and truly, too! My belly, Queenish girly-girl must eat now and suck the blood like berry wine to douse the terrible fires. *Ow!*" Pigg felt Toy strike him again inside. Sweat poured over Pigg's brow. "Show me or I shall have to eat you as you are! But, I think that was the last from that bad toy." Pigg frowned and smiled. "Yes."

"Put the stick between my teats," said Neuvia.

"Tasty teatsy-weetsy-weets, tweedly-toodly-doodly-doo," Pigg sang.

Neuvia hoped he would touch the scepter, for she knew it would protect itself, if she was truly its master, and hoped it would give this beast a terrible bite.

But Pigg pushed her breasts with scraggly fingers to move the scepter off her chest without touching it. It slid off to her side on the bed and she smiled at him with hidden rage.

What must she wait for? Where were all her forest friends now? What was there to save her? The sea eagle could not enter, for his wings were too broad. The squirrels were too few, and the birds wheeling outside did not daunt this animal. Indeed they stayed away as though an orb of fear surrounded it. Only a few brave sparrows flew into the room, aiming at Pigg's eye, but Pigg dashed them away with magical motions, not pulling his hot eyes from Neuvia's sweet flesh; for he was entranced by her and charged with wild purpose by the sight and scent of her.

She tried to think of the Spell of Protection. She felt certain she could still use it since the scepter's gem was touching her side.

Pigg drew the line straight like a boy learning geometry. "How far should I draw it? What other cuts are there?" he asked. His head bobbed without any rhythm. "The breasts split—like a chicken-wicky? And how do I cook these then? What should I add? What spices!"

"Too fast and hasty to last and be tasty, O, Tim!" winked Neuvia. She reclined regally beneath him and smiled. "There are many cuts. You must prepare for a week of feasts! You mustn't ruin your opportunity to eat a Queen. You must plan it out and do it right. Something to remember—that's far enough."

"Yes! Something to remember!" Pigg jumped on top of her and danced, his cloven hind hooves scratching her skin.

"You're marking up my skin. You're bruising it."

"Yes, yes!"

"If you care about tenderness in your meat," she sighed, "it is very bad. Especially when it is cooked in a marinade of eucalyptus and red butter."

"What?" Pigg's nostrils flared. "What's that?"

"Just a recipe."

He stepped off her to each side, squatting low. "Eh?"

"A special way to prepare the Queen's flesh for your palate. But perhaps you don't care how you eat your meals, after all. I think you don't care about eating very much, if this is how you would eat a Queen!" Neuvia rolled her eyes and shook her head.

"I do, I do! I care!"

"Then stop hemming and hawing! Finish drawing!"

"Yes! Well, now where? You know, Father wants the King's body for himself. But he gave me yours! Yours is much better, I think. Where should I draw, milady now, if you please?"

"Around the top of the thigh. Each thigh is a ham, and should be prepared accordingly."

"*Mmm!*" Pigg drew the sooty stick around each leg, biting his protruding gray tongue. "Now what?" he asked.

Neuvia guided him as he drew and drooled, marking her torso with an improvised design.

"Now, before you draw the shoulder cuts, I must ask you," said Neuvia. "What are your intentions as to herbs?"

"What?" asked Pigg.

"Surely you have the herbs for the meal—what could you have been thinking?"

Pigg blinked his tiny eyes. "Herbs?"

There was a commotion in the forest. The chimes moved up a scale of notes as someone passed down the main path. Trinadol must be awake, Neuvia realized. She thought of crying out but Pigg covered her mouth with his filthy fingers.

"We mustn't bother the King!" he whispered, holding his knife to her throat.

*   *   *

Trinadol did not stop running as he had passed through the forest and emerged on the oceanic fields, exhausted but filled with a fury that still compelled him forward. When he came before the North Cliff, gouged a mile short of the original coastline, he fell to his knees on the high ledge looking over the sea toward Ameulas.

Finally, he marched some distance from the edge and raised the Scepter before him, half at the sky and half toward Ameulas. He spoke the spell unlocking the intermediary gates between the worlds inside the island's rock, and as though a giant hammer smote the Dimmrock, a great piece clove off and a wall of steam rose before Trinadol.

Larger than any of Trinadol's previous creations, the new island slid away from the Dimmrock as its mighty fundament rose, molten, from of the sea.

And as the burning island rumbled away to the west to fill the last chink in his armor, Trinadol smiled in dark peace and fell into a deathly sleep in the grass beside the Dimmrock's smoldering edge.

* * *

"You fancy yourself a food lover? *Pshaw!*" Neuvia looked sidelong out the window. "Am I to be eaten by a crass fool who would not savor each succulent morsel?"

"Herbs?" asked Pigg.

"Of course!"

"I'm sorry, my lady-wady, I didn't think about that."

"Why am I being eaten by this fool!" she cried, as if to the Gairanor. "He has no love of food!"

Pigg saw the brilliant tear that spilled from her eye, and dabbed it on a finger, tasting it. "Tell me the herbs! I'll find them triple-quick. I'll have herbs in a few heartbeats, at your pleasure, my lady!"

"You have Tincair and Rosemary, of course. And without Lock of Gargoyle, what is a meal? Ginger would be nice. And Thyme. And hurry it up, will you, then? You say you've been planning this for years. *Hmmph!*"

Pigg kicked his heels. "Yes, my juicy Queen!" he leaped onto the ladder and rode it down to the base of the tree.

Neuvia heard him scrabbling off through the forest. Lock of Gargoyle would not be easy to find this time of year.

A hard summer squall pattered the roof.

She heard distant clapping. The beaver was slapping his tail against a tree upstream, near his dam.

The chimes in the forest jangled and the heavy branches of the enryd tree swayed, knocking purple enryds to the ground.

Neuvia saw a crimson orb of light in the window arching over the forest, and a thunder shook the island instead of the sky, tolling the heavy storm bell in the forest's heart. The entire forest wailed at once in a mournful chorus of chimes and reeds, which died away as the island settled.

Was this what it came to, she thought. Her precious Toy dead, as well as her other loyal guardians, and this wretched beast in their place? And now Trinadol was returning to *Wyndor,* where she could not follow him…

The rope ladder jerked and reeled something in. Neuvia looked as Pigg appeared in the doorway, soaked with rain and grasping uprooted weeds in his fingers. He hopped into the room from the ladder and danced as dirt clods splattered on the old rug from the roots of the many herbs he had picked.

"I got everything, milady! All the herbs for the feasty-weast!"

"I do trust you have the spices," she said with concerned hopefulness.

"Spices? I've got all these!" He threw down the thrashed specimens.

"Good! But those are herbs," said Neuvia.

"Herbs? Yes!" Pigg danced a few quick steps. "Herbs and Spices, Herbs and Spices!" he sang.

"Herbs aren't spices."

"What about these?" Pigg raised the limp weeds in his hands.

"Those are herbs!" Neuvia sighed, and she looked sadly out the window, seeing that the rain had stopped. But the thunder still rumbled and the room was still swaying on its mighty branch. "After ripening for 24 years, will I be eaten without spices?" She let herself weep now, which was easy to do given the circumstances. "And what are herbs without spices?" she cried in outrage and despair.

Pigg cocked his shriveled head at her.

"I shall be ruined!" she sobbed.

"No…I'll cook you so beautiful, don't ever to worry, dear Queen! What spices? I'll grab them—and dance around! Which ones, now? You're so sad! What are the spices you want to be cooked in nowny-now-now-now?"

"You don't seem to care," she turned her head away, haughtily, "*how* I taste!"

He jumped up and down. "Pigg cares! Don't ever you worry! What spices, my lady?"

"Put the herbs down, then," she said, wiping a tear from her eye.

Pigg threw them down in the floor, nodding.

"First of all, what about salt and pepper? There's some in the first floor of the King's Tower. Also, what about curry? Turmeric and coriander are in season. And honey will be essential."

"Oh! Honey…" Pigg jumped up and down, scratching his head. Never mind it wasn't a spice, he thought. He had never imagined such a feast! It was a royal feast, in his honor, and the Queen herself was the hostess, the cook, and the meal! "Coriander…all right, then! And what else?"

"Cinnamon!"

"Yes! I know where they all be! I will be back so soon, not to let you get sadder at all, never to worry, for my dear sweet Queeny-ween, I will cook you up so soony-woony-woon, don't worry about it now!"

"Remember Paprika and Sage!"

Pigg turned, his eyes slitted. "Yes. Why so *many* spices, milady?"

"It's a large meal, remember. At least seven sittings to finish! Each cut is seasoned differently to bring out every nuance in the meat's flavor with special gravies and sauces."

"*Hmmm.*"

"For instance, my tongue in paprika, cinnamon and honey, fried in butter, O Pigg? Can you imagine it now, hearing my tongue in your ears?"

Pigg's eyes glazed. "Toodly-doodly-doo!" he yelled as he hopped onto the rope ladder and rode it to the ground.

The forest groaned like a wounded animal. Neuvia heard the beaver, again, rapping his tail against a tree. For a moment she thought of trying to call him, but she despaired to be at his mercy in her predicament.

The rope ladder suddenly drew Pigg up and slammed his head against the ceiling. He hopped off the ladder, biting his lip and dumping handfuls of spices, barks and dried leaves, and even part of a beehive from which he had eaten all the tasty bees, which had only made his stomach feel worse. "Done!" he cried, spreading his arms. "Done-done-yum-yummy grand Lady-Yummy-Queen-Supper-Yum-Yum-Yay! Huzzah and…hitherto! How delightful! In actual fact! Righteo! *Ow!*"

Pigg shrieked and kneeled by the window overlooking the brook as he retched. A glistening cord as black as tar emerged from his mouth, spiraling into one of her tall boots. He coughed once and it was out, and then he grinned at her. "Now we can take our time. That nasty toy is broken. I'll cook you proper, don't you fear. Tweedle-dee-dee!"

Neuvia stared at her black boot, an incredulous tear on her cheek. Where were her friends? Where was Trinadol? Had he returned to *Wyndor?* "So what about the butchering part, then?" she asked.

"*Yes! Yes!* The Queen picked the word right off my tonguey-wung!"

"You'll lose all the blood."

Pigg winced and gripped his fists. "No, the blackberry wine!"

"You must get pots and pans!"

"Yes!"

"I can tell you how to make a pudding. But you must get pots, pans and a stick of butter. Don't look a coward at me. You've been lolling about for long enough now! The King is away from the Tower. Below the kitchen there is butter in the larder, which is full of glacier ice from Poldur Gwylor. Run in and get a stick. The King will not be back for some time."

"How do you know?" grinned Pigg with a crooked smile.

"The Queen knows! Stop lollidolloping!"

Pigg frowned and shrugged. "Righteo! Off I go! Tally-*hooooooo!*"

He tripped, bounced on his bottom and rolled backwards out the door.

The rope ladder whirled and stopped with a crash and a yelp down below.

Neuvia listened for Trinadol. Had Trinadol fallen asleep on the cliff side, as he did after casting his spells? She saw the sea eagle circling the tree house. The brave bird could not fly into the room, nor could it fight Pigg in such close quarters. She hoped it would attack him as he crossed the greensward to the Tower.

She heard the beaver again, cracking his tail against a tree. This time, she decided to call him. She made a fist and found she could knock it against the wall. She rapped the wood as loudly as she could, bruising her knuckles. But still it was not very loud and almost as soon as she started the birds and beasts of the forest cried a warning to Neuvia that Trinadol was approaching, this time heading south back to the Tower to go to *Wynderne*.

Neuvia wondered if she should use the Spell of Protection, and wondered, suddenly, what the words of the spell were.

She couldn't remember the spell! As many times as she read it, committed it to her memory, now it was gone.

Pigg would soon return.

"Toy! What is the Spell of Protection?" she whispered, for she still could not believe that he was gone.

Trinadol passed near the tree house, and the forest seemed to shake and tremble, the bells and rattles shivering. Then the noise receded and the branches were still.

O, Trinadol! she cried inside. Why can't I call you? Wouldn't the red stain be washed away if you saw me before you?

She drew in a breath to shout when she heard the shrill whoop of Pigg spurring his elk through the forest as he clutched a dripping stick of butter from the King's larder.

She sighed. How long can I wait, she wondered. Then she remembered the Spell of Protection. "Yes!" she cried and laughed, but when her hip barely nudged the scepter, it tumbled off the bed and *thunked* onto the floor. "No!"

Hooves thudded and splashed below.

The whole forest began to howl and clang. The eagle pealed, wheeling, and all the birds took flight, swarming over the creaking woods.

The rope ladder coiled on its dowel, and a tear fell from her eye as, grinning as his head was slammed against the roof, Pigg appeared in the doorway and tumbled forward onto the floor.

"*Ack, ack, ack*!" he spat, and dumped the pots and pans on the floor, letting the mangled stick of butter ooze from his fingers into a small saucepan. "The King is in a fury! I saw him coming down the broadway and ducked into the woods! He looks like a burning rose and the ground is all ashakey-wake!"

"You brought pots and pans, I see."

"Yes, and buttery-wutter-wut, tee-hee!"

"You have no suitable knife?" asked Neuvia.

"The sharpest!" grinned Pigg, producing his iron knife that he had stolen long ago and kept sharpened on a river stone.

Neuvia looked out the window overlooking the stream. The Spell of Protection was clear in her mind now, but the scepter was out of her reach. She heard the beaver's tail cracking a tree in the distance. "Who is your father, Pigg, may I ask?" she said.

"Him. He is my father," nodded Pigg, gesturing to nothing.

The windmill started turning, but the motion wasn't smooth. The ropes of the windmill seemed to lunge along as though someone was drawing it hand over hand.

Neuvia turned her head from the window.

"Come then, Pigg. Now for the butchering part," she smiled, looking him in the eyes.

Pigg trembled in reverence. He bowed and groveled.

She saw the rope surge behind his shoulder, and she noticed that a bucket was missing from its hook on the rope. Her heart pounded. "Allow me to explain how to prepare these dishes, my dear Pigg, since I will be dead after the butchering is over!"

"Oh." Pigg jumped on top of her with his knife. "Explain!" he drooled, his eyes crossing.

The pulley made the tiniest squeak in the window and Pigg's head jerked around.

"You'll want to slice the flanks off separately, of course…"

"What was that noise? The flanksies, yes?" Pigg grinned looking back at her.

"Yes, the flanksies," she winked.

The pulley squeaked again.

"How do I make the saucy-sauces?" asked Pigg, waving his knife.

"*Shhh!*" Neuvia hissed.

"*Hmm?*"

She gambled: "Something is coming!"

Pigg looked around slowly and saw the rope moving. "A-ha! Another friend of the Queen's, perhaps? Thank you for telling me, my lady-wady, now!"

Pigg leaped across the room and crouched beneath the window with his knife.

"The knife won't help you against the Dimmrock Lion," said Neuvia.

"Eh?"

"The earthquakes woke it up."

"What be coming, then?" Pigg's hackles bristled.

"Smite him in the mouth when he gets to the top. That will stun him and down he'll fall! But mind his teeth! *Poison!*"

"Well, what do I do?" Pigg was confused.

"The smallest nip is fatal, and he has a hundred fangs!" whispered Neuvia. "Put your hand in the boot and smite him with that!"

"Yes, yes! Sweet Queen!" Pigg reached his hand into the boot and stopped. He turned and leered at her. "A-ha!" he smiled, and he drew out a shriveled black snake. "Not much left of your toy, tee-hee!" Pigg tossed it aside and reached into the boot again. "A-ha!" he cried again, and he pulled out another shriveled snake, this one gray. Pigg's face screwed in puzzlement.

Four long hands tufted with orange fur grabbed the frame of the window. Pigg screamed as the Orange Man's face looked over the sill.

Pigg reached his hand into the boot again but as he swung it hard at the surprised ape's face he froze, dropped the boot, and fell onto his back.

"You tricked me!" Pigg squealed, pulling his right hand from the boot as his left hand waved his grimy dagger at her.

The Orange Man climbed into the room and grabbed both of Pigg's wrists and, almost playfully, he squeezed the knife into his long third hand at the end of his leg. Then he pinned Pigg to the ground with a callused knee and glanced at Neuvia.

He reached a long arm out with the knife and cut one of Neuvia's hands free and gave her the knife. Then he turned and grunted a call out the window.

Through all four windows marmosets of all stripes poured into the room, and they stuffed Pigg's head into the bucket of the windmill and wound its cord around the wiggling Pigg.

Then the Orange Man picked Pigg up and threw him out the window.

Pigg cruised headfirst down the line as the windmill spun, and the bucket smashed into its anchor stone in the brook.

But the bucket held together, and Pigg still kicked and struggled below.

The Orange Man howled in anger as Neuvia freed herself and she could smell his rich forest musk as she looked through the window beside him.

Pigg struggled out of the rope, though his head was still stuck in the bucket against the rock in midstream. The marmosets climbed down the windmill's ropes to attack him.

Neuvia heard the beaver's tail clapping far away and a noise like rushing wind suddenly rose through the trees.

The marmosets retreated up the ropes, and a wave of water like shattered quartz rushed down the Chuckling Wee, washing over its high banks.

Pigg squealed as the wave swept him downstream. He was not able to pry the bucket from his head until he was sliding over the brink of the great western falls.

Pigg cried feebly and shook his fists. Then he noticed a dark root protruding from the bank and grabbed it, kicking his cloven feet in joy.

The current was strong over him, and Pigg couldn't pull himself up. He sucked air through his snout as he held on. A white fish jumped and bit him on the nose, locking on and flipping. Pigg cursed, but finally, unable to stand the taste of Pigg, the fish let go and Pigg bit into its belly.

With a fierce cry, the sea eagle dipped from the sky and swooped down with talons forward.

Pigg shouted as the eagle seized his wrists and wrenched his hands from the root just as the whole cliff cracked and a giant wall of slate leaned out from the island and crumbled into the sea.

Revealed on the new cliff-face was a school of red fossils, giant nautilus embedded in the stone eons ago.

All along the cliff giant slabs were now sheering off the Dimmrock.

Pigg gripped the eagle's legs and thought he'd make it, after all, if the bird's wings could hold out.

They sank beside the waterfall, the eagle's cry echoing across the cracking cliff.

Pigg clicked his heels and fish scales spluttered from his chortling mouth just as he saw the eagle's beak flash and stab his eye.

He gasped and watched in horror with his right eye as the eagle stabbed it, too, and erased the world.

He howled and let go of the eagle, falling endlessly into the dark.

And Pigg's last thought before dying, as he lay mangled and blind on jagged rubble, was of Neuvia's ear, fried in butter, cinnamon, and paprika.

*   *   *

After the flood had passed, the Orange Man turned to Neuvia and felt her hair in his long hand.

He smiled and his turquoise eyes were full of thoughts.

Gracefully, he bowed his head, then, and climbed through the window. And he lowered himself on the windmill's rope as 50 marmosets still huddled in her room, shivering and looking up at her.

She heard a strange thunder rising, coming from all directions.

"The Queen must reach the King!" Toy hissed as he emerged snow-white from her boot, and the marmosets parted as the serpent passed across the floor to her.

Toy climbed Neuvia's arm and coiled around her neck as she slipped on her moccasins. She took Gieron's scepter in her hand and climbed onto the ladder.

The iron bell was clanging as she rode the swaying ladder to the ground and found the beaver waiting for her, holding Pigg's elk.

She reached out a fearless hand and stroked the beaver's head.

He spluttered a toothy chortle and trotted through the trembling woods to repair his dam.

She mounted the elk and urged it slightly, and it sprang toward the Lightstone Tower.

She found the main path, and flew south down the overgrown avenue.

The bells and chimes clashed like a pitched battle around her, their tones overlapping in a menacing drone. Riding radiant through the forest, her hair blown like a storm, Toy at her throat, and black lines of soot inscribing her naked body, Neuvia held Gieron's golden scepter high as the Spell of Protection rang clear in her mind. She saw the light at the end of the path and spurred the good elk forward, gripping its antlers to keep it steady.

When she reached the edge of the forest, she saw Trinadol in his red robe passing over the broken gate of the Tower's stairway.

The trees and clouds tore open as she emerged on the rumbling sun-smitten field and the elk did not lose its footing on the undulating ground as the marble statues of Poladoris Martharr toppled from their pedestals around her.

Trinadol ascended the stairs to the Tower as cracks streaked the stone around him.

The stampeding flock of sheep headed Neuvia off from Trinadol on the far side of the greensward and she spurred her leaping mount, hoping to beat them to the stairs.

A moan rose from the Lightstone Tower as it rippled in the sky.

The bleating charge of sheep sped ahead of her at the finish line of their race and she pulled back, cursing, as a chasm opened in the field and devoured the entire flock in a single swallow. Steam walled off her view of Trinadol on the stairs above.

The terrorized elk threw her and fled across the field.

The wall of steam dissipated as the gaping crack wrenched wider. Then she saw him sitting in the middle of the stairway above.

The stoneworks were cracking and falling away around him, even as pieces of the Dimmrock sheered off its shores and slashed into the sea.

The blue horizon climbed higher around them.

The island was sinking.

* * *

Chapter 16

Checkmate

He pointed the Scepter at the quavering Tower—but the Cronus Star was cold, his power bled. Trinadol slumped on the steps as the red steam subsided and only then did he see her, on the other side of the yawning crack. "It is you!" he gasped.

She met his eyes and sighed.

"You were here?" he cried.

"You never saw me!"

"Did I see you *there?*"

"Yes! It was I, my Love. Run to the Tower! Meet me *there* again before it is too late!"

Another wall of steam vented angry red eddies, and she raised the scepter of Gieron, incanting the Spell of Protection.

And it was the very sounds, so enunciated, that seemed to set in motion an agreement between light, the diamond, the Ring of Queen, the sky, and the trembling earth below, combing these forces into a channel of power that poured forth in purple light from her scepter's stone into the tip of the Lightstone Tower, and the Tower was set aglow like a candle.

The Tower's high-pitched drone was muffled, and made to seem distant, though the ground still shook beneath it. The lavender arch of light shifted then, pouring into the quaking gorge that opened between them.

Deep into the Dimmrock's roots did her nourishing will flow, binding, mending, and fusing the rock, so that the Dimmrock itself was calmed and brought from the brink.

But the broken piece of the Dimmrock upon which Trinadol stood slid away from the island even as the light in her scepter faded, leaving her spent and pale.

She fell to her knees and looked over the chasm as two foaming waves rolled slowly as though made of oil into the rift below. Four hundred feet down they smashed into each other and a thunder of mist blasted into the sky. A gravelly roar grated under the new channel as the new island slid into the frothing sea.

"Run to the Tower!" Neuvia cried to him.

"I will not!" His voice echoed over the gorge between them. He clung to the cracking marble stairs of the Tower.

"You will be safe!"

"My love, my love! What kept us apart?"

"I waited too long!" she cried.

"I deserve to die!"

"How dare you say it?"

He jumped down the steps, as though to leap into the abyss before her eyes. He stumbled and rolled, catching hold on the brink.

"Go to the Tower," she cried. "Or I shall hate you forever!"

He climbed onto the last step. "I betrayed you!" he said. "I betrayed everything!"

"It's the fear you began with! Save yourself!"

"Alas, I will! But only for you." He turned and lunged over the last steps even as they crumbled under his feet, and he hugged the edge of broken rock, pulling himself onto the marble verandah.

He looked at her one last time, and then ran through the doors of the Lightstone Tower, which slammed closed behind him, shimmering with the purple seal of Neuvia's magic.

* * *

The southern shore of the Dimmrock continued to slide into the sea as the sun sank into a bloody cloud on the west horizon.

Neuvia sat in the grass at the Dimmrock's smoking edge, weak and dazed as she watched the waves breach the cliffs around the Lightstone Tower and roll against the stoneworks. The sea gradually filled the courtyard and then closed over the verandah, lapping around the base of the Tower itself.

Dusk fell, and she could still see the weak red light of Trinadol's Scepter corkscrewing through the Tower as it descended. A long wake streamed behind the pinnacle as it slid down the deep trench between the Dimmrock and the southern reefs.

With sudden speed, the pinnacle was swallowed up, just as the glow of Trinadol's scepter reached the top of the Tower.

Night fell, and she could see no trace of the Tower in the dark sea. The stars raked the sky above and the silver crescent of the First Moon rose before she shook herself. "Toy, what shall I do?" She bowed her head. "I waited too long."

"He is safe. Go home and join him in *Wynder!*"

She sobbed as she ran across the field to find her secret home, which, alas, she had hidden too well from him.

*   *   *

Clutching the bloody Scepter, he fell on his bed into ferocious nightmares that seemed a sanctuary from the awful truth.

When Trinadol woke he did not know how long he had been asleep, or even if he had been sleeping. In the dark, he made out a dappled blue radiance edging the chamber.

Was he in *Wynder?*

The room was tilted and only his desk and chair stood upright in the center of the floor. The four windows were shuttered. The air was bitter cold. He stared through the ceiling till his eyes penetrated it.

He saw a fine gold filigree of cloud high up in the sky. Then he knew that it was not cloud but currents on the surface of the sea, hundreds of feet above him.

Dawn was coming.

He covered his eyes.

The Cronus Star turned black over his heart and the Scepter turned so cold it burned his hands.

He dropped it on the silken carpet as he sat on his bed, dumbstruck.

By degrees, he became aware that someone else was present in the room with him.

A hulking, umber ghost with 30 avid eyes appeared sitting in his chair by his desk, and it grinned with seven greedy mouths at Trinadol. All seven mouths frowned, then, and all 30 eyes closed. *"I am Drugor, sad King,"* he whispered.

Trinadol felt his heart seize and his sinews freeze.

The phantom played with the six black nipples on his crimson chest with his nine-fingered hands. *"I am the Khalwairn General of Nekkros, Drugor Enalis Akiol, slayer of* Elwyn, *your mother* Conilair *when she bore you into this world, your doltish father* Senadol *who spent his years gawking at the future, and even your bastard brother whom you will never know. And when you are gone, your grandfather's curse shall finally be lifted and I shall be set free. For when the last of* **Elwyn**'s *bloodline runs out, so will his curse. You never did solve your riddle, did you now, young King?"*

Trinadol could not form a single word with his white breath.

"I called you in the Serrid Strait...*Do you remember? I surprised you, hiding in the diamond crown of an ancient* Winteg. *I would have had you then, for you would have found the crown and tried it on. But the Gairanor intervened and sent a wave to bring you away, and I followed, filling your sail all the way to the* Dimmrock. *I tricked the Gairanor into thinking I was the ghost of the* Winteg

king. *I was the wind that tore* Senadol's *stubborn grip from* Hala *that night. He had a few words for you at the end. That riddle he left you. You never found that riddle's answer, I guess...?"*

Trinadol stared at him in frozen dread.

"What was the thing closest to Trinadol's *heart?"* Drugor *mused. "Do you know that now—at the end? I think I know."*

Trinadol did not know, even now.

"Have you thought, perhaps, it was your vainglory, young Gheldron?" Drugor *suggested. "Your dearest love of power?"* He snorted. *"It was your insatiable lust for stones of magic, after all, that troubled your own teachers. It was destined to bring about your destruction! You gave up all else when you got your hands on the* Scepter."

Trinadol nodded, persuaded easily by this verdict.

"Yes, yes," Drugor *laughed softly. "Such honesty befits a* Gheldron! *But perhaps, O King, I am wrong? For surely, it was not lust for power but love for your Queen that kept you here, always fighting to get back to* Wynder. *The Queen was ever closest to your heart, after all, and 'twas she you followed to this grim end."*

Trinadol trembled, numb before this demon's reason.

"Or was it for love of **Ameulas** *that you banished yourself, fearing that you would harm your fair realm?"*

Trinadol felt himself acquiescing to each suggestion in the slow chaos of his mind.

"Or none of these? Was your love of Wynder *dearest to your heart? Surely you sacrificed* Hala *for your precious moments in that dream-world and now lo, and behold...here are the wages of that sinful trade!"*

Trinadol felt a helplessness he never imagined with the power of the stars in his veins, for this phantom was invincibly confident and trifling, it seemed, with his complicated heart as though it were a toy made out of glass. "Alas, Demon! Are you playing a game?"

Drugor laughed, flashing his 91 ruby fangs. *"Your conceit is complete—innocence itself! But have you not thought, righteous King, that your dearest love is the secret you fear most of all? Perhaps your deepest love is of evil, righteous King! It was, after all, your lust to harm this* Hala World *with fiery violence that has left you isolated and doomed. Behold the horror you have wrought!"*

Trinadol was pale as a corpse before the glistening ghost who peeled his flesh with scornful omniscience, and he nodded in shame.

Drugor clapped his broad hands once, and laughed. *"Vain fool! 'Twas not* Ameulas *nor* Wynder *nor* Neuvia *nor power nor evil that were dearest to you, poor* Trinadol*,"* he sneered. *"I had only to cast one aspersion on your young soul, one stain on a stone, and your closest love, your consuming love, your crowning love of goodness, proud King, made you give up all, including yourself! Only one who loves goodness more than all else would worry that his soul was full of sin and sentence himself to life in exile! An evil man would not care, indeed would require victims. I had merely to hint what evil you might cause, in any direction that you turned, and you closed the trap upon yourself, my most dull* Gheldron*! You held onto your moral pride lest it be spotted with any sin, whilst the walls grew taller around your freedom, your love, alas, your very life. You gave up all the world lest you bruise your precious honor. And you gave the world to me."*

Drugor noticed Trinadol had stopped trembling.

"You are evil," murmured Trinadol.

Drugor laughed. *"Indeed, my* Hala *child! That is the very power I have over this world. Whilst the good wonder, doubting their own hearts, I reach in, take all, and laugh in their amazed faces as I demand more, and point the finger of blame at them! Their hesitation, the moment when they consider right and wrong—that, my sad idealist, is the moment I use to slash their throats, steal them blind, take their wives and make them my slaves! Can you not see it? Even now?"* Drugor looked with awesome pity at him.

"You are evil," repeated Trinadol, as though it were a revelation.

Drugor's mouths frowned. *"Hala is not my home,"* he explained, feeling generous. *"I cannot abide its sluggish matter always grounding my winged whims. The largeness of my dreams is impossible here. It is impossible for me to survive by men's petty rules or nature's stingy laws. Hala was made to be sacrificed to my desires. Indeed, it is curious and gratifying how easy it is to convince mortals of this. Truly, this notion of morality might be your greatest strength, but it is your greatest weakness, too. The conscience you value so much is a beast that is easily burdened."*

"How long can you survive by preying on virtue, like the parasite upon its host?" Trinadol looked at *Drugor* anew.

"I am the predator, cleverer, faster, stronger, and you are my prey. Somewhere men are always amassing loot for me to plunder."

"We are more than you," said Trinadol, meeting his many eyes now. "Or you would not need us."

"Bah!"

"You feed on the virtue of men," said Trinadol. "Without it there would be nothing to steal, except men's meat and bones, and that would not get you far. Without virtue you are nothing. Yet you are the greatest threat to virtue. You must live in terror, dull demon. You are the worst enemy of everything that sustains you and gives you whatever purpose that you have." Trinadol smiled and his eyes blazed as he looked at *Drugor*. His mind cleared for the first time in many years.

"Ah! A sharp tongue. A philosophic mind. Good brains that I shall find useful when you die and they are mine! Then your dear Ameulas, *that you were so afraid to harm, will see a new*

king. Where you hesitated, I will seek out ways to cause it agony. I have no doubts about my soul, as do you. I, good sir, am pure. You are the one so easily thrown into doubt."

A bright peace settled over Trinadol's heart, an abiding sense of his power that was without any shadow of guilt, like the sun itself. Goodness must and would overcome this villain's victory, even if his own life were lost. It made him strong to know he would die soon; it made him fearless. "Hide, now, inside a doorway," smiled Trinadol, waving his hand as though he could fan *Drugor* away like smoke. "Lest you be seen by the watching Gairanor. They will see you soon, old ghost!"

Drugor bared his teeth in livid wrath to hear Trinadol invoke their name. *"They won't see me in the* Cronus Star,*"* he said.

"Much may be said of evil's strengths, its sure strokes, its swift mind, its simplicity. But one thing is sure: it has no future that is not full of horror."

"The centuries won't save you, Cirilen.*"*

"Good lives on in ways evil cannot destroy."

Drugor snorted phantom flames. *"That is more false than you know. And pain is less punishment than you believe."*

"The good is remembered."

"Less than you know."

"Evil destroys its future."

"The good may have the future."

"The good is truth. You cannot escape it."

"The truth is what I make it, until I stop."

Trinadol laughed. "Until it stops you."

"It won't matter then."

"All is against you."

"I am against all."

"Is it anger, Demon? What grievous pain has the world done you?"

"You'd vest me with a conscience now?" Drugor recoiled and lashed Trinadol with contemptuous laughter.

"I know something of your dilemma, Demon," said Trinadol. "For what I have done is evil, and so I have some kinship with you, if not much. I have pitted myself against all, and all against myself. And in so doing, I condemned myself. You have done the same."

"Your council is deliciously comic. Don't forget how you were bested!"

"That is the very council I would give you."

"Well. Before the Gairanor spy me through this wall of sea, mad King, it's time I retire to the Cronus Star and await your death in safety. While your corpse is fresh, I will take it for mine. And I then will walk the earth as you."

Trinadol eyed *Drugor* inquisitively. "This Cronus Star was a fine home, I imagine?"

"Indeed, it has suited my needs quite nicely." Drugor studied him slyly out of a hundred squinting eyes.

"Where did you hide in the stone? I never saw you," Trinadol mused, with an air of morbid curiosity. "The chair was always empty."

"I was the chair."

Trinadol nodded, and then he raised the Scepter. It glittered for a moment between them, reflecting in *Drugor's* hundred eyes. Then, on the naked *lightstone* floor at the edge of the carpet, he smashed the diamond, and an explosion of light and sound severed past from present. The Cronus Star tumbled in seven fragments on the snowy carpet at *Drugor's* feet, and the world was forever different with the loss of that stone.

"Now, Demon," Trinadol said. "You have no home."

Drugor looked in awe at the shattered diamond.

"The Gairanor will see you soon even here beneath the sea," said Trinadol. "Before I die, at least. And they will seal Elwyn's curse. We shall both be destroyed, together, when their mighty blow comes down to scatter you from both the realms."

In warring silence the two stared into each other's eyes, testing the certainty there and finding it ever more challenging.

At last, *Drugor* whispered, *"Checkmate."*

Trinadol scoffed.

"Sad King," said *Drugor, "I may hide inside your grandfather's tower. It is wondrous that way." Drugor* actually looked sorrowful for a moment. *"And now you have no diamond. My trap is only now complete. I saw this last in a dream—you would doom yourself, if it meant my doom. If you thought the* Cronus Star *was my only refuge, you would destroy it. In truth, I thought it the single flaw in my stratagem. For with the* **Scepter**...*well! No matter. When you are dead, the last of your grandfather's issue will be gone and his curse will be lifted. Since I will take your body, you will never reach your precious Gairanor. And know that once I have conquered* Ameulas, *I will take an army of dead* Ameulentians *to vanquish* Trillan, *which I will be able to see, at last, with your* Cirilen *eyes. The* Cirilen's *reign on* Hala *will come to an end and everyone will assume that I am you. Even the Gairanor, and your father, mother and grandfather, will never be sure that I am not! Then I shall sire a new breed of Khalwairn-*Cirilen, *and we will rule* Hala, *forever. Good night, brief king."*

Drugor's specter drained away into the shadows of his chamber.

Trinadol looked down at the shards of the Cronus Star scattered on the carpet and wondered what color his true soul may have been inside it. The finality and totality of his trap dawned on him in every direction as far as his mind could see.

The sun's groping green fingers reached down and tipped the Tower with sunbeams.

The sea became brilliant, and he saw creatures swimming and, silhouetted high above, he saw wandering shoals of fish followed by sharks, like lions.

Then he thought he saw a boat, a tiny mote on the surface of the sea.

He aimed his spyglass through the ceiling: *Stargazer* was tossing on the waves above!

She dropped her anchor and it flashed, far, far out of his reach. He sighed, lowering his spyglass and staring at the shattered star on the carpet.

What a splendid world he had lost, he thought, as though the universe had pierced him, converging from all directions upon his center. It was from this world he shunned that he must ask salvation now. Now he must believe in hope, instead of doom. Now, alas!

And yet, untroubled, he opened his arms to the glorious sight all around him, for it was not hard to believe in the good of Hala now, as it was no longer hard to believe in the good inside himself.

He took a sharp fragment of the Cronus Star in his hand and walked to the north window overlooking the ruined stairway and courtyard, obscured in dim fathoms below.

He opened the shutter as Neuvia's magic held back the sea.

He sat on the deep silk carpet, crossing his legs. Pressing the sharp fragment of diamond to his forehead, he closed his eyes, and a bead of blood painted a line down his nose to his lips where it spread right and left.

When he opened his eyes he saw shoals of red minnows, packs of yellow tuna, wings of green turtles, and circling squads of opalescent squid gathering around the radiant pinnacle from across the undersea world. Two mighty black whales even stared through the wall at him.

He threw the chip of the Cronus Star through the purple window and it left a milky scar behind it in the water.

With a pop of light it vanished, and, as if they were scalded, the myriad creatures scattered in the sea.

*　　　　　*　　　　　*

Chapter 17

▼

A Message Heard

The sun was red at dawn as the sailors gripped callused hands on the trawl to haul their livelihood from the deep.

The sea was soft, oily and gray, embossed with fuzzy red smiles and frowns on that misty morning. The net rose from briny fathoms and the shoal of minnows glimmered red under the gray water.

The pink-and-silver fish shattered the surface. Flipping and pounding, the catch spilled over the taffrail from the trawl, rising up to the men's knees in seconds. They yelled as they shoved and gaffed the fish into the open sea doors, filling the ice-lined hold in a building, quickening rhythm.

The mates of the *Barnacle* grinned at each other as they rounded up the stragglers and gathered in the net.

The *Barnacle* was a far drop from Captain Bik Bohtum's previous vessel that had shipped 25 men, 18 of which had to be let go after Blox's dock tax was levied. Bik's last boat was called the *Oyster*, and she had drafted 25 tons and sported four sails, two of which had been designed by Nil Ramesis and had given the *Oyster* the edge in reaching the Early Market.

Times certainly had changed in the last long year. Storm after storm had stricken Gwylor, hiding the sun through summer, fall, winter and spring. The rain had eroded the roads and churned the sea. A different spirit seemed to inhabit the city since Blox had become mayor.

His taxes were scandalous, but enforced on pain of imprisonment and hard labor. Gold had fled the city, and Blox made noises about starting a national currency, with a value he and his administration would set, stamped in tin, to finally eliminate "this pestilent gold," as he referred to it, which to his mind was too ridiculously scarce a commodity to base an entire nation's business upon, a preposterous limitation on his power that seemed to thwart him at every turn. Through his various machinations the new mayor of Gwylor was busily prying the destiny of the Ameulentians out of their hands, a little more every day.

If Bik's *Barnacle* was a modest ship compared to his *Oyster*, she was sturdy and kept tidy by her proud crew of black sheep. Bik traditionally hired down-and-outers, out-of-towners and up-and-comers, believing them hungrier than the wealthy young men who came to him thirsting for salt and romance on the sea. "Stick with me and you'll earn a hearth and home for your name, and a wife and children to carry it on," he was fond of daring prospective recruits, and those eager young pikes who took his bait, men whose fathers had made no name for them, soon found they had a friend and reliable living out of Bik Bohtum. Bik performed their weddings and was godfather to their babes, as well as a father over their vices and a mother over their injuries.

One of Bik's "sons" had been Nil Ramesis, who was perhaps most dear to him from all the crews he had tended like litters of puppies over the years. Nil had not betrayed the name of his house when he signed on, and indeed after it became known to Bik that he was of Castle Martharr, Nil insisted that he make his own name, Ramesis, for his own house, and be given no advantage on another man's name. Bik took special pride in this disciplined shipmate who turned out to be a prince—for Nil had wanted to start on the same deck as the rest. Though Nil had moved on to bigger things, he had never looked down at Bik or his former mates.

"We caught a terrapin, Cappy!" cried one sailor who held onto a sea turtle rowing its paddles on the slippery deck.

Captain Bohtum closed the sea doors, wiping the white swirls of hair from his sweaty brow. "What?" he grunted, and he looked at the green turtle the sailor had in tow, and he smiled, flashing his pearly teeth in his white beard. "A sign of good luck, lads! Terrapins are the bringers of good fortune, don'tcha know!"

"Hurrah! The *Barnacle*'s blessed!" shouted buck-toothed Ed, from atop the bridge.

"I think she's been catched before! Someone's etched their diddy on her back, Cappy, parchment-like, and such!" said Larby.

"What! What are you thinkin', boy? Gimme a look-see!"

Captain Bohtum's boots pounded the deck as he went to inspect the beast.

"It's on her shell! Maybe I can't read, but that's writin', Cappy, fer sure! Ain't it?"

"Move aside, Larby!" Captain Bohtum seized the edges of the turtle and looked at its shell. "Thunderous squalls! Yer right as rain, laddy! P'raps a castaway scratched it in!" After a moment, he looked up at his crew with wide eyes.

"What's it say, Cappy?"

"Well, I can't quite believe it, boys. Let me chew it awhile."

The men gathered around as the captain moved his lips silently, his great mane hanging around his ruddy face and over the boulder of his back. At last he let loose the turtle and it grabbed on the deck, paddling toward the transom. There was a dumbstruck look in his topaz eyes and some of the crew thought he may have seen the ghost of his long-departed wife, once again.

"What's the matter, Cappy?" shouted Ed from the bridge, screwing his head to see.

"Lads, clew the canvas and drop the stone. We've got a mighty care to tend to right away, and no delay!"

"Drop the stone?"

"The market! The market!" shouted Ed. Captain Bohtum never let anything interfere with beating the other captains to market.

Bik waved a hand. "It's a heavier care we've got than the Early Market, lads! Do as I say, and the sooner you'll know the whys and wherefores. Now, by Lightning! And you'd better beat the thunder!" he growled.

And the men, hardly believing their ears, jumped to action only after his familiar command.

* * *

Just past noon, Bik hitched his piebald mare to a wagon and drove her from his driveway over rutted roads down the foothills east of Gwylor proper.

The seventh in a succession of storms was just moving in over the bay, and the slate clouds drizzled as Bik banged the wagon over the pot-holed cobblestone streets of the city. He took side streets he favored because they had weathered the storms, the ones rimmed by the pink-flowered oaks that showed their fall blossoms despite the gray season. Bik crossed the bridge built by Tormerick Martharr over the Thurnal River that split Gwylor and then he turned south onto Gieron Way.

He finally came to Bartering Square, which was really a circle nearly half a mile wide around which Gieron Way split, curving on ramparts that met again on the south side of the "square."

Bik turned right and passed around the western edge of Bartering Square. Before the square's northern wall were three rounded stone terraces, two at the lower level and a taller one in the center. It was from this top terrace that the King or the Mayor addressed the citizenry as his voice echoed off the curving wall at his back.

Below the square, Bik went south on Gieron Way across the estuary to the old embarcadero, where he turned west.

Bik saw some of Blox's monks ahead, dressed in burlap and surrounded by members of the Gwylorian Guard in their tattered red-and-gold uniforms that were more decorative than durable after centuries of ceremonial purpose. They were thrashed by heavy duty now, for the Guard had been pressed into service as strong-arms for the righteous young monks who roamed the streets looking for people and things to fine, penalize, and condemn. Bik was careful not to scowl in their direction.

The West Shore was the low-rent seafront; its coast was rocky and its buildings less fashionable than those east of Gieron Way. Nil Ramesis owned a small shipyard here that was wedged between a cliff on the west and a brick warehouse on its east. In the center of the property was a natural gorge in a broad rampart of rock that reached out into the sea. A squared, sloping channel had been fashioned out of this gorge, filled with placid seawater. At the end of this long pit were huge wooden sea doors that kept back the waves. The great launch was too large to serve the needs of most shipyards, which favored several smaller launches, yet it was perfect for the considerable vessel Nil Ramesis was wrighting.

Bik arrived at the shipyard and found a tall, solid fence with a locked gate covering the only narrow view of the ship beyond. The boathouse looked like no more than a storefront, and one that had gone out of business, like so many others on this road.

After hitching the wagon to a rail, Bik entered the front door carrying the terrapin's shell wrapped in one of his tunics.

A brass bell clanked. Bik set down the shell and stood with his cap in his hand, his huge mane of white hair spilling over the shoulders of his charcoal greatcoat.

The room was empty and built of bare planks, but it was warm, as though someone had just been there. A door was not quite closed on the other side of the room. "'Tis Bik!" he said. "Bik Bohtum! Captain of the *Barnacle!*"

"Then come in and stop yer hollerin', Bik Bohtum!" hollered a gravelly voice.

Bik recognized the voice of Lince Neery-Atton and grinned.

"Come on in," said the voice, yet nobody appeared in the doorway to greet him.

Bik strode through the door and Lince grabbed him from behind around his shoulders, and only a man such as Lince could have cinched Bik Bohtum in such a grip. Both men giggled like schoolboys even as they struggled, and soon the armlock became an embrace and a few stout pounds on the back.

"Lince, you limpid-assed, bow-legged, bottom-scraping fraud of a philanderin' dogfish—how be you?"

"Well, hullo there, Barnacle Bik!" Lince grinned a scimitar's slash. The blue eye tattooed on his shiny bald head had faded from sunburns since Bik last saw him, but it still kept its heavenward vigil.

Bik punched Lince on the ham of his arm with his chop-sized fist. "Don't be bad-mouthin' the *Barnacle* or I'll be swabbin' her bilge with yer gut-whiskers, Neery-Atton!" Bik warned.

"Aye, come along then. What's the story? Yer not bringin' fried chicken and beer. What pries you out of yer oyster, Bik? And what's that you brought us, in yonder room?"

Bik only now recognized this office, with its many-paned window that overlooked the shipyard, but he had not seen what was in the window before. "I'll be sunk! What in the world is Nil wrighting! A whale, is it?" A great vessel was draped in a patchwork of tarps.

"Aye, a sea monster is the *Sea Mare*." Lince had a way of screwing his head away from a person and cranking his eyebrows to glare from a sinister angle and this, whether Lince knew it or not, tilted the tattoo on the top of his head just slightly enough to give a third look at the subject of his scrutiny. "You'll be beggin' to buff her decks with yer belly-whiskers, Bik Bohtum, aye, ya miserable bunglefish! Now, what in Hala is that thing you brought us in yonder room?"

Bik fetched it and lugged it in. "It's something—"

"I've a feeling it should be said away from that street that seems so loaded down with ears of late!" Lince winked. He reached out and hoisted the turtle shell. "Close the curtains and follow me."

Bik drew the dark drapes across the window and followed Lince through the far door.

The door opened onto a covered wooden stairway to another door that opened into a large, odd-shaped warehouse built of stone quarried from the cliff that overshadowed the western border of the yard. The wooden roof was pitched, and covered with tarred canvas. Cheap and strange was the building, though it seemed sturdy and well laid out. Lumber, rope, canvas, barrels of pine sap, tar and a number of shop areas equipped with lathes and other tools were scattered across the cascading floors of the boathouse. Several windows were spaced along the east wall overlooking the ship that was under construction. The yardhouse seemed like a many-decked ship, this being the aft deck—which was Nil Ramesis's office. Bik recognized Nil sitting at his desk, like a captain, writing vigorously by the light of a lantern.

Nil looked around from the kerosene glow. He set down his quill in its stand and swiveled in his chair, gripping its arms as he looked at his former captain. They appraised each other wordlessly.

Nil put his hands on the knees of his dark gray breeches and heaved his tall and trim frame up. His eyes were winter-blue beside a fierce, chiseled nose pointing over his strong jaw, bearded in rich black coils. His lips had a stern downturn, and his cheeks the challenge of endurance. He was taller than his elders, if not broader, and his features were as fierce as one of Poladoris Martharr's sculptures or one of Senjessi Tillow's canvases. Indeed, Nil had been the model, without his knowledge, for both those artists' works, having grown up before their eyes in Castle Martharr.

As he built his ship and word got out among the loyalists of Ameulas, the weight of the nation had rested more and more heavily on Nil's shoulders. He knew that by taking on this burden, however, he had lost the love that would have made any burden bearable. His feelings had become too irreconcilable for him to feel over the last year, and he applied himself mechanically to each successive task before him, as though the skills and virtues of his character had become nothing but a complicated machine that he could switch on painlessly and joylessly. One would never know from looking in the young mariner's calm and steady eyes what dilemmas tried his soul.

"What brings you here today, Cappy?" smiled Nil.

"Why—after seeing that beautiful beast in the window and her splendid captain, I nearly forgot, Nilly! Someday, when the tarps are pulled off her, I'd like to see if there's a ship under there and not a mountain of rumors!"

Nil chuckled. "I could use an extra pair of eyes to light her decks—she's coming out of a fog as it is, Bik."

"Bah! You've got my eyes at your service from this day forward, and the crew of the *Barnacle* for extra hands, and all out of my own pocket." Bik leaned forward, cocking his topaz eye at Nil and then at Lince. "Trinadol's sent the word, at last. And not a week's delay if he's to be saved!"

Bik pulled the shirt off the turtle's shell.

* * *

Tecwyn and Acceber bayed as Nil's black stallion, Indigo, neighed outside the castle doors. They were mountain hounds with opal eyes and long fur like maple syrup. Lelinair glared at them, hating them for loving and missing Nil so much. She hated them for being free to howl, aloud and innocent, expressing a love that betrayed her own. "*Shhh!*" she hissed. They turned their heads to catch her withering look, and ran skulking toward the door, wagging their tails as the porter raised the bolts.

Nil slipped through the door and exchanged a few jovial sarcasms about the weather with Rumbard, the porter, as she watched from the doorway. She had visited the larder for a cup of warm milk to help her sleep and was padding back in her deerskin slippers and mink-lined robe when the dogs had bolted past her.

Nil had not visited in many weeks, cloistered with his suicidal pursuits in his insane shipyard, which she could see from the Even Tower through the powerful spyglass there. She scoffed and took a step back in the corridor that led to the castle armory. A tear suddenly, weakly, she thought, sprang from her eye and splashed on her lip. She tasted it, swallowed it.

She opened her hand, and looked at the piece of *lightstone* that she had hurled from the Even Tower a year ago. She had searched for the crystal for three weeks in the rain and then, when the clouds broke for a moment, a pink ray fell on the grass near the temple, and she had seen it. She ran down and plucked the half-pebble, like a flower off the grass, and shook off the rain, holding it to her breast.

Ten years after breaking the pebble, her half was now grown twice its original size. The fracture looked impossibly intricate and exaggerated now, and she could not see how her half could ever fit Nil's half again. But still, she had kept it.

Nil rolled the hounds with his outstretched arms as roared like a bear as he lowered to his knee and let them plaster his beard with a few adroit licks. "Up!" he said, lifting his arms, and they stood up on their hind legs until Nil brought down his hands. "Good girls," he said as he produced a boiled hamhock for each of them, which were wrapped in paper and stuffed into his pockets of his coat.

It was past midnight. What was he doing here? Lelinair wondered. What would possess him to take Indigo out on a night like this, with the roads treacherous and sliding into the sea?

Nil saw her by the candle that she had forgotten she was holding, and he called to her and strode quickly toward her.

"Lelinair! Wake Poladoris and Teldon. We have news from Trinadol that is most urgent! Go now. There's no time to tell it twice!" Nil squeezed her shoulders, and it was purely for Ameulas that he urged her, and she allowed it for that reason only and hurried up the stairs to the upper rooms. But she felt bitterness tugging her feet, as any duty to save the world seemed only to mock her.

Nil and Rumbard lit a few lamps in the conservatory, stoked the fires, and made coffee and brandy ready as Lelinair rallied the august house to wakefulness.

*   *   *

Senjessi and his wife Merania had been staying at Castle Martharr since the attack. Some of Blox's hired thugs had waylaid Senjessi, at last, on his way home nearly a year ago. They pinned the old artist down and cut his right hand from his wrist. Though it had been a dark day, indeed, for Ameulas, the Nekkrosites had openly celebrated the deed, for they had proclaimed Senjessi's art evil.

Senji had survived, however, thanks to his young wife's quick resourcefulness. Yet the tool of his soul had been stolen away from him. Merania was his right hand now, and she completed her tutelage by finishing her husband's masterpiece in one of the castle's great rooms. Merania felt his desire in her hand, steering her strokes in his style, and thus, both their spirits had survived Blox's savage blow.

The midnight company rubbed eyes and tied robes, with Senjessi and Merania leading the drowsy crowd.

Old Poladoris looked especially groggy, and bushy-haired Teldon yawned as they straggled behind. Last, diminutive and dour-faced, came the Queen Mother. She wore an elaborate sleeping hat over her high-braided hair arrangement, and a blue, white, and red silk robe. Nardleen had at last accepted the habits of royalty, and wore them well. She was a practical woman beneath the regal trappings, legitimizing them somehow instead of the reverse. She chose the chair next to Lelinair near the fire, and the others fanned out before the hearth.

Rumbard the porter served them coffee and brandy.

Poladoris growled, "Why in Hala did you wake us up, Nil?"

Everyone else grunted.

"Forgive me, lord," Nil said, "but I must ask you all to forget sleep, for the moment. Word has come from Trinadol that he is trapped in Elwyn's Tower under the sea. Trapped in the Lightstone Tower beneath the sea, I say again for foggy minds, the King even now barely clings to his life!"

"How came you by this news?" asked Senjessi.

Nil produced a package from his pocket, unwrapped the paper and showed them all a red minnow. The scorched letters of Trinadol's message were clearly visible on its silvery scales. "Sea creatures bearing the King's message have been found. This fish was caught by one of my men from the Lightstone Jetty today. Another message was emblazoned on the back of a sea turtle. The word has been passed among the captains and dock masters that any like messages be disposed of at sea, lest one of Blox's eyes might see it. Trinadol claims he has been tricked by an ancient enemy, just as Artimeer said!"

"Let me see!" said Senjessi. Nil handed the fish to him and he took it with his left hand. "Nil is right! Trinadol says he was tricked to his doom by *Drugor* himself!" cried Senjessi.

"You shouldn't say that word, Senji," said Merania.

"Captain Bohtum has donated his crew and put out the word for other volunteers," said Nil. "We should have a few dozen new hands, I would wager, by the time I return. We are working through the night and need materials of all kinds to finish the *Sea Mare*."

Lelinair gasped. "No!"

"Yes," said Poladoris, glancing crossly at his daughter. "Do you think she'll be seaworthy in time, Nil?"

"With help."

"Don't worry about that," said Senjessi. "I will give you enough gold tonight to buy much of what you need."

"And I will send men with you tonight with enough gold to cover the rest for now, and tomorrow many will avail their gold and services to the *Sea Mare*," said Poladoris.

"No one can know all of it. Blox can hear none of it. The Council…" Nil shook his head.

"The Council tomorrow!" Poladoris nodded, reminded only now. "We shall all attend, and we shall not show a sign of what we know. Our best chance is if Blox never knows what we know."

"Then let us retire and look well-rested tomorrow," said Senjessi. "We know what to do."

"I'm going back to the shipyard," said Nil. "I will meet you all on the southern verandah of the Council Hall, by the skull of Knot."

"You're going back tonight? You'll break your neck!" said Lelinair. "You idiotic…idiot!"

Nil looked at her with faint surprise. "Indigo will take care of me. The second coin gilds the way through the cloud now. Can you arrange for your couriers, lord?"

"Yes. Rumbard, go rouse the Stablemaster and have him pick his best horsemen."

Rumbard, the plump old porter, left with a wave.

"I will have the gold brought down to you. Go make sure your horse is watered and not warming up too much. Better yet, take my new charger, Star."

"Yes, I will, and many thanks, lord. Indigo probably misses his stable. And Lelinair." Nil smiled at her.

She smiled back for a tiny moment. "I will not stand for this!" she cried, looking away.

"Lelinair!" cried Poladoris. "What in Hala is chewing your toes? For the love of Ameulas, we must all do what we can! You as well, as a Council member, tomorrow!"

"I will not do a single thing to aid in Nil's suicide, even if it means letting this whole rotting country fall down in ruins!"

Poladoris gasped. "Lelinair! You could never mean it!"

"Ameulas be damned if she would take him from me! I will not sign your death warrant, Nil Ramesis! It is I who should be Lelinair Ramesis, Father, and not Nil who should be Nil Martharr! Don't you know it?" She wept, a thing her father could not recall ever seeing, and she ran from the conservatory.

Poladoris gave Nil a puzzled look.

"You old fool," Senjessi muttered.

"What's that?" Poladoris pointed at Senji.

"It's before your eyes for twenty years, and it's not enough to bore through that thick brain?" The old painter shook his head pitifully.

"Yes…wait…Senjessi, if you suspected, why did you never mention it? I am cross that you did not!"

"Nil never showed it, but Lelinair did," said Senjessi. "A woman doesn't avoid looking or speaking to a man for ten years unless she loves him like happiness itself."

"Oh, Nil showed it, all right," confirmed Nardleen with a chuckle.

"I never saw it…"

"Father, it is true!" said Nil, bending to one knee. "What Senji and the Queen Mother have perceived you have not. I forsook your name, and I regret you never knew it was because I love Lelinair, and not because I disown you! I love her, and I have always meant to have her, whatever the cost. I have tried to make my own name—but, alas! Now it's poison to her lips."

"Am I dreaming? So do dreams in the middle of the night reveal much to closed eyes. I bid you go in peace, Lord Ramesis, and with my blessing, whether you are my son by one law, or by another!" Poladoris glanced after his daughter. "I will speak to her."

"Where is the red minnow?" asked Nil. "We should burn it in the fire."

For a moment all eyes looked around the room as the hounds gnawed on their bones.

"Too late," said Senjessi. "Tecwyn must have eaten it. He's partial to fish."

"Very well." Nil paused, his coat still dripping rain and steaming with the fire at his back. "I will see you all tomorrow! Sweet sleep. Good speed!" Nil swallowed the rest of his coffee and brandy, his beard catching the drips. Then he went to Poladoris and bowed, clasping his hand.

The Queen Mother moved forward and took his hand from Poladoris.

"My lady," murmured Nil.

"Thank you, Nil Ramesis," Nardleen said, giving his hand a firm pull and kissing his brow. Then she turned and left to seek her bed as Rumbard came rushing into the room.

"Lord Martharr!" the porter cried. "Lelinair has taken Indigo! She's ridden off into the storm!"

"Blast it!" said Poladoris.

"I'll go after her," said Nil.

"No, my son. Indigo will not let her be followed if she wishes not to be found. I would not stop her—nor should you. Indigo will see no harm comes to her. You have more pressing business."

Nil left in great strides as he pulled his oilcloth topcoat over his shoulders. "Until tomorrow!" he called, and Tecwyn and Acceber groaned as he pulled the great door closed behind him.

*   *   *

Blox sat in his office in the unfinished mansion he was building for himself above the Council Hall of Gwylor. He could see the whole bay over the copper roof of the hall. Lit by intermittent lightning, pieces of the bay appeared like fragments of a great bronze shield under the menacing clouds.

The Gold Coin, now just the smallest sliver, set a southern cloud aglow in the window as morning neared.

The good Lady Martharr had retired after her long, hard ride over the highlands to Blox's mansion. He had graciously extended his hospitality to her and stabled her splendid stallion. He had other plans for the spirited and lovely Lelinair, when the time was ripe. However, she had forestalled those plans by her loyalty tonight.

On the table before Blox was a smelly red minnow.

*   *   *

A week had passed since Trinadol sent his message.

He put on a thick tiger coat from his dressing chamber and descended the spiral stair.

All the rooms and all the things in them were dusky and luminous, glowing and cold. It was somewhat soothing not to have the world plunged in red twilight anymore. Trinadol wandered with his yellow candle, poking into the forgotten libraries and bedchambers and parlors and hallways and galleries and baths, for what he knew not.

This was the extent of his world now, and he found himself curious about it, for the first time. Some rooms were strangely undisturbed and others thrown completely askew. There were knickknacks Ameulentians left behind seven years ago, reading spectacles, an opened book of court etiquette, a silver platter on which a petrified wedge of cheese and dusty crackers were arrayed. Some rooms seemed to be haunted. He heard laughs and glimpsed specters. The cold sliced through him and fear set into his bones as he ventured lower and lower in the Tower, needing now to check all the rooms to make sure no demon was lurking anywhere inside the Tower with him. When he got to the bottom, he noted with relief that it was dry.

He found himself drawn to the Throne Room.

He made his way down the curving corridor and opened the door.

A blue-green lacework of light undulated in the high walls. As he looked at the great doors, a dark crack streaked the *lightstone* over them and spouts of seawater arched onto the floor.

He cursed and set his jaw. A fuse was burning!

The highest spout grew slightly stronger, reaching farther out onto the floor.

Without the Scepter he was powerless against such forces. Without the Scepter he could not even go to *Wynderne* to see Neuvia one last time.

The waterspouts grew weaker, as though Neuvia's incantation was struggling against the awesome force of the sea. He must trust in her now...

He went to the larder and raised all the tins of food, dry goods and fresh water he would need for two months and bade them follow him in a train.

Water spread over the floor of the corridor as Trinadol reached the stairway. And as he climbed the stairs with his supplies in tow, he tried to calculate how long it would take for the sea to fill the Tower.

He deposited his provisions in the three floors below his bedchamber.

Then he climbed the ladder, and closed the heavy trap door.

Trinadol pulled back the white silk carpet and touched a fragment of the Cronus Star to the floor. A *lightstone* block glowed hot, and he crossed his legs and sat rubbing his hands over the bright stone, gazing through the ceiling at the surface of the sea, so far above. He might have a week—maybe two.

*   *   *

Chapter 18

The Council of Ameulas

A cold drizzle seeped from the rigid clouds and stained the city of Gwylor gray. The ceaseless rains seemed to have washed all colors away.

The city was built on a delta between a giant wedge of steep cliffs extending out onto the ocean. The same force that carved this valley had cut the Gulf of Gwylor, leaving palisades on either side. The southern coast was virtually uninhabited except at this great delta of the Thurnal River, where Gieron had founded the capital city of Ameulas.

From where Nil stood, he commanded a spectacular view. The marble verandah of the Council Hall glistened under him at the edge of the mighty cliff on which the hall was built. A tributary of the Thurnal River, the Feather, fell like white thunder from the cliff east of the Hall as the highlands sloughed off the unending rains.

The swollen Thurnal River threaded the city's many stone bridges below and filled the canals and the fresh water estuary dammed by the broad embarcadero. The fresh water poured from the embarcadero through hundreds of tunnels whose mouths were shaped like jolly fishes, carving channels into the long beach. The Lightstone Jetty reached out from the embarcadero, over the beach, and onto the bay for three miles; the giant sewer pipes of the city were laid alongside the jetty so that they issued into the deep sea beyond. To either side of the jetty, Nil could see the piers and wharfs reaching out over the misty bay.

"Pondering glory, Nil?" came a voice.

Nil turned, startled, to see his friend Hallot, with whom he had been schooled by Artimeer and Poladoris as a boy. Hallot was a learned man who, if given the chance, could flash a gilded tongue. He was short, beardless, and of a wide girth. His receding long hair was chestnut brown.

"How did you know?" Nil laughed, darkly.

"You usually are," said Hallot, dryly. "It's not a risk to wager that Nil Ramesis is dreaming of his name engraved in the halls of resplendence." Hallot laughed to see Nil blush. But his expression soured. "Someday, Nil," he said, his brows low like the sad clouds, "you may find that glory is unattainable. Perhaps that day will be today, my friend."

Nil nodded, a quick anger springing to life in his eyes as if it had waited for something to give it cause. "Have you heard something I have not? If you have, tell it to me!"

Hallot was taken aback. "What could I have heard, Nil?"

"Rumors of Blox, and what else?" A steel edge shone in the mariner's eyes.

Hallot stirred uncomfortably. He was of fair standing in the Council, having been a member for eight years, and so he was reluctant to speak. "I have heard many rumors, Nil," he finally said. His face became sad and homely and his eyes sank as he seemed to gaze at something shameful. "Blox has even corrupted Rishen, our own schoolmate, to do his bidding. Did you know?" Hallot shrugged. "Yet even if all these rumors are true, Nil, is Ameulas really ill-served by Blox, who is so consumed by mercy for the unfortunate? Think of the wrong Trinadol has done Ameulas! I am not sure how to weigh virtue anymore: all seems gray, does it not?"

Nil's eyes burned. "Why have you carried your voice to this place if you do not intend to use it?"

"Nil! Talk like that is both foolhardy…and admirable." Hallot looked over his shoulder. "We live in interesting times. You have no wife, no children, as do I. It is easy for a man such as you to be simple in the midst of the complicated. Do not count your courage too noble, my friend. For I have heard all the rumors you have, yet rumors about wives and children may not concern you as much as those men who have taken a wife and brought children into this world."

"If I had a wife, and she had borne me children, I would fight with my own strength ten times the lion against Blox—having heard those same rumors, Hallot! Do not look hither and thither for the wayward eye or lingering ear, old friend. For my fight, always, is for the wives and children of Ameulas, and to claim that my incentive may endanger them amounts to letting the tiger eat them slowly instead of attempting their rescue. To that I say die in slow anguish, Hallot, and see if it is more merciful than a courageous death! But if you are ready to be a Councilman today and not a toad, then buck yourself up, and stand ready. That is the right you have been given by proud Ameulentians who've entrusted you to use it here today!" Nil turned from Hallot in contempt, leaving him staring over the bay in the same place where he had stood.

Nil walked down the veranda of the great hall to the skull of Knot. The monster's skull had been cast in bronze and mounted on a polished malachite pedestal. Nil touched a fierce tooth, remembering that day, when he was startled by a voice.

"Hello, Nil!" A thin, black-haired man whose height did not quite match the mariner's smiled at Nil. His face was pale and beardless, his features sharp, clever and vital. Upon his body were rich robes of white.

Nil, who wore only boots, trousers, tunic and a black leather greatcoat, stood proud before the regal Lord Rishen. "Hello, Ree-Ree," he smiled, using Rishen's childhood nickname.

"Blast this rain, anyway," said Rishen, ignoring the barb good-naturedly. "The hunting will be rough-going through the underbrush next season. The forests will be thick."

Nil nodded. "The game will be rich. Well worth the struggle."

Rishen cocked his head, a wry light in his eyes. "More bears will come down from the mountains. An added risk."

"When the incentive is great, a bear can be dinner. With a team of good Ameulentian dogs."

"A bear is more powerful than a dog," Rishen said. "I have heard of a bear dashing a dozen hounds in five minutes."

"But the dogs will be hungry, and the bears will be fat."

Cold wind whipped over them, rifling their coats.

Rishen looked into Nil's menacing, oceanic eyes, and he smiled. "Come, come now. I have not even congratulated you on your election to the Council, Nil! We must save the hunt for later. You are held in great esteem by your fellow…*mariners*…it seems."

"It seems so. It is with their voice I shall speak today."

Rishen nodded. "I am sure! As it is with the voices of the downtrodden and the ill fortuned and the hungry and the shelter-less that I shall speak today, Nil Ramesis. For if the High Counselors do not remember them, they are sadly voiceless here."

"Many who were once in my constituency are now in yours, my lord," nodded Nil.

Rishen laughed softly. "Is it not very dangerous these days in the southern waters, with the King's terrors crowding the seaways?"

"A quick tongue to name what is merely mysterious to the eye, and quicker still at the expense of the King," marked Nil.

"Seven years do not fit inside 'quickness,' Nil," said Rishen. "Although they might with you. With each successive year the southern waters become more treacherous. How many seafarers have been lost to those hellish guardians around our most suspicious King?"

"What suspicious thing might be keeping us from the King? You doubt him first and I do not. He feared some great and powerful evil—and keeps us away so he may wrestle it alone and spare Ameulas its wrath. Does evil refuse power? I think not, Rishen! Without power, evil would perish as fast as nature would punish it."

Lightning flickered in the sky.

"My. We are staying up nights. With Artimeer, perchance? What hot, bright things you've been smelting in that coal-burning forge of yours!"

Thunder rolled in the clouds above.

"It's pouring," said Nil. "Let's go inside."

The sudden cloudburst cleared the long verandah.

Once inside, the crush of people elbowing each other as they took off their cloaks and topcoats and mufflers and hats made continuing the last thought impossible. The Counselors hung their rain-sprinkled garments on the Olix horns that ornamented every part of the walls and ceiling of the long hall. They also hung their swords and knives on the horns as the Mayoral Guard bulled through the crowd, rudely checking everyone to make sure they had put aside all weapons before coming to the table. This had never been done before and stirred cross comment.

Nil saw the ochre-and-black Olix horns patterned in the mortar between the beams in the ceiling and ringing two sky-lighted domes through which a cold violet light emanated above. In the wall overlooking the bay was a broad window, double-paned to insulate the great room from the cold. Almost all of the bay of Gwylor and most of the city could be seen like a mosaic through this great window, though the tips of the bay were lost in mist. In the center of the window rose the marble back of Gieron, washed and glimmering. Nil found himself taking in the Hall as Rishen tapped him on the shoulder.

"We'll talk later, Nil!" said Rishen over the hubbub. "Welcome to the Council!" He disappeared through the sea of Counselors, attendants, and uniformed Mayoral Guards.

Though this hall hosted the Council of Ameulas once every two years, it was the City Hall of Gwylor the remainder of the time, and it was traditional that the ancient Gwylorian Guard, now ten thousand strong since Blox had been elected Mayor, had jurisdiction over the Hall. The red-and-silver uniforms were certainly too plentiful to represent the population of Ameulas, however. Nil felt another hand on his shoulder and turned to see Bulgar Bedrosium winking beside the natural monument of his nose.

"All is provided," said Bulgar. "We met before the Hall. All except for you and Lelinair."

"Where is she?" asked Nil.

"We thought she was with you until we saw you talking to Rishen. That was a fright, son! I trust you stepped smartly. He's a clever one, soft though he may seem."

"He has not a wit. Power is all he has, which is proof that he's a weakling!" Nil looked around the room. "I wonder where she is?"

"We'll soon see, Nil. There's the first bell. Let's try to find our seats. We needn't sit yet. But it's always best to know where you're going." Bulgar winked.

Nil nodded and followed Bulgar, looking over the tossing sea of heads for her.

* * *

Rishen didn't slow his step as he approached the doors of the Mayoral chamber west of the Hall, and the guards sprang to open them before he ran right into them.

Rishen was stunned to see Lelinair Martharr.

She and Blox were seated in two of the ubiquitous Olix bone and fur chairs before the small fireplace. They were having coffee together!

Blox grinned at Rishen. "You should see your expression, Lord Rishen! Surely it is uncouth to show such surprise at our Lady's fealty. She sees as do we the futility of loyalty to royalty. Oh, I am so poetic—eh, my dear?"

Lelinair smiled at Blox's banality and blinked demurely, glancing at Rishen, whom she had always disdained in favor of Nil when they were schoolmates long ago; she sensed Rishen had not forgotten it.

"Indeed?" Rishen studied her eyes that had scorned him so many times. "I thought you a Loyalist, Lelinair! If I show surprise it may be because I was just chatting with Nil." He looked for any sign of the love for Nil he had always seen there. "It is clear Master Ramesis is quite the stubborn Loyalist," Rishen pressed. "It appears he is, indeed, seditiously and treacherously so. I tell you, Blox, and you, fair Lady Martharr, if now we may trust you on pain of death, as all trust must be based, that Nil Ramesis will make trouble if he is given the slightest chance. He has power, that Nil. He cuts a dashing figure, with a hero's dark mantle over a champion's reckless edge. His is a presence we must contend with. I put it to you, Lord Mayor, that he must be watched and quickly put down if he takes flight this afternoon. He could be a lightning rod. What say you to that, Lelinair?"

"I say that Nil intends to captain a vessel on a voyage to rescue Trinadol and bring him back to wreak vengeance on Blox and yourself."

Blox was delighted by his aristocratic lackey's shocked expression.

"Ah," said Rishen with a numb smile. "There it is, then!"

"Even now," Lelinair went on lightly, as though it was old news to her and Blox, "Nil is building a wondrous sea-craft in which to do the deed."

Blox nodded. "Lelinair has been the bringer of much news, Rishen. What we have smelled but not seen for days now, she has delivered to us! We can trust the beautiful Lady Martharr. In fact, she will sit at my side today. What a powerful signal it shall send that a Martharr should show her support for Nekkros, the King who shall come, so nigh, to Ameulas." Blox laughed, his teeth clenched. "Perhaps, even, a fitting future queen, eh, Rishen? Look at her so symbolically laid bare for all to see in sheer fabric! I approve of your raiment, my dear! I can plainly see you are concealing no weapons," he laughed.

"Indeed!" Rishen stared at Lelinair, who had dressed in a bolt of gossamer silk that revealed her shocking beauty. "Your devotion intrigues, Lady. I look forward to fighting together to lay the path for the Messiah—and to ridding Nil Ramesis from that path." Rishen fixed her eyes.

"Surely any voyage Nil plans can be forbidden," smiled Lelinair. "Now that it is known."

"And surely any traitor can be executed," smiled Rishen, holding her eyes, "now that he is known. For it is not deeds but the people who do them that are dangerous, or beneficial." Rishen had learned well from his master.

Rishen saw the promise of pleasure in Lelinair's eyes suddenly, an impossible thing that dazzled him after craving her darkly since he was a boy.

"Yet why martyr a lightning rod, my lord?" she said.

"Of course, my dear!" laughed Blox. He took Lelinair's hand in his invisible hand as he rose.

She felt Blox's ghostly fingers pull her to her feet and covered her surprise with an assured smile.

"Let us convene this Council!" said Blox. "We'll be rid of Ramesis as soon as the Council is concluded. His horse will spill him on the way to Gwylor. Preparations to strike his shipyard are underway."

Lelinair missed her footing but recovered gracefully.

"My lady looks pale?" whispered Rishen as he walked beside her. "Or is it just that your skin is not used to so much cloud?"

Lelinair looked at Rishen and pouted. "You find my skin unappealing?"

"I find it lucent as the purest alabaster!"

She smiled, reaching out for his hand and taking it. And so each of Lelinair's hands was grasped in one of theirs as she passed through the doors into the Council Hall.

*   *   *

The final bell tolled and 80 Counselors were swept away in separate currents toward their seats. Their attendants left, the great doors were shut, and the bolts were thrown.

As fate had it, Nil's seat was at Artimeer's right hand; Artimeer had surreptitiously switched the seating cards to suit him all around the table. Nil greeted the old philosopher and looked over the expanse of polished mahogany.

The table was curiously grooved and inlaid with green abalone. Three high-backed chairs rose at the western point of the triangular council table for the Mayor of Gwylor and his two High Counselors. Normally, the King sat in Blox's chair with the mayor to his right.

Nil looked at Artimeer, in whom so many here today had placed their hope. He was now a very old man. His features had finally taken on the razor-edge of those nearing a natural end, his face a delicate, wind-carved thing, the arches over his eyes blade-thin and near collapse. He conserved his energy these days so that he could put his whole effort into the things that mattered. He responded to no courteous conversation of any kind anymore, and spoke only when a single axiom could undo a plethora of dilemmas.

Artimeer saw echoes of faces he knew in the room. The houses of Rentallen, Veniciud, Dynuk-Tull, Ardile, Edo, and Nop were represented today, Ameulentians true who had harbored those displaced and persecuted by Blox. It was the House of Ardile that had issued forth Senadol's queen, Conilair, and Trinadol's grandparents, who had died long before he was born. The great family of the red Lion of Tunce was also represented today, by his red-haired daughter, the tall, muscular and imposingly beautiful Senthellzia. Her distant grandmother Apriscia had been Elwyn's queen, and her distant grandfather had been King of Ameulas. Senthellzia was a fiery one and seemed more fierce than usual in the sad absence of her father, who was rumored to be gravely ill. Her pet falcon Harm sat on her hard shoulder.

Most of the Nekkrosites at this table were individuals of no personal achievement, characters used to hawking things in common squares by day and flying by night, people who had popular but no personal appeal; individuals without name, fortune, friends or future to preserve who had banded together in one cause that had promised them power.

Yet there was also a growing Nekkrosite movement among the children of the great. Some of these rebellious youths were present, with shorn hair and sackcloth robes, depressing their haggard parents, who represented the Loyalist or at least opposition faction at that table.

Artimeer noticed a wondrous sight that brightened his heart. The young prince from far-off Demold sat across the table, having traveled with Captain Skylar on the *Green Ghost*. The only son of Demold's King, Ryndillym Skyaarmindu-Kaaryn, Prince Rollum was tall and tanned, with no beard on his square jaw and long blond hair cut straight over blue eyes. He wore a mantle of woven gold over a shirt of green silk—something from Demold and something from Ameulas, a good will gesture toward the land with which his country had once been united.

"Where is Lelinair," Nil asked Artimeer.

Artimeer shook his head.

The double doors between the fireplaces opened, and Blox entered.

Between Blox and Rishen, holding each of their hands, strode Lelinair.

A collective sigh of dismay filled the room.

Blox and Rishen walked forward, as though presenting Lelinair, yet the people supposed her to be Blox's captive, and Nil, fists clenched on the table, made to rise.

But then Lelinair smiled, coolly, as though she were in her natural place, and all watched in dazed silence as Blox reached his seat and Rishen sat on his right and Lelinair sat on his left.

Blox did not sit in the King's chair, which was the Mayor's chair when the King was absent. Instead, Blox remained standing and surveyed the faces in the hall.

He was not tall compared to Ameulentians, but his garb was fantastic. For one devoted to the poor, Blox wore his wealth with a garish and intimidating boldness. His face was different to everyone who looked at it; and his eyes seemed to ward off the timid eye, leaving his features shrouded in regal distance. Only his closest allies and bitterest enemies saw Blox as he really was—a gray, lumpy creature with red stubble on his head. He did not mind that his most intelligent enemies could see him truly; it made them seem like alarmists to the majority of Ameulentians, which was all that mattered in a democracy.

Blox smiled, glancing indulgently at Artimeer who, Blox knew, could see him most clearly. Then Blox saw Poladoris Martharr, who was faint and being assisted by those around him—good! Senjessi Tillow's fierce eyes had turned sad and weak at the sight of Lelinair…Blox blinked and looked again at Nil Ramesis, who was looking right at him with the unflinching eyes of a wolf!

Blox raised one of the Voice Stones, white opals that emanated cool radiance when they were held. The smooth stones were ancient, brought with Gieron's people from the land before Ameulas. To speak at the Council, one must hold one of the three Voice Stones; Artimeer and Poladoris held the other two.

Blox held his Voice Stone high and spoke: "As we convene this 512th Council of Ameulas, my dear friends, a matter most dire has been brought to my attention by the fair Lady Martharr, a matter to which we must all pay immediate attention."

Blox raised his invisible right arm—suspended over its stump floated a red minnow. "Trinadol has contacted Ameulas!" he cried.

Artimeer felt the room darken. He squeezed a hand into a fist around his Voice Stone as he squinted down the table at Blox, whose true face was smiling at him.

"Trinadol," Blox went on, "our King who would not be King, whose evil eruptions mar our southern waters and threaten our trade now writes on the skin of these bewitched messengers that he lies trapped in the ruin of the Dimmrock at the bottom of the sea by his own wicked devices. The poisonous King of the Tintilisair asks that we travel through his evil maze to save him, after forsaking us so coldly! Methinks he wants a trial run so he can see how all his monsters work! O, wonder of wonders, Ameulentians—he asks us to risk those dangers in order to *rescue* him! I, for one, am insulted! Ameulas, even it if were true that Trinadol is trapped and cannot escape his fate, is this not cause for celebration at this 512th Council? Prepare the feast and light the torches! For if the King should die, might not our southern waters live again? Might not the storm clouds lift? And then the way shall be laid for Nekkros, who shall come when the sun returns to Ameulas. So shall He come. Make no mistake! As Mayor of great Gwylor, I must remind those still dissenting that much of Ameulas has already sworn fealty to Nekkros, and wisely so. For He shall be the great equalizer. Those righteous in His eyes shall ascend. Those unworthy shall be cast down. The law of Nekkros shall be manifest! If this Council were to condone a rescue of King Trinadol, who bears the mighty Cronus Star he bloodied, there would be a clash of giants over Ameulas such as to rent Hala in two! For Nekkros will see the necessity of destroying our renegade king, even if we do not let him perish when nature would serve our interest. I ask only: Consider! How much grief will be visited upon Ameulas, let alone on the men who attempt such a voyage, if we elect to rescue Trinadol?"

With Blox's first stroke, he had called for a vote.

The meagerest murmur could be heard as the fires crackled.

"Good Ameulentians, I do not mean to interrupt your debate, however, I wonder what debate there could be?" Blox waved the fish in his invisible hand, and Lelinair smiled mildly beside him. The combined image rendered listless all opposition, for the whispered rumors of Blox's invisible hand were now chillingly confirmed.

Nil glared at Blox and Blox felt the mariner's murderous gaze, for that kind of gaze is unmistakable between men.

Nil looked away from him at Lelinair who, once again, refused to meet his eye, and the anger in his heart nearly burst Nil's chest.

Artimeer rose and held up his long-fingered right hand, the white opal pinched and glowing through his fingertips. "I do indeed debate, not anything, but everything in your statement, Mayor of Gwylor! It would be best if you show patience, therefore, and hear argument on this as well as all the many other matters that lie before us over the next two days. Councils are formed so disagreements may be heard and violence avoided, after all. No, do not be alarmed, young man, at my talk of Ameulentian traditions, or seek to make much of my frankness. If you lived as long as I your ear would be as frank as my tongue!"

A fracture of laughter broke the glacial silence.

Blox smiled respectfully, but Artimeer could clearly see the hateful frown on Blox's true face.

Artimeer flourished the Voice Stone. "There is much to say on this matter with which you have chosen to begin this 512th Council, O Mayor, and I, Artimeer of Nop, as well as many others whom I will name and call in due time, have much to say and much to argue. It is, I agree, most urgent—so urgent that it requires this Council's fullest examination, in all its regards, in exhaustive detail, to avoid any missteps in its handling which may result from hasty votes. Those in favor of debating this vote therefore say 'Aye!'"

Artimeer raised his hand, and it seemed even those in Blox's camp cried "Aye!" at his imperious gesture.

"Those against, say 'Nay!'" said Blox.

A spasm of "Nays" spluttered out.

"Motion carried by Artimeer of Nop," Blox smiled.

Artimeer smiled back at him, and took his seat.

"Let me begin then," said Blox. "It seems a review of the facts is necessary to some at this table. Let me remind us that our young King has not once set foot upon the mainland of his Kingdom! He does not wish to be King! He scorns Ameulas! And my great Lord Nekkros, in whose shadow I humbly wait, bends all of His power to make the way for His gracious descent to our abandoned Throne. Ameulas has not left Nekkros's thoughts since He gazed from on high and saw our orphaned land, and He has chosen to come down from that realm of immortals to walk in flesh among us. Do we repay that divine grace by dragging our derelict King from the depths of his depravity to place in Nekkros's way, and insult this great god who shall come to us in love so that He must find insult sitting in His seat?"

Artimeer grumbled and raised a square-knuckled old finger. "This great god you speak of, young man," he said, knowing how it must annoy Blox, who was older than years could tell if he was from the *Wynder World*. "You do make much of your far away champion, don't you, eh?"

There was a two-edged growl in the air.

"I make much of more, old philosopher! Nekkros shall show His face soon. And may mercy save the unbeliever from His terrible eye!"

"Always the threat," marked Artimeer. "The Ameulentian heart does not shy from threats, young Mayor! Nay, and call it foolish if you will, it does not even shy away from those threats made by gods. You would do better to remember it. But answer me this: Why does Nekkros demand love at the point of a sword?"

Both of Blox's faces looked nervous for a moment. I should have silenced this old man's tongue long ago, he thought. "I do not judge Nekkros. Perhaps there are those who would here today. They will have their chance to make plain where they stand, and their names will be recorded and remembered."

"Thank you, Mister Mayor, we are all aware of the consequences we look forward to from your god who would be King. We know how eager he is to come to punish those who would not obey him, yet we wonder what keeps him? Does a god have affairs to close up when relocating to Hala?"

There was a wave of laughter.

Blox smiled. "You are old, Artimeer. It is easy to make such talk when the security of the grave is like an open door to the impregnable castle of death in which one might hide from harm. There are those younger here, and generations unborn. They should not do well to take your example and make light talk of Nekkros."

"And let you not make light talk of the *present* King of Ameulas: King Trinadol Gheldron, the son of Senadol, and grandson of Elwyn, who vanquished the Black Wrath and banished that dark god from Hala!" said Artimeer.

Blox seemed to resent the mention of these names, as Artimeer had expected.

Artimeer went on. "You have thought to digest that fish you hold so tightly and spit out only the sharp bones! The King did not mean that fish to feed but one man, but his entire Kingdom with his news. It is good I have my own draft of the King's missive, Mister Mayor, so I may read it in its entirety to this Council today!" From his robes, Artimeer produced a small black nautilus shell, engraved with white letters, which had been found in the belly of a shark. He peered through a magnifying crystal at the words twisting on its spiral, turning the shell as he read the words aloud:

> "O, Ameulas! I have wronged you and myself to the profit of an ancient evil that preys on us both. I have delivered myself to Drugor, and can but warn you of his coming. If you brave my terrible sea and pull me from the Lightstone Tower toppled beneath the waves off Dimmrock, I promise you justice!"

Artimeer lifted the shell for all to see.

"What great power hath the King! For he conjured a legion of sea creatures and embossed this message on their sleek hides, counting on the mariners to bring them forth inside their nets. And so we know that he is trapped beneath the waves in his toppled tower, full of remorse. He is the quarry the horrors in our southern seas were meant to trap! And deeply ensnared in that trap he now lies. The Terrors stand between him and us, mocking us, daring Ameulas to do a thing to aid our king! Trinadol warns us of an ancient evil—indeed he uses a name not spoken in centuries, one Elwyn himself would not speak. For it was *Drugor* who took Elwyn from us almost four centuries ago!"

A wave of fear swept the room and the undecided vote began shifting.

"We should heed such news from a Cirilen," cried Artimeer, waving the nautilus.

Blox smirked, yet he realized he must disguise his contempt.

"Imagine what advantage this ancient evil has had over such a young King," Artimeer continued. "I am convinced that Trinadol is the prey of something cool, old, and wicked, O Ameulas! A Cirilen may live a thousand years—we are not finished with Trinadol yet. And it seems uncharitable and even uncivilized for our Mayoral host to ready his successor's breakfast before the King's last supper! Indeed, the chances of rescuing King Trinadol are small, as a further examination of the Terrors will surely show, and, without Trinadol, the Throne will certainly be vulnerable to any god that chooses to descend, good or evil! The odds are with Blox's messiah in any event, so why not give Ameulas a precious option to the tyrant he predicts will fly upon us willy-nilly without the courtesy Elwyn showed us when he went down on bended knee to ask if Ameulentians would have him for their liege. With King Gustomeer's blessing, Elwyn married Gustomeer's daughter Apriscia, who was descended from Gieron himself! Let us not forget the deep allegiance we have to the Gheldrons."

The Loyalists clamored in agreement, and many Nekkrosites complained that Artimeer was talking too much.

"Let Blox speak!" yelled one.

"Let Lelinair speak!" cried another.

A mixed chorus agreed, but Blox did not yield the stone, as Artimeer had that option also.

"Artimeer should make stained glass," Blox said. "So do his words paint windows with pretty pictures. Come, let us wipe the window clean and look together into Truth's garden so ripe with facts he cannot deny! After seven years, Trinadol invents a reason for us to attempt his rescue, and an ancient evil is easily offered as his excuse! This is all supposing Trinadol is in some danger. I cannot help but wonder if he is not merely issuing an invitation, now that his hideous carnival has been completed. With the latest monster placed so, come on with your best, our young King dares!

Could we elect to satisfy him and send our best into harm's way? I don't think it is anything an Ameulentian would do, not for a king, or a god!"

This shook the undecided, couched cleverly in terms Artimeer had just used.

Artimeer sensed it. "I call upon Marnik of the Highlands to give his testimonial," he said and he threw the fiery opal with expert precision across the table to the Counselor from the Wirtun Downs—Artimeer never used the grooves in the table.

A carrying "Aye!" confirmed his pass as Marnik swallowed and caught the stone, which glowed brighter as he touched it. He was a simple man, a farmer who had invented a more efficient plow and gained a small fortune manufacturing them. "If not for Trinadol, our children would have been murdered by the Nekkrosites!" he said, raking his beautiful green eyes across everyone at the table. "Trinadol scared them off, and no less, the night they were taken by Blox's followers! He came out of the sky and set upon their midnight gathering and stopped their sacrifice and sent them running over the hills casting off their cursed robes! And so our children came back to us, and they spoke of Trinadol. My beautiful twins, boy and girl, whom they were to sacrifice that night three years ago."

"Ha!" Blox shook his head, wearily. "Thank you, Marnik of Wirtun Downs! We have noted your views, and your name, I assure you. Sacrifices, indeed! Children we now have to add to the witnesses for Trinadol. Now let us hear the testimony of adults, if you please. Let us hear from our mariners and their tales of terror on our southern seas!"

No mariner would answer.

A miscalculation, thought Artimeer, smiling at Blox.

Yet Captain Skylar of the *Green Ghost* that shipped spun gold and rare fruit trees from Demold garnered enough votes for Poladoris's stone and he took it. "I can speak as well as any mariner, Mister Mayor! Fewer sailors have died in the southern waters since Trinadol was crowned King."

"What?" Blox appeared annoyed. "Nonsense!"

Captain Skylar smiled and shrugged. He was broad, though not tall, and had a swarthy, amicable face with green eyes and straight hair like burnished bronze combed back from his high brow. "I have a copy of the *King's Maritime Almanac* right here!" Skylar showed the councilors the book, opened it to where his thumb marked a page, and consulted a chart: "There were 127 men lost in the southern waters in the last seven years. There were 368 in the seven years prior to that. In fact, the only time there were as few deaths in those waters was when Trinadol was a lad living on the Dimmrock, when the King's dreaming spirit saved many a wretched sailor from the deep." He winked and closed the book. "The truth is, no one ventures into those cursed waters 'less brought by misfortune, or some calculated risk, out of respect for the King. More men die in the surrounding waters, and that is the fact of the matter, round and neat. His islands, if they're his, mark almost all the dangerous reefs. And the great monster Knot was slain by Trinadol, seven years ago. That's saved an untold number, in addition to those who were saved by Trinadol's dream-ghost, which is still said to come down from the heavens to aid a foundering caravel, even to this day!"

Blox sneered. "Superstitious speculations of salty sea dogs we now have to add to the tales of children! Thanks for that, Captain Skylar!" he glanced at Rishen and Rishen put Skylar's name on his list.

"Be that as it may," said Skylar, undaunted by the Mayor's malice. "The Almanac doesn't lie!" Skylar shook the book. "Fewer men have died in the southern waters since Trinadol has been King!" The captain smiled, bowed, and took his seat.

"Well then, what about commerce?" cried Blox, as though he cared about commerce. He had quickly learned to use any argument that suited the moment, and found it so easy to do that he wondered why his foes did not do it also. "Our fishers have suffered, our trade routes are blocked!"

Skylar slid his stone down the table to Bulgar Bedrosium, who had chartered many of his expeditions, and a solid voice vote sanctioned his pass.

"I can speak to that," said Bulgar, waving the Voice Stone. He stood, not increasing his height much, but revealing his great girth. "As the largest merchant of Gwylor—with the most ships trading—I can vouch that the obstacles surrounding the Dimmrock have been less harm to our industry than the endless storms and taxes besieging our land. The inclement weather claims more mariners and the taxes take more trade than the terrors that have trapped our King."

"Trapped? Trapped?" cried Blox. "It seems Lord Bedrosium believes as does Artimeer that Trinadol's is not a trap of his own making! That rather than setting a trap for Ameulas, he is himself trapped by some elaborate design!"

"Quite so. That is what I was going to say, but you said it much better!" said Bulgar, bowing with a flourish as he took his seat.

Blox nodded as Rishen wrote down Bulgar Bedrosium's name.

"Let Rishen speak!"

A number of votes came from the Nekkrosites.

"Let Lelinair speak!"

A number of voices agreed.

Blox waffled and passed the Voice Stone to Rishen.

All the Nekkrosites seconded the motion.

Lelinair smiled inscrutably beside Blox and even met his eyes reassuringly as he sat down.

Many saw it.

"I think it necessary to point out the futility of debating this issue in the first place," said Rishen. "The Wizard's Archipelago is impenetrable! We only know of a few of the Terrors for certain. The others we do not know of are surely equally dangerous. The Rollock cracks ships and feasts on their crews. A crystal colossus like a giant lobster snatches vessels in its claws. Some say three islands peak from under a permanent veil of fog from which no ship has ever returned. Southeast of the Dimmrock lay two islands, one of ice and one of fire, with a strait of ice between them like dragon's teeth. Ravenous currents sweep wayward ships through this strait, where they are doomed or dashed over the reefs south of the Dimmrock. With all of that, how little do we know? Captain Skylar has shown how seldom traveled these waters are! To sacrifice one life for this young King who has forsaken his subjects is outrageous enough. But to allow a rescue mission to be launched, knowing how desperate and, indeed, futile the mission would be, would be cruel and treacherous. Remember, there were three expeditions to the Dimmrock in the past; all came to a bitter end!"

"Bah! It isn't hopeless!" Nil growled, despite his better mind and his lack of a Voice Stone. No politician was Nil Ramesis.

Rishen thought he noticed Lelinair start at Nil's voice. He took the opportunity of Nil's interjection to invite him into the debate. "Please, Mariner. Nil Ramesis, of the House of Martharr, our new representative of the southern mariners. What have you to add to our debate?"

"Nothing. I speak without a stone, and beg forgiveness," said Nil, nodding his head to the gathering.

Rishen slid his stone over the long table. Nil took it as it passed, and the Nekkrosites and some Loyalists carried Rishen's motion.

"Tell us, Mariner, why you think the rescue of Trinadol is possible," said Rishen. "It is of obvious interest to us all!"

Nil rose and impressed the gathering, modestly dressed though he was. He leveled his dark eyes at Lelinair who smiled vaguely, looking at the wall over Nil. "My tongue is too rough, perhaps, for this place," said Nil. "As a mariner, I tell you anything is possible on the sea. Let us hear what the Lady Lelinair has to tell this Council. I wish to hear whether she approves of such a mission. What say you, Lady Martharr?" Nil slid the stone down the table in the sleek groove.

She took the smoldering stone and rose as the voice vote resoundingly approved Nil's motion. "I wish to hear from you instead, Nil Ramesis." With a fluid stroke she slid the stone back along the polished gutter to Nil.

As Nil caught the stone he felt a rough edge.

It was her half of their *lightstone* pebble.

He looked at her, but she still did not meet his eye.

"Mariner? Twice the stone has been offered to you and you do not use it," said Rishen. "What have you to say with the voice of your constituency?"

"Bulgar," said Artimeer. "Give your stone to Blox and let him speak."

Bulgar's eyes bulged in incomprehension, but with a look from Artimeer he slid his stone from the base of the pyramid in the central groove.

It spun backwards down the length of the table to the Mayor.

In perplexed gratitude Blox grabbed the stone but had nothing prepared to say, and Artimeer rose with his stone and stole the moment, again.

"We have an ambassador of great significance to this Council where so many of his predecessors called this hearth a home when Elwyn ruled our lands in common. Rollum Skyaarmindu-Kaaryn, Prince of Demold, has come great distance, and not for idle reasons, I think. Let us ask his opinion of this crisis confronting this 512th Council." Artimeer flung his stone to Rollum.

Rollum rose and caught it smartly, looking around the room with a gentle manner as a near unanimous vote welcomed his testimony.

"Good Mayor of Gwylor and gracious host of this Council, I am coming to Gieron's table to tell of omens that are besieging the dreaming of our wise women, who are feeling a great enemy preparing to be storming the world from the south. So disturbing have been their dreaming they are refusing to be eating for 40 days until the King is promising to send me, his eldest son, to be telling Gieron's table."

"There, you see?" said Blox. "The prospect of Trinadol's salvation is dreaded by Demoldan prophets! You were right to travel here, young Prince! Your action might well have prevented these grim prophecies from coming true by convincing this gathering to give up this wild notion of rescuing Trinadol, once and for all!"

"Yet the prophets were speaking of ancient evil," said Rollum. "Even as your young King is speaking of the most ancient evil Himself, which Demold is remembering too well. The wise women were saying the enemy's color is being red, like blood, like the Crimson Fire—like *Drugor*, long ago."

"That is Trinadol, good Prince!" laughed Blox. "His scepter is blood-red!"

"Yet Trinadol is not being ancient," shrugged Rollum. "He is being only my own age."

"Red is the ancient color of evil and Trinadol is merely its youngest heir," Blox smiled.

"I am giving the stone to Artimeer now," said Rollum.

Artimeer caught the stone from the groove, but Rollum's pass was challenged.

"Five for the Red Lion's daughter!"

"10 for Rishen!"

"25 for Rishen!"

"37 for Artimeer!"

Artimeer smiled as the debate warmed up.

"I believe a vote should be taken. What more can we debate?" shouted Blox.

The Red Lion's daughter, Senthellzia, caught Artimeer's eye and he threw her his Voice Stone across the table. Her falcon, Harm, caught the stone in his talon and blinked dryly as he dropped it into Senthellzia's hand.

A voice vote confirmed the pass, if only to extend the debate.

"I, like Nil Ramesis, wish to hear Lelinair Martharr," said Senthellzia. "Why do you forsake your noble father, and sit with Blox here today?"

"She has joined with the truth and given her allegiance to the future King. Does that anger you, Daughter of Gustomeer?" said Blox.

"It devastates me." Senthellzia slid her stone down the groove to Lelinair. "I ask as many here will I am sure, what is it, Lady Martharr, that brings you to the side of Blox?"

A unanimous vote confirmed her pass, as all there were curious.

Lelinair lifted the stone. "I tell you that Nil Ramesis plans a voyage to rescue Trinadol in a ship he is building for that purpose, and he will go whether this Council votes Yea, or Nay."

"Lelinair!" cried Poladoris, as though a sword had run him through.

Harm hissed on Senthellzia's shoulder.

Nil squeezed his fists over each half of their *lightstone* pebble, cutting his palms.

Artimeer swooned and Nil rose and steadied his arm.

Lelinair looked at Nil and it shook him. Nil wondered at the clear and confident light in her eyes. Then he looked at the halves of *lightstone* in his palms, and Artimeer saw them, too.

"Let us not tarry on this point," cried Blox. "Let us vote! Good Ameulas, let us vote now to forbid any rescue of Trinadol. The fate he faces is that of the wicked. Hala herself would perish him now. Since we can make sure Nil Ramesis won't circumnavigate this Council's will, why not take the simplest course of action to insure a just fate? Let us wait with good hearts and hope for the new King who would come to us, innocent and with open arms, eager heart, and unblemished loyalty. He will seem like Trinadol, only He will bear no stain! His scepter will be pure, multi-colored as all creation under the sun. And He will come so very soon, alas!" Blox flung his stone unexpectedly down the table to Artimeer. "Take the Voice Stone, Artimeer. Say what you will, and let us take this vote!"

Artimeer took the Voice Stone in his hand and noticed that it felt cold in his fingers. "Before we vote, I shall make my final statement to this Council," he said. Then, as it burned like ice in his hand, Artimeer knew that Blox had poisoned the Voice Stone. "Ameulas," Artimeer sighed. "I have watched many seasons and seen the face…of this great land in many lights down the decades. Having counseled Senadol for 50 years and Trinadol, alas, a few precious days, I learned much about this dynasty. The responsibilities that weigh on their gracious heads are heavy. They concern things otherworldly that threaten to overwhelm us mortal men in this simple world of modest means and hard-won gains. A noble folk are the Cirilen, splendid, modest, furious and wise, and longer lived than we.

"I say to you now...that each of these Cirilen-Lords has been indeed reluctant to rule his subjects. Protectorates instead have these Kings been, allowing Ameulentian life, art, industry, and charity to flourish...cultivating the goodness in our people by letting it grow and cutting back only evil. Theirs has been a healthy garden. Rich have these Kings left us and heroically have they protected us from foreign harm...Now Blox boasts his 'messiah' is eager to rule us. Eager? O, Ameulas! Beware the eager hand of rule! *Drugor* was most eager to rule us! That Trinadol refused to take our Throne should be his highest recommendation. That this 'Nekkros' seems so willing...Ameulas...should be your gravest doubt!"

Artimeer felt his chest squeezed, as if between two mighty hands as he looked at Blox, and Blox's face changed before him. As though his head were clay, it molded into a boar's head with a long snout and laughing, slitted eyes. Though his mind was composed, a cold sweat poured over the old philosopher's brow, channeling in the deep arches over his eyes. His hand shook as he held the stone and his eyes watered. "An ancient evil has followed the Gheldrons since Elwyn brought his family out of Sentad," he said.

All leaned forward in perfect silence to hear Artimeer.

"The evil that preyed on Senadol is the same that hastens our young liege to his grave. First, King; then, Kingdom. Ameulas! Do not listen to this foreign tyrant who may seem comely to you! Blox is the agent of a super-evil, a thing beyond our modest imagination or even his, who seeks entrance to this world by taking the body and visage of our rightful King!" Artimeer paused and caught his breath. "Even now, Blox bargains away our last opportunity...Alas! *I am poisoned!*"

The Loyalists hissed to see Artimeer fall.

Nil helped him into his chair, and tears streaked like lightning under his dark brows. He looked at Lelinair; and she was smiling, avoiding his eyes. He wished her damnation and in the same moment he thought no—*it was not possible!* He opened his hands.

"Nil," Artimeer whispered. "Join the stone!"

"Let us vote!" cried Blox, taking the hidden Voice Stone from Lelinair's hand. "Artimeer has said all he will say, and seems in uncertain health! All those who would forbid any rescue of Trinadol and choose to greet Nekkros with love and not hatred, I ask you now to say 'Aye!'"

Most of the Council uttered "Aye" at Blox's call.

"Say 'Nay?'" he said, cocking his left hand behind his ear with the Voice Stone suspended above his severed wrist.

The voices were too few, too weak.

"The motion is carried!" cried Rishen.

Nil tried the broken halves of the *lightstone* pebble. They slipped across each other, jagged and clashing and slipping finally into a slight concrescence, locking into a round, smooth stone that shrunk in Nil's hand and burned like a star. And as the halo of its light spread, it revealed colors no one had ever seen before in the things around them.

The Counselors gasped as they watched the eminence spread down the table from Nil's palm, and before the light reached him, Blox recognized the force inside the love-star, and he cringed. As the benevolent light touched Blox's true face it was made stark, and it was a wretched, childish face like clay poked with greedy nostrils. And as the radiance grew, his face flickered, and a bloody boar's head snarled in sudden surprise as it was exposed in the true glow of love.

Artimeer gripped Nil's shoulder. "Now all can see!" he hissed in Nil's ear. "Hold up this love-stone whose light is truth and finish the day, Nil Ramesis." Artimeer sighed, and he slumped in his chair.

Nil rose and turned to the guards at his back, holding the shining stone before them. They retreated as Nil strode forward and took his sword from the Olix horn on which it hung.

He unsheathed the blade and then leaped onto the Council table, pointing the shining sword at the Mayor who sat at the point of the pyramid.

Rishen took Blox's Voice Stone and rallied the guards. "The mariner has bared his blade in the Hall! Kill him where he stands!"

"Nay, he holds a Voice Stone!" said Hallot, and he was echoed by half of those present.

Nil looked at those around him at that table and cried, "I would gladly die, run through on this very table, my blood draining in its grooves to drip in each lap if there is not one man in this company who would stand with me against this evil made so plain before us now!"

"His sword is bare! The law is clear!" cried Rishen. "Guards! Strike him where he stands!"

Some of the guards at the Counselors backs drew their swords.

"At ease!" said Blox.

All eyes turned to the Mayor.

Lelinair had climbed onto Blox's chair behind him and she held a curving, crystal dagger to Blox's quivering throat; she had concealed the weapon under her naked breast. "If there is only one soul brave enough in all of Ameulas to stand with you, Nil Ramesis, it is I!" said Lelinair.

Rollum rose. "The men of Demold cannot be watching a woman's courage unassisted!" He leaped onto the Council table to stand by Nil.

"Count me by your side, Rollum!" cried Leoned of Nop, a shaven-headed Nekkrosite who stepped onto the table beside the Demoldan and the mariner, having seen Blox's true face for the first time and siding now against him.

"And me, Hallot of Gwylor," said the portly Counselor, who now joined them on the table.

"Tairen of Brin stands with you, too, Lady Martharr!" said another, who climbed onto the table, as well.

Senthellzia sent her falcon with a whisper into the vault of the room where it wheeled and swooped over Rishen, snatching the Voice Stone from his hand and returning it to her. "Take these mercenaries from this Hall, Mayor!" she cried, raising the stone, and to this a resounding "Aye!" shook the rafters.

Lelinair let the paper-thin edge of her dagger nibble Blox's throat. "Take your mercenaries from this Hall, Mayor!" she whispered in his ear.

"Be gone, you men-at-arms, from this Hall, and repair you to your armory!" quailed Blox, his Adam's Apple scraping Lelinair's blade.

The guardians backed away, and they left the Council Hall and closed the east doors behind them, listening closely on the other side.

At once, half the Counselors rose and claimed their weapons from the Olix horns where they hung.

Nil, Rollum, Hallot, Tairen and Leoned, another Nekkrosite dressed in burlap robes, walked forward now over the table toward Blox, and Nil pointed the tip of his sword at the mayor's eye as the light illuminated both of Blox's hideous faces at once before all who looked.

"This is revolution, young Mariner," Blox growled. "Treason!"

Most of Blox's followers were horrified to see his craven self revealed before their eyes, though there were yet some present that did not cringe nor abandon their loyalty to Blox, seeing only what they had known all along.

"So be it!" said Nil. "Let us draw the battle lines today, rather than let the tide of evil slowly drown us! Here is the line, Blox! No further shall you pass! See who wins this siege of Ameulas when it is quickened and an honest fight begun!"

Artimeer heard the roar that filled the hall then as he was comforted by the noble lords and ladies around him. And, as a smile of hope softened his vigilant face, he died in their embrace.

*   *   *

Chapter 19

Revolution

Fifty Counselors, their entourage, and some one hundred or more of the Mayoral Guard rode over the Alder Road descending east and curving south from the acropolis of the Council Hall toward the valley below.

Thundering hooves, billowing capes and glinting scabbards flew like the wind over that stone highway. Carriages and wagons pulled by Polwairn teams charged behind the procession, their spokes a blur. Senthellzia's long red hair flowed back in the wind as she rode and her falcon Harm soared, crying high over the rushing company.

One carriage bore Artimeer's body, tended by a weeping Senjessi and Poladoris, yet their tears were mixed with happiness as the sun chinked a high chip out of the cloud and three gold fingers pointed over the distant bay. A last shimmering rain swirled over the city as the storm finally broke.

Nil and Lelinair rode Star and Indigo, and the white and black stallions led the way, their nostrils snorting and eyes bulging as they felt the great force chasing them into Gwylor. The clattering hooves, jangling armor, and grinding wheels startled the somber countryside, and the stallions neighed at the horses behind, challenging them to match their speed, making a final charge for the stone bridge that spanned the Feather River at Gwylor's northern gate.

Noting the distant hue and cry, people gathered along the streets of Gwylor to watch the multicolored comet soaring down the highland road until the company crashed over the bridge and under the arch onto Gieron Way.

The citizens of Gwylor, having grown cautious under unrelenting storms, were amazed at the sunlit arrival of these joyous nobles who hailed from the Council Hall. At first they were worried, thinking them Blox's messengers and marking the uniforms of the Mayoral Guard among them, but when they saw them laughing out loud and with such good heart, they knew some great news must have finally come. They threw down their axes, their brooms, their hammers and rolling pins and ran out to join the charge, not knowing its cause, but guessing its goal well enough.

The train lengthened to a thousand as bells rolled and rang over the city. Shivering birds took to the sky as the clouds caught fire and burned away above.

Bulgar, on his shorter, tan steed, drew up beside Nil and Lelinair and flashed a toothy grin as his jewels sparkled. "Well done, Lord Ramesis!"

Behind him came Prince Rollum astride an ashen stallion, his blond hair whipping his swarthy brow. "Lord Ramesis!" he said. "On behalf of Demold, my service and allegiance!"

"I shall need them both!" said Nil.

"My father, King of Demold, has been sending friendly and…urgent blessings to your young King. I am offering my blade to you!"

"Many thanks, young Prince! It will be tested."

Rollum flashed a grin. "That's how I am liking it!"

"Good," said Nil. "I hope you're as fierce with a saw!" He winked and reined Star to the right as they came to the embarcadero, and Nil led the procession down the western seafront.

The street narrowed, and the train of followers strung out behind Nil and Lelinair, filling the gloomy avenue. The love-star, now in Lelinair's hand, illuminated the street on which Nil's humble shipyard crouched, making it seem not so dingy and dull. She met his warm gaze in relish and fear, and he turned and yelled over the wall of his yard: "Lince, heave to those gates, and make it quick! An army's come to launch the Lady, mate! Believe it, sure as your ears!"

"*Naw!* I heard the bells?" came a gravelly voice behind the fence. A winch grinded and two wide sections of the fence opened inwards.

Nil and Lelinair rode in and reared before the yardhouse, waving the people through the gate. The coaches and wagons stopped along the street and crowds poured into the yard.

Resting in stocks upon thick beech logs, pointing down a broad stone skidway, rose the mighty *Sea Mare*.

Lelinair's heart grew cold as she assessed the ship's proud beauty. The crowds gossiped in awe at her size, 143 feet from stern to prow, without the bowsprit that had yet to be mounted.

With a wedge-shaped fo'c's'le, a long main deck, and a stately aftercastle, the *Sea Mare* was graceful despite her unprecedented size. With cunning lines made to cut through air and sea, her hull was wrought of hard oak five inches thick and ballasted with sand. She sat high in her stocks and a close look revealed spikes on her keel, one particularly thick one astern.

The two masts would not be fitted until the ship was launched. Before where the mainmast would be was a narrow, two-story cabin and on top was the ship's wheel, one of Nil's invention. Another wheel in the first mate's cabin was afforded a wide view through a forward window. A third, emergency wheel was in the Captain's cabin below. The wheels' windlass turned a gear in the steerage box on the Green Deck below, which in turn winched the ship's rudder.

Rails had yet to be added and there were no companionways to the lower decks—or bunks, portals, storage closets, benches and tables below, as yet. She was much more and much less than everyone expected.

Nil rode through the parting crowds to the *Sea Mare* and climbed off his horse over the ways to the main deck.

He raised his arms to the people on the aftercastle, and they cheered and threw their hats as the bay turned blue under the opening sky.

"Blox lost a battle today!" he cried.

Cheers jeered the distant tyrant.

"But we must be vigilant! His invisible hand is still strong. Those who fear him should leave now, in peace."

The people only laughed, as though Blox's time had already passed.

"Not more than ten days we have to finish this vessel, and not more than that should it take, if we work hard and smart. Let our steel warn off Blox's guard, yet do not seek blood. For we do not wish war now, but peace, and time! Therefore, spread the word and let all know this is the moment to stand together against Blox. Let Blox's guard know that if it give provocation, we will be defiant! That will stay his hand, long enough for our task to be done. Then, I, Nil Ramesis, will take this ship to find the King and pull him from his watery grave, as he did so many of us mariners. I shall need a crew of noble hearts with unmatched skill. Fifty is the number I need to brave this voyage from which none may return. The risk is great; but the prize is freedom!"

The people cheered and threw their hats in the air, if they still had them.

"Those under my pay shall now be foremen, directing the labors of those who would join us," said Nil. "Those who are not carpenters or skilled shipwrights I ask to stand aside so suitable work may be found for you. The *Sea Mare* needs many supplies: lumber, food, water, ale, rope, blankets, stoves, hammocks and even plates, cups, and silverware. If any can find Ameulentians who would be willing to lay on these supplies, you would be of great service, indeed. Some should become deliverers, for there is much to cart there and back. However, I am afraid I will not be able to pay more than those already under my hire."

Nil held out empty hands, but a small man with long gray hair who had climbed up onto the main deck cried, "You, sir, have paid us more than any could! Our work is simple gratitude for freeing us from him!" He pointed north to the Council Hall on the cliff that was lit now by a new ray of sun.

"Whether I have freed anyone, we have yet to see! In the meantime, I accept your service, and I hope to repay you with the King's return! If I fail, good sir, you and all who help me will be in grave peril."

The crowd exalted him, accepting the challenge, and Lelinair wept in strange joy, confessing her love to him only now, when it was never more perilous to do so.

*   *   *

Nil had his men set up tables in front of the boathouse so they could take names and assign volunteers to special details, according to their skills and the *Sea Mare*'s needs. Many turned out to be craftsmen, and as the tools in Nil's yard were soon used up, they left to fetch more tools from their own shops. Nil realized that the skills and resources of ten large shipyards would soon be employed on every joint and trimming of the *Sea Mare*.

Nil's foremen laid out the plans of the ship so the enterprise could be overseen and divided. To his great delight, there were so many captains and master shipwrights present that the task organized itself quickly, and each took one part of the ship and studied the plans. Soon they knew what needed to be done and each enlisted a contingency to set about a job. Nil's men were relegated to supply acquisitions in order to feed the many-armed beast undulating around the ship, creating rather than devouring her, with equal hunger.

In all Ameulas, this was the longest ship ever built, and the only ship over 100 feet to bear two masts. Many mariners less wise than Nil scoffed at the *Sea Mare*'s design, saying she would capsize, or travel in circles, or not move at all. But the distinguished captains from the Council of Ameulas who stood before the vessel now praised her ingenuity, innovation and beauty, expressing not much surprise and not a little envy. Nil listened to their words, preferring to wait for the sea's compliments, but he smiled with pride as they divided into the crowds to lend their able hands and heads to her completion.

Two more captains approached. One was almost as tall as Nil, and beneath a straight, dubious nose, a large mustache curled. He carried a dark green cape on his shoulders. A gem-studded sword hilt was at his left hip. He bowed and introduced himself. "I am Tarsus Flint, Captain of the *South's Pride*, sir. I wish to offer my congratulations and gratitude for not only the doings of this day but for the months you have labored upon this craft. She's a worthy vessel, sir, to be the flagship of our lord." Again, he bowed.

Then Captain Skylar of the *Green Ghost* spoke. "I am Nop Skylar, Nil Ramesis, and I have heard your name as you have heard mine, I am sure. I also offer my congratulations and allegiance. Yet I wish also, by your leave, to install a sail such as this lateen aboard the *Green Ghost*, should it prove successful. Would you allow me to study your plans and follow your example?"

"Why, yes," said Nil. He had heard much of Skylar and his ship, said to be the fastest ship on the seas. "Yet," said Nil, "even with this added sail, the *Green Ghost* shall never outrun the *Sea Mare*."

Ire flashed in the dark captains' eyes as they held each other's stare. But Skylar, the smaller man and good-humored, grinned and laughed, and Nil laughed, too.

"Some day," said Skylar, "we'll race." He winked, and with a nod he left to prepare the *Sea Mare*'s chainplates.

Nil felt a tap on his shoulder and turned to catch Lelinair's lips. She stroked the tense curls on his noble head and smiled. "What shall we ladies of Ameulas do for the *Sea Mare*?" she asked, with a chorus of women at her back.

For a long moment the mariner puzzled over what they might do. The idea of so many women in his shipyard had never occurred to him, so his consternation was a little more apparent than he might have wished.

"Nil!" laughed Lelinair. "How will your great ship move?"

"By sail, of course," he grumbled as he cogitated.

A great round woman who had flung down her broom and dashed out to join the noble rebels over the squawks of her tiny husband now shouldered her way through the rest. "Show us your needles and yarn and we'll make your sails, Master! We'll see if women belong in a shipyard!"

Nil laughed. "Very well, mother! A small start has been made but plenty more must be done. Have my man in there give you the measures and materials."

"We'll take care of it, Captain!" said Lelinair, and their look lingered as she left, and Nil looked after her, half in joy and, only now, half in dread, as she led the others to the boathouse to stitch the sails.

The sun was bright and warm, and people shed their coats as they dug into their work. The shipyard fairly hummed with happy noise, and old salts sang work shanties.

Nil made the rounds answering questions and giving advice. Common laborers, merchants, and aristocrats worked side by side in his shipyard, sweating in the newborn sun. The renegade detachment of the Mayoral Guard stood vigil outside the yard, not changing their uniforms, and some escorted the wagons that were departing to fetch goods and supplies and tools. Nil lent a hand here and there, but he was overwhelmed and almost rendered idle by the passion of his fellow revolutionaries.

*   *   *

As the sun rolled past noon, the work on the *Sea Mare* buzzed. The bowsprit was hoisted into place and its block and tackle fastened. A hundred carpenters built the companionways and beveled the rails. The hull was coated three times with hard lacquer, and scuttles were cut to ventilate the Green Deck.

Meals were served in shifts to the hungry laborers, another chore taken over by the women, and when all had eaten and the sun dipped two hours before setting, Nil climbed the aftercastle and announced that it was time to launch the ship.

"Captain Ramesis!" cried a voice.

The mariner turned and saw Poladoris Martharr and Senjessi Tillow.

"You've come in time to lend a hand!" hailed Nil. "Now we shall see if the *Sea Mare* floats!"

"Ah! What a wonder she is!" cried Senjessi. "Look at her, Merania! You must paint her!"

"I will!" said Merania, her dark eyes huge as she memorized the ship and imagined her at sea.

"Now, people, I ask you all to gather 'round and seize the ways," said Nil. "Two teams of horses will pull, and together we'll take her down the skidway. Are the horses ready, Mister Neery-Atton?"

Lince had the reins of the two lead horses, which headed two lines of five Polwairns that had been harnessed to the stocks. The lead horses snorted and stamped the ground before the stocky mariner.

"Wait!" cried a voice, and everyone saw the old, silver-haired man who had thanked Nil for freeing Gwylor from Blox. Nimbly, he climbed the stocks to the main deck, carrying a great bundle wrapped in rags on his back. He ran to the bowsprit and jumped onto the scaffold beneath the thrusting spar. Drawing his cape to hide his actions, he worked furiously and everyone could hear him filing and pounding and wondered what the devil he was up to when he finally drew back his cape.

Pegged to the knighthead beneath the bowsprit neighed the head of a mare, carved passionately in wood and painted blazing white with eyes and nostrils black and wild, and Nil's heart thrilled to see the figurehead that would lead the *Sea Mare*. The silver-haired artisan jumped down then to help launch the ship, and Poladoris Martharr himself praised his work.

All took hold as Nil, standing on the prow, signaled the horses.

Everyone pushed at once, including Poladoris and Senjessi who put shoulder to stock behind the athletic Lady Senthellzia Tunn and Lelinair, who also helped push. A grating rumble rose as the ship in its wooden cradle inched forward down the stone channel.

Teams of men laid down logs before her, and the horses strained with shoulders bulging as they climbed onto the thick seawalls of the dock. The *Sea Mare* rolled forward faster now between them and met the water, leveling and rising off her stocks to a roar of applause.

She streamed forward as the men on the walls moored her to the right side of the dock.

The Polwairns dragged the ways back up the skidway as the foremen swarmed over the ship's plans on the dock to direct the great force of builders who now boarded the vessel.

Teams of shipwrights conferred as they began stepping the masts and securing the standing rigging.

Before the sun retired, the network of the *Sea Mare*'s companionways was installed and finished. Port and starboard, ladderways descended from the aftercastle to the main deck. Between these, two wide doors opened into the galley and to either side two more ladderways descended to the Green Deck—the long, wide deck where the crew was berthed. Below this was the long hold.

The crane on the dock lowered the two masts into place and the cordage was strung in the twilight. Men painted it with tar between the chainplates as the yards were rigged above.

Before nightfall, the first wagonloads of goods began filling the completed portions of the *Sea Mare*'s hold, gradually replacing the bags of sand that had temporarily provided her ballast. As the sun's victorious signature faded over the western mountains, Nil stood on the aftercastle and called the industrious laborers together. "Thank you all for the miraculous work you have done today! Now, as light leaves us, it's time for rest. Go home to your beds and sleep with the decision you've made."

There was a murmuring and, stepping forth, a tall young man, who was the very likeness of Nil fifteen years ago, said, "I am Lanning, Captain, sailor of the *White Shark*. Many of my friends wish to stay and continue working. Lanterns may be fetched and hung 'round. I don't feel the sun's weariness, though we've fought and won a battle as hard as it has fought today. I wish to stay, and finish this craft!"

The entire crowd echoed agreement, and Nil laughed, a little in awe at Lanning's resemblance to himself, and at the obstinacy of his new employees. "So be it! By my leave, stay, as I of course will, but take care not to tip a lantern and burn her down, though I doubt any would be so careless. Fetch lights from the yardhouse!"

And so, accommodated by both full moons and a warm wind, they worked throughout the night.

* * *

"My Lord Mayor," said Rishen. "Intelligence reports that Nil Ramesis and his rebels work diligently, taking no rest, presenting no opportunity for a surprise attack as a well-armed guard surrounds the shipyard. Argosies such as the *Green Ghost* and the *White Shark* have gone renegade, it seems, and lie anchored fully manned off the coast of Ramesis's shipyard, flying the flag of Gheldron."

Blox sat in his chair at the head of the Council Table, looking at the dark city flecked with lights like the clear sky above.

"Shall we attack?" urged Rishen. "Even without the advantage of surprise? Our numbers can surely crush these few renegades!"

"Don't be so sure, Rishen," Blox mused. "Let them toil away. Let them launch their meager hope. Let their ship enter the King's labyrinth. My Master would not have sprung his trap until it was complete! The Seven Terrors are impenetrable. The mission will fail. Their heroes will perish but in the meantime the people of Ameulas will cling to false hope. It will make them complacent. When Nekkros comes, they will be unprepared."

Rishen bowed before Blox. "In your wisdom, my Mayor."

* * *

The hold of the *Sea Mare* was quite spacious. In order to maintain the correct ballast, supplies had to be carefully distributed, and barrels must be filled with water and moved to keep the ballast even as supplies were consumed—in Nil's theory, at least. Nil designed the storage bins to manage the ship's ballast and allow barrels to roll from one side to another over the passageway.

Five men toiled in the hold to finish these bins now: Bultin, a great muscle-bound sailor with rounded shoulders; Rawley, a bald, red-bearded carpenter with a wooden leg; Rollum the fair-haired Demoldan prince; Tintil, another giant seemingly made of boulders; and Lanning, who might be mistaken for a younger brother of Nil Ramesis.

Tintil sawed the last frame, Rawley filed the last edge, Bultin drove the last peg, Rollum fitted the last brass handle, and Lanning painted the last spot with varnish. The two gleaming rows of storage compartments matched the ship's plans covered in shavings and varnish at their feet. Their shirts were stained with sweat and grime and their beards were flecked with sawdust. They gazed at their handiwork as they walked back along the bowed deck past others who were already loading supplies in the compartments, even as the varnish dried.

Near the stern, a thick shaft rose, cocked in wooden bolts like a crossbow with an iron spring coiled above it. It pierced the hull point-down and apparently could be released by knocking out a chock wedged in its side. The top of the shaft was curious—there was a deep groove lathed into the harpoon and above this the shaft flared wider like a cork. The men shrugged as they walked around it, careful not to give it a nudge.

They climbed past the Green Deck where Nil and others were installing hammocks and tables. The watertight bulkheads were being built on this deck, as well. The weary team of men passed the bare galley and finally emerged on the main deck, plated by the Gold Coin. They climbed to the aft deck and looked at the sea.

The wind caught the spray of the waves, sending gold dust over the gates of the dock across the prow of the gleaming vessel, and their hearts quickened. For on this great ship they felt equal to any challenge the sea might offer.

*   *   *

The sun found the most prominent captains, counselors, artists, artisans, merchants, lords, ladies and even lawyers of Ameulas strewn in slumber across the decks of the *Sea Mare*.

But this was not the greatest surprise—overnight a ship had materialized where only a hull had been the day before. Those who sought a few hours of sleep now cast off blankets and stretched, smelling the bacon and coffee that the women, who had slept in shifts, were now preparing in the yardhouse.

Others, who had chosen to sleep in a bed, woke to breakfast in the many hamlets of Gwylor, and they ate heartily, laughing, and all around them wondered at their easy gaiety that had been stifled in public places over the last year. Some passersby were wary to hear them insult Blox without care, for they had not yet heard of Blox's defeat at the Council, though these were fewer and fewer, and a sleeping spirit rekindled the ancient city.

By mid-morning, all were back to their labors, and there was a haggard camaraderie in the company.

Young sailors sprang up the rigging, pulling lines aloft with their teeth, in preparation for hoisting the main yard. After a score of men was positioned along the cordage and all their lines were fastened to the thick spar, they gave great heaves and the yard surged over the main deck.

From the crow's nest, Lince helped Bultin and Tintil, who hung on the shrouds to each side, hoist and guide the yard. Lince pulled the two cable loops of the yard through brasures in the crow's nest and hooked them over great cleats on each side of the mast, and they all let the yard hang, then, while securing the stays.

Wherever he was in the shipyard men came to Nil and applied for duty aboard the *Sea Mare*. One was Dillon Tobbs, a self-proclaimed naturalist whose father Nil had consulted concerning the Rollock several years back. The learned old man had explained to him how a rollock caught and killed its prey, the black nautilus, and Nil had devised defenses for it with his help. "If we succeed it will mean fortune and fame for you, young man," said Nil to eager young Tobbs. "If we fail…it will mean death. But still fame, maybe." Nil grinned.

"I don't seek fame, fortune or death, but knowledge, sir! And that is what I will give to the future, living on in that way," said Tobbs.

"You've a courageous heart and good judgment to go with it, young Tobbs! Pack your chattel. We'll give you a berth in the fo'c's'le so you can stow your instruments."

"Thank you, sir—er, Captain!"

"Now I suppose you read and write?" asked Nil.

"Why, of course! I've had the best edu—"

"You write a fair phrase, I'll warrant?"

"Yes, sir!"

"Your main charge will be to keep a detailed journal of the voyage. I want you to record everything you see, each night. I have devised buoys that will keep safe your writings and bear our news to the mainland, should we founder. And it will be your job to determine when those buoys should be tossed to preserve our record." Nil pressed his pointed finger on the lad's forehead.

"Yes, sir!" cried Dillon Tobbs, his pudgy, bread-dough face very serious. He slicked back his black hair and bowed solemnly, then swiveled on a heel and ran to collect his books and instruments.

"Ha!" said Lince. "He'll lose a long lunch when the fo'c's'le starts heavin'. Thirty-foot plunges in a hammock at midnight'll grow his eyeballs, some!"

Nil chuckled. "He'll serve a good purpose."

"Aye. Look yonder, Captain, 'tis that Sarkish doctor, coming our way!"

Indeed, a Sarkish man with skin as black as midnight and kinked reddish hair cropped short presented himself with a raised hand. He was a handsome and ageless man who bore scars of sword-strokes on his strong arms. He was dressed in a shirt of green wool and yellow pants with faint purple patterns that were gathered at the ankles above his sleek moccasins. He wore a leather cape, fringed with color-swirled glass beads. "I am Bruthru Zee, sir," he said in perfect Ardeyon. "A physician. I have experience dressing battle wounds. Would you have need of me?"

"We would," said Nil. "Where do you hail from, Bruthru Zee?"

"Call me Zee, sir, for that is the custom in my native Sarkland, lost to anarchy, as you know. I was one of those who fought with Prince Tylur to restore order, but Sarkland was too burdened by laws and debt when the earthquake struck, alas. There was nothing saved in anyone's coffers for that evil day. Order broke, and the savages took over. I escaped over the sea, and chanced upon Ameulas along with a few other families of my kind. We are thankful to be welcomed as citizens in this land where we have prospered, offering our special knowledge and skills while marveling at the wise freedom of this youthful kingdom. I will fight for that freedom. I have, before, and do not wish to see it lost again."

"Consider yourself the new ship's surgeon," said Nil.

"Aye, Zee. Welcome aboard!" nodded Lince gruffly, shaking his hand.

"I'll get my things, gentlemen." Zee bowed and left them.

Lince smiled. "A royal crew we'll be havin', it looks like, Nilly!"

"Yes. And here comes a Monkey Sailor to prove your point!"

A diminutive man in a suit striped yellow-and-blue strode up to them with a monkey, literally, on his back.

"Hello, good sir! A Monkey Sailor?" Lince smiled.

"Indeed, sir. He's of the best pedigree. Trained him myself since I was a boy. That's 15 years. Finished first at the Logger's Head heats last spring. Strong, too! He can carry a backstay 35 feet up, he can."

"What's your name, sir?" asked Nil.

"Feferl, and the monkey's Jootle."

Jootle tipped his little hat.

"Sign up at the desk. On my say! Welcome aboard, Feferl. A monkey will come in handy—so long as it doesn't cross paths with Lince's cat."

"He's smarter than a cat, I assure you!" laughed Feferl.

"We'll see," growled Lince.

*   *   *

That day, more was done aloft than alow, for all below was completed by noon.

Lince, Bultin, Tintil, and Bat, another huge man who had a baby's nose and ears and confused little eyes, hung the *Sea Mare*'s great lateen yard on her mizzenmast. Then men fastened the stays and painted boiled sap on all the lines.

At dusk, Nil announced the crew that he and Lince had selected out of the multitude of volunteers. Among them were Rawley, who would be the ship's carpenter, Lanning, who would lead the second watch, Bultin, Bat, Tintil, the Demoldan prince Rollum, and the imposing Senthellzia Tunn with her falcon Harm, who was the best archer to bend a bow in Ameulas. Of course, Lince was first mate, Nil was Captain, and Karlock Isopika was second mate.

Most of those who were chosen went home to pack for the voyage and rest.

Then Nil went to the yardhouse to inquire about the sails. Inside, he approached the ring of women as their young and old hands double-stitched the great lateen sail, 50feet long at the yard.

"How?" Nil laughed. "How could you have done so much?"

The lady nearest him, the great, round one who had spoken up before, turned to him and laughed a gentle mother's laugh. "My boy, we didn't quit last night as many of the men did. We worked straight through." She took a corner of the thick material. "Strong sails, these."

Nil looked at her hands, raw from working the needle all night. "Good as gold, I'm sure." He glanced around the room for Lelinair. "Where is the Lady Martharr?"

"We finally had to put that one to bed! She led the circle, and a fierce taskmaster, too!" she chuckled. "There she is, wrapped in yonder sail."

Nil walked over and he gazed at her, her hair sprayed in mahogany curls over the canvas cascades of the mainsail. She was peaceful as an effigy, and he knelt to take her hand and feel its warmth. Her eyes fluttered and he withdrew his hand, not knowing why. "Your hands are pierced and chafed," he said.

She smiled, reaching out and clasping his hand. "So are yours," she said. "Yet something else stops you from touching me. What, Nil?"

He rose. He wished to speak, but a terrible fear tied his tongue. He was no coward, Nil Ramesis, and this strange dread confounded him. It occurred to him suddenly that perhaps she was right to have scorned him all these years. He could bear risking his own life, but not hers. Making the kind of love to her that he had yearned and planned and needed to make all his life would be the cruelest of lies should he never return.

"I must supervise the rigging," he said, brandishing a troubled smile. He turned, and before leaving he asked the round old woman to have the sails brought forth upon completion, and she laughed heartily, for at that moment they were done.

Lelinair looked after him. It was crueler for her, she thought, for she would live even if he died. And yet, oddly, she felt less fear now than ever before.

*   *   *

The sails were brought out and fastened in the moonlight.

Teldon Martharr arrived and delivered a chart he had drafted of the southern waters. Though filled with question marks and speculation, it was the most complete chart of the strange battlements surrounding the

Dimmrock in existence, and Nil thanked him warmly, asking him to meet him in the morning for final counsel. Teldon promised he would and told him that Senjessi and Poladoris were coming as well, having attended to Artimeer by laying him to rest in his tomb on the estate of Castle Martharr. Then Teldon rolled up his sleeves and went to work on the ship through the night with the others, and Nil, at last, fell asleep at his desk in the yardhouse.

And in a murky dream he fought off chimeras and sea demons, and each stroke of his sword seemed only to wound Lelinair. He pulled his blows, but the monsters only grew, battling him with multiplying arms, and when he woke he felt only wearier for his rest.

*   *   *

At dawn, a gathering of captains and leaders of Ameulas met in Nil's office. Lince wasn't present as he supervised victualing the ship.

Captains Skylar, Tarsus Flint, Karlock Isopika, Bik Bohtum and Teldon, Poladoris, Bulgar, and Prince Rollum of Demold gave Nil counsel, and Teldon described everything that was known of the terrors surrounding the Dimmrock. Then each gripped Nil's hand and bid him farewell, leaving him to pack his sea chests with final necessities and last notions for the voyage.

Poladoris stayed after the rest had left and handed Nil a leather case. "My son, here is a treasure Artimeer told me to keep from Blox's hand when he won the seat of Mayor from me. It has been secreted for centuries in a vault deep under the Council Hall." Poladoris opened the top of a slender case and drew out a regal scepter whose diamond was the size of an apple, cut into many facets. "This ancient asterix is one of the Crown Jewels, Nil. If ever the King was to lose his scepter, this was to serve him in its stead. Stow it aboard the *Sea Mare*, for surely Trinadol must be in need of it now."

Nil took the case and closed the lid over the star. "Thank you, lord. I depended on it!"

Poladoris kissed his forehead. Tears were in his old, violet eyes, but his mouth was firm under his hawk's nose. "All blessings to you, so that I should see you safely home."

* * *

On that crisp day a sky blue as a mountain lake shone above as the sails were rigged, clewed, and furled. Everyone gathered around the ship, which had not taken ten days or even five to complete, but only three days as so many had toiled day and night.

Carpenters painted the crow's nest green above. A wooden statue of Trinadol donated by Karlock had been fixed atop the mainmast, the very statue Trinadol had charmed after catching Knot aboard the *White Shark*.

As a rosy castle of layered clouds burned against a yellow sunset, Nil climbed the ladder on the wall of his cabin to the bridge. He took the helm wheel as the sea doors were swung wide before the *Sea Mare*.

Open sea faced her.

The men climbed aloft and released her mainsail at Nil's command.

The men on the seawalls threw off her moorings as the wind cracked her canvas and filled it taut as a drum. She surged over a swell like a steed leaping a wall, and Nil felt her power like a beast grabbing hold of the sea beneath her.

"She's frightful pretty, Lince!" cried Nil.

Lince jumped up and down on the seawall in envy as she hauled out over the sea.

The *Sea Mare* plowed the waves as though she were on the verge of taking flight.

Yet only a few hundred yards out, Nil ordered her sails furled, and she was moored to a sturdy buoy, her wings clipped.

The sun sank and the stars appeared as a procession of longboats headed out to feed the newborn bird of prey with her final provisions.

*   *   *

Nil paced the deck in the Silver Coin's light as supplies and men arrived.

He inspected the catapults on the aftercastle that also housed double-crossbows.

Nil climbed the fo'c's'le and inspected the port and starboard crossbows there, each loaded with a single harpoon. They had been donated by Karlock and designed by Nil for the *White Shark*. One of them was the legendary crossbow Trinadol had used to slay Knot, which had always shot true, though hitting unintended targets sometimes that always had some excellent effect. In the center of the foredeck was the capstan and windlass that would set the flying jibs.

Nil descended the port ladder to the main deck and passed the forward sea doors and bridge to the row of millstones secured behind the mainmast, each as tall as a man. He rested a hand on the last millstone.

Just then, Nil noticed Pickle, the grim genius he hired on as ship's cook, clambering aboard with his clattering pots and pans. The sour-faced Pickle inspected and fondled his new stoves that had been acquired and installed in the aftercastle galley at the last possible moment. His perennial assistant Bombo backed right into Pickle, causing him to spill an arm-full of utensils and sparking the cook's indecipherable outburst. Nil entered the galley and greeted Pickle heartily, for he knew a good cook made for the best morale.

"I would feign prevaricate to annunciate my exaltation, Captain Ramesis!" Pickle bowed, flourishing a ladle.

"His varicose veins are feeling better," winked Bombo confidentially, ever quick to translate his master's obscure communications.

"Never mind this lolloping rublet's pulings; I offer hieratic magirics to this argosy upon my verisimilitudinous pollicitation!" The cook bowed solemnly.

"He says his brains are swollen just a tad—but it's spring fever, is all it is," Bombo whispered, shielding his lips from the cook with a plump hand.

The harried cook hurried off to catch a boat back to the shore as Bombo piled in behind him, for Pickle still had many more provisions to fetch for his galley.

Nil went below to oversee the loading in the hold as the last supplies arrived, and then he inspected the hull as she creaked, the sea cracking into the varnish and swelling the *Sea Mare*'s virgin timbers, tightening her seams.

At last, Nil stared at the shore from the aftercastle. She must choose, he thought.

It was ten o'clock when Nil finally left Lince in charge and went to his cabin.

She must come to him.

* * *

Lelinair ran down the broad wall of the dock to see if she could still catch a boat out to the *Sea Mare*, for she had finally realized what Nil was doing. She stood at the end of the rock rampart surrounded by the huffing and swelling water. No boat was in sight.

She let herself look at Nil's ship and for a moment grief and terror overpowered her. She fell to her knees before the swelling, hissing sea.

She looked at the love-star, smooth and whole in her hand. Its light had dimmed as the *Sea Mare* had carried Nil out to sea earlier that afternoon. Now the stone was barely glimmering.

Lelinair covered her face with her hands and sobbed. She knew he was leaving the choice up to her, and that she must go to him, but she dreaded her helplessness now. Though there was no limit to her courage, there was no way it could protect him from the fates rushing upon him now.

Silhouetted against the moonlit sea, Lelinair spied a cunning skiff with a three-pointed sail; a cloaked figure tended its tiller.

"Hullo!" Lelinair cried, waving. The skiff turned and came in her direction, swinging about and landing broadside against the dock ever so gently. "Good sir, could you take me out to yonder vessel?" said Lelinair.

A woman's voice responded. "In return for telling me what yonder ship is, I will."

"Thank you!" Lelinair climbed into the unusual little craft and sat on the forward thwart. "The ship is the *Sea Mare*," she said.

"I have heard that is the ship that is going to rescue King Trinadol," said the cloaked woman, her face in shadow. "If so, then I am very much in approval of its mission. Who is the captain?"

"Nil Ramesis."

"Ah! I know him! A worthy ship for a worthy captain."

"The ship is as worthy as he; he built it."

"I see!"

"My name is Lelinair Martharr, Lady. What is yours, if I may ask?"

The skiff's pilot guided the tiller out over the dark swells toward the great ship. "You may," she said, and she pulled back her cloak. "I am Neuvia."

Lelinair gasped, looking at the pale, beautiful face of the Queen.

"This is Trinadol's boat," said Neuvia. "He made it with his own hands. It is a magical boat; only it may pass the defenses around the Dimmrock unharmed. Alas, there is no way a boat of this size can reach Trinadol where he is now. Only a ship such as the *Sea Mare*, with a very long anchor line, will be able to reach him in the Lightstone Tower."

"Milady!" said Lelinair. "Why have you not made your presence known in Ameulas? Our land has suffered in your absence! Gwylor's evil mayor would have to stand aside if you took your rightful place!"

"If I was to show myself on Ameulas, milady, that is exactly what would happen. Then I could not leave, and help Nil Ramesis now."

"How would you help him?" Lelinair asked.

"You care about Nil Ramesis, I think?"

"I love him like my life!" said Lelinair.

A tear sparkled on Neuvia's cheek. "I am sorry, milady! I know what it is like to watch the one you love embark on a perilous journey."

"How would you help him, my Queen? What would you do?"

"I'm not sure. But I must do something. Trinadol and I hid from the world and its dangers these last seven years so that we could be with each other. But you can only hide from the world so long before the world comes crashing down, no matter how high the walls you build around you."

Lelinair laughed, wiping a tear from her own cheek.

"What is it, milady?" asked Neuvia.

"My Queen, I insisted that Nil Ramesis conquer the world first and make our home in it before I would give him a place in my heart. I wish I had done what you did, instead, for the last ten years have been filled with nothing but loneliness. Now I may lose him, never to know the kind of happiness you had." The love-star grew brighter in her hand as they drew near the giant *Sea Mare* on the waves.

Neuvia looked at Lelinair in sad surprise. "And yet," she said gently. "If Trinadol is saved, you and Nil Ramesis will be able to spend the rest of your lives together with no more fears to menace you."

Lelinair nodded. "And if Nil succeeds, will you and Trinadol come out of exile and into the world again?"

Neuvia clasped Lelinair's hand warmly, nodding. "We have a mutual interest, Lady Martharr."

"What can we do, milady?"

Neuvia smiled. "It is time that both of us stopped waiting, I think. It is time for us to act."

Lelinair kissed Neuvia's ring, and tears of gratitude anointed her hand.

Stargazer turned sharply from the *Sea Mare*'s nodding prow and raced out over the bay of Gwylor. And the *lightstone* pebble, which grew brighter as they approached the great ship, dimmed on Lelinair's palm as they sped away into the darkness.

*   *   *

Chapter 20

Under Way

Long banners of pink and orange cloud streamed over the eastern cliffs of the bay into the cobalt sky just before dawn.

Lince stood on the maindeck in a wool and leather tunic with a dagger stitched over his breastbone. Two additional daggers were stitched to his skin-tight leather pants below his hips. He wore a thick belt with a big brass buckle and thick-soled moccasins.

He wet his finger and raised it in the air. There was no wind and the sea was smooth and calm.

The men stood ready. They had been assigned to three watches: the first watch to man the port sheets, the second the starboard sheets, and the third the lateen sail. These were their home positions, but the watches would be rotated at regular intervals. They waited for the first command.

To their surprise, onlookers lined the three-mile Lightstone Jetty and the embarcadero, and were crowding onto the piers. Boats of all description raced out from the docks along the seafront to see the renegade warship off, including most of the fishing boats of Ameulas, whose captains had suspended this day's chores.

Nil stood at the helm wheel on top of the two-story cabin that rose before the mainmast, and he looked at the Council Hall seething darkly under a wrathful cloud on its palisade above the city. A soft wind rippled his long woolen coat and twisted the spirals of hair over his deep-etched brow. He wondered if Lelinair were somewhere among those cheering.

She had not come to say farewell, and he accepted her choice. But his heart was heavy.

"The people are with us, Cappy!" cried Lince.

"Let's get her off, Mister Mate!" Nil nodded to the bald first mate who stood patiently coiled on the deck before the bridge with his hands clasped behind his broad back.

Lince wheeled like a spring unwinding. "Unfurl 'em! Take 'em down, get 'em out, get her off! Go! Go! Go! Go!"

The men of the second watch, led by Lanning, jumped over the dark cordage into the dawning heavens.

The Monkey Sailor, Jootle, scampered aloft to check the lines, ready to scream and point if the rigging were in danger of breaking.

The men mounted the main yard and pulled off the brass gaskets that held the sail, sliding them down the stay lines to the deck.

"Cut us loose, Mister Sowernut! That's right, you, sir! Take out yer knife and cut that mooring line yonder!" yelled Lince.

The dignified Sowernut jumped and ran to the stern rail. With relish he pulled out his knife and cut through the thick mooring cable tied to the stern cleat as all waited. With a lunging bound, the *Sea Mare* was set free, and almost tossed Sowernut over the transom.

Lince yelled, "Drop the clews, mains'l, lateen, *arrrr*, ya rusty suckers, get a grip now, let 'em go. Ah! Welcome aboard Mister Sowernut, now git yer ass to that lateen line and get a hold—hold on, boys!"

The sails fell and the wind and sun smote them at once, like thunder and lightning.

They heard the people cheering along the shore and the shining jetty, and the crew hailed them, waving their hats from the rigging as she shipped out.

Nil ordered the long green banner of Ameulas raised above both masts, and another cheer rose from the shore as the emerald flags streamed over the *Sea Mare*.

"Hard port," said Nil as he spun the wheel.

"Heave 'em to, starboard, mates!" barked Lince. "Get 'em over, go-go-go-go!"

The *Sea Mare*'s massive sails shifted as she turned, hauling out toward the Lightstone Jetty. She rode higher as she picked up speed, leaving a narrow wake over the mild waves as the morning wind kicked up.

"Ah! The sea always smells like watermelon after a good rain!" Lince breathed in, patting his chest and winking at Nil and Karlock.

They grinned on the bridge.

"The wind's playing her like a fiddle, Nilly, and a fair tune it is!" said Karlock.

"A song!" cried young Lanning. "Let's have a song to start the voyage, Captain!"

Nil nodded, and Karlock raised his hand and brought his cane down on the railing as he raised his voice and led the crew in a line-pulling chantey:

> *O, it's sun so warm*
> *It's merciful rain*
> *And breeze on a summer day,*
> *It brings us harm*
> *And hurricanes*
> *And blows us all away!*
>
> *How fair and foul the cappin'*
> *That fills our sails with air,*
> *That fills our sails with air and so*
> *Keeps 'em full and flappin'*
> *O'er the seas so fair, so fair*
> *That Gieron's known for mappin'!*
>
> *Pullin' us fast*
> *And lightin' the way*

And guidin' us by the stars,
The sky, alas,
Will dark the day,
And knock us on our arse!
For sure as it pulls us over the blue
Givin' us reason to grin
It gives us a blow, so we're heavin' ho
Right into the muck again, O—

The canticle repeated and collapsed in a rubble of laughter as they passed the crowds thronging the seafront, who sang the song back in a round that echoed from the shore.

Then Nil conned her starboard, bringing her on a course that paralleled the Lightstone Jetty as the crew shifted the sails port—for he thought she might be waiting for him at the end of the jetty.

The muscular Senthellzia leaned against the galley under the port ladder as the great and gracious ship bounded gently over the big waves. Her falcon, Harm, looked disdainfully, or hungrily, from her shoulder at the seabirds flocking around the rigging. The Sarkish ship's surgeon, Bruthru Zee, sipped black coffee beside her as they watched the men trimming the sails around them with respectful awe.

The people lining the Lightstone Jetty waved as the ship passed, picking up speed as she headed now toward the open sea. They passed many ships whose decks were crowded with cheering people, bidding them farewell, and these ships flanked the *Sea Mare* and followed in her wake as she flew south. Some of the crew were lucky enough to spot their loved ones among those cheering well-wishers, though Nil saw no sign of Lelinair as he searched the ships and the jetty. For a moment he thought he saw her standing at the end of the jetty. But it was not her, after all.

Their cheering escort followed them far out, not wishing to lose sight of the great windjammer that crashed indomitably through the seas with a proud mare's head rampant beneath her bowsprit.

Only Captain Skylar on the *Green Ghost* was able to keep pace with her in the end, bearing down at the helm fiercely with his heavy one-sailed ship, and it was only because of the drag of the spikes pointing down from the *Sea Mare*'s keel that she did not outrun the *Green Ghost*.

Nil smiled. "Set the jibs!" he bayed like a hound. He grinned grimly at Karlock. "Hang on."

Lince, on the deck before the bridge, where he would relay the Captain's orders for the duration of the voyage, screamed, "Set the jibs, ya dockwallopers!" and he convulsed as he shook a massive fist above him.

Two men each from watches one and two hoisted the jibs, which lifted nearly effortlessly from slits in the fore deck and they filled like giant slings before the mainsail.

The men had to catch their footing as the *Sea Mare* hauled out.

The *Green Ghost* couldn't keep up, and Captain Skylar reined in his stallion, finally, and threw his hat in concession, laughing and shaking his fist.

Nil gave him a last wave. "Lince! Start the watch games!"

"Right, Captain!"

Lince gripped his hands behind his back and planted his feet wide on the deck just starboard of the bridge where the men minding the lateen sail could also see him. As if waiting for its cue, Lince's cat swaggered out, having hopped down the ladder from Lince's cabin. It was a shorthaired, tail-less cat which everyone called "the Creature." Striped black-and-gray, the Creature had a rusty hull and was covered in white scars from ratting. All those on deck couldn't help but watch the bow-legged cat lie down six feet behind Lince's right leg and perch its chin on a paw as it sneered at the men.

"We're goin' to do some pullin'!" snarled Lince. "And we'll find out who the sailors are and who the sorry suckers are! First watch take the port sheet; second watch, starboard; third watch, lateen! Now, by Golly's god-awful gut-whiskers, not the day after tomorrow, you puke-gargling scallywags, Go, Go, Go! You there, I caught that dirty look, Mister Bultin!" The Creature licked its fist behind Lince. "I'll be watchin' you!" Lince tapped the tattooed eye on top of his head. "You, Rawley, you've idle hands, not bein' on a watch as you carpenters aren't! So why don't you teach the cook and the Lady Senthellzia how to mind the jibs, eh Mister Wuhdoo-Ayedoo? It's just a windlass, and all you have to do is crank it one way or t'other, I'll tell ya which and when! Now get to it, you three, you heard me, Pickle, lurkin' in yer shadow, we'll taste yer breakfast soon enough—"

"Spare the cook!" ordered Nil from the bridge.

"Then Bombo will get his pork barrel out on deck fer a jib drill!" stomped Lince.

Nil chuckled.

Bombo trotted out from the aftercastle, none-too-thrilled.

"All right, we get everybody in on the act today, including the monkey, Mister Feferl. How's the rigging then?"

"Jootle's calm, sir! The rigging's sound!" reported Feferl.

"Good! We're not resting today till we're ticking like a clock! Rawley, you git your hollow leg to that windlass and commence teachin'!"

Rawley looked like a wet cat. The wily carpenter had a red beard and a balding head, a gold tooth, and a wooden leg with a spring-loaded knee, which he had made himself. "Mister Neery-Atton, I don't know the first thing about pulling a jib!"

"That's a lie, but I've a better place fer ya, then, Mister Tricky-Fellow! I've heard of yer mischief aboard ship, sir, and I'll be watchin' you even when it seems I'm not, and mark my words for your own sake, sir. Now take a place on the second watch at the starboard sheet and double-quick, no delay that means! We'll have no dockwollopers on this ship, carpenter or no, eh, now? Ed, you show the clodhoppers the ropes at the jib, eh boy?"

"Yes, sir!" said buck-toothed Ed, who came recommended from Bik Bohtum's *Barnacle*. He could handle the windlass of the ship's two highflying jibs with ease, and was a good teacher, too. Meanwhile, Rawley would have some honest work, thought Lince, leg or no.

Senthellzia sent Harm up to the crow's nest and rolled up her sleeves, eager to start her midshipman's training. The tall, strong-armed

Senthellzia tied her long red hair back in a ponytail and wound it under a tight cap. Bombo looked worried as he followed her up the ladderway to the fo'c's'le.

"I'm not touching that line," Rawley said to the men of watch two by the starboard sheet. Rawley had built a handle onto his wooden right leg that helped him move and bend it. He hooked his hand in the handle, locked his wooden knee, and leaned his weight on the wooden leg. "I'm the ship's carpenter, not a deck hand! Lince is crazy putting me on a watch!"

"You were just assigned to my watch, Mister," said Lanning. "And you will grab that line, plant that stump, and give your dainty little palms a good blistering!"

"Lanning, my dear lad, I can do much better than that." Rawley winked. "Hey, Bultin, I meant to tell you earlier, but with all the hurrahs and such…Do ya see that big clown over there on the first watch?" Rawley pointed at Tintil, a man who stood a good head taller and about a foot wider than his mates on that watch. "Do you know what Tintil's been saying about you?"

"Huh?" asked Bultin. "Tintil not a clown! What he say about me?"

"He said yer a bungle-fish, Bultin; he said that you're soft as a toad and couldn't lift a spoon without rippin' yer gut-whiskers. Now how do you suppose he'd know a thing like that about you?"

Bultin grunted. The big man's face with his crooked teeth looked permanently confused, anyway, but even more so, now. "Tintil say that?" His brows were like a caved-in thatched roof.

Lanning approved of the carpenter's contribution. "Grab hold, Bultin, ya gonna let Tintil's watch beat us?"

"After he be calling you that?" asked Rollum.

Bultin nearly pulverized the line in his hands, his jaws grinding like millstones.

The watches were in position.

Karlock held a long stick poised over the bridge rail.

Nil nodded from the bridge.

"Heave the main yard port!" Lince yelled, and with the rhythmic rap of Karlock's stick the first watch frantically heaved the port sheet in long, aftward motions, tilting the yardarm above. Tintil led the watch, reeling in the line as his companions cheered him on, more or less pretending to help. Karlock's stick stopped on the eleventh rap.

"Eleven, sir!" said Karlock.

"Thank you, sir!" said Lince.

The ship tacked starboard, southwest over the sea.

"Hey, Bultin: ya see that big idiot abaft?" whispered Lanning in Bultin's ear, for Lanning was directly behind him on the hauling line. Lanning pointed to an enormous man on the aftercastle who might even be larger than Bultin and who surely surpassed him in simplicity. He had a baby's face with the tiniest ears and nose. He was beardless, like Bultin, and strong as an ox.

"Bat?" said Bultin. "He not an idiot! What he say?"

"Bat said you got big eating dumplings and that yer weaker than a baby under all that blubber." Lanning poked Bultin's tunic. "Is that true?"

"It's a mighty shame if those two beat us!" said Rawley. "'Kind of prove their point, I'd guess it would. 'Show which watch got the short end, as it were."

Bultin quaked and the others smiled and got a grip behind him.

Lince shouted, "Lateen starboard! Mind the jibs!"

There was a mad confusion since the third watch had been in the midst of changing their line order. Bat finally flung everyone aside and dove at the line, smashing his head on the aft rail. Moaning, the huge sailor pulled the lateen sheet through the smoking halyard and the sail shifted until the high end came down on the other side, and they rigged the triangular sail starboard.

The *Sea Mare* leveled as she tacked port.

The third watch cheered arrogantly, for despite their rocky start, only ten raps had sounded.

Bultin gripped the line. "Bultin," whispered Lanning. "Was your daddy half-donkey? My gosh! Because that's what Tintil and Bat were telling…"
"Oh, Tintil!" Bultin bellowed.
"Heave the mainsail starboard, *arrgh!*" growled Lince.
Bultin ripped loose, knocking the others on their backsides as he sucked the line out of the sky and wrenched the main yard starboard in *eight beats!*
The members of the second watch hooted and jeered at the others, flocking around Bultin who scoffed boldly at Bat and Tintil.
"First watch: man the lateen! Third watch: man the port sheet! Second watch: stand by!"
The Creature yawned and stretched behind Lince, looking at the men with cold, unimpressed eyes as the watches rotated stations.
The watches organized their lines. The third watch would have to beat Bultin's eight, but Bat, quite over his anger, was swooning from his collision with the aft rail, and was grasping his head like a nutcracker. His fellows pushed him and desperately gave him the line, but Bat groaned and shoved them away. In vain, they pulled the sheet themselves, disjointedly, and the final count was twenty-one.
For a ripe moment the third watch was battered with jeers, until Lince cut it short: "Lateen, starboard!" he growled.
This time, Tintil braced himself and pulled the lateen yard over in a formidable five beats, and they trimmed the sail in three more.
Above boos and whistles, Lince called the next order. "First watch: starboard sheet! Second watch: lateen! Third watch: stand by!"
The first and second watches traded places.
Bultin took the line, and the others in watch two lined up behind him. "Lateen aport!"
Bultin groaned and gave a dangerous heave but the yard did not budge. He pulled again, this time causing the lateen yard to bow slightly, but it did not move.
"Check the line!" yelled Rollum.

Rawley eagerly dropped the line and ran to the halyard. "They've cinched it with a slip-knot!" Rawley reached down and unraveled the knot with a tug and all the force Bultin was exerting was released. The lateen swung and settled over in four beats and they quickly trimmed the sail—but the final count was a dismal *eleven*.

"Of course, this means war," muttered Lanning, glaring at the men of the first watch who were squirming and snickering furtively.

Karlock tallied up the scores. "It's a tie between watch one and watch two!"

"First and second watches take the port and starboard sheets," barked Lince. "Third watch, go to the poop deck and watch some real seamanship!"

"Lanning!" hissed Rawley.

"What, what!" snapped Lanning, still disgusted by the first watch's backhanded tactics.

"We can retaliate."

"What?" asked Lanning. "Don't tell me!" Lanning frowned and closed his eyes. "Just go."

Rawley strolled over the deck in a bouncing gait on his spring-loaded leg. He wielded a file as though he was going to smooth a rough spot on the port rail. He was the ship's carpenter and was within his rights, so Lince could not object. Naturally, Rawley's inspection brought him close to the men of the first watch.

"Heave the mainsail starboard!" yelled Lince.

The second watch—or Bultin—wrenched the sail starboard at fair speed, finishing the job in 10 beats.

Meanwhile, the men of the first watch took notice of the ship's carpenter who looked horrified as he scrutinized the block and tackle the men were about to try—a sight none too comforting.

Rept turned from his place on the line to study the carpenter's terrified expression.

"*Noooo* way!" Rawley shook his head. "One good pull and she'll snap like a whip!"

The men dropped the line and scrutinized the tackle for the fatal defect.

"Heave the mainsail starboard!" yelled Lince.

But the men of watch one did not budge, for the ship's carpenter had pronounced the rigging unfit.

The beat of Karlock's stick compelled them, but Rawley's word was weighty.

When the Captain saw the hazard Rawley had spotted, their turn would not be counted.

Rawley had bent down suddenly, opened a compartment in his leg, and pulled out a wooden mallet.

He bounced over to the railing and pounded in a loose belaying pin near the chainplates. "That'll do her!" he smiled, and winked at the men.

For a moment the men of the first watch gaped uncomprehending at the carpenter. Rept moaned then and turned to lift the line, and in a scrambling surge the men retrieved it, but the ensuing effort was painful to behold.

Twenty-three beats later, they were done, and they turned in rage at Rawley, who whistled as he looked over this and that, tweaking and filing like the responsible carpenter that he was. Then they cursed themselves, for the treacherous scoundrel had never actually claimed the rigging was unfit.

Rawley winked at Lanning across the deck when suddenly Lince's cat crossed his path. Lince appeared next, and the first mate's three eyes burned the grin off Rawley's face.

"A fine day for sailin', sir!" said Rawley, limping out from under Lince's glare.

When Rawley returned to the men of the second watch, they were doing the honors of grinding salt into the other watches' wounds. Bultin had been hoisted onto the shoulders of about seven men, and, as etiquette allowed, he was now abusing Bat and Tintil with a series of especially lewd gestures.

"Lince was watching you like a hawk, Rawley," whispered Lanning. "And so was that bloody Creature of his. They talk to each other, they say."

"I don't doubt it," Rawley snorted.

Nil rang the bell. "The victor of the watch games is the second watch, who will now possess certain privileges that shall be posted on my cabin door!" he announced from the bridge.

Bitterly, the other watches endured a renewed outburst of gloating.

"Now men, and Lady Tunn, this ship needs both sailors and fighters," said Nil. "Many among you are skilled in the arts of war, in swordplay and the like. Even as the sailors train you in seafare, you must train the sailors in warfare, for we will need both skills for our mission. Fix a course due south and go to a light watch, taking your morning mess in shifts, and rotate to the aftercastle for training in fencing and hand-to-hand combat. Two from each watch should join me on the main deck. These millstones behind the mainmast are to be tied to the nets clewed amidships. In the event we come across a sea beast, I will call these men to release the millstones to weigh down the nets. Other men shall be assigned to the harpoons that will cast the nets over whatever terrors might attack us. The catapults abaft the harpoons will fire the clay urns of oil stored beside them, and four men from each watch shall learn how to fire them.

"Lince, Karlock and I will show all of you in groups how to work these weapons, and everyone will be assigned a battle station, and a secondary battle station, and a third. We are heading into mystery, men. All that is certain is that great dangers are waiting for us ahead. Therefore, everyone must learn everything about how to run this ship's defenses so that we will be ready as a crew for any turn of fortune. Garner, leader of the third watch, will take the conn."

"Second watch: take yer mess!" barked Lince. "First watch: take the mainsail port and catch this southeasterly! Third watch: take the lateen port. We're on a heading due south, now, aye! Mr. Feferl, I want Jootle to watch that lateen and squeak if there's a thing wrong with it, eh, sir? When the second watch is finished with mess git to the poop deck for fencing and archery lessons, and those that know will do the teachin'. Then the first watch can take its mess. Watch three will bring up the rear! Now move, and be quick about it, Mister, I see you draggin' yer feet and scratchin' yer head there, ya lug-butt, Mister Bat!"

* * *

The *Sea Mare* cut a swath over the rolling seas.

The going was smooth, the sky was clear, and the spring wind was warm. For hours the men moved from one task to another and took their mess in shifts, a delicious breakfast of fried ham and egg fritters with a draught of black tea and apple juice. Each in their turn was assigned a battle station and each took a sword and bow.

They sailed south six hours through the gulf of Gwylor, minding not to tarry too far west where the reefs were, and keeping an eye forward for the cloud that marked the beginning of the Terrors.

At noon, they were a hundred miles from their starting point, the *Sea Mare* handling like a champion falcon as it winged over the waves, steady and swift. Nil rotated the men off their watches to take their mess, a meal of crispy rolls stuffed with creamed leeks and lamb, a big ripe orange, and a wedge of hard yellow cheese.

Pickle was outdoing himself.

After lunch, Rollum, the subject of Senthellzia's admiring eyes, capered and bragged to the Ameulentians on the aftercastle about how his countrymen soared on boards across the sea. The Ameulentian sailors had heard of the practice and expressed doubt that it was possible. Rollum eagerly disappeared below deck and returned in a flash with his polished "sea-board," carved out of Demoldan teak. He tied its long coiled line to the taffrail and before everyone's amazed eyes he hurled it overboard onto the *Sea Mare*'s wake, diving in after it.

Rollum plunged into the creamy sea and emerged, shaking his long golden hair. He grabbed the silken line and slid down as it unwound to the sea-board, which he caught with practiced ease. He flipped onto the board on his knees and rode the wooden shield over the water, much to the Ameulentians' astonishment. Moreover, Rollum was able to steer the board by lifting either edge, cutting to and fro across the wake while brashly striking comical poses.

Lince was soon on the scene. "You haul in that man, and that means now and NO OTHER INSTANT!" he roared.

The men nearby grabbed hold of Rollum's line and hauled him in. The Demoldan seemed to see what had happened, and yet he smiled, relaxing as he rode the sea-board, enjoying the ride while it still lasted.

They pulled the Demoldan aboard and Lince greeted him. "You may be a prince in yonder lands, Mister, but on this vessel yer startin' to become grit in my eye!"

"Yes, sir!" nodded Rollum, smiling and dripping on the deck, holding his slick sea-board and looking achingly handsome to Senthellzia, who had watched him riding the wake with awe.

"No more of that outlandish behavior, you hear, your highness?"

"No, sir," nodded Rollum.

Lince frowned but accepted Rollum's answer. "Stow this thing and get back to your post!"

"I am doing it even now!"

"Right you are, your Majesty!"

In the rigging aloft, Jootle suddenly screamed, causing Harm to take flight.

The Creature growled at Lince's heel.

Nil lifted his spyglass.

A wall of white cloud had risen over the southern horizon.

*   *   *

Part Three

Chapter 21

▼

The Fog Lifts

An immense wedge of cloud thrust at the *Sea Mare*, covering the entire southern waters and pointing, directly it seemed, at the *Sea Mare*'s bowsprit.

Though the sun was now overhead and hot, it did not cut this fog.

"A big cloud, eh, Lince?" said Nil.

"Aye, a queer bit of weather."

"Get a man aloft," said Nil. "Cut her speed."

"Ed, get down the jibs and man the crow's nest! You, Lady Tunn and Bombo, get back out of the way now. Clew the mainsail by half, men, do it right, and right quick! Yes, indeed, that's it and yes, yes, yes, man! Well done, 'twas! Tell us what ya see, Ed, once yer up now! Take it easy up there, spread out, get your feet right! Mr. Feferl, Jootle will howl if he sees a speck of land now, eh, sir?"

"Yes, Mr. Neery-Atton!" said Feferl, signaling the monkey who was still perched in the lateen shrouds. Jootle swung along the stay lines to the crow's nest.

"Right!"

The *Sea Mare* slowed on the glistening swells as her sails were trimmed.

Even the wind seemed to hold its breath as they approached the thick cloud.

"This cloud is much bigger than Teldon's chart shows, eh?" murmured Nil to Karlock beside him on the bridge.

"For sure. Whatever's beneath that cloud doesn't spread so far east, nor so far west, Nil. The question is, where do we cut in?"

"There's three islands rumored to lie due south beneath the fog. No one knows where, exactly."

"Aye," sighed Karlock.

"We'll approach slow," Nil said. "And take it easy. We'll see if the cloud burns off enough to see something."

"Aye, Captain!" said Lince below. "Keep a Sharpeye, Ed! The first sign of land, Feferl, sir, I want that monkey hollerin' his head off!"

"What can Harm do, Lady Tunn?" asked Nil.

Senthellzia looked up from beside the forecastle's ladderway where she had gone to get out of the way of the sailors. "Harm can see farther than a monkey or a man, sir! I'll send him aloft to look for land. He'll come back with a bird if there be land ahead, and he'll pipe how many leagues he flew to get it!" Senthellzia imitated the muted cry of the falcon, clicking her tongue as she stroked the sleek bird three times, and Harm took off, slipping up through the rigging.

"The cloud approaches, Captain," said Lince. "It's coming at us a bit now."

Harm disappeared over the fog.

Jootle screamed and at the same time Ed yelled, "Land!" from the crow's nest. "Two leagues to the southeast!"

Karlock took the conn as Nil looked through his spyglass down the eastern edge of the wedge of cloud. "An islet is all, revealed by the receding fog there. The sun's burning it off."

The corner of the cloud was fast approaching when Nil, at the last moment, conned the *Sea Mare* port along the eastern border.

Lince had the men trim the sails as they shipped past the misty wall toward the small island peaking from under the murk ahead.

With a peal, Harm dove down through the lines and dropped a petrel at Senthellzia's feet, piping once. "Less than a mile, Captain Ramesis!" she shouted. "Due south, there is land."

The fog off the starboard bow thinned and a rocky cliff appeared perilously close to the *Sea Mare*.

Nil conned her aport, and they safely passed the tall, round islet at the edge of the fog, seeing the tortured stone on its cliffs that seemed filled with mouths and eyes.

The mist lifted like a series of curtains now to the south, revealing another islet jutting out of the gray only a league distant.

"These may be the three islands on Teldon's map, Captain!" said Lince.

"Yes," said Nil. "Perhaps the forbidding fog is a bluff." Nil rubbed his thick beard, trying to second-guess Trinadol's design.

"Where there's two or three islands there could be many," cautioned Karlock. "And where there's a cloud, there's land. This cloud mounts pretty high due south of us, Nil. I'd say there's something under it. These small isles we see can't be all this fog conceals."

"Maybe, Karlock. But a cut through the fog could give us a quicker route and better cover at the same time until we are out of the Rollock's range."

"Who knows what we'll find in that fog?" said Lanning.

"Maybe this fog and our fear are setting a course for us, Lanning!" said Nil. "I don't like the fog charting our course."

"Aye, I get your meaning, Captain," said Karlock. "But let's proceed a bit more toward yonder isle. The fog is good cover, if only on one flank."

"Aye, for cover to the south at least, but a quick cut south of yonder isle might be a good move, Karlock."

"A good move, maybe, aye." Karlock frowned.

"Arm yourselves!" said Lince, never stingy with caution. "Sairkon, Overly, and Sowernut, haul the ship's store of arrows to the main deck. Rept, get a team of eight and batten the flood bulkheads in the castles and the Green Deck! Right now, and when else were you thinking, Mister Overly? Get goin'!"

The virgin vessel streamed beside the fog bank, catching the south wind with the lateen and only half the mainsail showing.

Ed peered from the crow's nest through his spyglass farther down along the edge of the cloud to the east.

They neared the second island jutting out of the fog and saw bubbles frozen as they burst in the pockmarked rock.

Nil took Karlock's advice and they passed north of the grotesque island along the border of the cloud.

Jootle yodeled alarm aloft.

"Land!" Feferl cried. "Another island, Captain, five leagues or more to the southeast, at the edge of the cloud!"

"Fifteen miles?" said Lince. "That would be the island of the Crystal Dragon, according to the charts, Captain!"

"We are being led by the nose," Nil said. "The fog rules a course connecting these four isles."

The statue of Trinadol as a boy mounted over Ed's head in the crow's nest lit like a white ember over the decks, and Ed cringed beneath it. "Captain!" Ed cried, covering his eyes in the near-blinding light.

Karlock looked up with wonder at the statue, for this was the one Trinadol had charmed the day they slew the sea monster Knot, and Karlock had donated it to the *Sea Mare*. "Nilly, it works! It's never flashed before!"

"Good! Trinadol must be alive!" said Nil. "But it means we're in danger, men!"

"Battle stations!" Lince shouted.

The men quickly manned the harpoons, catapults, weights and nets as light watches minded the sails.

The men's weapons were hoisted on a flat through the aft sea doors, and the men armed themselves, rotating off their stations.

Then, around the rocky cliff of the approaching isle, only a few hundred yards off their bow, came a creature beyond their dreaming.

For a moment they were too confused by what they saw to believe their own eyes: a crystal monster reaching pincered arms like giant cranes at the

Sea Mare as fins rippled furiously along its long, glassen tail like the oars of a galley.

Longer than the *Sea Mare*, the creature emitted a chilling scream like a choir of crickets as it propelled itself around the jutting isle and reached its arms in all directions, lunging forward to snip at the ship's rigging with its crystal scissors as she passed.

Dillon Tobbs gripped the rail near the bowsprit by Lanning. He and Lanning had been assigned to load the starboard crossbow with harpoons during battle. Tobbs yelled out, suddenly, "I think this is a lobster baby, Captain! It looks like the larval stage of a lobster that swims free in the ocean! Only this one's bigger than the ship, somehow!"

"Yes, Mister Tobbs, record it in your journal, now hard starboard, mates!" bayed Nil, and the crew heaved the mainyard port to cup the southerly as Nil wheeled the rudder south, yawing the *Sea Mare* straight into the wall of fog.

* * *

As if preparing for a dive, the crew drew a breath, and their eyes were suddenly blinded by the cotton-thick mist beating warm against their cheeks.

Nil held his hand before him, incredulous at the fog's density, but he could not see his own hand at any distance from his eyes. He dropped his arm and gripped the helm-wheel as if to make sure it was really there.

"Hold the helm steady!" said Lince, and his voice rang loud in the white blindness.

"Aye," said Nil, holding the wheel fast, and as the sound of his voice ended, the fog wrapped folds around the *Sea Mare*'s crew, separating each from the next.

Lanning stood beside Tobbs, but after a while he began to wonder where he stood, and even if the ship was still beneath him. There was a distant, steady roar like surf against a shore. Lanning's eyes searched the white fog with growing worry, looking for the rest of the *Sea Mare*, the rest of the crew.

The deck lurched, and then leveled.

The men looked toward the Captain where the bridge had been before the fog erased it.

"What was that?" Lanning asked, startled by the volume of his own voice.

He needed to reassure himself that the others were still there.

"That was the strangest jolt I've ever felt in my life!" said Overly.

"I've felt stranger," said Sowernut, warily.

"Can Harm get a bird's eye, Senthellzia?" asked Nil.

All heard Senthellzia's strange, intimate clucking and the falcon sang an ascending scale as its wings clapped like footsteps up a spiral stair. "He'll get above and have a look, Captain!" she promised.

"Thank you, milady. If only it were I."

The deck lurched, again.

"What's going on, Nil?" Karlock asked.

"I'm not sure," said a wary Nil.

Again the deck reeled and righted itself.

The hull shuddered and a ghastly sensation grew in the pit of the crew's stomachs. The *Sea Mare* was no longer moving forward, but *sideways*.

A vicious jolt shook her decks, flinging many off their feet as the ship tilted starboard.

A queer gurgling sound boiled around them on the sea, and the crew peered in dread into the impenetrable fog.

Nil tried the wheel, but it was stuck. The rudder had frozen somehow.

The ship moved spasmodically beneath them, as though pulled by a pack of unseen wolves in the water. Her portside rose as though pushed from below.

"Ho! Ah!" cried Lanning.

The mariners looked toward the prow of the ship and heard a splash.

The star of light from Trinadol's statue finally started burning away the mist above, and a gray light filtered down.

Then they could see the ship once more.

Lince dashed over the deck to the starboard rail. "What has caught us, then?" he shouted. Drawing a breath, he climbed over the rail, and jumped.

Even as he did, the white mist lifted and revealed a squirming mass of kelp below him.

Lince crashed into the slimy sea through the snaking tendrils. Kicking, he pushed his head up against a wriggling knot that tightened over him, and he pried at the fleshy cords, thrashing and clawing as he tried to tear an opening in the matted vines. He pulled his knife from the scabbard stitched to his tunic and slashed the vines in a last, berserk stroke.

A short slit opened, and Lince pulled it wide, thrusting his head into the air.

He filled his lungs and looked at the *Sea Mare*.

Her hull was snarled with the grasping fingers of a living sea vine that had converged around her. Red, black, and green tendrils coiled thick around her bowsprit and railings. Lince saw that she was being dragged, but toward what he did not know.

He turned and slashed a phalanx of vines reaching out of the water at him like cobras and he heard a gargled scream behind him. He turned to see Lanning several yards away, wrapped by the sinewy kelp. He was heaving himself to and fro, trying to tear free. Lince slashed through the grisly vines and plowed toward him through the water.

Lanning's arms and legs were in an iron grip, and he finally yielded to the will of the seaweed as it dragged him under the greasy sea.

"Hold on, kid!" Lince slitted his eyes as he met the vines with his knife, but when he felled the last, he saw Lanning had succumbed.

He dove and pulled himself down by the weird roots to slash at the bonds of the young sailor until the kelp's hold was weakened and it recoiled.

He jerked Lanning loose and swam to the surface. Lanning gasped and coughed as Lince cut the last clinging vines from his shoulders. Then Lince swam laboriously toward the *Sea Mare* as Lanning gripped him around his neck.

Another large bed of seaweed sensed their thrashing and streamed forward to cut them off. Lince was near exhaustion and he could not fight another fight. Sighing bitterly, he flung his knife through the air.

The knifepoint pierced a membranous bulb in the center of the seaweed cluster and, with an oily spray of purple, the bulb popped and the entire cluster around it was pulled under the sea.

The bulbs kept the writhing vines afloat, Lince realized, as a cord struck him on the back of the head. He wheeled to see the end of a line thrown by Nil from the deck, and he grabbed it and, with Lanning in tow, Nil pulled them both in.

"Wearin' boots, are ya, boy?" Lince chided Lanning as they drew closer the *Sea Mare*'s broadside. "Always wear light shoes. Wear moccasins, if need be, with tough soles, like mine. Makes it easier to swim."

When Lince got to the side of the ship, Nil and some others lifted him and Lanning, whose boots were brimming with water, out of the water over the vines. They fell over the rail on the deck in a heap, and Lanning crawled to his knees.

The Creature walked on Lince's chest and ground its face into Lince's nose.

"Are you all right?" asked Nil.

The two laughed weakly.

"Good! Then take a sword and fight!" Nil chopped at the vines on the rail beside Bruthru Zee.

As they stood catching their breath and gathering their wits, Lince and Lanning saw beds of seaweed converging all around them over the bay. To the south, shrouded in sunlit clouds of mist, a great waterfall flowed over a towering gray cliff into the bay.

"Archers take yer bows and aim at those blasted ugly bulbs!" shouted Lince. "Pierce those buoys, men, and the vines'll sink!"

Senthellzia took aim on the fo'c's'le with three men she had chosen as the best archers. Other men, also familiar with the bow, fired from the aftercastle at the targets Lince suggested.

"Look!" cried Lanning.

In the misty distance the two jagged cliffs that formed the wedge-shaped bay met behind the roaring falls. A distant peak of stone towered above, overflowing dense white cloud like a foaming tankard of beer. Rivulets of water ran down the slopes of this great peak, forming rivers that joined the great waterfall that veiled a brooding cave.

"They weren't two islands at all," said Lanning.

Lince saw that the two cliffs that joined behind the waterfall and formed the arms of the wedge-shaped bay ended in two peaked points, the round "islands" they had seen reaching out of the fog.

The deck reeled, and the *Sea Mare* lurched sideways.

"Toward the falls," Lince muttered.

Senthellzia and the other archers started making progress puncturing the purple bulbs. Sinking the gas-filled floats helped clear the kelp beds from around the *Sea Mare*, but the kelp that already wrapped thick around her hull was tying itself to the spikes on her keel and grasping up at her rail and rigging.

Young Nofair of the first watch cinched a line around his ankles and had his watch mates lower him over the fo'c's'le. He slashed at the vines as they swung him to and fro. The trick worked as Nofair flayed deep layers of vines back from the bow.

Lince fetched a weapon, but Lanning stood staring as more clusters came to the side of the *Sea Mare*, each with a thousand more vines. The whole, wriggling bay was embracing the ship like a giant, single being. She was being pulled fast now, though the falls were still a mile distant.

Lanning saw the seaweed's shining trunk, as wide as a man was tall, thrusting out of the cave under the pounding falls. All the beds of seaweed seemed to branch out into the bay from this root.

"You see the cave?" cried a voice and a hand clapped Lanning's shoulder, startling him.

It was Dillon Tobbs, the young ship's scientist.

"Yes, lad?"

"That's where the beast's stomach is."

"Oh," nodded Lanning. "Thanks!" Lanning ran to fetch a sword.

*   *   *

The sea had filled half the Lightstone Tower.

The level was rising faster now, over three inches an hour.

Trinadol had just come back from measuring the time he had left in his hourglass, and he confirmed his conclusion that the water would rise faster as the Tower's girth tapered. He had four days, maybe five.

Trinadol sat cross-legged on the white carpet of his room with the six remaining pieces of the Cronus Star glimmering darkly before him. His candle burned beside his bed, its heat alone warming the room.

One of the six fragments of the Cronus Star suddenly sparkled with a faceted blue fire.

He opened his eyes and seized the shard in the same motion. He focused on a single facet on its bevel.

Trinadol gradually distinguished an image, a view from a ship's mast. He could see men fighting on the decks below.

The facet was too small so he used his spyglass to peer into the diamond.

Now Trinadol could see a battle ensuing. The men on the ship were fighting one of his own creations.

"By what right can I ask for pity?" Trinadol cried aloud. "Behold the evil Trinadol has wrought! And now there is a man, I see, swinging valiantly on a rope to hew the terrible weed—dragged away and drowned by my own pitiless hand! Do they fight for me? Against my own wickedness?"

Trinadol watched the gruesome spectacle through the shattered gem as though witnessing his own soul condemned before his eyes.

*   *   *

Drugor smiled with Trinadol's *face in the Wynderne World.*

"The Sea Mare *shall be devoured," he announced, looking into the pool of* Halarian *water with a few of his unhappy advisors.*

"I want more knocking about, eh, Theosophiclar? Everyone, I mean each and everyone, is to fight and batter each other and struggle in combat on this greensward. I want this greensward black with blood," he cried. The grass turned black at his notion. "And everyone bloody, dripping red! Let the bloodletting begin!"

"Yes, lord," quailed Theosophiclar, the three-eyed court engineer who was bewildered and embittered after having tasted the sweet sanity of King Trinadol *who now seemed so mad and full of bitterness since he had returned, this time without* Neuvia.

Trinadol's *Wyndernalia subjects engaged in a hideous waltz of carnage much to Drugor's satisfaction and he looked down again into the pool and slapped his knee. "I put Senix in this one..." he said, rubbing his chin, unlike* Trinadol, *and glancing at the sky.*

"Who, lord?" asked Theosophiclar.

"Senix is one of the greatest Wynder demons, fool! I persuaded him to take the form of the seaweed. You'll see how diabolical a demon can be!" He raised his arms, fingering the air. "What sport! I haven't felt this way in ages."

Theosophiclar knew this was the Sixth Isle Trinadol *raised in* Hala, *and that by this time good and noble subjects were ready and willing to serve him in the* Hala World *when he called for* them. It was Telniquair, Theosophiclar thought, who had answered the call when **Trinadol** created this island. Theosophiclar knew of no Senix!

The crimson king raved on lustily. "He'll see how pitiful are these mortals he loves so much! And so will you see, Wynderne fools! You think these lowly Hala creatures noble, I know! Watch then! See how weak they are!" He leered at the Wyndernes, a dark Trinadol who mocked every bright memory of him they cherished.

*   *   *

Nofair's mates swung him over the hull so he could reap the vines with his sword when several slimy tendrils coiled around his arm and yanked him with such force that his shoes came off, and he slipped out of the cinch knot around his ankles and fell headfirst into the grasping twists of kelp girding the *Sea Mare*.

Cries of pity rang over the deck as the weed convulsed, surging over Nofair like a thousand pythons.

Nil climbed the bridge and stood there for precious moments as he thought. The rain of arrows was stopping most of the advancing clusters, but the weed already had a purchase on the *Sea Mare* and was weighing her down as its leathery cables hauled her toward the deadly cascade.

A party headed by Rollum charged the aftercastle. Senthellzia shot more arrows into the bulbs as Rollum leaned over the balustrade near her, sweeping his blade through the groping tendrils like a reaper. Barnel, another sailor, followed the strong Demoldan's example and leaned beside him.

"What sombrous entwinements!" lamented Pickle as he swung his old bronze sword.

"What a fix!" cried Bombo, wielding a meat cleaver.

They fought with the others on the main deck, prying vines from the shrouds and cutting them, careful not to sever the ship's rigging as the falls grew louder off the starboard rail.

Lanning, scraping the vines from the rail and catapults futilely, turned and ran to the ladder of the bridge. "Captain!" he said as he reached the top.

Nil turned sharply. "What, Mister?"

"Tobbs says the seaweed's stomach is in yonder cave!"

"Tobbs! Get to the bridge!" yelled Lince who had ears in the back of his head, as well as the extra eye on top.

The biologist, who had been neatly cutting the vines from the fo'c's'le, dashed to the bridge.

"Tobbs, you say its stomach is in the cave, behind the fall?" asked Nil.

"Yes, sir! I think so."

"And this seaweed issues from that cave?"

"Yes! From pools of acid, maybe, where it digests its victims…"

Nil smacked his lips. They were less than half a mile from the falls. The large vines grew thicker and joined together into five great branches that seemed to join at the wrist of this monstrous hand before the waterfall. "I wonder…" Nil muttered, rubbing his thick beard. "Bultin! Tintil! Report to the bridge!"

Both big men ran down the deck. They knew special dangers were a strong man's burden at sea, the battening of hatches against a storm, the reefing of a wild sail, the untangling broken spars to reach a sheet that could right a gale-crushed vessel. They stood ready now before their captain.

"Look there, men!" said Nil, pointing toward the looming tower of water. "Beyond that fall's a cave! The root of this weed sprouts from it. Men strong enough to chop that trunk are needed now! It might be possible to climb on top of the main branches to the base of the falls. Maybe a man could dive under then and climb up into yonder grotto. There, perhaps, this great hand might be severed at the wrist. What say you men? Are you up to it?"

"If there's a chance, we'll do it!" said Bultin.

"Aye! But how?" Tintil scratched his head.

Lanning looked through Nil's spyglass and saw what looked like Nofair's drowned body being dragged toward the falls, passed from vine to vine beside the central trunk.

"With knives ya should be able to get a purchase on the backs of these big branches, and climb along," said Lince. "You'll have to wave your sword a mite to keep off the reachers. They come out of the water at ya. But you can pull yerself forward by the knives and slide along to the main branches. Then you'll have to dive fer it, and kick under the falls to get to the cave."

"How do we get past this muck wrapped all around us?"

"Maybe we can get a harpoon into one of the main branches," said Nil. "Then you can slide down the line."

"You heard the Captain, you men at the starboard harpoon!"

The contingent there, minus Lanning and Dillon Tobbs, scrambled to assign new loaders.

"String up a harpoon and aim at one of the big branches! Bury it deep, bowman."

"Aye, sir!" cried Rept, who sat in the bowman's chair, eyeing the mark. This was the harpoon that slew Knot, and Rept let go the harpoon and it sang true carrying its twirling line as it plunged into a branch five feet thick. Other men pulled the harpoon line through a block and made it fast.

"May the Gairanor go with you," said Nil.

"Yassir!" they both yelled, and Tintil and Bultin ran to the fo'c's'le.

Lanning had the conn as Nil descended the bridge, and ran to the fo'c's'le behind Lince.

"Keep the arrows comin', and aim for that slippery branch we've harpooned! Put as many in her as far as you can shoot!" said Lince. "That'll give our men somethin' to grab onto!"

"Mind not hit us!" said Bultin, putting on sealskin gloves and grabbing the line of the harpoon, and he pulled his legs up around it. He slid himself down, his heavy sword sheathed at his hip and two knives slung around his neck.

Bultin crossed over the winding vines encasing the *Sea Mare*'s hull and out over the water. The harpoon, biting into the greasy flesh of the branch with its barbed point, held firm till he reached the stalk and straddled it. Tintil grabbed hold of the line behind him and shimmied across as Bultin had done.

Bultin pulled both knives out of their scabbards and, gripping them sideways, planted the blades into the greasy brown flesh of the vine to pull himself forward. The vine Bultin embraced suddenly lurched toward the *Sea Mare*, relaxing the harpoon line and dropping Tintil onto the thick mat of vines wound around the hull.

The vines were packed solidly, and it was only for the hull's strength, fitted with iron reinforcements, that the *Sea Mare* was not crushed by their combined strength. Tintil unwound his legs from the line and climbed to his feet on the tight mesh of kelp and then he let go of the line and ran toward Bultin, meaning to leap onto the branch behind him. But even as he ran, the hard vines beneath him loosened like noodles, and Tintil fell through. The kelp closed over him so fast it sent a spray of water into the air and Tintil was buried under the churning mass.

Bultin turned to the task ahead, tears streaming down his face. The thick stalk floated so high only his feet touched the sea. The musclebound giant clawed his way forward, planting one knife after another, mindful of the kelp beds streaming toward him.

Those on the *Sea Mare* looked ominously at Bultin every chance they could. The first nodding waves stirred by the waterfall nudged the *Sea Mare*'s broadside. Mist chilled her decks as the cave loomed wider behind the thundering curtain.

The vine was too slippery for Bultin and he nearly fell over the side, but he gripped his legs and dug in his heels to right himself. At times he had to pause, and cut off a random feeler that caught his ankle, but he tried to move forward as fast as possible. The vine was slow to react, gathering behind him against the branch as he moved forward.

It was exhausting to move like this, though, and even Bultin was hard-pressed. The branch grew thicker, making it harder to straddle.

He came to a fork and climbed on top of a broader stalk. He tried to crawl on hands and knees, which worked for about ten yards before he started to slide off. He desperately spread his legs and arms to grab his balance. A vine whipped around his throat and he slashed it with his knife. He pried it from his neck and threw it into the sea, planting a knife with his left hand and pulling himself forward.

Another fork was ahead, and the great pillar of water drenched him in its sweat, rocking the branch and making it slicker. Bultin had made it to within 50 yards of the falls.

He looked behind him and saw the *Sea Mare* was being pulled faster now. He charged ahead, hand over hand.

He came to another joint and the trunk became knottier, wider, not as slick. Again, he got on all fours and scrambled forward, splaying out and planting both knives whenever a wave knocked him off balance. Finally, he made it to one of the five main branches that joined at the base of the falls.

Bultin tried running on the back of the great branch between swells, diving down and driving in the knives when he lost his balance.

"By the Gairanor, he's a champion!" said Rawley, impressed.

Lanning nodded.

Bultin rose between waves to run again across the heaving branch. He made it 20 feet before losing his balance. He fell over the left side, clawed with his knife and missed, stabbing his own leg, but with his left hand he pulled his sword from its hilt and planted it in the side of the branch.

He fell over the hilt, holding onto the bending sword as his legs splashed in the water.

"That bloody beautiful brute!" said Rawley, stomping his wooden leg on the deck.

Bultin gripped both hands on the hilt of his sword, and swung from side to side. On the third swing, he got back astride the branch. He worked out the blade, holding on with the one knife he had left. When he got the sword loose he used it to rake along the side of the vine and steady himself as he crawled forward on bloody knees.

He crossed the last distance to the trunk.

He looked up at the billowing waterfall, clinging to the brown neck of the weed-beast. Behind him, Bultin could hear shouts of encouragement. The knotted trunk bent down into the water before him, ducking under the crushing weight of the falls.

Bultin was not sure he could swim to the other side, but he knew he had no choice and started breathing in and out very fast, a trick his father had taught him. He put his sword in its scabbard and held his knife in his left hand, continuing to breathe until he was dizzy. Then he sucked in a barrel-full of air and dove into the sea.

The fall beat Bultin's back, sending him deeper as he kicked through a blinding white haze of bubbles. The force seemed endless, and he kicked deeper till he thought he could never get to the surface again. He ran into a wall of rock, and climbed up across it, kicking and pulling, and he burst out of the sea onto a black ledge of rock pocked with holes.

The thunder of the falls filled the high cavern. The trunk of the seaweed rose beside him out of the sea, draped over the ledge.

On the other side of the ledge, Bultin saw a wide pool reaching into the cave, steaming with wisps of acrid fumes. Large pads of plant-flesh layered the bottom of the pool from which innumerable cords sprouted and joined to form the gigantic trunk. Bultin saw the pale, shredded form of a dolphin and other fish on the bottom of the stinking pool. Then he saw what appeared to be Nofair, but his body was already melting away.

Bultin drew his sword and ran at the trunk.

He landed his first blow across the shoulder of the vine and shuddered from the resistance he met. Nevertheless, the trunk had never been so scathed, and vines across the entire bay convulsed.

He tore the blade from the slit and lifted it again.

Another stroke, and a wedge was opened. Frantically, he hacked down, cutting chunks from the mass of the trunk. Between strokes, he glanced at the thundering wall to his right.

Mowing like a windmill, Bultin soon ran out of steam. An impressive gouge had been gashed, but it was a scratch compared to the whole.

By this time, though Bultin could not know it, the bay had gone wild, and the fist of weed began reeling in its catch much faster. An angry dispatch of kelp beds were heading toward the falls.

Bultin was blind to these events, but a bestial urgency lit his eyes and he bared his teeth, his muscles twisting and quaking with rage as with one flex of his body he plunged the blade down to the halfway point. He pried it loose, and with a frightful stroke matched his previous stroke, opening a wedge. A quarter of the vine was severed.

A flow of brown liquid spluttered from the wound, stinking of rotting vegetation and flesh. He sighed and lifted his blade for another thrust.

A cluster of vines reached under the fall beside him, knotted into a thick fist, and slammed against his side. He staggered, caught off guard, and teetered over the black pool. From behind, the tendrils bashed him again, and he fell forward.

The deathly waters spread wide, but he reached behind and grabbed a few of the vines. As soon as they sensed where they were being dragged, they pulled taut, and saved Bultin from the pool. He pulled himself back onto the ledge and abruptly swung his sword, severing the vines, and they retreated against the falls.

Bultin struck the trunk twice more when the trailers hit him again, more numerous now. He fell to his knees, swinging wildly at them, and they retreated.

He did not know how close the grisly fist was to victory until the *Sea Mare*'s shadow fell across the falls.

Bultin heard shouts in the water's thunder as he turned to the trunk and with two heart-bursting lunges cut another deep wedge in the far side of the trunk.

Since trying to cut all at once was wasting his strength, he concentrated on the side nearest him now. He whittled the gap down with rapid blows until at last he struck the rocky ledge. Only the far half of the trunk remained.

He moved forward into the gash, doused by the rancid blood of the beast that spurted from its grievous wound. His dripping eyes fixed on the notch before him as though he were a tool with a single purpose. A scream tore through the falls, and Bultin's mind swam. He detached from his spent body, viewing the spectacle of his own exhaustion as he swung and swung again. Then a few cords whipped around the blade and pulled it out of his hands, and other vines grabbed his arm and his waist and pulled him onto his back. A fist of bunched vines gathered and bashed into his side, knocking him off the ledge.

He struck the still waters of the pool and plunged deep into its shadow.

Strange arms reached for him on the bottom of the pool and he saw a glowing splinter of light. The tendrils grabbed hold and pulled him down, but a crystal that erupted from the bottom of the pool transfixed him, and he kicked his feet to reach it as he sank.

He saw that the crystal was formed, as if by nature's elements in her slow way, into a perfect sword of melted minerals clear and pure, with a handle connected by brittle fingers to the living rock.

He swung his hand at the hilt, and it broke off into his grip.

With a weak swing, he sliced through the fleshy arms that gripped him and pushed off the bottom.

He climbed out of the poisoned waters, unsteady and choking, as the bowsprit of the *Sea Mare* pierced the fall before him.

He sobbed and staggered toward the wounded trunk of the monster with the luminous blade hoisted high, and he fell forward, his weak stroke slicing straight through the vine as though through cake, the crystal blade sparking on the stone.

He lay on the rocky ledge, soaked by the spraying blood of the creature as his sight went dark and the shadow of the trunk slid away beside him into the sea.

*   *   *

As the *Sea Mare* withdrew from the waterfall, the men hacking at the weed noticed its grip loosen and when they saw the severed end of the trunk emerge from under the falls, they cheered Bultin's miraculous deed.

The beds of kelp began disappearing across the entire bay.

Nil ordered the sails clewed and had a boat put down to rescue Bultin.

The boat crossed to land unmolested by the vines, and a number of men climbed over the rock to the ledge behind the falls. They emerged carrying Bultin and they passed the burly sailor to the men waiting in the boat.

They rowed back to the *Sea Mare*, greeted by cheers and songs as the mariners produced various instruments. But when the boat clunked against the *Sea Mare*'s hull, all could see that Bultin was fast asleep.

They hoisted him with block and tackle over the rail and laid him out to dry on the deck. The sailor was deep in slumber and snoring loudly, clutching a shimmering crystal sword, which the men beheld with awe. He was covered in the sticky brown blood of the vine and Nil had some water brought up to wash him down. Nil splashed a bucket over Bultin's face and another over his chest. To his surprise, the sailor only smiled and smacked his lips over his crooked teeth, wiggling around for a better angle on the deck as he snoozed, gripping his mysterious weapon.

Nil shrugged and said, "Three cheers for him anyway!"

And the men cheered the snoring sailor three times, as the musicians in the crowd began composing songs to remember his deed.

They dropped the lateen sail and started tacking out of the bay against the mild southerly as the sun slanted over the western point. The *Sea Mare* tore loose of the dying vines as she picked up speed, but Nil decided to turn the bay to a good use.

"Lince, let's drop anchor and have this bay for the night."

"Aye, Captain, a good idea. Hear it, men! And Missy, aye!" winked Lince at Senthellzia. "We'll clew the sail in one more league and drop anchor here tonight!"

A hearty approval came up from the decks as Karlock climbed the bridge to join Nil.

"Good thinking, Captain," said Karlock. "I wonder if that other beast is around the corner, and no light left to see it, either."

"We'll tackle that one tomorrow. What a champion is our man Bultin! Mister Zee, have you tended to him?"

The Sarkish physician looked up from Bultin's side. "He is most healthy but quite tired, Captain," said Zee. "I stitched up his leg, but he felt no pain!"

"Thanks, Doctor," smiled Nil. "Mr. Pickle, I hope dinner is on the way, sir!"

"Dinner is on the way, sir!" Bombo called from the galley, and all aboard applauded, giddy just to have another supper after that day.

"Captain!"

"Yes, Mister Tobbs?"

"I tossed the buoy." Tobbs's paper-white skin seemed to invent several new shades of red.

"Tobbs tossed the buoy!" cried Ed from the crow's nest, and everyone had a good laugh.

Nil nodded, suppressing a grin. "Bad luck that we survived, then, Mister Tobbs. You'll have to rewrite everything, I guess."

The crew laughed at Tobbs's expense. He seemed to be on the verge of tears for a moment as the ridicule rained down on him. Then the look of determination that normally possessed his face doubled its intensity. "I have a perfect memory, Captain! My father will tell you. I remember every letter of every word, every stroke of every drawing, every blotch of ink I spilled. I'll write everything back just the way it was!"

"And you'll have another tale to add at the end," Nil smiled. "I guess you better get going before you start forgetting every little spot, Mister Tobbs!" Nil folded his arms, tapping his elbow.

"Yes, sir! I mean, Captain!" Tobbs ran off to his task to the knee-slapping merriment of the crew.

*   *   *

When the anchor bit the sea bottom, and the *Sea Mare* was furled in the bay she had tamed that day, twilight charged the sky with a lavender glow. A spark of summer was in the air as the brightest stars lit their torches.

Lince joined Nil and Karlock on the bridge as the men were allowed free time to socialize.

"We came close, eh, Lince?" said Nil.

"Aye, we lost young Nofair, and Tintil."

"We did, Nilly, and hindsight though it be, it was still a shrewd move to cut into the fog and avoid that other fierce beast," said Karlock.

"Tobbs says it was a lobster fry, made huge," mused Nil grimly.

"Huh?" said Lince. "Whatever it was, Captain, we tricked it, and won the battle here, as well! Boy, is Bultin a lad! And isn't that for sure?" Lince sniffed the air and grinned. "That crazy cook's a sorcerer, I think, Nilly!"

"I've got a bone to pick, Lince Neery-Atton," said Nil. "I never want to see you risk your neck like that again and that's an order!"

Lince smiled, blushing. "Captain," he said. "It's not as though I said 'Hey, risk yer neck!' to myself and then jumped in. It takes hold all of a sudden. I can't help nor hinder it. I saw Lanning fall in and thought 'he's a good lad, a lot like Nilly, and he ought not to die,' is all. And then I was jumping in. I lived."

"Make sure you're not around when someone else needs saving. I need you alive, and so does everyone on this ship."

Lince shrugged.

"By the Gairanor," Nil breathed. "The smell of that dinner does enchant the mind! Pickle is some kind of sorcerer, Lince," he laughed.

The sun lit clouds like fiery plumage over the barren arm of the bay as the dinner bell rang, and all except for a scant watch of grumbling sailors left for mess.

The men took their pewter plates and mugs and filed through the galley as Pickle and Bombo dished out the courses. Fresh veal cooked in thick, spiced gravy with nuts and onions, mashed Enryd and butter, and a healthy portion of grated spinach and leek. Fresh rolls of corn meal with dollops of sour cream crowned the absurdly opulent meal Pickle had conjured. Yet it was the icy bock beer that the men found most satisfying.

Pickle noticed the smiles on the men's faces, and all the wrinkles on his serious face vanished. This was the only time the wild-haired Pickle ever smiled—when he was watching the stunned delight on his audience's faces.

Bultin was finally roused and he was served at the head of the central table, opposite Nil. He blushed brightly and grinned wide as the men sang the songs they had written to remember his deed. He was given a whole dripping shank of veal with stuffing and extra gravy and a tiny silver spoon for the marrow, and his eyes and mouth grew wide. He attacked it like a crooked-toothed lion, topping his feast off with a flagon of the ship's finest mead.

As a final gesture, Pickle and Bombo distributed dessert, a peach cobbler steaming with cinnamon and butter. The meal ended amidst revelry, and Lince suggested it was time to clear the mess for a few hours of free time while the men on watch took their mess.

The mariners grouped in clusters across the decks in the warm, breezy evening. The First Moon waxed silver just shy of full as the stars appeared above.

At sea, watch assignments tended to delineate social groups more than previous friendships. Bultin, Lanning, Rawley, and the other members of the second watch gathered around on the fo'c's'le as they listened to Rollum strum soft chords on his mandolin.

Senthellzia smiled wide at the handsome Demoldan, and he smiled back, his blue eyes openly amorous.

Rawley lit his pipe in the dusk and the match illuminated his right thumb, which seemed thick and weird to Lanning's eye for an instant. He thought he saw a scar around the base of the thumb, but he couldn't be sure. Rawley blew out the match and winked at him. Lanning decided to have a look at Rawley's thumb in the daylight some time.

"So, tell us again how ya found that sword, Bultin," said Overly.

"'Twas at the bottom of the pool," said Bultin.

"And?" said the others.

Lince's cat was playing with a piece of wiggling seaweed on the deck, knocking it around and gnawing on it with its ears tucked back.

"That's where I got it," said Bultin, smiling.

"Well, what did it look like? On the bottom there?"

"All grabby like. Sticky thicket."

"So whatcha do?" asked Lanning.

"So I's aimed for the sword. Bright as a sunray!"

"What was?" asked Rawley.

"It!" said Bultin, holding it up.

They wouldn't get much out of Bultin.

"'Twas Trinadol that put it there!" said Lanning.

"Yep!" Bultin nodded vigorously.

"A stroke of mercy," said Rawley, blowing a stream of smoke. "He gave a way out, though not an easy one. It's a good sign, though."

Rollum and Senthellzia flirted behind the group now, and Harm leaped up with a scornful cry, landing on the shoulder of a surprised Sowernut in the crow's nest.

"May I see your sword, Bultin?" asked Bruthru Zee. He had gone around to check on the other men he had tended that day before coming to see the great sailor.

"Sure," said Bultin, offering the hilt of his crystal sword to the mysterious physician. "Careful, it's sharp, but it doesn't cut me."

Zee pulled it out and looked into the blade, smiling as the dazzle shone over his face. "Wondrous, wondrous," he murmured. "Your sword is living, Sir Bultin." He handed back the crystal blade.

Bultin's head jerked. "Eh?"

"It has life, and a will. Keep it always. You are meant for great things."

"How do you know?" asked Rawley, scratching his bald head as he bit down on his pipe.

"My Sarkish King's sword was passed down to him from Cirilen-Lords. Before my people lived in Sarkland, Trinadol's ancestors reigned over a different people there, before the plague. When my people arrived in Sarkland, many centuries later, they found the sword while digging in the ruins of an ancient city. It, too, possessed a spirit, like this one does. The Lord Trinadol must have made this, for he is a Gheldron, like the founders of Sarkland. It was made by the same gem, I believe, the Cronus Star."

"Gimme it back then," said Bultin, taking the hilt. "Trinadol gave it to me."

"Yes, Bultin." Zee smiled. "Always guard it; it is your responsibility now!"

Alone on the bridge, Nil looked at the Silver Coin in the clear night sky. The King's trap was as much his own, he ruminated. Thoughts of Lelinair stirred the embers in his heart. Then he heard Bruthru Zee on the fo'c's'le singing and drumming a long, toned drum with his rolling fingertips:

King Oru was a bad king
Who ordered men to die
He wasn't such a bad king
The axe was made of lye,
He ordered women hung
But the rope was made of dung.
He flogged the children hard
With a whip made out of lard!
Oh, Oru was a strange King
Oru was!

Nil smiled; the doctor's silly song had cured his heartache.

Lince strode onto the main deck below. "All right, now, stow it in, it's time to hit the hammocks! We'll have plenty of fun tomorrow!"

And so, after one day at sea, all but the night watch took their hard-earned sleep.

*   *   *

Chapter 22

▼

The Race Is On!

The *Sea Mare* weighed anchor before dawn.

The men aloft let the mainsail out, clewed by a third and they tacked against a light wind coming from the northwest and here, especially, the lateen gave the ship legs.

A carpet of mist slid down the slopes of the conical peak behind them, spilling over the waterfall into the bay. The island was shrouding itself again.

They made the eastern point of the bay and turned with the wind. A rose of cloud bloomed orange and pink over the eastern horizon.

The fog had nearly obscured the island again, yet for a moment they could see that it was shaped like a great trident pointing at Gwylor, with only its three rounded points exposed at the edge of the cloud.

The seas were heavier now. They could see on the eastern horizon the horseshoe island that was the home of the sea dragon they encountered the day before. The mouth of its bay faced the Illusion Sea to the south, so named just recently, from fresh reports of its existence. It was said to be a place of madness, though very little was known of it. They must somehow pass between these two terrors, but it better than facing the Rollock, whose island lay in the other direction, to the southwest of the isle they had encountered yesterday.

Nil ordered the jibs set to make the passage as fast as possible, at least, yet he kept the mainsail clewed by a third.

The day was brilliant, and terror seemed far away for the moment. A school of dolphins sewed the shining waves in front of them and filled the air with cheerful squeaks. Smacks of purple jellyfish blossomed across the sea like flowers.

The wind was steady and Lince rotated the watches off the lines to mess. Pickle served a wholesome breakfast of scrambled eggs and chopped tomato, black biscuits, gravy and potato sausage, topped with coffee and lemonade. It was a bracing, fortifying meal and set the crew's mood right as they faced their labors.

Senthellzia sat next to Rollum at the mess, as all politely noted. It was rather nice having the enticing but imposing Lady around, and the sailors of the second watch took it as further proof of their superiority over the other watches. But Senthellzia clearly had eyes only for Rollum.

She was not much for romance and had managed to avoid it for the most part. Some might call Senthellzia an old maid at 34, yet she laughed at that notion, seeing herself rather as a complete person, with an expertise and career of her own. Though her father was a wealthy merchant and social scion who could pay an opulent dowry and richly support her, she had chosen to make use of herself, and this seemed to take her away from the course of love with its promise of motherhood. There had been only a few affairs of the heart for her, fleeting expressions with other women, who admired her for her strength. Until now, she had always competed with men rather than acquiesce to them.

Rollum was from Demold, where chivalry found its home. Women were worshipped in that neighboring kingdom, and their strengths were readily admired and served by the men of that society. The power of creation and pleasure in women was the religion of the Demoldans, and with it came the sanctity of a woman's judgment, good or bad. There was no marriage in Demold. Women chose the men who would father their children, and each man was responsible, on pain of death, for supporting the child he fathered. There were women of great power in Demold, presiding over houses with the children of many successful men. It was natural for the handsome and polite Rollum to shower the accomplished Senthellzia with respect, bowing low and kissing her hand whenever she approached.

Senthellzia, with her tanned face and green eyes and long red hair, looked on Rollum always with a smile, as she did now while she ate breakfast with the second watch in the mess. She was dressed in earthen tones, with a suede vest of brown kidskin, a tight-sleeved shirt of purplish-brown, and black pants of eelskin tucked into tall black boots.

Meanwhile, Harm waited on the crow's nest for his meal, annoyed at his mistress's new affection, preening his feathers disdainfully and looking in disgust at the frowning Jootle, who lolled about in the rigging staring at him curiously.

"You can't understand a word he says, but Pickle's cooking is like poetry!" said Lanning, smacking his lips.

Rollum grunted agreement, and looked out at the fanning wake of the *Sea Mare* that was framed in the wide stern ports.

Senthellzia caught Rollum's left wrist as he brought a forkful to his lips. "What's the cooking like in Demold, eh? How do you like this fare? It's a good sample of what our kitchens offer."

Rollum smiled. "This is tasting like a dream, strange and wonderful. I am liking it, my marvelous Lady," he bowed his swarthy head, the blond strands gesturing on his brow. "I do not miss my homeland's recipes…yet." He smiled, taking the bite.

The Ameulentians laughed and thumped the table.

They heard Lince's growl through the breezeway of the galley: "Git yer bun-skins out of the mess! Finish it up and stretch yer legs!"

All groaned and shoveled down the last morsels, swigging their coffee and juice.

They left through the galley, thanking Pickle profusely, though Bombo took all the credit, and the third watch piled in behind them. The members of the second watch climbed the aftercastle to take a stretch.

Harm flew down and perched jealously on Senthellzia's shoulder.

Soon, all had messed and were on the decks, enjoying the gallant steed's brisk canter over the sea. Nil kept the mainsail clewed by a third as the wind kicked up and he bade Jootle keep an eye on the rig since this was the strongest blow yet she had encountered. The strong sails were proving their worth.

Lince sent Ed up to man the crow's nest, which suited the sharp-eyed sailor fine. Ed kept one eye always on the horseshoe island three points off their port bow for any sign of its resident.

Dillon Tobbs climbed the aft companion ladder and approached the starboard contingent of the second watch, comprising Lanning, Bultin, Rawley, Overly, Sowernut and three others. "Lanning!" he said cheerily, his pale, pudgy cheeks florid. His oily black hair was a mess.

"How are you faring, good scientist?"

"I'm a naturalist, sir, though science it certainly is. It was a wonder what yonder Bultin did, yesterday! Wouldn't you say?"

"Aw, we don't want to give him a big *head*, too!" laughed Lanning, glancing at the blushing brute. "He did the job, all right."

"Well, I just wanted to say hello and offer my congratulations. I guess I'll be of no further bother. Good day," Tobbs said earnestly.

"Oh, knock it off, ya knobby-kneed weed-sucker!" Rawley laughed, resting his weight on his shapely wooden leg, which sprang and creaked at the knee as the deck pitched. He puffed his pipe. "Stick around and make friends."

"All right," said Tobbs, "I will!"

"The *Sea Mare's* really flyin', boys!" said Bultin, grinning his puzzled teeth.

The lateen was set and there was smooth sailing ahead.

"She's the biggest ship I've ever seen, and the fastest, too!"

"Yes, Overly, we know," said Lanning.

"I've been on faster," said Sowernut.

"Name the faster ship!" bellowed Bultin.

Sowernut balked. "Maybe not," he shrugged.

"That's right!" said Bultin.

Lince's cat climbed the companionway with its bowed legs and looked derisively at the men as it jumped onto the rail over the galley. Three of its muscular legs gripped the balustrade as it licked its right paw, basking in the sun.

The men shivered a bit at the sight of the feisty feline.

"What did you say that beastie we saw yesterday was, Doc?" Overly asked Tobbs.

"A microscopic lobster fry. My father was the first to catalog the tiny creatures of the sea, invisible to our naked eyes, by using a microscope. Many are the children of common creatures like lobsters, coral, crabs and octopus."

"So the King made it big, then?" asked Bultin, confused.

"That was the biggest migro-lopic lobster thing I've ever seen!" said Overly without irony, to Sowernut's chagrin, and Sowernut burst out laughing, confounded by the twisted loops Overly's gratuitous enthusiasm always seemed to create. Somehow, Overly and Sowernut always seemed to ship out together, which made for amusing entanglements of their temperaments.

"*Microscopic*," Tobbs corrected. "Tiny."

"But it was big!" said Bultin.

Tobbs looked up at Bultin, despairing at the predicament of explaining anything to him.

"And the wretched kelp? What was that, eh?" Lanning asked.

"It seemed to be a blend of two creatures, Lanning. A microscopic seaweed that gobbles up other tiny animals. And common kelp, which uses bulbs to stay afloat and bask in the sun."

"There was some evil in it, too," said Lanning, remembering its grip.

"That's why Trinadol gave me this," smiled Bultin, resting his hand on the crystal hilt of his sword, which he had slid into a suitable bronze scabbard he bartered from a shipmate after the sword sliced through two copper scabbards.

"That's right, Bultin. And his statue lit," said Lanning.

"Aye, when there was danger, he warned us true. Good signs, all," said Rawley. He lit his pipe and Lanning noticed the terrible scar on his big right thumb.

Tobbs noticed it too, and marked politely to himself that it suited a carpenter.

Rawley winked at them both. "Hey, Tobbs, you ever heard of a three-headed fish?"

Tobbs jaw dropped. "A what?"

"A three-headed fish."

"Never!"

Rawley snorted smoke and raised a rusty brow over a pale green eye. "Well?"

"You mean yer dad never told ya about 'em?"

"No, sir. He most certainly did not."

"Well, that's the trouble with you scientists, I guess. You don't get out much."

"If you tell me what it is, I'll make sure to record it, sir."

"Well, it's work to bring 'em about, too much work fer a brainy-boy, p'r'aps."

"Sir, I am on this ship, aren't I? There are easier ways to learn, but I've chosen this one. Does that not count for anything?"

Rawley leaned forward with a sinister challenge in his eyes. "You have to shave yer eyebrows."

Lince made a quick rounds, checking the big millstones to see if they were secure, when he noticed Rawley on the aftercastle.

"Shave my eyebrows?" exclaimed Tobbs.

"Didn't think you'd have the stomach," grumbled Rawley.

"Please explain, sir. I assure you I'm game for any worthwhile scientific endeavor."

"Ya have to shave yer eyebrows off and sprinkle 'em in two cups o' brine. Set out the cups where they won't get spilled fer a day, then look inside and you'll be the first to discover, officially at least, the astounding three-headed fish."

"Why does it need eyebrows?"

"Why does it need eyebrows? There's tiny things smaller than yer father's ever seen livin' in yer eyebrows, man! Eatin' the skin and crumbs that gets trapped in 'em, even if you can't see 'em with yer naked eye."

"Ah! Do they regenerate in seawater?"

"Generate, they do, aye, indeed."

"Both eyebrows?" Tobbs frowned.

"Yep. But one would probably do the trick, too."

"Two must be better, though."

"*Mmm*, I should think so."

"Why two cups?"

"Because it doesn't work with one! Plus they gotta be kept side-by-side fer a day," said Rawley impatiently. "The weather's good fer it, right about now. That's some luck fer ya, laddy. If ya take it. But I guess science can always wait another day." Rawley winked and tossed a look skyward.

"Science cannot wait, sir! How big should the cups be?"

"The size you'd put coffee in."

"Do they need light?"

"It works best alow, but with a tiny bit of light, ya see. And it takes a whole day, no takin' 'em above deck to peek."

"Oh, I'm quite familiar with controlling experiments, Mister Skarmillion," said Tobbs.

Rawley shrugged. "Aye, you would be, of course."

"Well, good day to you mariners, and many thanks, Mister Skarmillion. I need to be off to make some entries in my journals about now."

The young naturalist made his way across the decks to his quarters in the fo'c's'le.

The Creature caught Rawley's twinkling eye, and its mouth curled in a threat. Rawley nodded sheepishly at the devilish cat, and swiveled on his wooden foot, shivering.

* * *

Karlock sat in the oaken pilot's chair in Lince's cabin under the bridge, tending the second helm wheel and conning against the wind that shifted from the northeast. The sails were trimmed, yet the *Sea Mare* galloped steady over the seas with only two-thirds of her mainsail showing.

Nil sat behind Karlock at the chart table, where he studied Teldon's map rolled out on the table's surface. Nil invited the ship's surgeon to sit with them in the cabin, which doubled as a bridge. The bay window was thick and wrapped around the corners for a full view. They had fixed the cabin door open and were all enjoying some hot coffee.

Since he had taken the wheel there was a boyish grin on Karlock's face. "By the Gairanor, Nilly, she handles!"

"She's a mite slow, with the spikes along her keel. But they'll slow down the Rollock, too, should we be that unlucky."

"She's got a cat's balance. She rolls a bit, but not like other vessels. The hold is perfectly ballasted. We'll have to make sure the men keep it right."

Zee was studying the chart intently. "The Illusion Sea? What is that, Captain, and how does one know where it starts and where it stops?" Zee asked, pointing to the portion of the chart that was directly off their starboard bow.

"One doesn't, really, Doctor," Nil said. "But we think it's south of us right now. If we catch an edge of it, the most important thing is to keep the wheel and the sails fixed. Then we'll pass out of it along its edge and should be all right."

"I've heard very little about it," said Zee. "And I read the local postings of the news faithfully, I assure you. Is it a place of nightmares, then?"

"You know as much about it as any. Nightmares and dreams, it has been said. There is only one report of it, only a few weeks old," said Nil. "Artimeer said it might be a *Wundery* place, a place where the *Wunder World* leaks through."

Jootle screamed and Ed called from the crow's nest. The Creature pounced through the door.

Lince's head appeared, eye-first, in the doorway. "That inforny-tassmic fried lobster tail's back, gentlemen!" His tattooed eye gave them one last glare as he went back down the ladder.

*   *   *

From the bridge above Lince's cabin, Nil screwed his spyglass on the beast that churned like a silvery eggbeater across the sea toward them.

It came from the mouth of its bay, four points off their port bow, and was clearly aiming to head them off to their present course. Nil saw that the beast was counting dearly on the *Sea Mare* staying her present speed. "Let fall the mainsail!" he bayed, and Lince volleyed his command below as the men climbed the shrouds to the mainyard.

As soon as they loosed the clews, the sail billowed under them and the whole yard floated up, weightless beneath them. They descended the shrouds as the others hauled in the sheets.

The ship leaped off the crest of a wave and flew through the air, her wings spread, and she alighted on the next wave like an eagle as her mainsail cracked.

"Ho! We'll see how fast yonder bug is!" Bultin bellowed from the stern, and the men hooted and hollered, hanging on as the *Sea Mare* rode the fierce easterly.

"These waves are getting bloody high," groused Karlock.

"Give me the conn. Keep an eye on it." Nil handed Karlock the spyglass and took the helm.

The wind shifted south of her beam, and they set the yards port to catch it.

"Ed, get out of the bloody crow's nest!" shouted Lince from the main deck.

"A bit late for that!" muttered Karlock.

Ed lowered himself through the hatch in the crow's nest and hung on to the shrouds as the *Sea Mare* kicked up over a wave, stringing Ed out over the deck. "*Agh*, Lince, I'm done for!" he cried.

In an instant, Lince grabbed hold of the shrouds and his crab-like figure scrabbled steadily up the webbing as the mast swung back and forth until he reached Ed and hauled him in by the top of his breeches. Ed shuddered as Lince clamped him tighter than the force of gravity against the shrouds, and they climbed down together. "Always wear a belt, kid," said Lince in his ear. "With a solid buckle. Somethin' to grab on to in a scrape."

The crew watched as Lince shepherded Ed to the deck in his crustacean embrace. "Now git to yer position at the jib, Mister!" growled Lince, booting him in the butt.

Lince climbed the ladder to the bridge.

"Ya left Ed aloft, ya did," grimaced Karlock.

"'Got him down, though," Lince grunted.

"What do you make of it?" Karlock handed Lince the spyglass.

Lince screwed his eye into the eyepiece, grabbing the rail with his left hand. His thin lips sliced over his long rows of teeth. "In a hurry to cut us off, eh?" he grinned. "Still two leagues, I'd say. Let's get the catapults, harpoons and nets rigged, Cappy, and batten the bulkheads!"

"Right as rain, Lince! I've a feeling we may not need it, though it's too nice a notion to go on," said Nil.

"Get it done, then!" yelled Karlock.

Lince lunged down the ladder to the deck. "Battle stations!" he boomed, and he pulled off the members of the watches assigned to man the harpoons and catapults, sending some to man the millstones. Lince had some others pull open the portion of the rails abaft the chainplates in order to let the millstones roll overboard, and he sent men below to close the bulkheads and bring up weapons, firebombs, and arrows from below.

Senthellzia and Zee found themselves tucked under the starboard companion ladder, hanging on for dear life as the men made the vessel ready for battle. They smiled at each other with wide eyes as they watched the artful drama aboard the hurling ship, and, suddenly, Bombo came out and gave them an extra pastry from Pickle's oven.

"Let's eat it quick," said Senthellzia, gobbling the small, juicy cinnamon roll and giving half of it to Harm.

Zee nodded, consuming the buttery confection in one bite as he looked at the strange creature plowing across the sea before them.

Tobbs trotted up.

"Oh no, son. What in Hala did you do?" asked Zee, noting the bald patches above the lad's eyes.

"It's part of an experiment, sir!" said Tobbs earnestly. "Yonder sea beast seems intent on intersecting our course."

"Yes," said Zee. "And you look more foolish than a circus clown."

The eyebrow-less Tobbs blushed wine-red. "'Tis for a good cause, Doctor, I assure you," he said.

"*Hmmm*," Zee frowned. "Boy, beware of sailors. They are a mischievous lot. You'd best find a place to hang on."

Feferl backed across the deck signaling and shouting to the intrepid monkey who climbed through the rigging as nimble as a spider. For this was the time a Monkey Sailor earned his board, when the sails were fully spread and the wind was hard and hitting the broadside. The new ship proved rigid as she shipped out at full tilt, and Feferl was gladdened to see Jootle's little face bored above.

The wind shifted further south of her beam, and they fought it a little to head off the steaming monster, though Nil took her port in the troughs to gain a little speed, gambling that they would outrun it in the end.

"We're beating it, Captain," said Karlock on the bridge, his eye screwed into the spyglass.

"Take the conn," Nil said, and he took the spyglass from Karlock. "It'll be close; too close to call."

"*Gaw!* Ya callin' me an optimist?"

"With this ship, aye!"

"Not without reason," said Karlock.

All clung to the galloping craft as she parted the heavy seas. The king's third creation rowed its many legs in a fury, and raised its crystalline arms, dotted with barnacles, out of the water like half a dozen cranes that obscured its head and joined in a point before it.

The waves grew steep, but the ship was taut as a bow. When the set of swells passed, Lince ordered Rept into the crow's nest, giving Rept's second-in-command a chance to run the watch. Rept climbed the shrouds, and almost as soon as he sat down, cried, "Aye, land ho! One-and-a-half points aport!"

Nil and Karlock fixed it a moment after. It was the Isle of the so-called "coral beast," lying gray like a clay brick on the sea, due east.

"We need never go near it," said Nil. "Hard to it, men: Get us by this fiend and we'll cut southeast past yonder isle, and then it's a quick cut southwest to the shore of the Dimmrock! But if we should tangle with this foe, be ready to pound it with fire and foul it with nets. Mind the millstones, Lince! I bet its pretty arms'll tangle good in our web, if it comes too close!" Nil combed his fingers back through his storm of hair, his dark eyes fixed on the furious chimera.

Everyone assumed battle stations.

The second watch manned the aftercastle, with Overly in charge.

Sowernut, Lanning, and Tobbs manned the starboard harpoon.

Bat was assigned to release the millstones, which could be rolled port or starboard over the reinforced deck. These stones weighed over two tons apiece and must be released only when the deck was not pitching or rolling too heavily. For stability in rough seas they were positioned to roll at an aftward angle.

The decks heaved over another set of swells from the south that smacked her broadside.

The heavy seas were working against the fulminating dragon that beat a dogged course to intercept them. It was now only a compass point off the port bow, climbing the waves like a giant wind-up toy only a thousand feet from them with its long arms pointed like a great bowsprit. They heard its voice over the waves now, like a shrieking plague of locusts.

They were heading toward a common point where neither could give another inch.

"Hold yer fire!" growled Lince, gripping his fist as his cat stood growling around his leg.

The monster charging over the waves was only 300 hundred yards away, four points off the port bow.

The strange noise rose to an ear-splitting pitch, like a thousand teapots whistling, as the dragon milled up a swell just off their port broadside, its crystal arms clawing the sky.

But the *Sea Mare* passed it by before it could catch her rigging, and the creature crossed her wake, its craning claws smashing into the sea.

"Too fast for the wretch!" nodded Karlock.

The beast turned in pursuit.

"Maybe," said Nil, craning his neck for a look around the mainmast.

"Fire at will!" Lince yelled, and the men on the aftercastle fired a round of firebombs lit with rag fuses, which shattered in flames on the craning ice-like arms of the creature.

The creature's great arms promptly plunged into the foaming sea behind them.

The monster slowed on their wake, exhausted, it seemed, and unable to go any further.

"Now we've done it!" said Nil.

The beast turned suddenly and rolled its hind oars, propelling itself away from the *Sea Mare* as fast as it could go.

Karlock hooted from the bridge and threw his gray hat into the wind.

The men cheered.

The statue of Trinadol flashed above the crow's nest.

They mounted the next swell, and three orange fingers reached out of the wave and grabbed them.

*   *   *

Chapter 23

▼

Caught

The *Sea Mare* moaned and yawed port as the Rollock closed its fingers on her hull and shuddered her timbers

"Battle stations!" Lince yelled. "Fire at will!"

Regaining their feet, all resumed their posts, and Senthellzia and her contingent of archers fanned out and fired at the massive arms closing on the starboard foredeck, the port main, and the starboard stern.

Milky tube-feet, ringed with purple lips, writhed and rippled on the underside of the muscular arms. These cups attached themselves to the *Sea Mare*'s hull as the arms pressed against her.

The hard back of the beast was bright orange, dotted with yellow and crimson studs. On the end of its muscular arms, purplish stalks reached in every direction, tipped with flat, black eyes ringed in gold and turquoise. They were studying the men on the decks below.

"Fire the oil-bombs at its underside, you there on the poop deck!" Lince ran at the arm that was closing in on the port side, threatening the mainmast's shrouds. He plunged his short, thick sword through the chain-plates into the onrushing arm and it sunk to the hilt, sending the arm reeling back in pain and pulling the sword out of Lince's hand.

"Damn, you spotty creep!" Lince spat at it; for it was his father's weapon.

The arm quaked as if enraged, and seemed about to rush at the ship in a timber-crushing blow. Rawley pogoed across the deck and made a nifty throw, striking the tender underside of the arm with a lit fire-bomb, and the clay pot shattered into dripping flames over the grasping tube-feet. Quickly the muscular arm bent back under the waves to douse the fire.

"Fire a net port, boys, and weight this one back!" yelled Lince.

The harpoon sailed over the tip of the arm as it rose and draped it with black net. The catapult on the aftercastle fired another spear over the Rollock's arm there, spreading the rest of the net on the water over the beast.

"Let her go!" Lince brayed, and Bat swung down his wooden mallet to knock out the chocks and release a millstone.

With a grinding drumbeat, the millstone rippled the deck planks on the tilting ship as it rolled overboard, glancing off the arm and plunging into the sea behind it.

"Hack the underside," shouted Nil. "Mind its strength!" He left the bridge to Karlock as the ship labored forward, yawing dangerously. "First and second watch, clew the mainsail two-thirds! Third watch, clew the lateen! You on the fo'c's'le, drop the jibs," shouted Nil and he jumped down the ladder as men scurried up the shrouds and spread out on the yard to clew the straining mainsail.

The men on the fo'c's'le managed to plunge a harpoon into the arm that was closing in on the starboard prow. The purple stalks of eyes waved frantically on its tip as Senthellzia pounded arrow after arrow into its soft tube-feet.

The three fingers around the ship turned sideways then, protecting themselves from the arrows, firebombs, harpoons, and sword strokes as the Rollock tried to get a purchase on the hull from below.

"Keep the arms off her at all costs!" cried Nil, sword drawn, surveying the entire ship as he felt her groaning under his boots. "Fire a net port and let a millstone go! Two from each watch go alow and jab it through the brasures! We've got to keep the beast's arms from closing on the *Sea Mare*'s broadsides, men, and we'll beat this thing, by the Gairanor!"

"Fire, you scum-suckers!" charged Lince, and his cat curled against his calf as the men fired another net port.

Bat sent another millstone over the port side.

The men aloft finished their work and came down. The *Sea Mare*'s sails no longer tipped her decks, yet still she moved forward, low in the water.

They fired a third net port side and it seemed the weight of three millstones was too much for the Rollock's arm to lift.

Nil saw that the two arms below were kicking, pushing them south—toward the Illusion Sea.

The arm over each castle closed in, and teams of men were ready with swords in hand. They hacked the undulating underside, ripping deep gashes in the tube-feet. Their assault was unbearable to the Rollock, and three men then tasted its wrath as its arms knocked two across the deck and one into the sea.

"Keep throwing the fire-bombs!" said Lince. "But mind you don't burn off the nets!"

Queto, of the third watch, leaped on the starboard rail of the aftercastle, waving his sword under the arm there. He whipped his sword mightily through the Rollock's flesh, shredding the grasping tubes into a quivering mass. The arm reeled and twisted, but Queto's blows were relentless. When the trembling limb drew back, pointing skyward, Queto turned to the others, and they cheered his deed.

Queto danced on the rail even as the creature's arm, with a sudden rage, came down over him and, smashing through the railing, drove him into the deck.

The Rollock's arm rose with Queto stuck to it, and he screamed as needles at the bottom of the tube-feet pumped venom into his back.

The arm curled forward under the ship before the men, and they could only guess what merciless fate awaited Queto in the Rollock's maw below.

In minutes, the arm bent back upward and Queto was gone.

Harm shrieked as he descended talons-first onto the arm's eyes, tearing at them and piercing their flat lenses with his beak. The arm swung back as a few white tubes grasped at the feral bird, but Harm easily lifted into the air, ripping off purple stalks and dodging and dipping to strike again.

The sinewy arms of the Rollock sent shudders through the ship as it shifted to get a tighter hold on her hull.

Off the port aftercastle and the starboard main deck, the Rollock's two other arms rose out of the sea.

* * *

Trinadol watched the crew fighting on the decks through a different fragment of the Cronus Star, which had sparkled when his statue lit over the decks of the *Sea Mare*.

He gazed, horrified by his own vicious creation but enthralled by the purpose these Ameulentians showed in the face of such danger. With death so fast all around, they worked with discipline, ingenuity, resourcefulness, and even pride as they deployed an elaborate attack on the Rollock.

Each lunge of the starfish made him shudder with self-loathing, yet each effort of these men to win the day warmed his heart with unexpected pride and awe. Though their mortal lives were short and precious, they risked them to save their kingdom. Though doom was all around them, they met it head on and fought with all their hearts and minds. As he watched them confront the deadliest beast he could imagine, their every defiant action taught him an abstract lesson he could never imagine. The hope they vested in him would not be in vain, he vowed.

"Get more nets out, that's it, beat it back off the stern!"

Trinadol's lonely cries echoed in his chamber as he peered with his spyglass through the diamond window.

* * *

"Get a grip!" Drugor sat on a block of stone over the viewing pool. "Why doesn't he just crush this vessel? What is Deevex waiting for?"

The King's advisors surrounded the pool, watching with hidden hope as the men of the Sea Mare *disproved their lord's mean predictions.*

"This is one of my fiercest recruits, Theosophiclar," Drugor grinned with Trinadol's face.

"Eh, lord?" asked Theosophiclar.

"At first, the young fool had no control over what passed from Wynder through his stone, he did not even know Wynder existed, thanks to his overcautious teachers. So I let through the stone a demon of Wynderne even you foolish Wyndernes must remember: Deevex."

The counselors, even though they had heard terrible legends about Deevex, showed no sign of it to Drugor. For they sensed this Trinadol was not the one they knew.

"What? You have never heard of Deevex?" he cried, enraged.

For a moment, Theosophiclar could see a different shape, crimson and hot, emanating beneath the shape of the King. "No, Lord, though we shall see his power soon, I'm sure," said the three-eyed engineer.

"There he goes!" cried Drugor, pointing at the pool. "Watch closely, now, foolish Wyndernes. See how unwise it is to put your faith in mortals. See how fragile they are and how easily their lives are whisked away, like so many ants!"

They all feigned boredom as they looked into the lightstone window.

* * *

The sailors fired another net port over the newly-risen arm there and let another millstone over the side. They shot a net starboard that draped over both the arm amidships and astern, and they rolled a millstone over the starboard side. The eyes waved on the tips of the arms through the netting, looking over the men.

The archers continued to rain arrows over the fingers of the great hand that gripped the ship, yet the tough orange hide deflected most of their arrows as the Rollock had learned to twist its tough side toward the decks as it closed its fingers.

Senthellzia took advantage of the tiniest opening, plunging arrow after arrow into the beast's soft underside. She knew that each arrow would make it more difficult for the Rollock to get a grip on the *Sea Mare* as it had to break the shafts off against her hull in order to attach its grisly suckers. Senthellzia and her archers had also managed to pierce some of the glistening eyes.

The men on the castles hurled firebombs at the arms there, sending them curling into the cold sea to douse the flames each time.

The spikes spaced along the *Sea Mare*'s keel prevented the Rollock from getting a solid enough hold to crush her hull. The crew could hear and feel the Rollock's maw grinding the spikes off under the ship, one by one, as it worked its way toward the stern.

Bultin charged the aftercastle holding his crystal sword high. He leaped into the air under the arm bending down over the deck, and his sword flashed. The entire tip of the arm landed on the deck, its eyes and feet still moving. The Rollock was jolted by the terrible sword-stroke, and its arms retreated from the *Sea Mare*.

Nil ran to open sea doors before his cabin.

The bleeding arm over the starboard fo'c's'le trembled as the men landed another firebomb on its underside. Then they pounded it with harpoons and arrows as it curled back under the sea.

And yet, this time, it burst from the water and rammed furiously into the prow.

Nil saw it bash the rail and smash through the deck. The proud horse's head snapped from its place under the bowsprit and bounced off the Rollock onto the foredeck and down the ladderway to the edge of the sea door.

Rept straddled the bowsprit right over the thrashing arm, which he gashed with his blade, and it surged up and knocked the sword from his hand.

Rept turned as Skillah threw another sword, but Rept's reach was overeager and he lost his balance. He slid from the top of the bowsprit and hung from it upside down.

The arm paused underneath him. Its last remaining eye bent up at him.

Rept cried out for another sword, but the arm rammed his back, and Rept screamed as the bowsprit bent above him and snapped in a roaring violence. He soared through the air, clutching the shattered spar and tumbling as the masts groaned, the forestay cut.

The inner jib floated up and tangled itself in the mainyard as Rept struck the deck across the sea doors from Nil. Rept stared at Nil with glazing eyes as blood welled over his lips.

Bultin rushed at the arm on the fo'c's'le, swinging his shining sword in a furious blow that lay open a deep gash in its hard orange hide. Another shockwave ran through the beast's muscles, rolling the timbers of the ship, and all five fingers backed away again, and stretched out straight, streaming wakes in the sea beside the *Sea Mare*.

But the Rollock was not surrendering.

Nil started down the ladder into the hold as the monster closed its fist.

The men fired arrows and firebombs at the converging arms, but they were not slowed down, and the ship bellowed as they slammed into her iron-ribbed sides. The arm with four millstones weighting it back was unable to close upon the *Sea Mare*, but the arm off the starboard side of the main deck, which was weighted with two millstones, slung them against the hull as it rushed forward. All heard the crunch, and the ugly gasp of the sea.

The hold flooded in seconds, and water lapped over the Green Deck. The horizon rose around the *Sea Mare*.

* * *

"Heel her port, Lince!" Nil cried, and he dove into the dark water through the sea doors.

The men were already dropping the clews and pulling the mainyard port as Lince repeated the order, and the men on the aftercastle shifted the lateen to catch the northeasterly and try to raise the breaches.

Nil plunged into the icy water, kicking as he remembered Lince's chiding advice about wearing boots. He saw two gaping holes in the starboard hull but the ship rolled port, the sloshing water shifting and providing a pocket of air to the starboard where light streamed through the breaches.

Nil surfaced and took some air. The mainsail had pulled the breaches above the waterline just in time, though the weight of the Rollock was resisting her and letting in surges of water.

The crew cranked the bailing lines at the sea doors fore and aft, pulling up a procession of buckets that emptied into wooden sluices under the main deck and poured over the sides.

Nil breathed in the pocket of air and looked along the gloomy hold. The water was filled with sliding debris and slicked by the Rollock's slime, rolling forward and aft as the *Sea Mare* pitched over the waves.

Nil kicked and pulled himself aft as the ship nodded over a swell, and a fresh wave curled at his back.

He grabbed a breath and dove under the water, swimming under the heaving flotsam.

The ship was down by the stern, and the water was now up to the overhead, so he kicked harder to get to his destination.

A millstone cracked beside him, lower on the hull, and the sea rushed in again. He saw the harpoon ahead, but a bolt of canvas wrapped around him and he turned upside down, kicking it off.

He spun, his lungs bursting, and kicked forward, reaching out to grasp the coiled spring of the harpoon.

Nil pulled himself in and looked into the glass eyepiece at the top of the shaft. Dreamily, he focused on the white, purple-rimmed suction cups of the starfish, which seemed strangely beautiful as they marched by in the lens. Peace settled over his mind, blocking out the groans of the ship. His heart beat slower and a kind of drugged clarity possessed him. The translucent cylinders undulated past the lens like a field of weird flowers, and his sight seemed to fade like a sunset.

Clunk!
Crunge!
Clunk!

Nil heard the millstones banging the hull, miles away. He briefly wondered if the venom of the starfish was drugging him. The crawling tubes suddenly parted to reveal a gnashing beak of crimson, which had arrived, at last, to gnaw off the largest spike.

Nil stared at the ravenous maw of the Rollock for a moment out of time, and, as if coming to the conclusion before he did, his whole body convulsed and he swung his right boot, knocking the chock from the mighty bronze-pointed shaft. It slammed down through the hull beside Nil, and its flared end corked the hole as the Rollock broke it off below.

Boots are useful too, Lince, Nil thought as he planted them on the deck and lunged backwards toward the blue light filtering through the churning water. He vomited his breath like poison, gasping in the sea. He sank back in dark water then, before he reached the surface, and he gave his last thought to Lelinair.

*   *   *

The men fired another net and sent the last millstone overboard. The weight of five stones overpowered the finger off the port main, bending it back as the rest gripped the ship tight.

The *Sea Mare* heeled painfully as the full mainsail was set almost parallel with her keel, though she limped over the swells, sinking.

With a tearful sigh, Tobbs hurled the buoy over the transom.

As the buoy splashed in the water, the Rollock's arms shot out bolt-straight, lifting the ship out of the water as they rippled to their very tips.

With a tremendous shudder it let go of the *Sea Mare*.

She lunged forward, nearly capsizing as she limped over the next wave, but the men of watch two were ready at the sheets and hauled the mainyard over and righted her just in the nick of time.

The bulkheads Nil had designed sealed enough parts of the Green Deck and castles from flooding to give them the time they needed, just as he had predicted.

Lince looked into the hold and saw a ghost of Nil reaching toward him through the dark water, and he jumped through the sea doors into the water.

Clasping Nil by the belt, Lince kicked up to the Green Deck and hauled the Captain out of the water.

Lince pounded his back until Nil gasped and retched the sea out of his lungs.

"Nilly!" Lince shouted. "You've done it, lad!"

Nil rose on his hands and knees, coughing. "Good!" he nodded.

*   *   *

The Rollock grasped upside-down on their wake, the heavy shaft plunged deep in its maw, having pierced its stomach, heart and brain with one stroke.

The motley band of seabirds that made a living off the Rollock's fortune turned with the wind now to tear scraps from its soft underside, and they fought each other as the leviathan sank.

Sharks appeared, swimming over the ravaged bottom of the Rollock, and joined in the frenzy as the millstones dragged the beast under.

One last orange arm thrust out of the water, and a dingy gull swooped in to tear at a tube-foot only to be sucked in and pierced by its poisonous needle—the Rollock's last victim, dragged with it into its deep grave.

"It's finished, Captain Ramesis! The blow to its heart did it in," cried Tobbs as Nil climbed out of the sea doors ahead of Lince. "My father was right!"

"Yes, Tobbs," said Nil. "Your father was right. Now what in Hala happened to your eyebrows?"

"It's—er—an experiment, Captain. See, I…"

"I trust you'll mark well today's events, lad," said Nil, grimacing as he straightened up on the deck. "Write it all down, Tobbs, with an eye for the details now," said Nil. "Leave out the eyebrows."

"Captain…I'm so sorry. I can't believe it, but, you see, sir—"

"What is it, lad?"

"I tossed the buoy again, sir. I just thought we were finished, for certain, sir!"

Nil raised a grim eyebrow at Tobbs. "Then I guess you'll be staying up late again, eh Mister Tobbs?"

"Yes, sir! As I mentioned, and it's a good thing, I have a perfect memory. I can picture every page, even where I spilled the ink…"

"'Ever thought of making a copy, Tobbs?" growled Nil.

"No, sir." Tobbs, who prided himself on being thorough, was shamed into an even deeper spiral of grief.

"Get crackin'!" growled Lince. "And don't spill the ink this time!"

The young naturalist ran off across the deck, happy to have an action before him that would remedy his shame, and Nil winced and shook his head at how foolish the earnest lad looked, alas, with no eyebrows.

When the Rollock struck the bottom of the sea, the limping *Sea Mare* was miles away.

Nothing remained of the orange hand but for a star-shaped mass of gnawed flesh, too tough even for the sharp daggers of the sharks. The fearsome fist that clutched the southern waters of Ameulas for seven years would do so nevermore.

* * *

Chapter 24

Healing Wounds

Rawley rigged the jibs to the port rail, and both were set to heel the ship so her wounds would not be exposed to the sea.

The *Sea Mare* rolled heavy with her broad canvas catching the true northerly, making due east as the sun grew heavy in the clear sky astern.

Her decks tilted steeply and the odd wave breached her port waist.

Rawley pogoed expertly over the tilting deck on his pivoting shoe to the starboard rail and he ordered the canvas and tar pots brought from below to tack the breaches.

As the fires were lit under the tar pots, the carpenter ordered Bat and Bultin aloft to carry a temporary stayline he had the men fo'c's'le rig to the cathead.

Rawley himself climbed the shrouds after them and pulled out a heavy hatchet from the toolbox in his wooden leg, which he used to chop the old stay line from the mast. Then he let Bultin and Bat fasten the temporary stays to the cleats on the mainmast, and he signaled the men on the fo'c's'le to heave the rig taut.

To everyone's relief, both masts stopped groaning against the ship's timbers as the stay was made fast.

"Now get some hot tar up here and you boys lay it on nice and thick, right?" winked Rawley, and he bounced down the shrouds on his nimble wooden foot.

Lince, meanwhile, had organized bailing lines out of both sea doors. Four men on the Green Deck filled buckets and passed them to four on the main, who emptied them overboard. He had two men above and below cranking the wooden gears of a bailing line that hauled buckets at the fore and aft sea doors. The men worked like a machine, and the statue of Trinadol, that had burned white-hot over them for nearly two hours, finally cooled and grew dark.

The wind kept up, keeling her generously as the red sun slanted through the *Sea Mare*'s rigging.

Rawley swung down on a line over the exposed starboard hull to tack canvas patches over the breaches. His wooden leg bent at the knee, which had a rubber pad shaped to grip the hull, and the top of his wooden thigh opened to reveal his chest of tools. He patched the three breaches with remarkable speed with tacks and canvas, and some sailors hung down beside him to paint the patches with hot tar as he finished. He had some men he trusted descend to tack on a second patch of canvas and tar.

Then Rawley went to the ravaged fo'c's'le to assay the damage there.

He ordered Bat and Bultin, and, in his sudden flush of authority, even Lince to help him fit out the new bowsprit.

Lince never liked it when the ship needed repair; for this was the only time the carpenter outranked the first mate.

Bultin had draped his greatcoat over Rept, the third watch leader, who was a good work of a man, sharp, hard, and true. The body of Tairnol was similarly draped with a sailor's coat, near the aft sea doors on the main deck—he had been bashed during one of the Rollock's rages and thrown across the deck onto his head. Fingers of blood reached port and starboard from under both coats on the main deck.

As the men cut the rigging from the bowsprit, clearing the snarls of line, the strongest men aboard came together to lift the shattered spar, and as they did they revealed the terrible wound that stove in Rept's chest, which filled with blood before unlucky eyes that lingered.

The men took the mast up the stern companion ladder over to the taffrail, and a number joined them as they launched it overboard into their wake.

Bruthru Zee had gotten the five injured men below to his spacious infirmary, which Nil had given special conveniences when designing his ship.

Now Zee tended to the bodies of the dead, washing them and wrapping them from head to toe in sheets of yellow cotton, as was the custom in far-off Sarkland. He enlisted a few sad mariners to help him carry the bodies and lay them under one of the aft ladderways. Once there, he lit two pieces of frankincense on golden coins, which he placed on their foreheads.

The bailing had emptied nearly half the hold when four men dropped into the hold to pass buckets up to the Green Deck and on up to the main deck, which slowed down the process. But the ship was riding higher as the sun slanted west, and since the Rollock had gnawed off most of the spikes on her keel, she was running fast on the sea. Indeed she was much lighter without the millstones, so Nil ordered 30 barrels filled with seawater to add ballast as the others continued bailing.

*   *   *

Everyone aboard was hard-tasked as the sun sank like a red rose whose petals burned golden as they shed.

Pickle and Bombo finally got their galley in order and started supper.

Rawley went below to loosen the bowsprit, assisted by Lanning.

Up to their hams in water, the men pulled the broken spar from its socket, backing it down into the hold to float the heavy mast to the aft sea doors. Tobbs paused to watch the tree-sized spar moving down the corner of his cabin as he furiously transcribed his log from memory.

The second bowsprit was lifted out of its bed beneath the hold's decking and the men floated it forward. Its lines were fixed and sent up to the fo'c's'le, where they were strung through deadeyes rigged to the end of the boomkins and fixed to the capstan.

The men on the foredeck cranked the capstan as the men below shoved.

When the bowsprit emerged, the men hooked the loop of the heavy mainstay over the sharp tip.

The men pushed below and pulled above as the mighty shaft thrust forward over the forking knighthead.

A jittery Jootle managed to do his job above and watch the rigging for any signs of giving way as the men loosened the new forestay and extended the spar.

Under Rawley's orders, various details repaired the foredeck and starboard rails, all while the ship was underway so that the wind would keep her breaches high.

Nil sent Tobbs to examine the tip of the Rollock's arm that continued to wander over the fo'c's'le on its suction tubes, seemingly unaware that its body had died. Tobbs pronounced it dead, amid much laughter. The naturalist turned nearly purple, but endured the mockery, explaining patiently that he had shaved his eyebrows for science, for he assumed by now that his lack of eyebrows was the reason for all laughter hurled at him aboard the ship. He employed the authority the Captain gave him, however, to select two men to help him pack the specimen with salt and wrap it in linens to preserve it, as Tobbs wished to bring the trophy back to his father for study.

Parting from Senthellzia with a warm smile and a stroke of her crimson mane, Rollum headed off to the damaged fo'c's'le to apply his own native skills as he sawed new deck planks handed up from below to mend the foredeck.

Senthellzia found herself in front of the galley again, the only place she felt out of the way. This time she was alone, as Zee was tending three badly wounded men below.

She leaned against the port companion ladder on the tilting deck, and Harm fluttered down from the crow's nest, to the relief of Sowernut who had the watch again. Senthellzia welcomed him onto the leather gauntlet of her right arm. But her green eyes were distant as she gazed at the yellow sunset, thinking of Rollum's blue eyes.

She looked at the bodies of the two men swathed in yellow shrouds near her and she smelled the pungent incense Zee had set burning upon their brows, one of which was streaked with blood even through the cotton swathing. Sadness filled her heart as she realized Rollum might be next to follow them.

The warm wind was frisky, and in the southwest, over what was rumored to be the Illusion Sea, distant lightning lit a silver lace of clouds.

Senthellzia was lost inside her heart as Pickle rushed out of the galley, with his perennial frown of brooding rage and crazed hair. He handed Senthellzia a small hot buttered scone. "An investiture for the mellifluous concord your presence superinduces," he smiled, bowing on the tilted deck.

"Thank you, good sir!" Senthellzia nodded uncertainly, and Harm took the biscuit out of her hand.

Pickle frowned, flummoxed, and ran back into his galley.

*   *   *

The *Sea Mare* flew due east as the men below, led by the dogged Rawley, repaired the starboard breaches. They lost the sun and the first stars appeared over the bowsprit.

Dead ahead lay the isle of the coral giant.

The bay of the crystal dragon gaped only a few leagues north off their stern, shrouded in cloud.

"That bloody lobster turned coward when it saw the Rollock, Lince," said Nil. "It may be spooked. Let's not proceed too close to yonder eastern isle. We'll bet on dusk for cover. Furl 'em and drop anchor three leagues hence. Make her ready!"

"Aye, Captain, a fair bet—I'll take it!" said Lince. "There's a deep reef ahead, part of the same reef this lobster's home is built upon. We can anchor there."

Karlock nodded. "The men are in need of a rest."

"Shift the ballast port," Nil ordered, and Lince descended the bridge, leaving Lince's cat curled around the rail by Nil and Karlock.

The hold was finally bailed and the last water mopped and sent over the side. The sea doors fore and abaft were left open to air the decks on the warm night. Lince led the men in rolling 200 great kegs of water to the port side of the hold as Nil ordered the mainsail heaved progressively starboard until the ballast was shifted.

Dusk was settling and lanterns were lit as the *Sea Mare* crossed a deep reef glowing with twinkling lights. With barely any sail showing, she streamed over the smooth water, slivering the First Moon's reflection into dancing splinters.

Lince climbed out of the fore sea doors and announced that the ballast had been shifted.

Nil ordered the sails furled and the anchor dropped.

When the anchor grabbed hold on the reef, she rested easy on her port side in a gentle sea.

Nil gave the nod to an impatient Pickle, and the cook nodded at Bombo, who finally rang the dinner bell.

The wafting fumes of ham and cornmeal stuffing with onion potatoes, which had enchanted the men for an hour, now dragged them to the mess. To Pickle's dismay, his masterful dinner was swallowed practically whole, and after swilling down their mug of mead, the men staggered out, sated but too dazed to appreciate what they had just ingested.

Fog wrapped around the northwest isle where the strange crystal lobster lived, and the crew of the *Sea Mare* slept on that strange monster's doorstep that night, after eluding it twice, and they were comforted to have the cover of cloud and darkness as Rawley rotated his own watch out of the others to repair the breaches through the night.

* * *

Rawley kept his conscripts working, and he taught each young sailor the finer points of carpentry as they went along. Since the hull patches kept back the seas occasionally slapping the starboard broadside, the men were able to work on the breaches without major incident. It was a seemingly endless ordeal, heating, clamping, bending, sawing, fitting, pitching and pegging the beams and planks. Nil hoped it would be completed by dawn, though Rawley was skeptical and enforced meticulous standards on the process.

Meanwhile, Nil reordered the supplies in the hold, which had been thrown into disarray by the breach. Stocks that needed to be dried were hauled up through the sea doors and laid out under Karlock's instruction. Those that were spoiled were thrown overboard. The warm wind was a welcome friend, toweling off the waterlogged ship, and they opened all the brasures, vents and ports to air out the decks.

The men above had no reprieve, either, as Lince ordered the lines and rigging inspected. He also made them scrub the decks, a particularly harsh assignment, which the exhausted crew wished dearly to finish by midnight, but, as Overly lamented, these were the biggest decks they'd ever seen. Lince would not have the blood of their fellows trodden on, however, nor would he have the blood of the Rollock fouling the ship.

Three men had been lost overboard, and so it was five who had died battling the Rollock that day. Two below were badly injured with head wounds, and three more nursed broken limbs and ribs.

* * *

Trinadol touched one of the last four fragments of the Cronus Star to the fragment he was peering through. In this way, he "lit" the new shard as the other waned so he could continue watching the *Sea Mare*.

The men were engaged in their intricate industry, effecting an incremental magic that was a revelation to him, attacking each problem's solution with such relentless purpose in the face of attack that they amazed his heart. This valiant crew met each puzzle with strength and guile, undoing each obstacle like a knot, and the vast array of objects and actions, quantities and qualities they had mastered thrilled, amazed and humbled him.

For the first time, Trinadol looked with adult eyes upon mortal men, whose daily tasks required perseverance and will, knowledge and skill, their minds undaunted by the range of nature's possibilities, instead harnessing them, engaging them in an intimate, seductive dance with nature that subtly, respectfully, and persuasively led her to their goal. Here was everything there was in magic! But it was played out on an even grander stage over a longer range with far greater organization, and leading to conclusions all the more miraculous. He awed at mortal man, then, as he felt a surge of confidence, for the first time, to know his fate was in their hands.

* * *

Drugor sneered in silence. He was bored. He was no longer amused by the show he saw. "They scramble like ants," *he muttered.*

"Industrious ants, lord!" *laughed Theosophiclar, risking torture.*

"Bah!" *Drugor spat.* "Stooping slaves of nature, flailing at death to postpone the inevitable, Theosophiclar. I detect a germ of admiration for these lowly things. I would torture you for your insolence...though it would bore me, too. You know too well what immortality means. What transpires below will be your punishment for your ill-placed faith. See you will that despite these arduous, tortuous efforts, men are mere grist in the merciless mill of Hala!"

"Yes, my lord," said Theosophiclar, *convinced now that this was not* Trinadol. *And the Wyndernal engineer who had helped* Elwyn, Senadol *and* Trinadol *direct their accomplishments in* Hala, *committed himself now to discovering this imposter's true identity.*

*   *   *

At about ten that night, the men finally finished scrubbing the decks of the *Sea Mare*.

The repairs above were completed, as well. The foredeck and new bowsprit were seamless and sturdy and the welcome smell of fresh pine tar, which sealed the ship's wounds, emanated from her decks.

Nil blew the whistle to call all hands on deck. All below put down their tools, coming above and gathering before the bridge as they shook off the sweat and sawdust and breathed the fresh air off the sea.

The First Moon shone over the mainmast and three lanterns swung over the crew on a line strung from the rail of the bridge to the rail of the fo'c's'le.

Nil stood on the bridge with Karlock, and Lince stood before the bridge on the main deck, clasping his hands behind his back, the Creature peering slyly around his leg.

"We've weathered a wicked storm no others have passed and lived," said Nil.

To his delight the assembly still had the energy to send up a hearty cheer.

"Five brothers we lost bitterly to the Rollock today. And now we lay two to rest in the sea. For Kazum, Tenwyn, Queto, Rept and Tairnol, let us win glory that will remember them forever!"

The crew shouted approval, and some stifled sobs as six men came forward bearing the wrapped bodies of the two men Zee had prepared, and they lowered them over the port side into the sea as the crew bid them, and the others, farewell.

"Now take a half hour of free time and then get some sleep," Nil said. "Rawley, rotate your men below, so they get some rest, as well. We weigh anchor at dawn."

Rawley sent only a small detachment of men back into the hold, letting the rest off for a while, Rollum among them.

Immediately, he joined Senthellzia on the aftercastle. Lince eyed them slipping stealthily up the aft companion ladder and grumbled to himself that this was the very reason women were bad luck aboard a vessel. And yet, later on, he shrugged and let them sneak into her fo'c's'le quarters, without official notice.

Tobbs, meanwhile, got his first lesson in the biology of men and women, as he couldn't resist a peek through a crack in the bulkhead between his and the Lady Senthellzia's cabin to see what all the sighs and cries were about. Tobbs's perfect memory preserved a series of lantern-lit portraits forever, and if he still had eyebrows, they would certainly have been singed off by what he saw.

*   *   *

The rest of the crew were so spent they practically collapsed over the decks as soon as they were relieved from duty by Nil, and they lay prone on the decks, groaning pathetically as Lince strutted and grumbled among them.

"First mate, sir!" said Nil from the bridge. "Come to the bridge, please, sir!"

Lince nodded his head and clenched his teeth as he turned back toward the bridge and climbed the ladder.

"Leave 'em be, now, ya mean bastard, ya!" growled Karlock.

"All right, I will, sir," Lince grumbled. He grabbed a knit cap out of the pocket of his greatcoat and stretched it over his head, reaching his arms out to grab the rail and noticing his own weary weight.

Zee poked his head over the deck of the bridge. "Gentlemen, I suggest you all join me in the first mate's cabin for some medicine. Doctor's orders."

"The good doctor took the breath out of my very mouth," said Lince.

"Mr. Feferl, put Jootle aloft. Let him yell if a beast comes our way tonight, eh?"

"Oh, yes, sir!" said Feferl, waking up the dozing monkey on his back, giving it a blanket and a bag of coffee beans to eat, and sending it up to the crow's nest.

"Let's have a nip of the Doctor's medicine," said Nil.

*   *   *

"*Oooeeeeaarrrryaaa-ugh!*" groaned Lanning as he staggered up to the other aching members of watch two, who lay wrecked over the foredeck. "A python's wrapped around my back. *Ow*, Hala!" he whined.

"Shut yer blubberin', ya—*ooogh!*" Bultin winced, the small of his back spasming like a bear trap.

The men of the second watch lay in ruins on the fo'c's'le.

Rollum was too tired to strum his mandolin as the beaming Senthellzia, her fiery hair let down over her shoulders, kneaded the prince's grateful muscles. All knew what had transpired there, and marked privately how princely the fair Demoldan had truly been to have had fire left for the considerable Senthellzia after this devilish day.

Rawley perched his left foot on the wedge on his inner shin and pogoed smartly up the companion ladder to the starboard fo'c's'le, his back erect and his pipe clenched in grinning teeth as he whistled a little tune.

He leaned against the rail and surveyed the men with a curious shrug. Shaking his head, the bald carpenter lit a punk off a lantern and fired up his pipe. He puffed away, and hummed a snappy little tune.

The men hefted their heads off the deck and twisted their necks to look in his direction, annoyed at the devil who had driven them mad all day, after fighting off the Rollock.

Rawley smiled at Bultin, who slumped beside him, and he blew a snake of blue smoke over the deck. "Look!" Rawley exclaimed. "Blue Niveron!" he pointed north and smiled.

"How can you sit there stargazing!" snapped Lanning. "Of course, it's Niveron. It's the North Star, you idiot!"

"I see no reason to be snippy about it, Lanning." Rawley sulked at the young sailor who lay on the deck, curled in a ball of pain.

Lanning cranked his head around, and it wavered on his weak neck as he saw the sinister carpenter's scarred thumb, red beard, and bald head. Lanning saw Rawley light his infernal pipe and wink at him before his neck gave out and his head banged on the deck. The young sailor groaned.

Rawley whistled an improvised medley of cheery little tunes.

"You are not being weary?" Rollum grunted.

"Weary? Why, not with a healing rock. *Nooo*, sir!" Rawley winked at the Demoldan prince and went back to his whistling.

That took a while to settle in, and Rawley gave it time, nibbling his pipe-stem, and whistling mighty poorly.

Bultin twitched. "What rock?"

Rawley brushed some sawdust off his elbow. "Works every time," he said, puffing on his pipe.

"What er you blabbin' about?" asked Lanning.

"What rock!" Bultin rumbled, a bronze chain vibrating on his massive chest.

"Why, the Cirilen-Stone I found. Nothing shoos a man's aches away faster than a genuine Cirilen-Stone." Rawley shook his head in appreciation, then he wiggled his body and lifted his arms to the sky. "Hala, I feel ten years younger!"

*   *   *

Watching Rawley from Lince's cabin, Nil chuckled. The others looked, too, wagering what the ship's carpenter was up to.

Lince was less jovial as he screwed his eyes on the wily fellow.

"A bit of larking might be good fer 'em, now, Mister Mate," said Karlock.

Lince rolled his eyes and gritted his teeth.

The Creature jumped from the table and climbed down the ladder.

Lince grinned in grim pride as his cat ran across the deck, up the companionway, and onto the foredeck.

"The cat smells a rat, I guess!" Zee giggled.

"That it did," Lince smiled, toasting his cat with a thimble of medicine.

"I wonder if this should be the Captain's cabin," said Nil.

"It pitches a bit," said Lince jealously. "Compared to alow."

"Yes, nicely, like a horse, I've noticed, Lince. Suits me fine. I wonder why I even wanted the lower cabin now. Check out yonder carpenter, Mister Mate!" Nil grinned and elbowed Lince.

*   *   *

"What's a Cirilen-Stone?" asked Lanning.

"Give it here!" bellowed Bultin.

Rawley shuddered to think of Bultin all lathered up, but he gambled on his own guile now, as he had so many times before. "You mean you fellows don't already use 'em? By gosh, they're about all the time, and you don't *use* 'em? Wait till I tell my grand-pappy Gilbobble back in the Blackberry Mountains where my kin are from, and then he'll have the meanest belly laugh you ever did witness, I declare! Cirilen-Stones come from the Blackberry Mountains, don't ya know, and everyone there knows they cure a man's aches and pains!"

"Where?" snarled Bultin.

Rawley relit his pipe carefully. "The Blackberry Mountains. Why, that's where my kin have lived for—"

"No!" yelled Bultin. "Where's the rock?"

Rawley flicked a finger.

The men's eyes followed it to an overturned bucket on the deck, and in a puddle next to it sat a porous, gray rock.

"'At's a scrubstone!" growled Bultin.

"That's a holystone, is all!" said Sowernut.

Bultin rumbled and bulged.

"Why do ya think they call it a 'holystone,' then, Mister know-it-all, if it's not a Cirilen-Stone, eh?" said Rawley.

Sowernut frowned.

"'Cause it's full of holes!" said Bultin.

"Oh, that's the stupidest thing I ever heard, Bultin," said Overly.

"I've heard *stupider*," grunted Sowernut.

"If ya take that yonder stone and rub it all over your aches and pains," nodded Rawley, widening his eyes, "they vanish like they never were there. *Hooo* Daddy! Do they ever. That is, if ya dig in and do it right, of course. Ya' gotta' get it in there, right where it counts, and go at it! *Aah!*" Rawley flicked a speck of sawdust from his shirt and patted his chest. "I feel fit as a Polwairn!"

There was a pause as the men of the second watch eyed the carpenter with hope and scorn. Rawley's face remained sincere—and so did the men's agony.

Someone made a step toward the bucket.

Then they all collided in a painful heap over the holystone.

Bultin rose from the pile, holding the rock. "Git yer own!" he yelled, shaking off the others who ran across the decks in search of holystones, to the amusement and amazement of the other watches.

All gathered back at the fo'c's'le before Rawley with their scrubstones in hand.

"Now," Rawley said, blowing a row of smoke rings. "Commence rubbin' those aches away!" He grinned, his gold tooth glinting in the Second Moon's light.

Bultin grunted as he reached back his arm to grind the rock into the small of his back.

The others twisted the rocks into sore muscles, resolved to endure immediate pain for the long-lasting relief that Rawley had guaranteed them.

Twisting, contorted, they drilled the rocks into painful hollows, sinews, and joints to get at that "one crick" where the pain was most intense. Even Sowernut gave it a vigorous try. Some flailed and lost their balance, crashing to the deck in pitiful piles, yet they continued to dig the rocks deeper into their sore flesh as they lay prostrate on the deck.

The other watches reacted with glee as the men of watch two engaged in their exotic dance on the fo'c's'le, stamping about in strange positions, flailing and moaning.

The sailor's faces burned as they noticed their mates' amusement, but ridicule was not their only worry: a gnawing suspicion was giving birth to a horrible realization.

"Harder, Mates!" said Rawley. "You've got to take a little to get a little!" The red-bearded carpenter lit another splint to spark his pipe.

The sailors gritted their teeth and buckled down, believing in Rawley if only to save themselves, and grinding the rocks deeper into their inflamed backs and shoulders and buttocks, scraping their skin raw, determined only more as they invested more shame and agony into the gruesome process.

Bultin grimaced, teetering before Rawley as he tried to dig the rock into his calf, and, like a mighty oak, the giant sailor tipped over and fell, crashing onto the deck.

He moaned in pain.

Rawley exploded in laughter and a volcano of sparks erupted from his pipe.

The dance ceased, its members frozen in unfortunate poses.

They turned their heads toward the chortling carpenter.

Sowernut closed his eyes.

"No," Lanning nodded, incredulous.

"He be doing it to us again!" Rollum said.

Behind Rollum, Senthellzia, who had wisely abstained from the proceedings, reclined against the rail and clucked in sad laughter.

"Rawley!" Lanning cried, and he lunged for him in fury. But Rawley was too quick. He was already sailing through the air off his spring-loaded leg and bouncing down the ladderway. The Creature hissed at him, having blended into the railing, and spooked Rawley for an instant as the men lumbered down the ladderway behind him.

Rawley turned to them on the lower deck.

"Many of you are too afraid to admit the power of the Cirilen-Stone!" he proclaimed. "And many more are too timid to believe that the power of the Cirilen-Stone is coursing through your veins, even now, repairing and replenishing all the weary parts as I speak! Alas, many will forever be blind to the power of the Cirilen-Stone, pity though it be!"

Overly touched his back. "Well…it's the most amazing thing I've ever felt in my life!"

"In a way!" growled Sowernut.

"I feel better, Rawley!" said Bultin, grinning and blinking his beady eyes.

Rawley winked. "Just ask Bultin!"

"Wait a minute, you shammy-tongued, fish-coated, slick-whistled hornswaggler!" said Lanning.

Just then, Lince strode up behind Rawley and tapped him on the shoulder. "Mister Carpenter, how are the repairs farin' alow?" he asked.

Rawley turned, and he never thought he would be so relieved to see the menacing first mate. "Well apace, Mister Neery-Atton."

"Then, Mister Skarmillion, the Captain invites you for a small libation in my cabin, sir."

Rawley grinned in the moonlight at the crew on the fo'c's'le. "Why, thank you, sir, I guess I will!" He turned with a salute to the men and walked in a springing limp beside Lince, stifling his glee.

The other watches applauded Rawley like a conquering hero as he passed.

"Can ya climb a ladder, Mister Skarmillion?" asked Lince.

"Why, yes, Mister Neery-Atton. Faster than most, thanks to my leg."

Rawley skillfully propelled himself up the ladder to the first mate's cabin where the Captain, second mate, and ship's surgeon all toasted him.

"Why, I thank you gentlemen most kindly. I don't think I've ever been so mean tired as I am right now!" Rawley laughed and pulled his cap from his bald head as he fell into a seat next to Zee behind Nil and Karlock.

"Good show," said Nil. "A fine job today and a splendid lark just now, sir!"

"Cheers, Rawley!" laughed Karlock, tipping his glass.

Lince put a drink in Rawley's hand. "Rawley, yer made of a crazy kind of stuff," said the first mate. "You've done a fine job today, but I'll bust ya in two if I catch you pullin' yer guff again on this ship, I do swear it by the Gairanor, sir!"

Zee had been chuckling ever since Rawley came into the room. "That was the finest joke I've seen for a dozen moons, Mister Carpenter," said the physician. "They looked a fine rafter of turkeys!"

And they all had a good a laugh and Rawley took his medicine before going below to oversee the repairs.

*   *   *

After the others went below, Nil and Lince looked at the chart spread on the table in the lantern glow. "Time, Lince," Nil murmured.

"Aye."

"Two days out, and we're not even halfway. Seven dead, five injured, Lince! We're down to 38."

"As long as Trinadol's statue lights up when we're in danger, I figure he's still alive," said Lince.

Nil nodded. "All the more reason we must hurry. Sleep now, my friend. We'll leave at dawn. Blast Rawley, I hope the repairs are done! I'll wake you." Nil stepped onto the ladder and climbed down to his cabin.

"Good night, Captain! I'll wake you." Lince winked and closed the door behind Nil.

Nil blew out the lantern by his bed and fell asleep in his clothes as he touched his head to the pillow.

But his brief sleep was filled with dreams of frantic action inside a trap of his own design made of endless battles and labors that required ever-more skill and concentration, growing more tedious and pressing until his eyes finally cracked open at Lince's stout knocking overhead.

* * *

Chapter 25

A Damsel in Distress

Dawn lit orange arms of cloud over the horizon like the ghost of the Rollock reaching over the sky. The isle to the north was still swathed in fog that burned off as a hot day cooked the air.

They weighed anchor before the repairs were finished, balancing the ballast in the hold as they rode against the grain of a gentle northeasterly. To keep the *Sea Mare* heeled, they were forced to make due east.

Rawley crawled on the new bowsprit and tied a thick line around it that was fastened to his belt. He swung under it, took the battered figurehead from Bultin, and, with his wooden knee planted against the bow, he pegged the neighing mare to the knighthead.

The men on the foredeck sent up a few hoorays as Rawley climbed back aboard.

Tobbs ran up the companionway to the foredeck, sending a spontaneous wave of laughter over the men there.

"Mister Skarmillion!" Tobbs cried, blushing.

Rawley ducked and pretended not to see him as he coiled a line for stowage.

"Mister Skarmillion, sir! It's been a full day!"

"Why the day's just begun, young Tobbs!" Rawley raised a hand at the sky, bringing a round of guffaws.

"No sir, I mean…Don't you remember, Mister Skarmillion? You do remember, sir, I'm sure you do, don't you?"

"You look a tad peaked, Tobbs!"

"The three-headed fish, sir!" Tobbs gestured haplessly with his pale hands.

"Ah! So, I guess yer cups must have spilled all over, with the way things have been goin', eh now, in the fo'c's'le, lad?"

"No, sir!" said Tobbs. "I devised a way to keep the cups from spilling by affixing them to a set of scales on a swivel base of my own design."

"Oh, and sure ya did now."

"Yes, sir! And it has worked marvelously, I must confess."

"Hmm, well, it should have, I guess!"

"I presume from what you told me that it is time to bring the specimens above deck for inspection. I can't seem to see anything below, but then the light is only partial, just as you instructed."

"You've done it right, after all, I see, Tobbs! Bring them up, and be careful not to spill, now. We'll all have a look-see. Gather 'round, men—we're going to get a rare look at the amazing, notorious, astounding and dumbfounding three-headed fish! Not to be missed, this!"

Rawley's spirited advertisement gave Tobbs a surge of confidence as he bolted to his cabin to retrieve his specimens.

The crew crowded forward as Tobbs emerged from the fo'c's'le with his two cups full of brine and eyebrow shavings. He glared confidently at the salty brutes who had routinely chided him, barely able to keep from stopping to let the water settle and have a look. But, now that an audience had gathered, he decided to proceed up the companionway to the fo'c's'le where Rawley was waiting and puffing his pipe. The going was rough up the companionway as the bow smote a set of sturdy seas, but Tobbs showed a remarkable sense of balance as he conveyed his precious cargo.

"Well, Mister Skarmillion, here they are!" he announced.

Rawley leaned forward and squinted, his gold tooth flashing. "Uh—hold the mugs side-by-side and peer down into them, with your eyes real wide, lad, and make sure to look as close as can be!"

Tobbs held the mugs side-by-side and squinted as he looked into the brine. The crew fell quiet.

"What do ya see? Open yer eyes real wide!"

"I can't see anything…wait! No. Just an eyebrow hair. No, yes, no…No, I'm afraid I can't see them, sir, I can't see them, at all…"

"You're looking too deep! Pull back a bit. What do you see, looking back at you out of the water, eh?"

Tobbs looked intently, his face distressed. "I see nothing."

"Hold them still. What do you see?" coaxed Rawley.

"Apart from my own reflections in the water, sir—nothing!" he said, exasperated.

"With no eyebrows?"

"Why, yes…"

"Like a fish has no eyebrows?"

"…Right."

"And yer mouth's open. Eh, laddy?"

"Yes…"

"And there's two of ya, side-by-side, now?"

"Well…"

"And plus yer own head, eh?"

"Uh, I'm not sure I'm…"

"Go like this." Rawley pursed his lips like he was blowing smoke rings. Tobbs mimicked him hopefully.

"Now look in the water."

Tobbs did, making O's with his lips.

Everybody exploded.

"Looks like a three-headed fish to me, ya lily-livered, land-lubbin' book-weevil! *Yooo-hoo-hoo!*" Rawley hooted, and laughter erupted from his fiery beard, cascading over his chest in waves as the crew joined in a chorus of rock-grinding jeers, pummeling the poor naturalist with heaps of burning mirth.

"Oh yes, I see, so fish have no eyebrows…so I'm the *fish*," nodded Tobbs, realizing, at last, it was a joke. "And my reflection…" He turned three shades of purple. Somehow, the pride and sense of humor his father had instilled in him made Tobbs concede that he had been made a perfect fool. And so he laughed, too, then, surrounded by the laughing sailors, and this won him their affection and respect perhaps more than any other thing might have.

Lince shot a look at Rawley from the maindeck as Bombo rang the mess with great enthusiasm, having witnessed Pickle's artistry that morning.

Awaiting each man was a breakfast of potato pancakes with shredded Enryd and garlic, apple preserves and eggs scrambled with smoked pork and sweet white cheese, along with a soft corn biscuit with a slab of butter, an orange, and strong coffee. Nil rotated the men off the watches to the galley and was glad to see their disposition change as they came out on deck.

The sharp-eyed Sowernut from the second watch took the crow's nest, relieving Beenay of the third watch who had relieved Jootle. Beenay finally took his breakfast, last and hungriest.

Feferl held Jootle is arms as he took him to his bed after his long vigil. "Jootle's been sorely tasked, Mister Neery-Atton," Feferl mentioned to Lince.

"Aye. He should rest."

"It's not right he should have been out all night. He's got the shakes from coffee beans, sir."

"All creatures on this ship will do their part in our survival, Mister!" barked Lince. The Creature growled with a surprisingly deep rumble as it came around Lince's calf and glanced at Feferl, and then it licked its chops in disgust.

"Aye, Mister Neery-Atton, I see that," nodded Feferl. "And your cat serves some crucial function, I'm sure!" He turned and strode toward the aft passageway to go below.

Lince produced a stuffed rat from a pocket in his battered black greatcoat and threw it toward Feferl. The Creature snarled and leaped though the air, catching the stuffed toy in its mouth before landing on the deck at

Feferl's heels. Feferl wheeled and saw the Creature rip into the toy at his feet with carnivorous lust in its wild eyes.

"You wouldn't want a rat gnawing on poor Jootle's nose while he's sleepin' now, would ya, Mister Feferl?" Lince chuckled. "Eh, sir?"

"Aye. The cat does its job, Mister Mate! No argument here."

Feferl went below to tend Jootle in his hammock, and he fed him a bottle of milk from the one sweet-goat they had aboard and sat with him until the monkey finally burned off the false energy of the coffee beans and fell asleep.

Everyone took their stations, with the second watch at the weather sheet, the first watch on the port sheet and the third at the lateen.

A small contingent from the first and second watches tended the jibs.

Every inch of sail was fixed to catch the northeasterly wind as Karlock conned her due east against the grain to keep her keeled.

The gray isle drew ominously near, straight ahead.

"Mister Carpenter!"

"Aye, Captain!" Rawley's voice rose through the sea doors.

"How bloody long do you need, sir?"

"As long as we can possibly get, sir! The pitch must set, if you please, before we roll her back under. We've only three planks to go on the highest breach."

"Very well, sir, then make haste, and we'll give you every last possible instant," said Nil. "Fine work, sir. All of your men are to be commended."

"Aye, sir," said Rawley.

Bloody ship's carpenters, Nil thought, furrowing his brows as he gave the conn to Karlock and climbed down the ladder to Lince's cabin in order to consult the chart.

Zee climbed in after him.

"Doctor, good to see you. Come in and have some coffee with me."

"Thank you, Captain. Of the five men in my infirmary, only two will be able seaman for the duration of the voyage. One has a broken arm, which I have splinted, and the other a badly broken foot, which I set and cast. The other has a head wound that is still grave. I am doing all I can to keep him with us."

"Thank you, Doctor." Nil looked grimly at the island after pouring Zee a mug of coffee.

"We seem to be heading straight for that island," said Zee.

"Yes."

"I believe a large beast is said to roam that island, a prisoner of its northern beach."

"So it's said, Zee."

"We're heading straight toward it."

"You mentioned that, I think."

"Yes."

"I'm hoping we'll pass it to the north. That should certainly give our carpenter time to complete his repairs. Then we'll tack southwest against the wind toward the Dimmrock."

"It seems we'll have an excellent view of the beast that lives there then, Captain," said Zee.

"You're right, Zee. We should have an excellent view. It can't be helped. If we luff around that isle—"

"Eh?"

"If we take her further north, with the wind, she'll yaw and breach the repairs. I only hope we won't run aground." Nil ran a stick of lead along a straight edge over the chart toward the island, just missing its northwest corner. "A ship is like a person, Zee. Wounds like the *Sea Mare*'s need time to heal."

Zee frowned.

"If you'll excuse me, Doctor. You're quite welcome to stay. I'm going up top."

"Thank you," said Zee. "I'm going below."

* * *

All noticed that the Lady Tunn looked ten years younger, with a blushing heat in her skin and the tiny wrinkles around her eyes all smoothed away. She beamed at Rollum with poetry in her eyes as he doted on her. All kept a discreet distance as the pair traded adventures, of which each had many, and they wove a braid of bold tales like a rosy bower that morning with their vivid yarns.

A halo of pride crowned the ship, and the mariners were all in approval that one of Ameulas's finest daughters had sparked love in the heart of the fair Demoldan prince; and they felt their mission blessed.

Harm sat disdainfully on the crow's nest, glaring at Rollum now and then.

From the blue sea the island loomed closer and closer, a gray slab so featureless and regular it was clearly not the work of nature. The western shore was 100 feet tall and 100 wide. The men saw the white spray of rollers against this its flat walls.

If they were going to pass by the corner of this great brick of an island, they would not pass it by much.

"Sowernut, shout when you see sign of a reef! Hear me, man?" yelled Nil.

"Aye, sir, a ring-reef, but broken dead ahead, just north of the island!"

"Mister Carpenter!" Nil bayed from the bridge.

His voice rang down the forward sea doors into Rawley's ear.

"Aye, Captain?" came Rawley's voice.

"When will you be satisfied, sir?"

"Half an hour, if you please, sir!"

"Damn your hide, man, I'll give it to you then!" Nil rapped on the overhead and took the helm from Karlock, vigorously spinning the wheel to conn her across the wind and luff her north in the troughs.

As the men came nearer they saw the word "NO" carved in 90-foot letters on the narrow end of the island.

They were little comforted to see how close the Captain was taking them.

The sun peaked as the *Sea Mare* passed the sharp corner of the island with barely ten ship-widths to spare. They crossed over a gap in the reef into the shallow lagoon that fronted the island's long beach.

The water was clear, and Sowernut did not see any place where the reef came too close to the surface within the oval lagoon. Placid waves foamed on the beach off their starboard rail, and the wind swept over the island and down to meet them at a steady angle, fortunately, so they were still able to keep the ship heeled on her port side.

They saw words stretching into the gray distance carved along the entire length of the island:

NEVER JOURNEY HERE

At last, Rawley gave the signal that the breaches were repaired, and Nil pulled the helm a quarter north and ordered the sails clewed so they could search for an exit from this lagoon at a slower clip.

The ship righted herself, at last, and weary cheers below confirmed that the repairs were holding. Then the men started shifting the ballast in the hold.

The *Sea Mare* streamed over the aquamarine waters of the coral atoll whose gentle waves had pushed a pink sand beach against the island's stark cliff.

The heat and salt shimmered in the air as they cruised close to the beach's breakwater. Between the words "NEVER" and "JOURNEY," obscured in curling sun-struck mists, a mass of rock loomed as if it had split off from the cliff. Sowernut studied it as the shoulders of the outcrop shrugged, and vast arms appeared at its sides. Sowernut gave a yell, more of surprise than fear, and he pointed incredulously at the colossus. Yet, after a roar from its cavernous mouth, the rest of the crew saw it, too.

Draped in seaweed, covered with barnacles and reef fragments with cactus growing on its head, the lurching giant shambled into the surf and pointed at Sowernut in the crow's nest.

Nil turned the wheel port to avoid a course too near the giant, which seemed pathetic, if powerful, wandering in the surf at the center of the beach. There was no reason to fear it since it moved so slowly and they would pass well out of its reach.

Nevertheless, Senthellzia nocked a lead-cored arrow in her bow, and Nil ordered the crew to battle stations.

Sowernut cried, "It's after a lady!"

Nil gouged his ear. "What, sir?"

A high, desperate cry lifted on the wind and as if in answer the beast growled like an earthquake and stepped deeper into the breakers.

A group of men on the foredeck shouted and motioned toward a spot on the sea before the giant.

Lince peered over the rail as another urgent cry guided his eyes, and he spied a maiden splashing in the water before the oncoming creature. "Aye, Captain, he's right!"

They heard a shrill scream, rising and falling, and Rollum saw the maid in the surf, her golden hair flashing in the sun as she thrashed. She lunged out of the water and the men could see her bare breasts. Her arms flew high, and she wailed a piercing scream as the beast waded in after her. She moved deeper into the sea toward the ship.

Rollum's eyes lit with quick fury and he turned to Senthellzia, kissing her brow. He ran like a hunting lion to the aftercastle and she followed even as he tied his Demoldan sea-board to the taffrail and hurled the board like a discus into the *Sea Mare*'s wake.

Senthellzia was too late to stop him from diving in after it. He grabbed the line of the sea-board and slid down until he had mounted it. Then he steered it expertly across the wake. Nil could see what he intended to do, and wheeled the *Sea Mare* starboard to bring them closer to the woman as they passed.

The fair Demoldan clutched the edges of the sleek board and bore down, steering along the heaving rollers. He saw the woman splashing before the hoary beast and heard another scream. Rollum tightened his grip as he swung wide, planning to hang onto the line with his left hand and catch her in his right arm as they passed. There would be no second chance, he knew, and he was grateful the Captain was steering the ship within range of his reach.

Senthellzia stood on the aftercastle and watched Rollum jet over the crystal water. She looked at the woman, thrashing and shrieking in the waves, with a mixed bitterness.

The beast sent another tremor through the sea as it planted a foot closer to its screaming quarry. It was encrusted with barnacles and muscles and kelp and cactus like a patchwork monster from a child's fantasy, yet it was horrible in the reasonable light of the day.

Senthellzia looked for something like an eye to aim at but found no vulnerable target. Seaweed hung from its closed mouth in great lengths that draped over its body into the sea.

Rollum steeled his eyes on the target, catching only brief glimpses of the woman's flaxen hair and pink nipples. He heard her scream again, loud and close, as he reached out his arm. Rollum skipped over the waves pushed by the giant's knees and he noticed her gray skin an instant before reaching her and he recoiled as she embraced him.

For an instant out of time, he saw her head, a stump with long blond hair that sprouted around a rude hole in its top, through which a weird scream whistled. Her arms were spongy plugs of sticky flesh that flailed on a pale trunk spotted with two bright pink spots. Another whistling shriek emitted from the hole, and the thing's neck quivered and spit as Rollum screamed. The creature's flesh was covered in some kind of glue and he could not let go.

Sighting the head of the beast, Senthellzia's green eye did not flinch, though she blinked away a burning tear.

The men watched from the ship and cheered as the gallant Rollum appeared to have gotten hold of the maiden.

But then he was jerked from the sea and lost hold of the sea-board.

He flew through the air before them, reeled in by the giant's tongue that had draped over its body with the random detritus that covered it. The "woman" was merely the lure of a monstrous angler.

The colossus opened its jaws like giant clamshells as Rollum flew backwards into its dark mouth, and Rollum glanced at the deck of the *Sea Mare* just as Senthellzia's arrow pierced his heart.

The giant crushed Rollum in its rocky jaws, and ground them cruelly, though Senthellzia's deadly aim had prevented her love from knowing that anguish. She fell to her knees and stared through the balusters of the aft rail at the sea-board skipping free on the *Sea Mare*'s wake below.

* * *

Drugor smiled.

* * *

The men on the aftercastle tried to comfort Senthellzia and they glanced crossly at the statue of Trinadol above them, which had not warned them of the tragic peril.

They noticed the beast staggering in the waves behind them.

It fell to its knees and founts of blood ran down its rocky jowls, staining the foaming sea. The Lady Senthellzia's heavy arrow must have struck a vital innard after piercing her lover's heart: a mean solace.

NEVER JOURNEY HERE, read the letters carved into the island's long cliff, mocking them in the aftermath of the senseless evil.

Nil held the helm steady as they searched for an eastern passage. Sowernut spotted a deep-water gap in the atoll a few points north of east and Nil took them toward it.

Zee went to Senthellzia as she knelt on the aftercastle, and she hugged the tall physician, burying her head in his scented orange robes. She sobbed, too proud to show the sailors all around, who hung their heads in grief.

Nil climbed down onto the main deck. He looked wrathfully at the isle they had passed, wondering why Trinadol's statue had not warned them.

"It's a cruel thing, Nilly," Karlock said from the bridge. "I don't see what to make of it."

"Perhaps Trinadol is dead." Nil looked resentfully south, toward the Dimmrock. "It's hard to see any good in him, now, anyway, Karlock," said Nil.

"'Twas the second thing the King did make," offered Karlock. "The Rollock and this seem the most merciless of his beasts."

"How can I rally them?"

"Rescuing the King is Ameulas's only hope, Nil. Artimeer himself died for this cause. There is no turning back, Captain. What do we have to turn back to?"

Nil looked at Karlock's steady eye. He looked at the words carved in the cliff. "He did warn us. We just didn't hear him." Nil climbed the ladder and took the helm as Karlock rang the bell.

The men gathered below.

"This was the second isle young Trinadol created," said Nil. "His power was less disciplined and reckless, and not entirely his own."

"'Twas a cruel thing, Captain!" said Lanning from the aftercastle near Senthellzia.

"Aye, Mister, you're right," said Nil, facing the aftercastle from the bridge. "The same cruel thing that traps our King!"

"Why didn't his statue light up?" asked Bultin.

"Maybe the King's dead!" said Sowernut from above.

"This is the time we're tested!" said Nil. "The ugliness of this beast was meant not to destroy us but to defeat our hearts and turn us back. There is mercy in that, though hard to see. Trinadol carved his warning that was right before us, alas! There is good in the King, though it is besieged by an ancient evil that is not from his heart. That evil comes for Ameulas, next, and only Trinadol can defeat it. The King is alive, without long to live. As long as we can save him, we must try!"

"You heard the Captain!" boomed Lince.

As soon as they passed the island, Karlock yawed the *Sea Mare* south.

It was four o'clock when a strong headwind challenged Nil's wish to go southwest. They began tacking arduously, crossing back and forth over the current that flowed southeast and aided greatly by the lateen sail. Nevertheless, the current pulled them toward the channel between the Isle of Ice and Snow and the Living Isle, which lie directly east of the Dimmrock.

Nil meant to cross this current as directly as possible while using it to bring them further south to skirt the Illusion Sea. He planned to escape the current just in time and cut southwest, straight to the Dimmrock. The unfavorable wind, however, would make the final cut difficult, and dangerous.

White clouds spread from the southwest, quickly closing over the sky. On their third tack, they came to a glowing deepwater reef. Nil reluctantly chose to anchor on the reef and rest for the evening as the crimson sun fell behind a gray horizon. Nil did not wish to reenter the current against the wind, or risk crossing into the Illusion Sea. In the morning, he decided regretfully, they would get their bearings and hope for a more favorable wind. Nil cursed inwardly. They could be at the Dimmrock in a matter of hours.

When the sails were furled and the *Sea Mare*'s great anchor bit into the reef, Nil climbed down from the bridge and followed the scent of dinner with the others.

He was approaching the men gathered before the galley when he saw Lelinair walking through the men toward him.

"Lelinair!" he cried, thunderstruck by the sight of her.

"Nil!" She smiled and she held their glowing love-star up in one hand.

Nil wanted to speak but he was speechless.

In her other hand, Lelinair waved a writhing green viper, and she started to dance, clicking her heels on the deck. She whirled around and around and her clothes and flesh shriveled on her bones and flew off until she was a white skeleton with flowing chestnut hair dancing before Nil on the deck. Her joints snapped and her bones rained down and shattered, and the love-star bounced into the empty socket of her eye and sparkled as her skull rose from the deck into the air. Her bony hand floated up, too, and her finger signaled silence against her grinning teeth.

*   *   *

CHAPTER 26

▼

Nightmares

"Captain!" called Lince.

"I know!" said Nil. "Weigh anchor!"

Several men screamed wildly. Others obeyed and cranked the capstan to pull the anchor from its grip on the coral. Then they all saw it.

A wave in the north was coming out of the ocean like a mountain.

"Pay it no heed!" said Nil.

The ship began rising on the wave's foothills and the cold shadow of its crest crossed over the decks.

All fell to their knees, clutching whatever hold was nearby.

The wave smashed through the rigging and sails, crushing the masts and sending Sowernut to the deck in a broken heap.

When the wave struck Nil, it felt cold and wet, but he felt no pain and gripped the bridge rail. Like water, the nightmare drained from the ship back into the sea and the astonished men saw calm waters around them and everything intact.

"Pay these visions no mind! We've entered the Illusion Sea, men," cried Nil.

"The sky's clear, Captain," said Sowernut. "And the sun—it's noon!"

"No! It's a lie!" growled Lince, pale after seeing the ghost of his father, which had just crawled over the rail of the main deck, drowned and tangled in seaweeds.

An upsurge roiled the sea off the starboard bow; all turned to look.

A green patch spread as it neared the surface and long after the men expected it to emerge, the shape continued to grow until it was many times larger than the *Sea Mare*. It tore the ocean wide then, sending waves in all directions as it rose.

The men forgot Nil's advice, shivering and choking as the foul breath of a giant dragonfly blasted over the decks. Slime streamed over the slopes of its vast green head as it glared at the tiny ship fluttering before its snout like a mosquito, and a terrible hunger burned in the crimson domes of the nightmare's eyes. Its mouth yawned like night tearing open, and everyone fell to the decks, covering their heads as its many jaws closed and they heard the squealing crunch of the *Sea Mare* splintering in ruin all around them in the blackness.

A moment later they looked up, and it was a clear night, cold and silent; they saw a meteor shower in the sky.

"Never mind what you see!" said Nil from the bridge.

"Listen to the Captain!" cried Karlock.

"Pay no attention to these dreams!" said Nil, but when they all turned to look at him they saw a skeleton standing on the bridge with a bearded skull over a flapping greatcoat that flashed pale ribs. "We will drift free of this sea as the current takes us southeast!" shouted the skull.

The next moment it was day. The sea was rough as clouds sped over the sky. Snow swirled over bitter waves.

"Go below!" shouted Nil. But all saw a terrible frog instead, with long slitted eyes. "Go below," it croaked. "Don't look at the sea or you'll go mad!"

One sailor shrieked as the grotesque captain climbed down to the deck. "Go below! Do as I say!" Nil cried, but all now backed away from him.

One man screamed as he looked at his friend beside him, for his friend had no face: a charred pit was dug into his head with the jutting teeth of a grin bridging the terrible wound. So hideous was the sight that it drove him mad, and with a raving laugh he flung himself overboard. With a cackle of triumph, the grinning apparition he had seen soared upward and exploded in sparks by the crow's nest. The sailor would never know his friend was still alive and unharmed as he swam with vigorous strokes toward the bottom of the sea, chased by demons that burst his heart in horror before he drowned.

"Below! Now!" warned the blue, reptilian Captain.

The men ran from him over the decks.

Senthellzia sat in a corner with her eyes closed, stroking Harm with Zee.

"Very well!" cried Nil. "I say again that all should go below before they are driven mad by what they see! Each of you must save yourself if we are to survive! Do not believe this world until it is believable again! Remember what you know is true!" Nil ran to the door of his cabin, and it transformed into a mirror wherein he saw the illusion that had been cast over him, and the image laughed at him even as Nil realized why the men had fled.

He reached for the knob and the brass handle became the head of a serpent, dripping venomous fangs. He gripped it tight, feeling its cold scales, twisting it and opening the door as he felt cold fangs stab his palm. He slammed closed the door behind him and jumped on his bed.

But it was not his bed—it was a mound of glistening maggots. He sunk into the squirming mass, feeling the worms trying to bore into his skin, and he screamed, but then he stopped, gritted his teeth, and closed his eyes.

The worms continued to wriggle against his flesh until his stubborn disbelief finally faded them away.

He opened his eyes, sighing, and found himself suspended over a chasm gouged right through the ship.

He grabbed the broken edge as the sea welled through the decks like a geyser. Nil scrambled for the door and stopped. It is not real, it cannot be real, he thought. He felt the water swashing around his legs, but when he straightened the bending thought, he was dry again. The hole was gone. His bed reappeared; but someone was lying on it.

It was Trinadol.

Nil leaped to his side and took his hand, but the Cirilen was dead, his eyes wide, dry and milky. Purple and green seaweed was tangled in his hair and trailed across his blue lips. His cheeks sank as Nil looked at him and his hand suddenly gripped Nil's. "I'm alive!" the dead king suddenly hissed, and his eyes flared with crimson fire as he leaped off the bed and grabbed Nil around the throat.

Nil stared at the phantom that clung to him, paralyzed with fear, or courage, and finally, in the face of his disbelief, the specter became fair, aglow with life, and the eyes cooled until they were clear and blue. "For a moment, I can reach you," said the apparition.

Nil shook his head, dizzy with the strain of disbelieving.

"Do not try to understand anything here, Nil! Weigh these words later. I am alive!" said Trinadol. "And your mission is not in vain. My power is dwindling, but I am alive."

"Are you real?"

"I am no illusion. I am a reflection. A reflection of the truth."

Nil shuddered. "Lord!" he gasped. "What can we do?"

"Have hope. For I have only this myself." For an instant the image faded into awful shape, then pulsed painfully back to life. "Beware this sea's borders. They are not what they seem. If you save me from the depths, I will save Ameulas. That I promise, noble mariner. Go to sleep." The ghost shifted, and then vanished.

Nil clasped his hands against his face, but could not feel his fingers. He pulled them back and saw ten earthworms sprouting from his wrists.

He could hear screams outside the cabin, and a queer thumping sound of heavy legs roaming the decks. But he could not give it a thought. He could not go out there.

Then the walls around him vanished and whatever shelter they had offered him was lost.

Myriad horrors swarmed around the *Sea Mare*. In the water danced a gallery of creatures. Green gargoyles stared from under the waves with evil, knowing grins. Nightmare beasts waltzed in the air, smiling at the men with animal heads. Beautiful mermaids with the heads of hags cavorted in the waves, blowing long silver trumpets. Seven-legged shaggy beasts with stupid, fearsome jaws shambled across the decks, gawking at the dazed mariners.

Enthralled by the wheeling terrors, Nil somehow conjured a thought. He struck a match and lit the wick of a long tallow candle that turned, before his eyes, into a caterpillar. The match turned into a praying mantis that snapped at his finger. He put the match in his mouth to make sure it was out and felt a pinch on his tongue. He spit the mantis out, bent low, and ran forward, aiming at what seemed to be a great island in the distance spewing molten comets at the *Sea Mare*.

His head struck air with a crush of pain. He fell to the floor as the wall became visible again and Nil sank into grateful unconsciousness.

*   *   *

Nil was wakened by Lince. He had no idea how many days or leagues had passed. He kneaded the knot on his forehead.

"Eh, Nilly? That's quite a bump on yer noggin!" grinned Lince, who had a few bloody bumps and scrapes on his own noggin.

"What happened?" said Nil.

"We drifted clear. We've sighted the Dimmrock, Nilly! Karlock is setting the sail."

Nil got to his feet and staggered toward the door, grabbing the hatchway to steady himself. "How long were we in? How are the men?"

"A minute after you went into your cabin, Captain, all the visions stopped."

Nil looked at the candle on his table. The candle had completely melted, its hardened drippings flowing down the table's leg. "What time is it, Lince?"

"That I don't know, Captain," Lince opened the door. "It seems about two."

"That's impossible. It must be night now, at least..."

"Well, Captain," Lince smiled. "All seems fair." He gestured out the door.

Nil went out and looked around the decks.

All the men were at their stations and the sun was tipping past noon. The *Sea Mare* seemed indeed to be mounting the southern horizon and the ship's sails were spread to catch an ideal nor'easterly. The cliffs of the Dimmrock rose out of the southern horizon.

"Ho, Captain! Are you all right?" asked Karlock from the bridge.

"Aye, how long has passed, Karlock?" Nil asked.

"Only a few minutes since you went into your cabin!"

Nil climbed up to the bridge and looked Karlock in the eye. He saw his face was bruised and scraped and his clothes rumpled. "How long was I in the cabin, Karlock?" he demanded.

Just then Nil felt a freezing gust of wind pass over the decks and shivered. He looked up at the summer sky and felt the sun on his own hands.

"Everything is fine now, Captain," Karlock smiled.

"Men!" roared Nil. "Furl the sails and drop anchor!"

"But Captain," Karlock smiled. "The Dimmrock is right ahead!"

"You heard me, Mister! Lince, get it done now, by the Gairanor, and not an instant later!"

Lince turned to Nil from the deck before the bridge. "Nilly, we'll make yonder isle before nightfall! Why drop anchor now?" The men hesitated.

Nil felt another chill whip over the decks as his breath spouted white from his black beard. "Do it NOW I SAY, or your Captain is mutinied, upon my death!"

Lince wheeled in surprise and growled at the men to follow the Captain's order, and the Creature growled at his heel.

The men moved against their instincts and weakly undertook the task of taking in the sails.

"Captain!" said Karlock. "You're still distracted by the Illusion Sea. It's behind us now, lad, and in our wake!"

"*Gah!* Don't defy me, man. Do as I say!" Nil took the helm from him.

The sails were clewed and at last the men released the anchor. As its chain was clanking over the bow they turned and looked at the Captain.

With a flash of white light Trinadol's statue ignited over the crow's nest.

Distant thunder rolled through the sky and a different world was lit up around them as though revealed by the statue's light.

The sky was knotted with iron clouds above. Nil now saw that most of the men were strewn across the *Sea Mare* with livid stares on their faces as a freezing wind rushed over the decks; only a few had actually helped haul in the sails and anchor, assisted by mere phantoms of their mates which had now vanished.

Karlock stared forward with a smile on his weathered face, unable to see the misty, frozen channel filled with jagged ice around them.

The ship was streaming toward the edge of an ice shelf that had frozen over the channel. The *Sea Mare*'s anchor line pulled taut just in time; she swung about and her starboard broadside crashed against the ledge of ice.

Chunks of ice flowed in her wake, and crowded into the passage through which she had come, compacting like a jigsaw puzzle against her port side. Her strong hull had not been breached.

Nil turned to Karlock. "Wake up, man!" he yelled. "We're out of it only now!"

Karlock stared.

Nil took him by the shoulders and gave him a shake and backhanded his cheek. "Karlock! I need you!"

Nil went down the ladder to the deck.

Lince shook his head as the Creature rubbed against his leg.

"Wake up, Lince!"

"I'm with ya, Captain! You were right as rain." Lince followed Nil across the deck, dazed and sad as he only now could see the truth again.

Lince helped Nil raise the men who lay lost in the places in their minds they had run to in order to escape the chaos around them. Soon, they revived Lanning and Sowernut, who, with a fully recovered Karlock, helped rouse the others.

"You men above, come down and help! You're not crazy, only confused! In times of confusion, listen to your Captain!" commanded Nil.

The men answered Nil's call, gratefully, climbing down to help the men who lay raving on the decks with inward stares.

Nil came to Senthellzia and Zee huddled under the port aft ladder. Both were stroking Harm with their eyes closed, and the bird turned to Nil and cried softly as if for help. Nil let the beautiful falcon clutch his forearm as he and Lince rubbed the arms and shoulders of Senthellzia and Zee and spoke to them, pulling them back to wakefulness. At last, each sobbed and hugged the other before hugging Lince and Nil, and Harm clucked in stern approval on Nil's shoulder.

Nil climbed the bridge where Karlock stood gripping the rail and staring at the cloud. Nil stood beside him, leaning on the rail and looking over the ice. The scurrying clouds rained sleet over the ship, frosting her lines. "Karlock," he said.

"Aye, ya sobered me up, Captain."

"This ice…is not going anywhere."

Karlock nodded. "No."

"And neither are we."

"No."

Nil's eyes wandered toward the strange, still island waiting to the west. Its brown, black, red and yellow shores spread pockmarked and grooved down to the ice. The mountains further inland were sharp and high—they would afford an excellent view of the Dimmrock, no doubt. "According to the charts, the Dimmrock is not far west of this island."

"The Living Isle, Nil?" frowned Karlock, for that was its fearsome name, though little was known of it.

"We won't stand idle," said Nil. "We must move!" He rang the bell over the bridge and mustered the crew, except for three who were unaccounted for.

Lince took his place staunchly before the bridge with the Creature at his heel as Nil addressed his haggard crew.

"We are out of the Illusion Sea only now, and now we are stuck in this frozen muck. The mountainous isle to our east, capped with snows and laced with savage clouds, is bitter with icy death, it's said. The dark mountains to our west are what some mariners have named the Living Isle, though not much is known of it, and it appears to be dead as it can be."

The men were shaken by all the private fears they had faced over the last days, and they stared with ashen faces, hearing the Captain's words with a distant self that was familiar and soothing. They were somehow calmed to hear words they trusted, despite the dangers they described.

"I know that Trinadol is still alive," said Nil. "He lies with powers dwindling under the sea south of the Dimmrock. He visited me in a vision. He warns us he has not long! Pickle and Bombo, set your galley straight and cook us a feast, for who knows how long it's been since we've had nourishment. We will eat our dinner though it appears to be only a little after noon above these cruel clouds. I think we have been at sea days we cannot count. Let's hope not too many! We are free of that sea of fears, mariners, though fresh fears await us. We must carry landing boats over this island to the west, and once we have scaled it, we should see the Dimmrock only one league west of here. Longboats could make the distance, provided we take them safely overland. Most of the crew should stay aboard the *Sea Mare* under Karlock's command in case she breaks free. Then we'll have two chances to reach Trinadol, one by land and one by sea, in case the *Sea Mare* should find a way, as well. Lince, assign the landing party, and Karlock, see to victualing the boats. The rest come with me as we tidy the decks until dinner is ready."

Karlock ordered the activities as two of the ship's four longboats were hauled on deck, and each of the 15-foot vessels was victualed.

Pickle's dinner of pork boiled in gravy with bacon and curry had an intoxicatingly sweet smell that wafted over the decks; and only then were they certain that they had passed from the Illusion Sea into the familiar Hala World again.

*   *   *

CHAPTER 27

The Living Isle

The *Sea Mare* was wedged against the unbroken sheet of ice to the south by the slob ice crowding against her starboard hull. The rugged island before her prow was jumbled with turned rock and soil. Red, yellow, and brown spattered and sprayed the island's ashen face. Rifts furrowed the slopes to the shore and black boulders rested deep in the hillsides. Not a living thing was visible as far as the eye could see, not even a gull resting on its way someplace else.

Nil had the men set bonfires on the ice aport. Rawley offered some of his precious lumber, and Lince allowed some barrels of oil to be poured over the smooth ice. The oil kept the meager fires burning, but the stubborn wind from the north sent an unceasing gale over them, damping the flames; the fires burned only light scars into the ten-foot thick ice.

Hoarfrost crystallized on the spars and lines, and relentless sleet, snow, and rain pelted the decks. Nil ordered the decks mopped with boiling water and decided that no more wood or oil should be used to burn the ice, but instead reserved for heating aboard the ship.

Karlock confronted Nil in his cabin then. "Nil, you should take the royal scepter so you might have a chance to deliver it to Trinadol."

Nil grasped Karlock's hand and squeezed it hard. "No. I think I know what we must do. I think I know, now, how we might pass. Don't ask me any questions, Karlock. Just know that I think the scepter should stay aboard the *Sea Mare*."

Karlock looked fiercely at Nil, and then embraced him, hiding his tears as he went with the Captain onto the main deck.

Nil asked Lince who he had assigned to the landing party.

Lince yelled out the roster. "Everyone pay attention, now, ya men and you woman, too! These sailors are on the landing party: Lanning, Bultin, Berrul, Sowernut, Overly, Rawley, Tunelle, Fodrick, Bat, Karul, Parnel, Erlair, Wicket and Lonair. Git yer sorry carcasses over here—we're goin' over yonder isle!"

"Aye, men," Nil nodded. "We'll have a look over that hill and see if we can reach the Dimmrock. The King has not much time left, nor do we, if we stay here."

The chosen crew gathered around the landing boats, paying special attention to what was packed in them.

Lanning was the first to climb down the rope ladder to the translucent ice, fearing as he put his weight on it that it would split underneath him. But it held like granite, which was even more depressing, and the rest climbed after him.

Rawley had improvised some sleds out of spars and rope on which the two boats could be hauled over the ice to the shore. Rawley had appointed Ed in his place as ship's carpenter, having measured and fitted him for the job. Rawley had not flinched at the rough duty Lince had assigned to him.

The men lowered the boats into the sleds and found they slid easily. Nil and Lince climbed down the ladder, and the Captain bade the crew of the *Sea Mare* farewell as the 16 men, dressed in their heaviest greatcoats, set off across the ice, leaving 23 behind.

Two men grabbed the line of each sled and pulled the landing boats over the slick ice. Many lost their footing and had painful landings as they got the hang of it the hard way.

On the shore ahead, a little to the south, an outcrop bulged out of the rock that looked a little like an old man's head. There was a blister of rock on its face that looked like a heavy-lidded eye.

Lanning walked with Lince, Rawley, and Nil at the head of the party, testing the ice. They had not felt firm ground for some time and looked forward to it as the desolate island extended its humble shores.

White steam hissed behind a ridge on the high slope of the island.

Lanning turned to Nil, warily. "Just how living is this isle, Captain?" he asked.

Nil looked at the island and walked on. "We'll avoid that mountain, I think," he said, pointing to a blackened cone smoldering dark fumes further inland that rose high over the other peaks to the north. "We'll climb straight west, if possible, as fast as we can."

With his springing gait, Rawley kept up with apparent ease.

Lince made sure the boats were secure as they slid over the ice.

They were more than half the distance to the shore when the bulging eye on the rocky outcrop's wizened face seemed to swell and redden.

A piercing white light brightened the overcast sky and they turned to see Trinadol's statue blazing over the crow's nest.

An orange gout of fire burst from the gnarled eye of the stone face overlooking the channel and the geyser shot a livid red stream over the crunching sheet of ice.

The gushing lava streaked toward the *Sea Mare* over the ice with alarming speed.

The men weren't sure which way to turn and Bat panicked, running back to the ship.

"No, Bat! Come this way!" Nil cried. But the lumbering sailor would not turn back, and Nil urged the men forward as fast as they could go.

Steam billowed from the streaking river of lava and cracks exploded in the ice to either side as it reached across the frozen channel.

Bat ran over the ice as the red river chased him, seeming to sense his movement and trying to head him off. He ran harder, bearing down, but at the last moment a finger of lava spurted from the main stream and crossed the sailor's path before him. He backpedaled, falling on his back, and slid through the fiery finger, only yards from the *Sea Mare*. He slid a few feet more over the ice and screamed, but his agony was short as the ice beneath him, and all around the *Sea Mare,* shattered like a glass plate. He fell into the water, and gushing lava poured in after him, sealing his tomb at the bottom of the channel.

The island trembled and white faults shot through the thick ice along its shores. More bloody founts appeared along the island's coast now, raining fire over the frozen channel, breaking it up even as it cut the landing party off from the ship.

Rawley, pogoing on his wooden leg, was far out ahead of the struggling men who hauled the boats. He splashed through the thin shattered ice at the island's shore and climbed onto its coarse black beach. He turned and urged the men ashore as he saw the ice crumbling in a rolling wave at their backs.

One team struggled to slide the landing boat and fell behind the other team. Lince ran behind the other boat, bulling it over the quaking ice, and when they finally made it to the shore he jumped into the shallow water by Rawley, grabbing the line himself to pull the boat aground.

"Come on!" Nil yelled to the remaining team, who had come to a standstill as they slipped and fell on the heaving ice. The ice had broken into puzzle pieces that still fit together though moving across them was treacherous.

The fountain of lava to their right spouted higher and shifted its aim to rain down over the men, five of them. A merciful cloud of steam covered the scene as their screams stabbed the sky.

The men on the shore howled at the painful sight, but Nil said, "Move!" and he turned them to the business of hauling the boat.

The ice in the channel broke apart before the *Sea Mare,* giving her new hope. The jagged slurry packed close to the shore, however, was impassable for the longboat and impossible to cross on foot.

On the slopes of the island, vermilion veins of fire dripped down toward them as though from wounds, a fiery maze they must read carefully to avoid being trapped.

"Six men under the boat!" Nil shouted. "Rawley, Lanning and Lince come ahead with me!"

The other six men grabbed hold of the boat and lifted it to their shoulders as the four ahead hurried a few hundred feet up the barren slope to a stable point safe from the languid streams of fire and with an open path above. They set the boat down and turned to look at the *Sea Mare*.

The veins of red sank through the ice before her bows as the frozen barrier crumbled.

Karlock had set sail and the landing party looked with envy as the *Sea Mare* picked up speed and tilted south toward clearer waters.

"Well," said Nil. "It's a race, then. Mister Neery-Atton, you manage the transport of the boat. Mister Skarmillion, you are in charge of the boat's repair should she be damaged. The boat is our life. Whatever we do on this island, we have to keep moving. We'll go up this slope to that low saddle above and see the view from there."

The men hoisted the landing boat onto their shoulders, Nil among them, and dug in their heels.

*   *   *

Cold water slowly swallowed one of his feet.

Trinadol woke on his tilted bed and saw himself reflected in the sea that was filling his chamber. It was not a dream. The sea was seeping through the cracks in the trap door.

He choked on the stale air. His candle floated, barely lit, on the surface of the water.

With the last fragment of the Cronus Star, Trinadol shaved off a layer of *lightstone* and held it in the air, closing his eyes and turning it slowly. The shard of stone seemed to evaporate into white smoke and the room freshened with new air.

Through his closed eyes he saw a glimmer of light. Opening them, he saw that the shard of the Cronus Star was glowing in his hand.

He turned over on the bed and peered through his spyglass into one of its facets.

Trinadol saw the *Sea Mare* trapped in ice as fire leaped from the island beside her—the island that lay immediately west of Trinadol. He watched as the noble ship broke free and the men who had reached the island, stranded, made their way up its forsaken shore. Even as the *Sea Mare* reached open waters to the south, Trinadol felt desolate. The piece of the Cronus Star dimmed in his hand.

His power was spent.

*   *   *

Nil and the others turned back to look at the *Sea Mare* a few more times, but she was soon lost in the mists to the south.

The men avoided the oozing streams of lava as Rawley read the branches correctly, but they felt the ground trembling, and Nil made them keep moving, pausing seldom and not for long.

Nil, Lince, and Lanning took turns relieving the men from the hard duty, but Rawley always stayed in front, climbing the hill tirelessly ahead of the others on his spring-loaded leg.

The chill of the bay gave way to the inner heat of the island itself, which seemed to increase as they rose higher, and the men shed their coats. At last they reached the saddle of the ridge and looked over a gray valley bereft of any living shoot or beetle.

On the other side of the valley, foothills scaled the base of a great peak. To the right of the peak was a ridge less than half its height.

Nil had them make for the ridge across the valley.

When they had crossed a few hundred paces across the valley floor, Rawley noticed a bulge in the earth some hundred paces ahead.

"Captain, more fire?" he asked.

Nil looked at the rise, and rolled his eyes. "Give it a wide berth!" he said.

Rawley headed a little to the left to skirt the swollen hill. The ground shuddered under their boots. Rawley tested it more gingerly with his wooden foot before shifting his full weight on it. A bubble rose in the dirt beside them and blew open like a belching mouth.

It startled the men, but they managed to keep hold of the boat as they choked on the acrid fumes.

Rawley stopped. He stared at the plain ahead and shook his head with a strange foreboding. "I don't like it."

Nil saw the whole plain was undulating now. The swollen hill behind them exploded gas through its side and collapsed like a pie-crust. "Hurry up, Mister," said Nil. "And step smartly!"

"Aye, Captain," Rawley grunted, with such ominous finality that the others winced as they carried the boat forward.

The going was slow, but there were no complaints; the bubbles swelled as though ready to burst and fling some infernal poison at them, and the steady rumble under their feet only deepened as they wound their way between the swelling "pie-crusts" in the valley

Occasionally, Rawley's pace would quicken as he found a path between two swells, but then he would stop and wait for a bubble to subside. They usually did, but one of them burst and sent clods of earth over the party, and a cloud of choking vapors. The men lowered the boat and tried to hold their breath. Those in front buried their face in their arms, having tasted that poisonous wind.

Rawley's guesses were shrewd enough to get them more than halfway across the trembling valley, and in the last hundred yards they passed no bulges when suddenly Rawley stopped, causing Bultin and some of the others carrying the boat to grumble.

He took a reluctant step forward and his wooden foot plunged through the ground, his shout fading in the gaping hole before them.

Nil let the boat slide from his shoulder and ran forward to look down the hole. "Back away!" he said to the others.

"Rawley!" called Lanning, who had been rotated to the leading three and now edged perilously close to the hole beside Nil. "He's on my watch, Captain!"

Bultin cried out bitterly and bolted from under the longboat, prompting the others to lower it completely as he ran to the hole. "Rawley, come back!" the sailor bellowed and he kneeled at the edge and pounded the ground until slivers of earth fell from its edges. "Come back!" he yelled.

"Bultin, get back or get a grip, man!" shouted Nil.

A deep, long gasp rose from below.

They fell silent and looked at each other.

"Rawley?" Bultin stared into the hole, wiping tears from his eyes, and he saw the carpenter lying on top of a black tower of rock that rose from a lake of simmering lava.

"Rawley!" Bultin grabbed the edge of the hole, which crumbled in his great fingers as wind sucked into the cavern, causing swirling red lines on the lake to glow below.

Fifty feet beneath them, Rawley climbed to his knees, having landed on his back in a layer of soft ash on a rock tower. Around him, a lava sea cooked, and the heat and ash made him choke. Surging through the hole above, a steady stream of cool air rushed down over him, dampening the blow of the heat. But he cried out in despair, knowing that he would not last long.

Sowernut threw a coiled line from the boat to Nil and Lanning, and Nil took hold of one end as Lanning threw the coil down the hole.

Rawley saw Bultin, Nil and Lanning around the hole above him, feeding a line down to him. "Get away, by the Gairanor!" he choked. "You want the whole roof to come down? Get away and be gone, you idiots!"

"You shut up, Rawley!" bellowed Bultin.

Rawley saw the uncoiling rope snap above him, its end too far above for him to reach. The gusts of air coming through the hole swung the rope out over the black-striped magma, where it caught fire. The men above tried to swing it over the island, but the wind was tossing it to and fro.

Nil reeled in the rope quickly and cut off the burning end. "Find a stone to tie on the end, Lince!" Nil and Lanning felt the ground lurch beneath their feet at the same time and they jumped from the edge of the hole as a few feet crumbled away. Lince tossed Nil a lumpy stone and Lanning tied it on, then Nil threw the stone down to Rawley from the edge of the widened hole.

"Take the boat, men, get off this plain and wait above on the saddle of the ridge," said Nil as he guided the rope toward Rawley. Even with the weight of the stone, the line began to swing, and Nil could not control it. Furthermore, since the edge had crumbled, they were not directly over Rawley now.

Rawley shouted, "Go, Captain, I won't make it!" and Nil heard the faintness in his voice as he hauled up the line to stabilize the swing. He lowered it again, and Rawley reached for it, stumbling, barely catching himself from falling over the edge as he missed the already flaming end of the rope. The stone fell off into the lava below.

Rawley noticed his beard was catching fire and he slapped at it to put it out. "Get away!" he howled.

Bultin, crouching on his knees at the edge of the hole, fell through as the shelf crumbled under his weight. His grip on the rope behind Nil was so firm he ripped it right out of Nil and Lanning's hands. The rest of the rope danced at Lince's heel.

Lince grabbed the end of the rope in an iron hand and dug in just as it paid out. He turned and ran from the hole, hauling the rope over his shoulder hand over hand as he did so.

Lanning and Nil grabbed the line, too, as Bultin's weight winched it downward. Together, they hauled it in as much as they could, and Nil and Lanning climbed back along the rope to the new edge of the hole to look down.

Rawley thought he was seeing double to see the two of them above. "Get away, Captain! Get Bultin up!" The cool breeze from the widening hole touched and teased the carpenter, keeping him barely alive.

Bultin swung on the rope halfway down to Rawley. "You shut up, Rawley!" he yelled.

"Bultin!" cried Nil.

"Yes, Cappy! My boots are smoking!"

Lince pulled in a few lengths of the rope when Nil stopped him. "Can you swing yourself over Rawley?" Nil shouted.

"Er—maybe…My boots are smoking!"

Nil and Lince, side by side, began paying out the rope to lower Bultin over the molten lake.

"My boots are smoking, Cappy!" Bultin bellowed.

"Swing yourself over Rawley!" growled Lince.

"Aye-aye!" Bultin quailed, swinging his feet smartly.

"Get away!" cried Rawley.

"Rawley, get up and grab hold of Bultin when he passes!" yelled Nil.

Bultin's swing was a kind of figure-eight that brought him out of Rawley's reach for the moment.

Rawley realized he had one more chance and might as well take it as Bultin passed around and near again. Bultin's swing would not cross over the island, but Rawley pulled together all his remaining will, and with a demonic cry, bounced on his wooden foot at the edge of the island and sprang over the lake.

He grabbed a surprised Bultin around the waist and slipped down before Bultin locked his legs around his chest. His wooden foot caught fire as Nil, Lanning, and Lince hauled in the line, the rope gouging the edge of the hole.

One wall of the cavern broke loose below, and yellow lava flooded over the lake as Bultin grabbed the ledge and the three men pulled Rawley over.

"Let's get out of here!" shouted Nil, pulling Rawley to his feet, and they ran over the heaving plain.

*   *   *

When they reached the foothills on the far side of the valley, the carbuncle had bubbled over on the swollen hill below, and a spray of gory fire shot from its peak.

Rawley collapsed, and Lince carried him on his back up the remaining slope to join the others. Bultin, too, fell down, for the heat had wasted them both. The men gave them water and poured some of their precious supply over their heads and chests and hands and feet, letting them rest as they watched the earth boil over in the valley below. The afternoon sun was getting heavy in the sky.

On the other side of the ridge, facing the sinking red sun, they saw another valley in which lay a maze of zigzagging walls. Upon these walls towers of rocks were stacked precariously over the crooked corridors.

On the other side of this valley rose another ridge and a tall, steep mountain to the south.

Rawley, whose red beard and eyebrows were singed and whose eyes were bloodshot, began to feel his mind clearing, and a strange euphoria washed over his body.

"How are ya, Rawley?" asked Lince.

"Good ol' Lince, ya crusty crab!" he said. "Fine and dandy I be!"

"Think ya can walk?"

"Sure I can walk! My foot's only a little charred." Lince and Nil helped Rawley to his feet and he smiled under his frizzled mustache. "I'm a toasted scone!" he giggled.

"You seem a little punchy," growled Lince.

"Let's go. I'll be fine, Mister Neery-Atton!"

"All right, go ahead with Lanning and Bultin while we bring the boat behind you."

Lanning took the lead as they descended the lifeless slope of ash and sand toward the rocky maze below.

"That's the craziest canyon I've ever seen in my life," said Overly as they approached the tangled valley.

"Me too," sighed Sowernut, behind him under the boat.

Lanning spotted one corridor that slanted all the way across the canyon, though stacks of rocks lined the walls along the way.

"Those rock towers wouldn't be standing if this place weren't stable," said Rawley, who was zigzagging down the hill effortlessly below them.

"This whole island is unnatural!" said Sowernut.

"Aye, 'tis!" said Lince.

"It's the most unnatural island I've ever seen in my life. Wouldn't you agree, Sowernut?" said Overly.

"Yes, yes, Overly, I would!" said Sowernut.

"I think it feels us, Captain. Like ants crawling over its skin," said Lanning.

"We should all get under the boat and run together as fast as we can down that corridor across this valley," said Lince.

"Yes, Lince, a good idea. In three legs," said Nil at the head of the boat. "It will have to be. We won't all make that kind of run in one haul."

"The sun won't be with us much longer, Captain," said Lanning.

"Look!" cried Overly, at the rear of the boat.

The hills behind them were swelling. A fissure opened in one of them, and a flow of molten rubies streamed from the gash, rolling and skipping down the hillside at their backs.

"Keep moving!" bayed Nil. "Lince! We'll climb down and turn the boat over, strap our packs and stores on top of the hull to protect it and use it as a shield as we charge down the canyon as far as we can go. Rawley, can you do that?"

"Why don't I ride on top? I can be your eyes," he said as he tacked down the hillside below.

"We'll be totin' yer lard-ass around!" Lince growled.

"I can't run! Not like a normal man, if you please, Mister Neery-Atton. I bounce, more like."

"Let him do it, Cappy!" said Bultin.

"Yes, Bultin, it's a good idea. The rest of us will have to carry him, but it's worth his weight to have his eyes."

At the bottom of the slope, the men tied their stowage to the hull and lowered the boat carefully down a crumbling escarpment into one of the crevices in the valley floor.

Rawley climbed on top of the boat and they lifted it onto their backs.

They took off down the canyon.

Rawley lit his pipe in the orange twilight as the men hustled under him, and he sipped smoke gingerly into his sore lungs, smiling as he hung onto his padded carriage.

What seemed like a free ride soon turned to rough duty, however. The ground began to shake and the crooked cliffs, which seemed to mirror each other, began to grate and turn the earth between them. Rocks tumbled into the path and Rawley was indeed busy, lying on his belly on the bottom of the boat, yelling which direction to turn to avoid the latest avalanche. At last, he saw a crouching gouge at the base of the cliff, under which was shelter, and he told the men to make for it.

The men collapsed under Rawley as they reached the overhang, and the boat ran aground into a bar of course pebbles as the men untangled themselves under her and caught their breath.

The earth continued to rumble and they knew they must rally themselves for another push.

"The canyon is narrower ahead," Lanning panted, his hands on his hips.

"We'll have the sun for only another minute!" said Overly.

"We must get to the other end of this valley. Then we'll climb up the other side and camp where we can," said Nil.

The earth quaked and murmured, and sharp slivers of rock fell from the ceiling above.

"Let's go!" said Lince.

Rawley climbed on the boat and they lifted the boat again.

The overhang under which they had huddled collapsed as they left it behind.

They rushed forward like some kind of many-legged beetle with Rawley, its fuzzy red head, scanning the cliffs for falling rocks. Twice, Rawley miscalculated, by a hair, and a sizable rock glanced off the bow, smashing some water flasks. But for the most part his weight was a worthy investment.

After staggering on without a break for what seemed an eternity, the men saw the sun disappearing over a sooty blade of rock above and the valley's end rising out of the rocky maze ahead.

Tall towers of boulders were stacked along the corridor the rest of the way. Rawley bade them wait and gather their strength before making the last run, but they insisted on going forward with much snorting and grunting below.

"Go then but be swift!" Rawley cried, and their boots crunched as the stacks of stones teetered and tipped overhead, toppling and ricocheting into the ravine whose walls, Rawley noticed, were now closing in, churning the earth between them.

Rawley tried to anticipate each cluster of falling rock as he steered them up the narrowing canyon. The ground was rising, however, as the walls closed in.

"Stop!" Rawley cried, and he almost flew off as they did, and a pile of stone landed before them. "Go!" he cried, and they were off again, climbing over the rubble through a tight squeeze in the ravine as another deposit of stone thudded behind them.

They staggered through the last narrow alley toward the valley's far slope, a hundred yards away.

Halfway across, they finally faltered under the burden of the boat. Rawley grimaced as it careened over the ground, dipping and scraping into the dirt. He could tell that the ground must be coming unhinged beneath the men and he cursed Trinadol then for fighting his own benefactors with such pitiless fury.

The walls splintered around them as they pressed closer, and all felt the same despair Rawley felt as he lunged back and forth on the boat to avoid the heavy stones pounding the seabags and stores that protected her hull.

Blasts of searing steam hissed through cracks in the cliffs beside them now, scalding them as they ran. Rawley cheered them on though he was himself stricken several times by the infernal jets. "We're almost there, lads, you've almost done it! Thirty feet more and we're there!" Rawley cried.

There was not a man under that boat who believed, by the time he got to the end of that corridor, that there was a shred of goodness in Trinadol's heart.

Within ten feet of the end of the canyon, one last rock pierced the port side of the hull, killing Parnel.

They dragged the damaged boat up the steep slope, leaving the cursed canyon behind along with Parnel's body, staved in by a 300-pound stone.

The walls converged behind them, squeezing the rubble of rock between them high above the walls, and when the walls separated again, piles of rocks were left standing on the walls, ready for their next quarry.

The men climbed to the top of the ridge in the twilight, and their hearts were heavy as they saw, at last, the western sea.

The Silver Coin, now three quarters full, shone upon the Dimmrock, whose cliffs had been ravaged by some horrible violence.

Yet fear and anger stifled any joy they might have felt to see that sight.

*   *   *

Bulgar Bedrosium flipped a gold Gieron in the air.

"Oh stop it!" yelled Nardleen Fenstridol, causing Bulgar to drop the coin.

There was complete silence then as the gathering looked at the sea through the window of Castle Martharr's great hall that evening. The three-quarter First Moon shone silver over the bay.

"When will we know? They should have been there already!" said Bulgar's wife, Ninny. "They should be back by now!"

Captain Skylar winked a green eye at Ninny over his rakish brown mustache. "It isn't time to give up on Nil Ramesis, milady. Not yet, I think."

"It's been seven days. They're three days overdue," said Senjessi.

"Nothing to be alarmed about," said Poladoris Martharr. "There are a few obstacles, after all."

"Blox is tightening his grip," said Bulgar. "His guards have taken residence in all the shops along Gieron Way, preparing for the coming of his messiah-king."

"The *Sea Mare* is a worthy vessel. She has many weapons and defenses," said Captain Skylar. "We should not count her lost too easily."

"But it's been seven days!" said Luxolair beside Teldon.

"Seven days could not undo a warrior like Nil Ramesis," said Hallot. "He still strives to reach Trinadol, I wager my fortune."

"As do we all," grunted Bulgar.

"But what of Trinadol?" asked Ninny.

Those who were worried felt worse now, and those who still had faith felt doubt as they all looked out the window at the Gulf of Gwylor.

* * *

"What kind of king would create a place like this, Captain?" asked Lanning as they gazed at the Dimmrock and felt the warm wind from the west.

"Never ask that, Lanning," growled Lince as they stood atop the ridge.

"Sometimes, ask it, Lanning," said Rawley.

"The King saved my life twice, and for that I say banish evil thoughts of him!" said Lince.

"No one knows his mercy as well as Lince," Nil said, as he doubted it now himself. Nil looked at the churned soil ahead. Then he noticed a single, orange flower, a Dimfire, beside his own thrashed boot.

Blown across the sea from the Dimmrock, a Dimfire seed had sprouted on the ridge.

Looking further along the ridge, Nil saw another flower spiraling in the wind.

Indeed, a clear trail marked by Dimfires led along the ridge and to the base of the mountain to their left and led around it toward a great turret of rock that thrust over the island's western slopes. The top of this strange buttress of rock was flared into a bowl.

"Let's follow this path. These are the first living things on this island that we have seen."

Nil had Lanning take his place under the boat as he, Rawley and a grateful Bultin took the lead.

The men moved on along the ridge to the base of the southern peak. Increasingly fringed with foliage, the path revealed itself to be the product of some kind of design as it brought its followers up stairways and over bridges in the cruel terrain.

They finally reached the butte thrusting over the valley and crossed a bridge reaching to a hole in its side.

They crossed the bridge, molded in molten minerals, and found a flower-rimmed spiral stairway inside the tunnel, lit with windows that looked like burst bubbles in the walls.

They emerged on a high hollow of sweet grass shining under the waxing First Moon. The air was sugared with the scent of gardenias. Dimfires ruffled in the dell around what appeared to be a great pool and fountain.

"This sweet glade is made for us!" Bultin exclaimed. "Trinadol put it here!" He gripped the hilt of his crystal sword and grinned. "Like my sword!" he nodded.

Nil looked at Lanning. "A stroke of mercy."

"Is that a fountain at the center of this glade?" asked Rawley, sighing.

"Yes!" said Overly, Bultin, and Sowernut in harmony as they set down the boat.

Some of the men carried Rawley over the lawn, and lowered him into the round pool around the gnarled stone fountain.

Then the rest dove into the water and their weary sinews were soothed and their scorched flesh was cooled by the waters of the charmed spring.

Nil had them build a fire near the fountain as the night revealed its glittering horde that swathed the sky behind the Silver Coin.

They came around the fire and the aroma of melting pork and beans wafted around the clovered bowl.

They ate their dinner, smoked pork ankles and honeyed, spiced beans, and it was like a banquet to them after that day. They swabbed their chins with golden flatbreads of corn and drank cool water from fat flasks filled by the spring.

After Rawley and a few others finished patching the hole in the landing boat with three layers of canvas and tar, Lince passed around a flask of red whiskey to the men.

Rawley lit his punk on the fire and stoked his pipe and, once again, Lanning noticed Rawley's strange, scarred thumb.

Lince eyed the carpenter. "Well, ya made it, by the Gairanor, Rawley, I'm glad ya did, sir!" he grinned, nudging Rawley on the shoulder.

"Thank you, Mister Neery-Atton, for helping to save my life," Rawley nodded.

"You know, now that we're ashore and off the ship, and yer life is saved…I'd like to ask yer a question or two, sir," Lince said.

Nil chuckled.

Rawley squinted at Lince and blew smoke out his nostrils. "What's that, sir?"

"I guess yer wondering why I don't approve of your hi-jinx aboard ship, Mister Carpenter?" said Lince.

"A bit," said Rawley, warily.

"He's going to tell it," said Overly, elbowing Sowernut.

"Indeed, I am going to tell it, young Overly," said Lince.

"The reason for the grudge?" smiled Rawley.

"More like the grudge's reason," said Lince.

Rawley smiled. "Tell it, then."

"For those who think discipline aboard ship naught matters a willy, let me tell ya's all a bloody horrible tale to right yer heads quick, fast, and in a hurry!" the barrel-chested mariner declared. "And may ye learn it now from me, the easy way, I say."

The others cringed.

Lince drew in a deep breath, and rolled down his stippled blue eye at the men as the fire creased his brow with deep shadows. "Here's the story why I got this eye aloft that watches you men and never blinks." He clasped his broad hands and seemed to look inward at a distant scene. "Half my life ago, when I was but 25, I was second mate aboard the *Coral Bay*. Captain Starr and first mate Pokkstridol were below in the chart room, and we were underway to Logger's Port after a gruesome storm that tore out our bowsprit and took two men."

The others grunted, sad.

"Aye, we had loosened the backstay and were taking a light wind on the mainsail to push the mainmast forward so the men could rig the new bowsprit. Men aloft were ready to clew the sail should the wind kick up and push the mast too far before the backstay could be tightened. Well, Jimmy the Jokester was making light on the mainyard.

"He was a fine lad, was Jimmy, don't ya know. Yes, he was smart, funny and full of high spirits. He played harmless pranks on the men, but they only loved him the more for it. Well, after the storm, I thought, let it go. I'll look away and let it go, just for the moment, right? It seemed right after what we'd just weathered. The men needed a break, I told myself, and something to brighten their spirits. The hard part was over anyway, I thought.

"Well, now, it seems Jimmy was tellin' the men that there were immortal *Wondry* birds that never land and spend their life in the sky, buildin' their nests in the clouds, and such, ya see. He said they looked like common kites, but their feathers changed colors to match the sky so a man can't see 'em. 'Hey!' Jimmy yelled, all of a sudden. 'One just landed on the end of the yard!' Well, Jimmy didn't expect it, but a kite did land on the end of the yard just as he said it. The men lunged toward it, to catch the magic, ya see, for Jimmy could weave a pretty spell with his tricky tongue..."

Lince cleared his throat. He nodded, and an angry grin spread on his anguished face as he looked at the others. "And just then the wind came ripping at our backs and I ordered the mainsail clewed. The yard, ya see, well, they didn't clew the sail on the port side, so the mainyard started to swing. The men held on, but as the men on the starboard yard tried to let out the sail to even the beam, the yard started knocking back and forth like a teeter-totter." Lince squinted into the fire. He lowered his head and the men saw the remorseless blue eye on his scalp, glaring at them.

Lince raised his own baleful eyes at them. "In five beats, all eight men were thrown from the yard. They landed on the deck around me. Six of them died, and the other two—they wished to the Gairanor they died. One lost his arms, and the other his jaw. When we got to port, only me knowing what had happened and how I turned a blind eye, I shaved my head and had Nincairia, the tattoo woman at Logger's Port—that's another story for another night—stipple this eye on my head, so that even when I look the other away the men aloft won't ever let their guard down. And don't for a minute think this eye doesn't see!" Lince glared at them all with all three eyes, then he nodded at the carpenter. "I don't approve of mischief aboard ship, sir, I do not. Humor, all right, and I'll contribute, but mischief, nay, and nay, sir, again. It backfires, and when it does, there's no excuse, and it's a pitiful thing to try and live with."

"Yes, Mister Mate, I hear you, sir," said Rawley, and it seemed he was content to leave it at that as he relit his pipe.

Lanning saw his thumb and the scar around the first joint illuminated by Rawley's splint. Emboldened by the drama of their day and the candor of Lince, he voiced his own peculiar curiosity. "Hey, what happened to your thumb, Rawley?"

"Yeah!" said Bultin. "I been wondering!"

"I've never been more curious about anything in my life!" said Overly.

"I'm a bit curious," said Sowernut.

"Well?" laughed Lanning, turning a piece of salt pork on a stick over the fire.

"You don't have to say if you don't want to, Rawley," said Nil.

Rawley raised his hand, with its thick, scarred thumb and closed a fist before the fire. "I guess I'll tell. 'Never told it before. Why not?" Rawley pursed his lips and stared into the fire as everyone pricked up their ears.

"I was 20 years old and fresh from the hills," he sighed, "when I went to Gwylor with a dream of running my own fishing business. Ha!" He shook his head, seeing some bitter past in the flames of the fire. "Too proud to take a lowly post as a common sailor, I held out, of course, airing out my purse and wandering along the embarcadero, holding out for a miracle.

"One day I wandered to the west waterfront. And, on a dark street corner, a tall, portly man in a shabby tweed topcoat and a purple stovepipe hat swung his black cane as he barked a pitch to the passersby. 'Be your own man!' he cried. 'You be the Captain! Fully-fitted one-man fishing vessels for unbelievably low cost! You could be the Captain!' he crowed, his huge mouth open in a smile as his beady little eyes darted over his shoulders.

"I was 20 and therefore looking for a way to kill myself. I walked straight up to the man, grinning from ear to ear, and tapped him on the shoulder. 'Well, well,' he said, his face lighting up and his voice a whisper. 'The smartest man on this street, I see!' His name was Bilk, though everyone called him the Commodore, he said, and he put his arm around me like the wing of an old raven and took me through a narrow alley to a shipyard.

"There were a number of broken boats laying about and piles of scrap and sawdust. Some workers were mending the hulls of boats that were shored up. There was a launch and a crooked little pier, and at the end two boats were tied, no bigger than 25 feet, and their hulls were painted black, and their masts were painted white, and I thought I'd never seen finer vessels, both of them just as neat as a pin!"

The others nodded, for they knew never to trust a boat with painted spars.

"Aye," Rawley laughed. "So Commodore Bilk took me for a stroll to the end of that pier and showed me the biggest of the two vessels. The *Sea Rose*, the hag was called, and she filled my head with dreams as soon as I saw her. She'd be the flagship of my fishing fleet, and I would haul the sea's treasure in like no one before me and pile mountains of gold to build my folks a castle to live in, and I would become the Mayor of my hometown in my old age with my wife and red-headed children. All my dreams seemed to live inside the boat clunking against that crooked dock.

"Well, Bilk smiled and said, 'How much of your father's money do you have left, young squire?' I was amazed at his insight, but shrewd enough to answer, 'How much are you asking?' He sized me up. 'Seven hundred Gierons,' he said.

"I was shocked, for I had only 337 left. Too proud, I said I would like to inspect the boat first. I was trained as a carpenter by my father, and had sailed on Lake Placiri often when I was young. I thought I knew what to look for. I noticed a patch on the bowsprit under the black paint and asked him about it. 'Demoldan teak—nothing stronger or better suited to the sea! Guess you don't see much of it so far inland,' he said. I noticed another patch on the mainmast. He said the same thing, rolling back on his heels and smiling.

"I thought I saw my chance. 'Well,' I said, 'strong or no, patches take the value down, I'd say.' 'Down? Why, the price is rock bottom!' he says. 'How do I know how strong Demoldan teak is, eh? It's an added risk, and that takes the value down!' I says. 'Well, maybe you'd be interested in this other vessel here, a bit smaller but—'

"Well, I wouldn't have it, of course. 'It's the bigger one or none at all!' I says. 'Ah, you'd make your father proud!' says the Commodore, cocking a shaggy brow over his beady eye. 'This ship is ready to sail, with nets and gaffs and all the fisherman's wares already stowed. I'd have to talk it over with my partners first. Why don't we go into the boathouse and palaver a bit!'

"So he took me back to the yard and in a shanty they called the 'boathouse' I sat at a table where they had some contracts and a quill. I waited a while as he talked with the others in the yard, which I thought was strange since they were just painters, and he came back with his arms wide and a great smile on his face.

"He sat in the chair across the table from me and said, 'I'm prepared to sell her to ya for 400 Gierons, son! A prince's deal!' I blushed and blurted out 'Three-hundred-and-thirty-seven!' leaving none to spare for anything. 'Done! Sign here!'

"Well, in a daze, I walked all the way back to the boarding house where I was staying and took my box of tools and chattel, slipping out and not paying my bill. I knew I could pay it later, with interest."

Rawley looked off at the sky, a sardonic smile on his lips. "I made it back to the shipyard and no one was there. My boat was there, though, and I had the deed in my hand, so I climbed aboard her, knowing that she was where my next meal was coming from. I busied about the boat, figuring it out as I worried over my future. Pretty soon, I couldn't resist taking her out to moor her offshore, so I could sit awhile and think things out.

"Once I got her out and made her fast to a float, I fished and pulled in a beautiful pink sheephead, and cooked a filet—the best dinner of my life.

"I felt happy, though I kept discovering little things about the *Sea Rose*. The gaff's handle was broken and bound up with flimsy canvas painted black. The sail was sturdy but old and stitched from patches. The lines were notched and streaked with tar as though cast off from other ships. But I counted myself lucky for being a carpenter because I could fix the weak spots in the boat. I slept with my head full of fears and plans.

"At dawn, I knew my life as a fisherman had started. I took her off the mooring float and set her sail as dark clouds rolled down over Gwylor at my back, kicking up a cold wind.

"She started making noises, but I told myself they were normal and for some reason I felt I couldn't turn back. The squall came fast behind me and other sailors shouted at me, heading in the other direction, but I was not intimidated, no, indeed! I clewed her sail and guarded the rudder, looking for fish. The ocean was a strong and strange beast to me. I felt like I had climbed on top of a wild bull after sailing the calm lakes of Gilbobble. But I rode the sea stubbornly, and I rigged up the net to the boom to lower it over the side when I spotted a shoal of minnows. The weather got worse and the sky fell gray all of a sudden. Rain slicked the deck. The mast creaked, and I leaned under the boom to haul the clews when I heard a squealing thunder.

"The top half of the mast broke and fell forward. It wasn't the mast so much as the boom that crushed my right leg. The mast struck the gunwale, and smashed my right thumb right off into the sea." Rawley smiled, peacefully. "Well, there I was, mates. Dead, and cursing the Commodore from my grave…And for a long time after the squall passed I lay there. And the more the pain burned into me, the more I saw the Commodore's face and truly 'twas hate that made me finally move as dusk fell, and I blinded my brain to the pain as I pulled myself out from under the spars. I tied a line around my thigh and dragged my tool chest out of the cabin. I took a half-full jug of whiskey one of the workers had left inside and went to work, with my left hand, under the light of a few candles."

Rawley leaned forward over the fire, blowing smoke out of his nostrils. "I sawed my leg off and sewed it up." He drew another drag. "Then, sittin' there, lookin' at my old foot, I thought I'd fix my thumb while I had the chance."

Rawley smiled, looking at each man in the eye. "So I sawed off my big toe and threw the rest of the leg overboard. Then I fixed my toe to my hand and dovetailed the ends of the bone, ya see, with my knife, and then I stitched the muscles together with thread and sewed up the skin, so that I could pull out the thread later. And I wrapped two splints around it.

"Somehow I lived for two days, pouring whiskey on my hand and leg, and sleeping, mostly, till a fine ship, the *Trade Wind*, sent out a boat to rescue me. The old hag hadn't sunk, and I'll give her that. A month later, I pulled out the string and took off the splint."

The others looked at him with open mouths as he flexed his hand and homemade thumb.

"What good's a carpenter without a thumb?" Rawley grinned, his eyebrows flaring devilishly over his eyes. He licked his lips and nodded his head, humbly. "So that's why I play a trick or two on naive youngsters and gullible sailors, Mister Neery-Atton, if you want to know my reason. To teach them to trust the world before their eyes more than the words of men."

"My grand-dad always said it's a damn thin pancake that doesn't have two sides," said Lince, grimly. "I see your angle now, sir. You're made of hard stuff, and nothing foolish about you. So just a last word of caution: good intentions can backfire aboard a vessel. Playing it straight is a valuable example, as well, and maybe more rare. And certainly safer, at sea. That is all."

"Aye, Mister Mate, and you've made your point tonight, as well. I'll bear it in mind, sir. I will."

The two shook hands over the fire, a sight the others never thought they'd see.

Then the landing party took their sleep under the stars, ready to spring up at first light.

Having taken the first watch, Nil stared after the other men dozed off at the tortured slopes below that descended and split into branching ravines leading down to a narrow bay enclosed by sharp cliffs.

He surveyed the island's tallest mountain that rose to the right of the bay. They had seen it even from the *Sea Mare* off the island's eastern coast. Streams of starlit steam curled across the starry sky from the black peak.

She does not love me, Nil said to himself. I'm nothing. I'm going to die a fool. This was a familiar litany he told himself countless times during the last years whenever he faced another mountain to climb between himself and Lelinair's heart. Somehow it had made it easier.

He wondered why, now, laughing sadly at himself. She had not seen him off, he thought, though she knew he might never return. She did not love him. He was nothing. He was going to die a fool. He set his eyes grimly on the bay below.

* * *

Lanning rallied them at dawn. The sun lit the eastern heavens with a swirling alloy of metallic hues spilling over the slopes before them.

Hastily the party packed and bid farewell to their comfortable haven.

They followed the spiral tunnel below the level of the bridge they had crossed the day before. The boat was just the right size to lower it through the corkscrewing passage. They finally came to an arch that opened at the base of the stone turret. Below, they saw the slopes falling into ravines leading down to the bay, which was shrouded in amber mists in the early light.

They started down the valley, moving briskly in the cool morning air. This time, Rawley was secured by a line around his chest, which was tied around Nil, who walked 15 yards behind Rawley.

The going was fast and easy for the first mile.

Then, as the sun got a purchase on the sky, the ground began to tremble.

Moreover, the ground became striped with vibrant colors: red, yellow, black, and white. Several times, Rawley suddenly found himself teetering over the brink of a pit that had hidden under pathways of rock winding amid the colorful patterns. Nil saved him more than once with a tug on his line over this treacherous maze, but somehow Rawley learned how to decipher the true path, and they safely found their way to the deepest ravine that led down to the bay.

To their right, the island's tallest peak loomed a few miles away, jetting plumes of sunlit steam into the sky.

A black pavement of frozen rock flowed down the floor of the canyon, snaking all the way down to the sea. They trotted down the ravine on this firm road as the walls rose around them and blocked their view of the bay.

As they wound their way down the curving canyon a sound against which all sounds could barely be measured split the sky above in two.

*   *   *

A flash blinded them and a fiery fountain gushed into the sky from the peak of the great mountain, which they could see above the canyon wall to their right.

A flow of fire streaked down the side of the mountain above like a bolt of lightning, and even as they ran forward it spewed over the cliff ahead of them into the canyon.

They buckled down and ran harder as a mighty thunderhead of ash and fire billowed above the mountain. Fine cracks spread under their feet in the black rock. The sky trembled with a steady roar.

Smoking rocks hailed down from the cloud and somehow missed them as they skirted the lava fall and raced down the ravine.

A molten river coursed down the narrow behind them.

They stopped for a moment to trade out two men from under the boat as Bultin and Lanning took their place.

Then they made their final charge.

The canyon zigzagged sharply right and left, and at each corner they could see the river of lava sloshing closer and heavier behind them. Fireballs ricocheted around them in the gorge, but the walls were too sheer to climb out of the ravine now.

Choking on the sharp dust in the air, they stumbled near exhaustion, only gravity pulling them down the ravine as they lost ground to the river at their back. They could already feel its heat as they turned down the last jog of the canyon that met the sea, which was shrouded under a thick bank of white fog.

They ran for it.

The red river appeared behind them, rushing fast and swollen.

To their joy, they saw a ramp of rock rising out of the canyon along its left wall and they headed for it.

They were relieved as they climbed up the rock ramp and saw that it led to a wide ledge along the canyon wall that widened and reached out into the sea. As they neared the top of the natural ramp, they laughed and yelled victory cries as they carried the boat. The lava pouring down the channel could not reach them now, and soon they would be off this island.

"Ah, this is the best little bay I've ever seen in my life!" said Overly.

And at this, everyone laughed heartily, letting the boat joggle on their shoulders, just for an instant.

Lince, bringing up the rear, saw a crack appear in the white vein of rock under the men's feet. "Look out!" he yelled.

Rawley and Nil looked back and saw the ledge slide away under the men carrying the boat as the river of lava swept down the ravine.

The men managed to leap and catch hold of what remained of the ledge, but the boat fell.

Lince spat and leaped off the ledge.

He landed seven feet down on the canyon floor and hoisted the boat by its keel onto his shoulders. Crouching his knees, sitting on his ankles, he gave a great lunge like a tiger, straightening out and hurling the vessel upward toward the ledge.

Miraculously, the men were able to catch the gunwale of the boat as the flood of bright lava swept around Lince's ribs.

"Lince, damn it, man!" Nil cursed.

Lince's face blanched as he looked up at Nil and Rawley, and he raised his fist as he fell forward, and his sleepless blue eye was the last of him they would ever see.

Rawley stared with unbelieving eyes as the river rushed over Lince and into the sea amid billows of steam.

The men holding on to the landing boat noticed that its hull was burning and they quickly dragged it onto the ledge and rolled it over to put out the flames.

Rawley stood where he had watched Lince die and turned to see the burning boat. The fire had charred holes in its timbers.

"To the shore!" shouted Nil. "Come on, Rawley! Take the boat!"

As Nil spoke, an orange wave of liquid rock slurped up the ledge of rock and seemed to leap through the air, staining the boat's bow, which caught fire again. More splashes of fire reached over the ledge like arms and their hands splattered molten fingers over the boat's hull as though the rock was imbued with a clever malice.

"Leave the boat!" said Nil. "Get to the shore!"

He and Rawley led the charge down the widening ledge of rock to the water and as they stepped into it they found it was boiling hot.

They turned and saw the lava pouring over the ledge behind them. They were hemmed in by the cliff on their right, the fiery river to their left, and the boiling sea at their backs.

They backed their heels into the scalding waves as the red flood flowed toward them.

Nil's mind ran out of options as his wild eyes took in their trap. "It comes to this," he said with sudden calm. "But the *Sea Mare* is free. My greatest admiration to you all. We must choose a way to die, it seems." Nil looked at each of them and he said something that shocked them. "We did all we could."

The molten mud tumbled and oozed down the ledge toward them.

"Which way will you choose, Captain?" asked Lanning.

"I..." Nil thought of Lelinair as he looked at the approaching fire. "I think I'll face the sea and fall back, Lanning, in the fire, when it reaches us."

"I'll do the same!"

"And I," said Rawley.

"Let's all do the same!" said Overly.

Sowernut gritted his teeth. "All right then."

The eight men turned together and faced the bay. They felt the heat rising behind them and waited for the hot nudge against their heels to fall backward into the flowing fire.

"Bye, Rawley!" sobbed Bultin. "Bye, Lanning, and Wicket, and Lonair, and Overly, and Sowernut. Bye, Captain!"

Nil looked at the men beside him, who grimaced now as they looked back at their unfinished journeys. His heart broke to bear the burden of their lives, and he told himself, in stern solace, that at least her heart had hardened to him after its brief madness. She did not love him. He would die a fool, after all, tricked by life's dream, and here was the proof of her heart's wisdom. Yet he wondered if her rejection at the end was a gift to make this moment easier, and the notion destroyed him. Despite Nil's wish to die gracefully, mechanically, in contempt for life's cruel illusion, tears streaked the ashes on the mariner's face as he looked into the thick steam over the boiling bay. So here it would end, he scoffed, and fate so foreign to justice would erase all accounts instead of settling them, burying him on a nameless shore, an unfinished man who would have been better unbegun. He felt the heat on his back as his coat began smoking. He grinned farewell to this wicked world and nodded, then, taking his last breath.

The others took their last breath, too, waiting for Nil's signal now.

They gazed into the swirling white mist over the bay one last time as they glimpsed a moving point of light there.

None remarked on it until it reappeared, shining brighter and closer.

"Captain," said Rawley.

"Captain, look!" said Lanning.

"I see it, lad." Nil was wary of all hope now.

Their heels smoldered. The heat blistered their backs as they bent forward, peering into the steam, but then the fog closed and the point of light faded away.

In bitter wrath, Nil folded his arms to fall backward, and then the curtains of steam parted, revealing a figure rushing over the water, like a dream.

With long chestnut hair flowing, Lelinair stood at the prow of a boat, peering through the mist. The nearer she came to them the brighter the love-star burned in her raised hand.

*   *   *

Chapter 28

Drugor

Trinadol floated with only his face above water as he felt the cold ocean with his swollen fingers, savoring his last moments in this tactile world—even the pain.

He wondered why no bubbles escaped into the sea over the Tower, though the water continued to rise inside. He shaved off a last curl of *lightstone* and whispered on it as it ignited and smoked fresh air, floating on the water. He breathed it in as he dropped the last piece of the Cronus Star. He felt his life flickering as the cold sea sapped the warmth from his very bones.

He would not let go, as his father had done before him. He would hang on until his corpse was useless to his nemesis. That, at least, he would bequeath his kingdom.

*   *   *

"Are we dreaming?" Nil asked. "Are we dead? Tell us quick, woman, for I know not!"

Lelinair climbed over the other eight men crammed in the narrow vessel to reach Nil at the prow. As she passed over them they embraced her legs in joy and she smiled, stroking their heads.

Then she sat in Nil's lap and embraced him. "You aren't dreaming, Nil, and you're not dead!"

The men turned, discreetly, to the other person on board, who was hooded and minded the tiller.

"And who be you, good stranger?" asked Lanning.

The person pulled back the hood and, shining in dull garments, they saw her face, serious and beautiful, with falcon eyes aimed forward and a precious serpent coiled around her throat. "I am Neuvia," she said. She appeared to be no more than 18 years old, and yet there was an ageless mist and timeless wisdom about her that seemed melancholy.

"We are honored, your majesty! How did you find us?" asked Lanning.

Only now did Nil recognize Trinadol's magical boat.

"It is I who is honored, brave men!" said Neuvia. "It was the Lady Martharr's magical stone that led us here. Now my husband needs your help. We cannot spare a moment, or Trinadol is lost."

"That's why we came, Lady!" nodded Bultin.

"Yes." Neuvia smiled, stroking Bultin's head. "I know."

Stargazer cut swiftly over the scalding waves of the bay, as though under some power of her own. The men looked in awe at the magical craft, which, though she barely held them, rode high in the water nevertheless as she clawed the sky with her talon-shaped sail.

"How did you get through the Terrors?" asked Rawley, having finally forced himself to believe that this was really happening.

Neuvia looked at Lelinair. "You tell it."

Lelinair looked pensive as she sat on Nil's lap at the prow facing the others.

"Tell us, woman!" laughed Nil, stroking his fingers through her hair and kissing her head. Tears streamed freely over his stern face now, washing away the ashes.

Lelinair wiped his face on her sleeve and stroked his head. "Before I came aboard this enchanted boat, the Queen sailed through the Terrors alone, invisible to its demons. This is the King's own craft and she may pass the islands unharmed."

"His Wizard's Shoe?" asked Nil.

"Yes!" nodded Neuvia. "*Stargazer* is her name."

Stargazer snapped her sail above them by way of introduction.

"*Stargazer* found the *Sea Mare* and the Queen waited on the bay until Toy, the royal pearl snake, sensed the love-star I was holding. Toy told Neuvia to go to the shore and seek me out."

Toy flicked his green tongue on Neuvia's throat in greeting to the men, who looked at the Queen with wide eyes.

"Nil, I was trying to catch a boat out to the *Sea Mare* to bid you farewell and resign myself to the worst fate there might be, when Neuvia came. I decided to go with her so we could keep a watchful eye, instead!" She sweetly brushed the tear from his cheek as she shed one of her own. "I knew that it would break your heart, but I thought that if you were to die with my heart in your hand it would be too terrible for you to bear."

He squeezed her hand. "I knew it, at the end, alas."

"But it is not the end," smiled Lelinair.

"Aye," laughed Nil.

"I told the Queen about the *Sea Mare*, and then the Queen—"

"If any should call me Neuvia, it is all of you," Neuvia interrupted, nodding. "Please do so, forever and from now on."

"Yes, your Ladyship," grinned Bultin around his crooked teeth.

Neuvia laughed, stroking his blushing head.

"I've found it hard to get used to calling her Neuvia, too, dear Bultin!" said Lelinair. "Neuvia and I followed the *Sea Mare,* and *Stargazer*'s magical sail kept us hidden from you. And luckily, someone aboard the *Sea Mare* is quite the pessimist!"

Neuvia interjected, covering her smile. "We found three of your buoys, Captain. The journals that were inside them told us all about your progress so far and let us know how you were faring after the previous disaster we had witnessed."

"When we hauled them aboard we couldn't wait to read the last dramatic sentence of doom scribbled in the log," said Lelinair. "For we already knew by the time we retrieved them that the *Sea Mare* was safe."

Lelinair and Neuvia glanced at each other and laughed.

"We were wondering how they could have been copied so exactly," said Neuvia. "It was rather odd, I think, Captain. Even the inkspots were quite precisely the same!"

Nil nodded. "You'll have to ask Tobbs about that, milady. Our young naturalist."

"Indeed?" said Neuvia. "'Twas his pessimism that gave us hope."

"He'll be glad to know it," said Nil. "How do you know Trinadol's condition, milady?"

Lelinair answered him. "Toy, the pearl snake that rides the Queen's neck, spies on Trinadol for us through the prism of the Lightstone Tower."

"Trinadol does not have long, Nil Ramesis!" said Neuvia. "Hours—even minutes."

"Do you know what has become of the *Sea Mare*?" he asked.

Neuvia closed her eyes as Toy whispered in her ear. "As we speak, she sails over the Lightstone Tower."

*   *   *

"Avast! Furl all sail! I see the King's Tower down below!"

Karlock called the order from the bridge, flushed from the success of navigating the southern reefs, which, more than once, the few remaining spikes on the *Sea Mare*'s keel had fended off.

Karlock made a slow approach as the men took all sail away and descended the shrouds.

"The water's too deep here to anchor, Zee," said Karlock to the physician, who nodded appreciatively beside him.

Senthellzia and Harm now joined Karlock on the bridge.

The Creature, who would not have tolerated Harm in its presence, especially on the bridge, had died a few hours ago. Whimpering and freezing, the proud cat closed its eyes and seemed to fall asleep. All took it as a dark sign, and Zee had given the feared and venerated cat a proper funeral, in honor of Lince.

Karlock called out a sharp series of orders now. "Rig the anchor and Captain Ramesis's floats overboard, you three groups, and check out what ya see off the starboard bow!"

Three teams of two jumped overboard on the gentle waves and kicked out on the floats Nil had designed. The floats were tied to the ship at the starboard rail. In the center of the each float was a glass window covered by a black umbrella through which the men could look down into the sea.

"Wow, Captain! It's a wonder! The Lord's Tower's lit up like a candle, ain't it right, lads?" cried young Skillah.

The others nodded as they looked down through the windows. "Aye, Captain!"

"Tie the royal scepter to the fluke of the starboard anchor, Ed," ordered Karlock.

With trustworthy hands, Ed took the royal scepter young Kandrus Flint now handed to him and he secured the crown jewel to the iron fluke of the starboard anchor with thick leather cord. "Ready, Captain!" he called, and the men let loose the anchor.

It plunged from the cathead into the sea as the windlass spun and paid out the vast hawser they had stowed for the job.

Karlock grinned at Senthellzia. "We're kingfishers now!" He winked.

She smiled back at the silver mariner, grateful for his light sense of humor over the last dark days.

The iron hook of the *Sea Mare*'s anchor, baited with the royal jewel, descended into the depths over the Lightstone Tower.

*   *   *

As they came around the shattered cliff of the Dimmrock, *Stargazer*'s passengers saw a sea dragon much like Knot, only bigger and more ferocious, embedded in the cliff—an ancient red skeleton buried in a grave of green shale eons before the island had risen, unearthed by the great violence that had been done the Dimmrock.

Spectacular as this sight was, it was the *Sea Mare* rising on the waves before the raw cliff that stole their attention.

Her sails were furled and she looked scarred and patched from her ordeals as she drifted on the high swells, her anchor hurling down into the deep sea.

Nil and the others hailed her, crying out and waving their arms.

*   *   *

Where is the air going, Trinadol wondered. No bubbles rose over the Tower…

Two hours had passed since Trinadol had stopped breathing.

The shrinking pocket of air above was dead.

His joints were cold in his still limbs, and he had no wish to move them again.

He floated in his room, his hands touching the vaulted ceiling as he peered upward with dimming sight. He looked at his own turgid fingers, knowing that his drowned Cirilen body was giving way to its destruction by tiny degrees. With each passing minute his body would be more useless to his nemesis.

He felt *Drugor* waiting impatiently for him to surrender. He saw him above, as though through a tunnel, ready to descend on him like a spider on a string to take his fallen young body. He understood his father's motives at the end now, and why he had lingered in his own corpse. But Trinadol could hold on no longer.

The last air was swallowed up above him, and the sea filled the Tower. Where, he wondered weakly. Where did the air go?

Only then did it occur to him. The air had leaked into the *Wynder World!*

Like a giant scepter, his grandfather's tower was a lens between the worlds.

He looked at *Drugor* preparing to pounce through the Tower's portal above, and Trinadol decided to use his grandfather's magical gateway to steal his last moment with Neuvia.

* * *

Stargazer slowed as she approached the *Sea Mare*, and Toy started raveling his braid around Neuvia's neck. "Yes?" Neuvia whispered, and Toy reached up to her ear.

"Ho, Karlock!" called Nil at the prow. "Can the men see the Tower?"

"Aye, Captain, a bloody wonderful sight to see," yelled Karlock, and the men on the decks cheered to see the landing party, diminished though it was, and borne by a strange craft.

"The King has gone to *Wynder*," hissed Toy in Neuvia's ear.

"What? Why?" Neuvia gasped softly.

"We've got a bite, Captain!" cried one man who peered through one of the floats on the sea, and the men at the other floats confirmed it.

"I think we hooked the tip of the Tower!"

"One of the top windows, Captain, I think!"

"Weigh anchor!" Nil yelled.

"It's coming up!" cried one man, floating on the waves.

"What is?" asked Nil as *Stargazer* paused before the *Sea Mare*.

"Aye!" cried the other men in the water as they looked down.

"What's coming up?" Nil roared.

"The top!" said one.

"The tip of the Tower, I think!" said another.

"Just the top, Captain, and it's coming up fast!"

"It's not Trinadol," Toy hissed in Neuvia's ear, and he turned bitter cold around her neck.

"Get away!" Neuvia shouted, standing at the stern of *Stargazer*.

The crew of both vessels and the men around the floats on the sea heard her voice pierce the air and somehow they knew who she was immediately.

"This is not the Lord Trinadol who rises now, Ameulentians. This is the fiend that was stalking him!" said Neuvia.

"We gave him a scepter," Karlock shouted from the bridge of the *Sea Mare*.

"Yes, that was our plan," said Nil. "How can you be sure, milady?"

"Get away from here as fast as you can!" cried Neuvia. "Dear mariner, I do know it, but I cannot explain to you how. You must believe me!"

Lelinair squeezed Nil's arm.

"You men in the water, get back to the *Sea Mare*!" shouted Nil. "Now, now, now, not a second later, Mister, you, yes, you, get it going! Go! Go!"

The men abandoned the buoys and pulled themselves back along their lines to the ship as the sea welled at their backs and bubbles filled with colored light burst on the roiling water.

The cone of the Lightstone Tower, with its tattered flag of the Cirilen, pierced the surface of the sea and rose on boiling foam, bobbing like an upside-down top on the sea.

Half the men on the decks were ready to cheer as they watched the windows of Trinadol's room for any sign of the King.

Then a window opened and he climbed up the Tower and stood on its pinnacle, hanging on the flagstaff as it pitched.

Some cheered to see him, others were chilled by his strange pallor, even from a distance.

Trinadol's long black hair twisted with seaweed around his neck and his eyes smoldered crimson. In one hand he held up the royal scepter, and its star suddenly lit with a thousand colors.

Then he dove into the sea as the tip of the Tower rolled and sank behind him under the waves.

He swam toward *Stargazer*.

* * *

Nil ordered the other men and Lelinair to swim for the *Sea Mare*. But Lelinair stayed with Nil as the others dove overboard. Lanning kicked off his boots and dove, pulling Rawley along after him through the water. Neuvia herself shed her cloak, drawing the Scepter of Gieron from a boot at her feet, and she dove, darting under the waves toward the *Sea Mare*.

As Nil and Lelinair stared at the face of Trinadol nearing them in the water, it became more gruesome than all their fears. *Stargazer*'s sail whispered to them: *"Swim! Swim!"* and finally they dove into the water and swam over the waves toward the *Sea Mare*.

Drugor climbed into *Stargazer*.

Her sail darkened somehow in the glow of his scepter, and he sneered at her. He pulled back his wet hair and leaned against her sternpost. He jerked with sudden laughter and seawater gurgled from his mouth. Then he turned and looked at the haggard crew of the *Sea Mare*.

To those on the *Sea Mare*, his pale face still seemed beautiful in the glow of his scepter.

Neuvia climbed up the ladder to the *Sea Mare*'s main deck as Toy caught his breath on top of her head.

Drugor spoke to her in Trinadol's voice, which made the air tremble on the verge of thunder. "My Queen, where are you going?"

The crew of the *Sea Mare* helped her aboard as the King waved the diamond they had given him.

Neuvia turned on the deck, holding the scepter of Gieron in both hands, hatred overpowering her fear, and yet she held her tongue as her wisdom intervened.

Fine bolts of rainbow hues flickered faintly from *Drugor*'s scepter in a great arch over the sky, and distant thunder rolled from the southwest where they seemed to touch the horizon.

Then Neuvia saw Trinadol's body turn and bow to her like a mawkish marionette on the deck of *Stargazer*. "My brave lady, my wife and loyal guardian," her beloved's voice said. "I am saved! Now at last we can be together, in Hala, my love!"

She measured her words. "You are not my husband. You are not Trinadol! You are a worm in his corpse, and we shall defy you, dead King, as did my husband."

"Your husband was a knave!" he said.

All marked it well and knew the truth.

The sharp-eyed Sowernut, still wet from his swim to the *Sea Mare*, shouted from the crow's nest: "Land ho!"

All were mystified how this could be so, until they looked southwest.

And there they saw the Seventh Isle of Ameulas.

And they knew why no one had been able to pinpoint its position on a chart, for it was moving.

* * *

They cringed as the island widened on the horizon, its cliffs glowing pink in the afternoon twilight off their port bow.

"You Ameulentians have come such a long way, alas," said the demon, who stood grasping *Stargazer*'s mast off their starboard main. "I owe you a debt of gratitude, for providing me with this rare stone. I will not destroy you myself, therefore. No, I shall let Trinadol's last creation do that for me; a fitting close to his sad story, I think!"

"'Twas you that plagued Trinadol's soul with guilt and led his goodness against himself," said Neuvia, and either her scepter or the truth she spoke magnified her voice over his.

Already the Seventh Isle was only two leagues distant, pushing a wall of water before it.

Drugor studied Neuvia. "You would have made a delicious Queen, proud woman." *Drugor* gestured with his scepter, and *Stargazer* turned, and bore him swiftly around the southwest corner of the Dimmrock.

"Get out the sails, men! Avast!" Nil bayed, and the men sprang to action.

"You heard the Captain, get it goin' er you'll have me to reckon with!" shouted Rawley. "Get it done, you nelly-legged rascal, I see ya wanderin' 'round, go forward, yes, that's where the windlass is, now go ahead and get a grip on the windlass with the others and WEIGH THE DAMNED ANCHOR!"

The certainty of Lince's presence was sorely missed, and yet Rawley had stepped up miraculously now to fill his shoes, and the crew was reassured as much as they were baffled at the carpenter's sudden transformation.

"Let's run him down, men!" Nil said from the bridge, and the mariners heartily dropped the sails and wound the long hawser on the fo'c's'le.

Neuvia felt faint and came to Lelinair's side.

"I must lie down," she whispered.

"Yes?"

"I must go see the King. He is in *Wynder*. He lives!"

Lelinair brought Neuvia to Nil's cabin with Bruthru Zee's help, and they sat beside her as she lied on Nil's bed, letting Toy take her yonder into the *Wunderl World*.

Nil flew full sail and caught a favorable wind as they gave chase to *Drugor*.

The Seventh Isle gained on their port broadside from the southwest as its pink and gray cliffs pushed a foaming hill of water.

The *Sea Mare* flew past the Dimmrock's mighty cliff, with its river of red dragon bones, and headed for a close shave by the island's southwest point, beyond which lay the Dimmrock's bay.

"Why are we giving him chase, Captain?" asked Karlock.

Nil winked.

The elder mariner smiled, reassured that Nil had a plan.

The *Sea Mare* gained on the perplexed *Drugor*, who looked back at the wave that was coming uncomfortably close before the island he had sent after the *Sea Mare*.

Drugor looked at Nil on the bridge as he pondered his strategy, for *Drugor* was the greatest general there had ever been, certainly outlasting all others, and strategies and tactics excited him more than anything else. He commanded more speed from *Stargazer*, and seemed to get some but not quite enough as he crossed before the mouth of the Dimmrock's bay.

Nil laughed. At 500 yards, he could see the scoundrel's dismay through his spyglass. The *Sea Mare* fairly galloped in hot pursuit as the giant wave of the Seventh Isle lifted her wake.

Drugor could, of course, demolish the *Sea Mare*. But that wouldn't solve his immediate problem, as she had lead the island he had summoned right on top of him.

As the *Sea Mare* passed the point of the bay, Nil yawed her starboard. With a swing of her sails and a twang of her lines she cut east into the Dimmrock's bay.

The wave behind her smashed into the arm of the bay and rolled over the *Sea Mare*'s wake toward *Drugor*.

Drugor sat on *Stargazer*'s taffrail with his legs crossed around the tiller, scratching his head and spinning the scepter; the island he had summoned against the Ameulentians was suddenly upon him. He tipped the diamond scepter at the isle and a faint lightning of many hues touched the approaching cliff.

The island stopped and reared up in the sea, pulling back the wave in front of it with a deep gasp.

The *Sea Mare* continued into the bay as *Drugor* waved goodbye and spurred *Stargazer* to the north.

Behind him, the Seventh Isle rotated.

Its girth was too broad to follow the *Sea Mare* into the bay, but its swirled palisades smashed against its points, trapping them.

Then the Seventh Isle finally came to rest.

Nil bent his head, gripping the rail. "He's won."

*   *   *

Chapter 29

Reunion

Neuvia *saw* Trinadol *sitting on the broken edge of the Wynderne Dimmrock, grasping his head. He was surrounded by his Wondyrnal subjects, who had rushed with joy and sadness to see their real king after their ordeal with Drugor.*

"I am here!" Neuvia *cried, and he looked up and ran to her, and they embraced long inside the vibrant dream; the Wyndernes trembled with happiness to see their overdue reunion, and encircled them now with loving embraces.*

She looked deep into his eyes, knowing the peril in which their love was trapped. "You are alive!" she said gratefully, burying her head in his chest.

He sighed. "It is only a matter of time before the Gairanor see me and take me away!"

"He took your body in Hala, *grievously harmed though it was,"* she wept.

"It is my grandfather's nemesis, Drugor himself..."

"I know. And the men who came to save you know it, too! But Trinadol, *why can't you do something?"*

"I have no earthly body. It is a matter of moments before the Gairanor know it, and banish me from Wynder."

"Can you not come to Hala? Is there no magic you can do?" she asked.

"Neuvia, *alas, there is no magic that can make a* Hala *body for me. If there were, Drugor would not have needed mine. The worst injustice of all, that ruins my heart and poisons my very senses,"* he looked into her eyes, *"is that there is no shred of hope left now for us to grasp—the very thing you honored this world and the next with, no matter how unlikely. Alas, by leaving* Hala *I have taken away all hope, though it seems if I had left you one grain of sand you could have made of it a beachhead, and then a garden of joy. For you are the miracle-worker, not I, and though I gave you less and less through these years somehow you made of it more and more! How can you ever forgive me, or I myself, for taking away, piece by piece, all the chances you had to work your magic, alas, leaving nothing now for you to grasp, nothing at all, as though to ridicule your wondrous nature and confound its hope with despair? Let me give you this last, stolen moment, then, for it is all I have left to give you."*

"Drugor has taken your body in Hala*!"*

"Do not speak his name anymore."

"He has taken your place and your crown and he will rule your kingdom in your flesh!"

"Yet he will not live long with what I left him. Know that, too. For as my father did before me, I made sure my flesh was greatly ruined before I gave it up so it would be of no use to him. Listen to me, and not in anger, for I surely have not long. And you will have a lifetime to hate me, if that be your final judgment."

"Then speak, but by your soul you leave me breath to make my answer!"

He nodded, flickering before her. *"Know always that I love you, and did in truth make full reform of my distrust of this world you never abandoned. For never was I more in love with* Hala *than when certain death replaced mere doubt. Alas, we were not to be more than we have been. Just as there is no poetry in fate,* there is no shame in defeat, for fate's author is often artless and without purpose. So let me kiss you and say my love directly on your lips that they might never forget." Trinadol took her in his arms and made an indelible impression on her lips that would defy time as tears streamed from her eyes like the hope she finally relinquished now.

She squeezed his hair in anger, expecting him to vanish at any moment. She wished to tell him that Drugor would not perish, that his scepter would overcome the damage done and carry him unopposed against fair **Ameulas** as Toy had warned her, yet there was no use in these tidings, no hope, no reason, no purpose now.

They embraced as though they become one being out of time until he softened in her grip, as though some ominous force was lessening him.

Neuvia *looked at him and dared not blink as tears blurred her Wynderne eyes. Toy whispered in her ear.*

Neuvia *extended her arm and pointed lovingly at* Trinadol's neck.

Toy *coursed over her hand and struck him, sinking sharp fangs into his throat.*

Trinadol *sighed, and then faded away.*

Neuvia *squeezed his hand until it was gone.*

Then she lie down upon the cliff as the Wyndornes wailed in grief.

*   *   *

Nil opened the door to his cabin. He saw Lelinair and Zee seated beside Neuvia, who was asleep on his bed.

Nil entered with Karlock and Senthellzia. "What has befallen her?" Nil whispered.

"She is in the other world, with the King," said Lelinair.

Karlock glanced at Nil.

Lelinair felt the heat on Neuvia's brow with the back of her fingers.

Toy moved on her throat and slid down, pushing back Neuvia's tunic over her left breast. Then he coiled around it, putting Nil and Karlock on guard.

"What is the serpent doing?" Nil asked.

"Leave him be," whispered Lelinair.

The snake struck Neuvia's nipple, sinking his crystal fangs deep and injecting some mystical venom.

"What has it done?" hissed Zee.

"Be still!" whispered Lelinair, tears welling in her eyes.

The Queen seemed to wake for an instant, but then she sank back into a fever dream as sweat broke on her brow.

Toy slithered around her throat again and, after braiding himself, he became very still.

Neuvia's face became ashen and her cheeks sank as the peace of death fell over her features.

They feared the worst when her skin flushed, and they noticed her belly was swelling.

Zee quickly bent down and examined her, feeling and looking with his educated hands and eyes. "It seems the *Sea Mare* is a fertile vessel," he said, rising. "Here is the second woman to become pregnant aboard her decks!"

Senthellzia slapped his arm.

"I am most sorry, milady," said the physician, deeply humbled. "I did not intend to betray your trust!"

Senthellzia frowned, but then smiled in awe as she looked at the body of the Queen ripening before their eyes in the space of a few minutes. And Senthellzia and Lelinair helped Zee bend her legs to deliver from her loins a glowing child, who came easily and effortlessly into the world.

Only now did Neuvia awake, exhausted and pale, and she looked upon her love, whose look she recognized in the infant's eyes, for he was infant only in form.

As the King suckled her, those present turned away; for he was not drawing her rich milk like a hungry babe, but like a starving lover.

They could not help but look again, however, as the infant grew with alarming speed, nourished by her magical milk.

*   *   *

Outside the cabin, the crew was gathered, trying to divine what was going on from the sounds they heard through the walls of Nil's cabin.

A great eagle suddenly swooped down through the rigging and landed on the rail of the bridge, startling Harm up into the crow's nest. The great eagle folded its wings and looked fiercely at the men on the deck, and they all took a step back from the cabin.

They thought they heard the shrill laugh of a child from inside Nil's cabin, and then they were utterly perplexed.

At last, the door of Nil's cabin opened, and the boy Trinadol, dressed in one of Nil's nightshirts, dashed out onto the deck and ran right up to the mariners.

With long black hair and sparkling eyes, he was the very image of the statue over the crow's nest, seeming no more than four years old, and yet he ran with an adult's nimble ease from man to man on the deck.

"I know you, Karlock," said Trinadol, shaking the amazed old sailor's hand. "You are the first mate of the *Eventide* who showed me around when I was a child, and you were the Captain of the *White Shark* when we hunted the sea monster, Knot. I am Trinadol, good sir, though for the moment I may seem to be a babe!"

"My lord, are you reborn?"

"Yes."

Trinadol greeted each of the awe-struck mariners. And as he ran from here to there he grew from toddler to child before their eyes. "I'm starving!" he suddenly cried.

Pickle had been preparing dinner and now he sent out a table and chair and a royal helping for the child-king. A dish of bacon, onions, butter and eggs with a pork-filled cake and creamed enryd was served to him by a bowing Bombo. Trinadol devoured the hearty fare and visibly grew taller with each swallow, his body building itself with Pickle's excellent victuals. Pickle sent out more food and Trinadol sucked down asparagus and lemon potatoes and sugar-fried lamb, and black grapes and baked bread and beef ribs and fried squid and pork and walnuts and oranges. He devoured them all to Pickle's delight as his galley crackled with all ovens blazing.

The King grew into Nil's nightshirt as he breakfasted on the deck before the bridge, with everyone gathered around him.

The eagle on the bridge spread its wings and cried as it lifted into the air.

Neuvia emerged from the cabin, having eaten her own royal breakfast from Pickle. She had recovered already from her magical pregnancy.

Trinadol swallowed the last morsel from his seventh plate of food and he turned, growing several inches. Then he threw down his fork, stood up and moved through the onlookers, many of whom were grinning with tears of wonder streaking their faces, and he thanked each of them as he made his way to Neuvia.

He bowed then at her feet, touching her toe with his hand.

When he rose, he looked exactly like the seventeen-year-old Prince she had married seven years ago, though taller, perhaps, from Pickle's cooking.

Tears sparkled on her face, and Trinadol tasted them in tentative ecstasy before he kissed her smiling lips.

The crew cheered around them at the miraculous sight.

"Here are some trousers, lord. You should wear them, I think, now that you are all grown up." She smiled wryly and handed him a pair of Nil's pants.

All laughed as Trinadol winked apologetically and pulled them on.

Then he turned and strode with Nil through the crew as he looked at the *Sea Mare*, examining the harpoons and catapults with appreciative wonder.

He climbed the forward companion ladder alone to the fo'c's'le and he turned to them.

"Lord!" Nil cried.

"Yes, brave Captain?" Trinadol turned to Nil, the cliffs of the Seventh Isle at his back.

"*Drugor* is reborn and makes for Ameulas."

Trinadol nodded. "Then we should follow him," he said.

Neuvia climbed to the fo'c's'le. "Take the scepter, my lord," said Neuvia, offering him the golden scepter of Gieron.

"Not yet," said Trinadol, and without it, he flourished his right hand.

At his back the Seventh Isle rose 200 feet above the waves.

The men looked at each other for confirmation of the deed, and then threw their hats in joy.

Rawley made sure they hustled up the shrouds and let out the sails as the second watch weighed anchor.

"Let 'em out, get her off!" Nil bayed, climbing the bridge.

"Go! Go! Go!" said Rawley.

The *Sea Mare* caught her sail and cantered over the placid bay, meeting the new rows of rollers that now passed freely under the island.

The men held their breath as they sailed under the shadow of the isle, which rained seawater from its undersurface over the decks. They kept glancing at the smiling Cirilen on the prow, who stood looking at the wine-stained sunset with Neuvia at his side.

The *Sea Mare* passed unharmed under the Seventh Isle, which lowered slowly behind her into the sea as they headed north.

Trinadol changed into some clothes given to him by the sailors, the drabbest he could find, to the men's chagrin. Then he spoke with Nil in Lince's cabin as all left them.

Neuvia, Zee, and Lelinair spoke with Senthellzia, who all on deck now knew was pregnant with the grandchild of the King of Demold.

There was hope now on those decks that had been so laden with grief. For the death of Lince, and so many others, was not in vain. And the men made songs to remember them as heroes.

* * *

"You may have my cabin below, lord. I will take this one," said Nil.

They sat at the chart table inside Lince's cabin and for a moment they regarded each other.

"You, mariner, fulfilled my worst fears," said Trinadol. "You rescued me."

They both laughed.

"I built as many walls, lord, between myself and happiness," said Nil. "In a way, your walls were mine."

"Now you have broken down the walls and slain all the monsters."

"There is one left, my lord," Nil said.

Trinadol nodded. "That one is left for me. Thank you for giving me your cabin. Now I command you to take one hour to be with your woman in your new cabin. Your second-in-command should be able to serve in your stead for that period of time, as we are in no danger, now."

Nil looked at him, as if he could not believe his ears. "Thank you, my lord!" Nil laughed, though tears shone in his eyes. "I believe I will do just that."

And for one hour sailors extended their ears, only to be frustrated by the shroud of silence Trinadol had conjured over the Captain's cabin.

* * *

Drugor crossed the Illusion Sea.

He was only fairly confident that he was immune to its effects. But he didn't trust this strange craft.

Stargazer appeared to be heading due north without any diversions, and yet he had been traveling too long by his calculations without seeing any islands to the north. *Drugor* worried that *Stargazer* was warping his perception of time or the perspective of distance around him.

The Second Moon, burning bright, peeked through a cloud and sprinkled its gold dust over the world.

Drugor grinned with blue lips at the smoldering Golden Coin. "On the morrow, I shall take Elwyn's crown!" he cried, and he laughed with mordant delight as he cruelly gripped *Stargazer*'s tiller.

    *   *   *

Chapter 30

The Fate of the World

Stargazer brought *Drugor* stubbornly north, arriving well after the expected rendezvous he had communicated to his minion, Blox.

When Trinadol flung Blox out of *Wynder*, *Drugor*, crouching inside the Cronus Star, had planted Blox's *Wyndernial* germ in a deliciously humorous body: a gray sea slug that had red stubble on its head and could disguise itself with pretty colors. It was in this lowly form that Blox had slithered out of the sea onto Gwylor's great beach at midnight, transforming until morning into a mockery of human shape amid the foaming waves. Such crude Hala forms as he had given Blox could never sustain the powers of a *Khalwairn* or a Cirilen, yet *Drugor* found they could mock mortal man sufficiently.

Blox was missing his right hand, however, because *Drugor* had not allowed it to pass through the sharp stone of the Scepter into his Hala form.

Drugor had "kept" Blox's hand inside the Scepter and through it he had communicated his will to Blox. Before Trinadol destroyed the Cronus Star, he had hidden Blox's hand in the *Winderl World*. As soon as he seized this new scepter, he retrieved the hand and pulled it into the jewel like a spider with its quarry.

He communicated his displeasure to Blox now as *Stargazer* finally streamed, unheralded, toward Gwylor.

Drugor arrived at dawn, deceived by *Stargazer*'s distortions. Only fishing vessels passed him, in the other direction. And, without his knowledge, *Stargazer*'s sail made him invisible even to these ships. She slipped beside the Lightstone Jetty to the shore, long after the crowds Blox had ordered to greet him had dispersed.

Drugor tied the recalcitrant vessel to the great pier west of the Lightstone Jetty, the less grand of the entrances, for the eastern landing was built of marble and had beautiful docks. *Drugor* did not want to draw a crowd too close to him now, since at close quarters illusion worked only on the weak-minded—a large number, though never quite enough, he had learned, in Ameulas.

He climbed the pier and strode fast among the Ameulentians, weaving an illusion around himself and hiding his scepter.

"There is the King, by the Gairanor, look!" cried one fisherman.

"He doesn't look well!" cried a fishwife.

"Well? He looks splendid!" said a weary stevedore.

His kingly robes had given him away more than anything else.

Drugor rushed down the pier and paused as he came to the intersection where Gieron Way joined the embarcadero. He raised his scepter and sent through it showers of glittering color to obscure his form.

Those passing were struck with awe and filled with dread to witness what seemed the truth of Blox's warnings coming to pass, after all. When Blox's messiah had not come yesterday, the people had laughed and wandered away.

But surely, here was Blox's terrible lord, for he looked like Trinadol and yet his scepter shone many colors instead of crimson, as Blox had prophesized. Word spread fast along the waterfront that Nekkros had arrived.

A company of seven Nekkrosites, with shaven heads, had waited loyally all night on the embarcadero, and now they mobilized and marched to greet their savior, having heard the gossip. They made their way through the passersby and saw him, and they quickly surrounded him, trembling to be near him, and he laughed and strode forward, reassured in their company even though he decided to kill them to make an example for his rude reception.

"Where is Blox?" he asked. "Fetch him!"

Two of them ran to do so.

The news spread fast, and a river of Nekkrosites and Loyalists alike flowed up Gieron Way, following the dazzling scepter of Nekkros as he headed toward the great circle of Bartering Square.

Blox and Rishen rushed to meet him down that avenue, and their improvised entourage of guards dropped to one knee and trumpeted a weak fanfare before him.

"Get up!" said *Drugor*.

"Lord Nekkros!" the Nekkrosites exclaimed, holding their arms in entreaty, more frightened of him, it seemed, than those who stood back in silent scrutiny all around.

All ten thousand of the Mayoral Guard had been mustering since Blox had gotten the message of his master, and they poured out of the quarters they had taken in buildings along Gieron Way, having displaced many shops and businesses there in order to await the new king's arrival. They hastily lined the street and surrounded Nekkros, at a frightful distance, as he marched north up the avenue.

A carriage was finally procured to convey *Drugor*. He climbed inside the coach with Blox and Rishen.

Heavily flanked, they rolled forward before a stream of followers and past the banks of onlookers that were collecting along the street.

When they reached Bartering Square, the thousands gathered there fell silent, seeing the strange light emitting from the carriage's windows as it made its way to the north end of the square where the high terrace rose.

Drugor said not a word to either of his horrified companions on the trip, and they dared not utter a sound. When they arrived at the terrace stairs, *Drugor* clenched blue fingers on the brass handle of the carriage door and snapped it open, stepping out into the sun.

Quickly, Blox, Rishen and a large contingent of Mayoral Guards and Nekkrosite monks closed in behind him as he climbed the stairs.

*   *   *

Before dawn, the *Sea Mare* had crossed the sea of terrors without incident, and the gulf of Gwylor welcomed her with wide arms.

All blessed Pickle, for the crew woke to an overpowering aroma of bacon, onions, and corn, and when they found all of the above in an omelet waiting for them, with black coffee and tomato juice, they felt revived and their attention was set upon the northern horizon with renewed vigor.

Trinadol addressed them from the aft deck, with Neuvia and Nil at each side.

Tobbs wrote down each word he spoke in his log.

"Soon, I shall meet the ancient shadow that has haunted this brave world from its beginning and walks among us now in the flesh that was mine. I cannot be sure to best his high craft so sharpened by eons of evil plotting. Surely he has imagined his next incantations for centuries. Yet I have a power he does not, mighty now that it is free and no longer shackled by his lies. Evil wields only the power of destruction, but good has the power of creation. When good doubts itself it gives the world to evil, but when good fights for itself, there is almost no obstacle that it cannot overcome. That I have learned from you."

Trinadol turned, closed his eyes, and extended his hand toward the south. Vivid threads of white light arced from his palm to a point touching somewhere over the horizon. "*Theosophiclar*, loyal friend," he whispered. "I summon you now!"

Then he opened his eyes, and his skin was radiant as a Cirilen child's. He turned and smiled at Nil. "The Seventh Isle may be of use to us."

"Ships to the north!" called Sowernut from the crow's nest.

"Let us raise the green buntings of Ameulas and take as many ships with us into Gwylor as we can!" said Trinadol. "We must make a great spectacle of our arrival, the likes of which he would have liked to have made, but could not make in *Stargazer*."

"Indeed, lord!" Nil grinned.

"There shall be no doubt who is the King of Ameulas!" cried Karlock.

The men ran up the colors, and the flag of the Cirilen, trumpeting instruments and ringing the ship's bell, and they tacked toward nearby vessels as they headed north over the gulf.

Soon the vessels that recognized her raised their colors, and signaled other ships to set their course to flank the *Sea Mare*.

All across the Gulf of Gwylor, vessels came to greet the returning warship. Fishing trawls and grand cargo ships and yachts and salvaging crews that doubled as rescue vessels—for a price—and the skiffs of pearl divers and even two Royal Science Schooners, which were measuring the weather and water, converged upon the *Sea Mare*, whose sails were stained and battered bows were patched.

The mariners of Ameulas were Trinadol's most loyal subjects, and they proved their loyalty now with a rowdy show as they raced alongside the *Sea Mare*, though none succeeded in keeping up with her for very long.

*   *   *

As he twisted a knob on the bronze telescope in the Even Tower of Castle Martharr, Teldon spied the *Sea Mare*, followed by the wakes of a hundred ships like a comet on the sea!

He soon had rallied the household, and they all set out for Bartering Square.

*   *   *

Trinadol stood at the prow with Neuvia at his side.

Nil and Lelinair were at the helm.

Neuvia raised Gieron's scepter and its star burned purple before the bows of the *Sea Mare* for all to see.

Fanfared by thunder, the rosy cliffs of the Seventh Isle appeared on the southern horizon, following the *Sea Mare*'s spontaneous regatta into Gwylor.

*   *   *

"Behold the new king!" cried Blox, as he stood with *Drugor* and Rishen on the high terrace of Bartering Square.

Guards and monks flanked them, with the curving wall at their backs that was carved by Poladoris Martharr with friezes of fishermen and butchers and bakers and seamstresses and coopers and all manner of entrepreneurs and artisans in symmetries that radiated from the high terrace around the "square." Graffiti had built up on the figures carved on the wall since Blox had declared all art by Poladoris Martharr or Senjessi Tillow sacrilegious and gave sanction to its defacement.

Drugor waited as more people filled the broad marketplace and lined the wall down both sides of the square to Gieron Way.

Then *Drugor*'s voice echoed off the great wall and filled the mile-wide amphitheater: "I have come, at last, as Blox has forewarned you!"

His voice seemed to grind against the sky.

"Ameulas is mine now." The words echoed over the silent masses. "And all of Ameulas shall be my body and my muscle and my bones, and it shall help me spread my cause across the globe until it closes around it, like a fist of iron."

All, including Blox and Rishen, were breathless at his words.

The Nekkrosites shrank back to stand behind him at a distance. Blox, alone among all witnesses, smiled in admiration at *Drugor*.

"All who are not believers in my cause shall be put to the sword," the new messiah roared, softly. "But first: where are the good people who came to greet me this morning? They are among this company, I believe?"

Drugor turned, and the seven Nekkrosites stepped forward, smiling in relief as they came before him on that dais. They bowed before him and *Drugor* touched his scepter to the back of each of their heads, and, as he did, their heads fell severed on the marble, splattering it with crimson as their bodies jumped up, erect.

Then *Drugor* picked up each head and placed it on the neck of a different body, and they smiled strange and vacant smiles before the horrified crowds.

"Now these men and women are redeemed and shall do my bidding without question, forevermore!" said *Drugor*, raising his hands over the balustrade at the crowd.

The Ameulentians churned across Bartering Square in horror, and the Nekkrosites among them were humbled completely before the spectacle.

Drugor spied a purple spark upon the sea, then, and he heard distant horns blowing along the seafront.

From Bartering Square all turned to see a marvelous sight. A great island with swirled pink cliffs had appeared on the horizon, and it crashed into the end of the Lightstone Jetty with a great spray of sparks and an echoing boom.

A foaming wave rolled down each side of the three-mile jetty toward the shore and on its back east of the jetty rode a great windjammer flying the long green bunting of Ameulas. She was flanked by a fleet of vessels on that spreading crest on both sides of the jetty, and a purple star burned at her prow.

It must be Neuvia, thought *Drugor* with unexpected delight.

*   *   *

The *Sea Mare* rode the foaming wave past cheering throngs running along the jetty, and then the wave curled before her bows and she pulled back as it crashed gently under the mighty stone piers and over the sea walls of the docks.

The *Sea Mare* docked at one of the great marble slips and all the craft in her wake docked. Their crews poured over the piers in the thousands and gathered on the embarcadero to greet the *Sea Mare*'s crew.

The multitude of mariners issuing onto the seafront became Trinadol's army now, marching before and behind his party as Trinadol strode among them dressed in simple sailor's clothing. He smiled, holding no scepter, and Neuvia kept Gieron's scepter hidden under her dull cloak as she strode beside Trinadol.

A coach came through the crowd, drawn by a stamping Polwairn. "Lord Trinadol!" cried the coachman. "Thank the Gairanor! Blox's terrible messiah has come, my lord!"

Trinadol nodded as the people looked to him now. "Let us go, then, and reckon with him," he said.

Then he, Neuvia, Nil and Lelinair climbed into the coach.

More carriages and wagons stopped to carry the crew of the *Sea Mare* on a procession of honor behind the King up Gieron Way.

"Lince…died?" asked Trinadol of Nil.

Nil nodded, bitterly.

"We shall do all we can for his kin."

"He had none, save his cat, and she died with him, lord," said Nil.

"There will be justice then." Trinadol looked out the window at the cheering crowds rushing along the street beside them. Then he looked at the others with him in the coach. "There are many guards surrounding him. We may have to fight through them, yet I hope our grand entrance will impress all to stand aside and let us pass. I do not wish to take Gieron's scepter until I am before him, for he can not imagine what my wife has done, it is so far beyond the reach of his own power." He smiled at Neuvia and kissed her hand, closing his eyes.

"Let it be a surprise," she agreed, smiling.

Trinadol pulled his fisherman's hood over his head, and it nearly covered his face. "His charming horror has enthralled his guards by now, and it is unsure which of our powers will prevail. Some will know what they see and choose our side, others will know and turn against us. These will turn the tide, the few who are truly good, and truly evil. For they know their minds and are immune to mere illusion. The others will merely follow whichever wins."

"There are more of those who know their mind in Gwylor than those who don't, my lord," said Lelinair.

Trinadol smiled. "Indeed, I am counting on it, milady. For of those who know their mind, more are good than evil."

The scepter shone violet in Neuvia's hand through the windows of the coach as it entered Bartering Square behind a phalanx of mariners, who parted the way for the royal company.

As the crowds saw who arrived, the loyalists among them quickly formed human walls to line an avenue so that the procession could pass. The coachman cried, "The Lord Trinadol approaches, stand aside and give him passage!" as they went.

Drugor saw the convulsion of people on the square below and laughed defiantly, for it was Neuvia who made this grand entrance, not Trinadol, and she had already spent her one spell, unwisely. He would make a public spectacle of her beheading, as soon as she climbed the stairs to the terrace. "Let her pass!" *Drugor* roared. "Let the Queen of Trinadol come forth before her people."

The company passed unmolested up the eastern stairway to the high terrace, the mariners not sheathing their blades or their glares as they climbed through the nervous guards and disciples who yielded now before them.

They reached the top of the stairs and Trinadol walked before Nekkros on the high terrace before all the people, unnoticed in his common clothes as Neuvia held Gieron's scepter behind him.

Drugor laughed loud now before the crowds and thrust his scepter straight at Neuvia as Trinadol took the scepter from her hand and the diamond ignited with a blue explosion.

Drugor stepped back, confused.

Neuvia stepped aside with the others and found herself beside Blox. Toy slipped down her arm toward Blox's sleeve.

Trinadol strode forward holding the scepter high as he cast back his hood. And in the light of its blazing star he saw his own ravaged corpse standing before him as though in a false mirror.

There was no magic *Drugor* knew that could account for Trinadol standing before him, and the mighty *Khalwairn* general doubted his eyes and glanced at Neuvia with rage and terror.

The people saw the two of them facing each other on that high stage, and they appeared to be contrary twins in regal robes and plain sailor's garb, with a scepter that shone all hues and another that shone pure as a mountain lake.

Then Trinadol's diamond burned through the fog of *Drugor*'s gem, stripping bare its crimson fire and revealing his wasted body for all to see.

Now, at last, the Gairanor themselves took notice and sensed that there were two Trinadols on Hala, and that some law was being violated there. They wondered if *Drugor* was defying Elwyn's curse, yet they could not determine which was Trinadol and which was not, as each seemed half of Trinadol.

Drugor would not wait for the Gairanor to make up their minds.

Neither would Trinadol; he pointed a finger at the Seventh Isle.

Light speared the sky above the isle at the end of the Lightstone Jetty, and the Lightstone Tower, trailing shimmering plumes of water, rose into the air and hung still for a moment before coming down with a distant toll on the island's rosy cliffs. Its pinnacle had been restored and it flew the flag of the Cirilen.

It was only *Drugor*'s fascination with tactics that made him pause and study this surprisingly empty spectacle.

What could this young Gheldron be imagining, if he were indeed real, with this meaningless ostentation?

Whatever it was, Trinadol would not have the chance to see it through, *Drugor* decided. He let his entire reservoir of ancient power flood through the diamond of his scepter in one decimating blow and he focused it on the young Cirilen's heart.

Trinadol did not resist it. He took the full force of the *Khalwairn*'s strike and redirected it through Gieron's diamond, along with his own power, toward the distant Lightstone Tower.

The Tower lit, one half sapphire and the other crimson, and *Theosophiclar*, his *Wynder* engineer whose spirit now imbued the Tower, channeled the two forces through the lens of *lightstone* like a cannon, and brilliant beams of blue and crimson blasted straight into the heavens, even beyond *Wyndernia*.

Drugor instantly withdrew his attack; an instant too late.

The Gairanor had clearly glimpsed their minds and knew their identities.

Drugor looked at the sky.

Blox trembled next to Neuvia.

Clouds emerged out of the blue over Gwylor.

A lash of lightning cracked the sky like a whip.

Drugor thought of escaping through the diamond of his scepter, but he wondered for a moment if a bolt from the Gairanor would also destroy the stone. He would have to make his way across *Wondyre* and emerge in another stone, the King's, perhaps, before their blow struck.

Blox ran to *Drugor*'s side, having seen the look of fear on his master's face, and he placed a hand on his shoulder.

Toy slipped down Blox's sleeve and bit *Drugor*'s neck.

Drugor dropped the scepter.

He turned and seized Blox around the throat as the cold poison froze his sinews and his hands snapped the mayor's windpipe.

The bolt thrown by the Gairanor dropped like a gossamer hammer-blow from the sky, almost too fast to see.

It smote them both where they stood and bounced upward from the terrace, dragging *Drugor* and Blox in red sparks across the sky. Then black cinders drifted down over the city.

The grinning Nekkrosites with switched heads fell to natural deaths upon the terrace.

The clouds dispersed with grumbles of far off thunder.

The Nekkrosites fled in shame, fear, or rage, and those who had committed crimes against their fellow Ameulentians under Blox's authority ran the fastest, though their reputations would forever chase them. Some, the most notorious, were caught, and their fate was certain and swift, at least.

The Mayoral Guard turned readily to Trinadol's service and seized Rishen, so that the high lord could be tried at council. Yet his crimes, his ghosts, and his enemies were too many for Rishen to face, and he stabbed himself in the chest with a dagger as he was dragged away. He died on the high terrace staring with hatred at Lelinair, who did not waste her eyes on him, looking instead at Nil Ramesis.

Neuvia looked for Toy and then found him around her neck, where he had surreptitiously returned.

Trinadol strode to the balustrade of the high terrace with her at his arm and he lifted his scepter to calm the crowds. Then, for the first time, he addressed them.

"Ameulas has suffered since I was made King."

His voice rang true and strong over the silent square.

"I doubted myself, and evil took my place. Come, Ameulentians, we have suffered long enough. The sky is clear, the tax is lifted, and tyranny tamed. I will defend the good and push back evil so this land of ours can be as beautiful and free as the world inside our hearts. Let us feast and celebrate tonight in this square, and bring all manner of extravagance to add to our pleasure. For we have weathered a great winter, and now the spring has come!"

The people were jubilant to hear his clear words, and many set out to fetch offerings for the celebration.

*   *   *

Torches were lit around the high terrace and the stone was washed of blood. Then three long tables were set out for the crew of the *Sea Mare* and the King and Queen.

Trinadol went to the balustrade and lifted Gieron's Star before the people, and the diamond shone blue like the North Star that pulled Trinadol to Ameulas so long ago.

"Good Ameulas!" he cried from the terrace. "If you are worried about insect aggressions," he closed his eyes. "There shall be none." he flourished the golden scepter.

The people applauded, full of mirth, across the broad square.

"We shall play a little game tonight!" said Trinadol. "Look at the sky!" He pointed upward with the Scepter, whose stone erupted sapphire sparks that seemed to reach out to every star.

All looked as the starry dome above seemed to detach and slowly spin free.

Hoots and cries and gasps rose as Trinadol laughed and waved his arms. "No, my people, it is only an illusion! I cannot move the stars! Only we in Gieron's Square can see a sky such as this tonight. Yet note the lion pouncing in the west, the ship tossing in the south, the horse galloping in the east and the bird flying in the north, for three times tonight they will be aligned to the compass and the stars will be right in the sky. Then all must say 'Cheers!' or drink twice what remains in their mug!"

Tears sparkled in Neuvia's eyes as she heard the crowds buzzing below.

"Ah, there! You missed it!" cried Trinadol as the gleaming icons passed their heavenly marks. "All must drink!"

There was a roar of approval as all toasted deep to Trinadol.

Trinadol sat between Neuvia and the Queen Mother, Nardleen, whose dour face had never been so bright, as a feast was served by smiling attendants.

All the guests of honor had been bathed and had dressed up for the occasion, and the *Sea Mare*'s 28 survivors were waited upon like royalty at the tables around the King.

Bultin shoveled food and bailed beer down his hatch, his mighty crystal sword gleaming at his hip.

Jootle kept stealing food right out of Feferl's mouth; both of them were dressed in fine suits of yellow velvet.

Bruthru Zee sat with a glowing Senthellzia, and Harm gripped the high back of her chair protectively.

Rawley had fitted his spare leg to his knee and had finally washed his sooty face and trimmed his fried beard and eyebrows.

Tobbs's eyebrows had filled in a bit, and his pale skin had turned tan, his baby fat burned off. He looked a man now, and the serving maids noticed.

Pickle frowned at Bombo's obsequious praise of every course that was served. But, as Bombo spoke with his mouth too full, and Pickle eagerly translated for him: "He says he's full of gas!"

In the most curious turn, Sowernut was heard exaggerating their adventures and Overly was heard deflating his accounts.

"The King has an announcement," said the Queen, tapping a glass.

"Nil Ramesis shall be Admiral of the Royal Navy," said Trinadol to his dinner party.

Nil smiled, but shook his head. "No, my lord. I should not want to be away at sea without Lelinair any longer. I beg a different post, with all respect!"

"Then you shall be Naval Architect and Honorary Admiral during your very infrequent times at sea, during which Lelinair should always be given a berth by your side."

"I approve, my lord!" said Lelinair. "It is the perfect arrangement!"

Nil laughed. "Aye, I think so, as well, lord!"

The minstrels on the lower tiers played a dashing melody to suit Trinadol's stargazing contest, and the people danced and sang across the great square.

Stealing away, Nil and Lelinair embraced as though the world no longer existed, now that the world was saved.

And, clasping hands, Trinadol and Neuvia looked over the moonlit Gulf of Gwylor. The Lightstone Tower glowed faintly on the Seventh Isle at the end of the Lightstone Jetty, guarding the great harbor now. They smiled, full of hope, for the world was like a dream that finally woke.

The End

Publisher's Note

Though we have striven to capture the text exactly as it has been delivered to us, we must admit that it is sometimes impossible to transmit any word having to do with the *Wynderli* realm without strange typographical errors occurring. We regret this, and can only warn readers that over time words that directly refer to the *Winder World* will slowly become distorted, even when printed firmly on paper here in the Hala World. When ordering this book from a local bookstore, therefore, please be assured that we will endeavor to provide the freshest copy available. Thank you.

About the Author

Casey Fahy was born and lives in southern California with his pug named Caesar. When he isn't writing, he's feeding Caesar, or sculpting, maintaining his website (escapingamerica.com), and making a general mess of his home, which Caesar never seems to do a dang thing about. He is the author of several novels, including *The Bot Story*, which is also available from Writers Club Press.